To Tammy,

You are a great
person and you have
a beautiful voice.
I wish you nothing but
the best love, happiness,
and great fortune.

Love,
Colidge
Jaime

Twisted Dream, Dead Moon

by

CHELSEA RAINE

iUniverse, Inc.

New York   Bloomington

iUniverse books may be ordered through booksellers or by contacting:

iUniverse
1663 Liberty Drive
Bloomington, IN 47403
www.iuniverse.com
1-800-Authors (1-800-288-4677)

Because of the dynamic nature of the Internet, any Web addresses or links contained in this book may have changed since publication and may no longer be valid. The views expressed in this work are solely those of the author and do not necessarily reflect the views of the publisher, and the publisher hereby disclaims any responsibility for them.

ISBN: 978-1-4502-1835-1 (sc)
ISBN: 978-1-4502-1837-5 (hc)
ISBN: 978-1-4502-1836-8 (ebook)

Library of Congress Control Number: 2010903725

Printed in the United States of America

iUniverse rev. date: 04/29/2010

In loving memory of Andrea Wakefield 1957-2009 I will always have you in my heart. I also dedicate this to: Barbie Willis an amazing person. Allen Damron my God father. I'll see you all again someday!

Contents

Chapter 1:   Night Out   1

Chapter 2:   A Trip   20

Chapter 3:   Just Another Day   31

Chapter 4:   Anticipation   37

Chapter 5:   The Outcome   45

Chapter 6:   The Castle Party   53

Chapter 7:   Darkness Over Me   68

Chapter 8:   Desperation   86

Chapter 9:   So Deeply   96

Chapter X: Take Me In The Sky   109

Chapter 11: Captured In A Dream   122

Chapter 12: In Heaven With You   134

Chapter 13: You Took My Heart   159

Chapter 14: The Fight Back   173

Chapter 15: My Awakening   189

Chapter 16: My Returned Heart   212

Chapter 17: Dream Dragon   231

Chapter 18: Don't Leave Me Now   244

Chapter 19: Come Back to Me   261

Chapter 20: Tears Kept Falling   278

Epilogue   302

Book 2 Islathon Chapter 1   321

Acknowledements   349

Preface

J OPENED MY EYES AND GASPED WHEN I realized what was happening to me. I thought about pinching myself. *This is a nightmare and any minute I'm going to wake up*, I told myself. He whispered in my ear his voice delicate, but hard at the same time. His breath caused my ear to throb. "I will take your life, your heart, or your soul ... you choose." Even his whisper oozed of evil. I tried to scream, but could barely breathe. He stood back and smiled in a deadly way. I could finally make out his face as he stepped out of a shadow into the flickering candlelight. Then like a two by four knocking me over the head it registered who he was. It was him, Sigrid. He had hair as black as onyx, long and shiny. His piercing black eyes cut through to my very soul. His words sliced into my core. I tried to break free from the thick rope around my wrists, but it was no use. He had me and that was it. I screamed my loves name over and over in my mind, hoping to get through so that he would rescue me. But, the music was too loud, there was no way he could possibly hear me, not even in his mind.

My abductor interrupted my thoughts. "I'm waiting." His voice was full of condescension as he glared at me. He was pale. To look at him hurt.

"What do you mean?" I cried out, but didn't really want to hear the introduction to my demise. I wanted so badly to wipe my eyes and nose with a tissue, but my hands were tied. My tears were not provoked by the pain I was in but merely the thought of never seeing him again. To feel his lips to mine or feel the cool tenderness of his touch. I was dying inside.

Sigrid circled the room and then headed straight for me. My whole body shook in tremors to see the evil approaching. Sigrid growled and sounded like a mad panther except lower and much scarier. My heart shook and my hair blew from his polar breath, he was so close.

He got right up in my face. His breath stunk of ancient antique and reddened my skin by his air. "I mean, I will go after everyone you know and love. You can die, or you can become what I am. DECIDE!!!"

Chapter 1

Night Out

I WAS IN AND OUT OF CONSCIOUSNESS, listening to the birds through my closed window whistling and singing their morning praise to the sun. I said a prayer and wished for an escape from the stagnant slumber my life had become. It was a month and then some, before my twenty-first birthday. The question that was repeatedly running through my mind was whether or not I would ever find love and if so what price would I pay for it. And would I really want it when I finally found it? Or was I going to be alone forever? This was probably going to be just another birthday. Having never really felt love, in that way, I dreamt and pined for a yearning of the sensation and wondered if it would ever come, my way. I pulled a pillow over my head and buried my face in the fluffy mattress.

I was startled awake when the light came on and my mom yelled, "Time to get up sleepy head. This is your last summer before you go off to college." As she threw open my dark red satin curtains and let the sun shine right in my eyeballs. I squinted, moaned and blocked the light by rolling over the other way. What she meant was, it had been three summers since I graduated high school. I went to beauty school, but that was not good enough for them. They wanted me to go to a real college. Have the real college experience.

"Funny. I can't decide where I want to go," I sighed lackadaisically as I peaked over the edge of my blanket to see her reaction. Her expression showed she was disgruntled at my words. I didn't care I was tired and could stay in bed forever. "Mom, I want to sleep some more, please," I begged, pulling the blanket up over my head and curling up in a little ball.

"You're a bum," she murmured, under her breath.

I yelled, "I am not!" (How dare she, I am the farthest thing from lazy.) I thought as I came up out of the covers and threw a pillow at her as she walked out the door and slammed it behind her. I shrugged her scolding and went somewhere else in my mind.

I lounged around a little bit longer, then the sun hit my eyes again and nearly blinded me. So I got up and staggered to the bathroom. I did what I had to do and shut the door behind me on my way back to my bedroom. I turned the TV on, sat on my bed and did my face. I watched an old movie for a minute or two, then decided to channel surf. Nothing good was on and I didn't feel like watching anything I had seen before.

My heart skipped a beat when I heard a clicking sound. Then I saw my phone vibrating on the bedside table and relaxed. Reaching for it I nearly fell off the bed. My bed was extra high off the floor. If I had fallen, it would've hurt.

"Hey Lizzy," I answered .

"Lets go out tonight. I want to go to Jaggers," her voice was anxious and excited.

"Sure, sounds like a plan. I don't want to go there, though. The people that hang out there are lazy, and they don't dance." Of course, she wanted to go to Jaggers. I really didn't like that place, but needed a night out. Even though I had never been there, I was aware of it's bizarre reputation.

"I'll see you at 8:00," I agreed. She wanted to drive because she didn't drink so I was happy to oblige her. Although, I didn't either. Well at least not legally, yet.

After getting off the phone, I piddled, worked on a poem, and listened to some music until about 6:30. After a relaxing bath I got dressed in my little black dress, styled my hair and went downstairs. "I'm going out with Lizzy," I said as I got to the bottom of the steps and entered the kitchen.

"I am so glad to see you're still hanging out with Lizzy, she is such a sweet girl," my mother said softly as she came into the room.. "Where are y'all going tonight?" she asked in a parenting tone.

"We're going to the Loft." I know, I lied, but she did not like Jaggers. Like mother, like daughter. She always said the people that hung out there were all dark and mean. I had heard nothing but bad things about Jaggers. The news had reported a girl missing from there a few years back. She was about the same age as me. It had stirred up quite a disturbance in the community. I didn't remember hearing if they had ever found her. Becoming a recluse at that time, wasn't my idea. But I didn't mind. I enjoyed being alone in my room.

I was sitting on the couch chatting with mom when Lizzy's horn interrupted our conversation.

I stood in front of the mirror by the door reapplying my lipstick. I had eaten a snack and it had worn off. I took a deep breath and told myself this would be a night to remember.

"Bye mom, see you around 1:30," I called out as I walked out the door. My eyes were clenched tight waiting for a negative response from her as I held the brass knob in my hand and slowly pulled the door to. She said nothing. I shook my head in disbelief and thought maybe I should have said 2:00 instead. Walking up to Lizzy's smoky black car I jumped in and gave her a hug. We were really close. I didn't have any siblings, so she was the closest thing I had to a sister. We were soul sisters.

"Hey girl, can we get something to eat before we go to Jaggers?" I asked as I placed my purse on the floorboard.

"Sure," she agreed then pushed down on the accelerator and we drove down the dim lit night road.

"How have you been?" I asked.

"Good. Things have been really crazy lately. I went on a date last night," she announced, leaning over to see what station the radio was on and then turning down the volume so we could talk.

"With who?" I asked as I looked at my nails, trying to scrape off some scratch ticket residue from a lottery ticket I had purchased the day before. Although I had wondered how it attached to my nail in the first place, since I had used a coin.

"Jordan Blair," she answered hesitantly, staring ahead without looking at my expression. Which was that of surprise.

"I thought you weren't interested in him," I replied, flabbergasted to hear his name since he had hurt her, literally. They had been involved in a car accident. Neither one of them knew the other existed until the wreck. They were both very lucky to have walked away with minor bruises and contusions. Lizzy went through some physical therapy for her back. But she recovered and hardly has a pain unless there was a storm coming. I called her the weather girl because she let me know when to run for cover.

"He's sweet and funny, and we have a *great* time together. He keeps me in stitches with his sense of humor. My gut always hurts from laughing afterwards," she explained. Her eyes lit up when she talked about him.

"I thought you were still in love with Jeff?" I declared, confused, but happy for her. Not like I wanted her to be with Jeff. I wanted her to find someone who would treat her with respect. Anybody that did that, had my approval.

"Jeff is a good guy, but he wouldn't commit and I wasn't going to have sloppy seconds," she stated with a grin as she glanced my way and then back at the road. We both giggled.

"Where do you want to eat?" she asked, changing the subject.

"I don't care. We can drive through McDonalds if you want."

McDonalds was just up a head, which was the reason I suggested it. Plus it was fast and they had good fries. And I knew my time of fried foods, well, at least fried fast food, was short lived. I couldn't eat that way forever.

We drove through. She ordered a burger and fries. I ordered the same. We got our food and sat in the parking lot and ate. My burger wasn't that good, but I was hungry so I ate it. After we scarfed down our food we made our way to Jaggers.

When we got there, I recognized some faces, but saw nobody I wanted to talk to. There were some girls I remembered from a party years back, standing at the bar. But they had been so snooty to me and some of my friends I didn't give them the time of day. They acknowledged me and then put their noses back in the air.

"Aren't we meeting Micha here?" I asked as we sat down in a dimly-lit booth. The tables were empty all around us. In fact there were very few patrons in the restaurant at all. Mostly it was populated by the staff. All the furniture was made of dark wood. The chairs were padded in a deep red velvet and had an elegant design up the back. There was a crystal clear candle holder with a lit candle on every table. The bar was black and dark wood with tall black and silver bar stools. Behind the bar the walls were mirrored with Jaggers in black print across it. The bottles of liquor were lined on shelves in front of the mirror with a slew of white lights under and behind them making the bottles glow. The place was so hazy it looked as if a cloud had lightly touched down.

"She should be here soon. When I text her she said she had to get gas and then she would be on her way," Lizzy answered staring at her phone, texting someone. Lizzy always had the phone in her hand. The phone had become an attachment to her arm.

About five minutes later Micha walked in and came over. She gave us both hugs. Micha was a really good person, and she had been through a lot. She was going through a bad breakup, and didn't know what she wanted. So a girl's night out was exactly what she needed. She had dark eyes and dark hair, really pretty and sweet too.

Lizzy was just as beautiful, she had dark sultry brown hair with golden highlights. Her dark chocolate brown eyes were warmed with a smile that brightened up my day. They both did.

"What's up girl? How are you doing?" I asked Micha as she settled in her seat and took off her jacket placing it next to her side.

"I'm doing good," she sighed with sad undertones. "I'm doing as good as can be expected. My heart is not healing that fast, though," she admitted with one corner of her mouth raised. Her eyes confirmed her confession. The light in them was murky and dull by the heartache she had experienced.

"It will get better girl, you just need some distractions. In time you will find someone worthy of you," I said cheerfully as I gently patted her arm.

"You just need to work on yourself and make yourself happy," Lizzy suggested. We all agreed. Lizzy and I comforted her the best we knew how.

I felt like an idiot. I was giving advice and I hadn't dated anyone in two years. Someone needed to be consoling me, advising me. But, I didn't want a pity party. I turned my eyes away from their view so they wouldn't see my anguish and boredom. The waitress approached our table and took our drink order. We asked for sodas, but we all wanted something a little stronger. None of us were twenty-one yet, though. The waitress returned with our drinks. She was an average height brunette with a shoulder length swing bob and a smile that seemed fake. She didn't look very happy to be there or to wait on us.

I sat there sipping my root beer thinking to myself, *Just one more month and I will be drinking legally. Yes! I can't wait!* (Not like I wanted to drink everyday or anything. As if I would go that far. I preferred to be sober, but I would enjoy having the option.)

Lizzy peered up from her phone, "Are they staring at us?" she asked sarcastically, holding the straw up to her lips as she downed the rest of her soda. She motioned with her eyes.

We looked to see three guys sitting not too far from us. They appeared out of nowhere. I didn't even see them sit down. I thought about it for a second or two and then shrugged my shoulders in acceptance that they appeared like magic. My eyes were on the prowl, but my head looked through and around them. Although, one of the guys did look interesting to me.

"Don't stare, I don't want them to come over," Micha demanded. She looked at them, and batted her long feathery eyelashes. She pretty much stood up and waved a white flag by the invitation of her body language.

The other guy closest to us nodded to his friends, then slowly scooted his chair out. He got up, came towards us. Lizzy put her phone down on the table and gripped my arm to announce his presence. I guess she thought I wasn't paying attention. He introduced himself.

"Hey, how are you ladies doing? My name is Rick Morris." He grinned boyishly as he pulled a chair from behind him up to the corner of our booth and straddled it.

He had dark hair, pale skin, and dark hazel eyes. He was pretty good looking, and seemed like a nice enough guy. We all introduced ourselves.

"Hi, I'm Jennifer," I said shyly.

"Hey, how are doing? I'm Betty." Micha shook his hand as she finished the last of her soda with the other hand. She stared at her hand after his fingers left hers.

"What's up? I'm Sarah," Lizzy smiled, shaking his hand, barely. Partly because she had noticed Micha's confused look. We decided to play our little game. We did this from time to time, just for fun. Although by the end of the night, if they were lucky, we would tell them our real names.

We were sitting there drinking our sodas, talking and having fun. Then the other guy, the one I thought was interesting looking, came over and started flirting blatantly with all of us. He was tall, had dark brown hair, a goatee, and mysteriously shaded brown eyes. He was muscular, but not too muscular in a semi-tight plain black shirt and black slacks. He introduced himself as Bill, but didn't give us his last name. In one swift motion he set his empty glass on the table in front of me and paused briefly before coming up. It was almost like he stopped to smell my hair. A warning sign began flashing in my head. I felt strange. I eyed his glass wondering what he had been drinking. It looked to be wine or some kind of deep red beverage.

Bill motioned for the cocktail waitress to come over. It was a different lady than our original waitress. "Drinks are on me," he offered, smiling at all of us.

The cocktail waitress came to find out what we wanted. I stood up next to him and leaned closer in a nonchalant way and whispered privately, "My birthday is next month."

"What day?" he asked, tickling my eardrum with the frequency of his dreamy voice.

"May twenty-fifth," I sighed, catching my breath somewhat ashamed of my youth. "I'm not twenty one yet," I admitted reluctantly. He put his arm around me in a friendly way, although I could tell he was attracted to me.

He whispered in my ear, "I own this place!" Then he stepped back, but didn't let go of me. I raised my hand and rubbed my ear, it was cold, which puzzled me. He held me really snug, embracing me tightly, but not painfully. I didn't know what to say. Actually, I felt drawn to him, in a weird way. My heart was pounding to the beat of the song on the jukebox and it felt as if it had moved into my head. The song was fast and powerful. And so were the feelings I was experiencing.

"You ladies have anything you want, it's on me," Bill announced, still holding me unyieldingly around my waist, but looking at Lizzy and Micha with a huge smile. His teeth gleamed and sparkled. I took a deep breath. Something was wrong. I could feel it deep down, way down inside, in the depth of my core that I was playing with fire. Taken by my dastardliness I withdrew. But, I couldn't stop admiring him. The wanting of love in my life made me desire to play Russian-roulette then and there.

Then I heard a strong deep voice inside my head say, *Drink one, be polite and get the heck out of there!"* Shivers ran up my spine. The sensation started from the tip of my big toe and ran through my body all the way to the very top of my head. My eyes told of my anxiety.

Lizzy could see I was in turmoil.

"Oh, Jennifer," Lizzy stood up trying to get my attention. "Girls, I've got to go. I have to be at work early in the morning," she said pulling the strap of her purse over her shoulder as she got up.

"Oh crap, that's right," I agreed, gathering my cigarettes up off the table and throwing them in my bag. I knew what she was attempting to do and I was grateful for her caring gesture.

He grabbed me and pulled me to his face. I was scared, but somehow lost in his eyes. I'd never seen such a handsomely beautiful face before in my life. They say eyes are the window to the soul. But I couldn't see any soul in those eyes. I assumed he had bad circulation, his hands felt so cold on my face. It was a shock to my system to feel his touch.

He kissed me hard. I felt euphoric, like I was floating then ... everything began to spin, making me feel nauseous and dizzy, but good. It was indescribable and unfamiliar to me.

Micha grabbed my arm and jerked me away too quickly, my head was spinning uncontrollably. Bewildered and dumbfounded, I looked around the room. Lizzy took my other arm and yanked me to her. They were playing tug-a-war with me. I suddenly felt torn, like I wanted to stay. But, I kept it to myself.

As we headed to the door a really big scary guy stopped us before we could get out the door. (His blood red tee-shirt accented his overly muscular torso and waist length dark hair.)

We all gasped, but Lizzy shouted at him, "Get out of our way! We're leaving ---Good night." She was firm and curt with her voice.

The dark eyed man stared at us. I was still out of it, but I heard Bill say, "Let them go! I will see you again, Isla." My eyes widened and I held my breath when I heard my name. He actually said my name right, it was pronounced exactly the way it was spelt Is La. I was totally thunderstruck that he knew my name. He spoke in that tranquil voice and my heart stopped. I turned to both of them with a look of shock across my face as we scurried out the door.

"How did he know my real name?" I asked out loud, once the door closed behind us. I glanced up at the crescent moon. The sky was fairly clear except for a few small clouds strewn throughout. The stars were bright and sparkly. I still felt strange and a bit dizzy.

We ran to the car, jumped in, and peeled out of the parking lot spraying the few cars there with gravel. I kept looking over my shoulder to see if anybody was following us.

"There isn't anyone chasing us, is there?" I asked as I faced forward and nervously bit the tips of my unnatural nails.

Micha answered sharply, "I hope not!" She turned and looked out the back window. I turned to see the worry in her eyes, even though the street was bare behind us.

"It doesn't look like it," Lizzy replied, eying the rearview mirror.

Lizzy had to be speeding because we were flying down the back roads. Flashes of Bill's face kept appearing in my brain. I got a chill thinking about that kiss and how it was as if the whole world disappeared around us.

When we pulled up to the curb in front of my house, the front porch light was still on, which meant my parents were up.

"We're not coming in. I really do work tomorrow, that was no lie," Lizzy admitted, smiling warmly. She worked as a receptionist for a lawyer in downtown Asheville and he was an early bird. He expected her to show up early as well.

She threw her arms around my neck and squeezed for a moment.

"Love ya, girl. We will have to do something next weekend. But don't worry we won't go to Jaggers," Lizzy said lovingly. When she hugged me I looked at her hair and noticed she had spit ends. Hairstylists do that. It doesn't matter where or who you are. We examine the hair and think *Man she needs highlights* or *She would look great with a lot of layers*. It's true, we can't help it. It's engraved in our blood. After my mind wandered into left field, it registered what Lizzy had said about not going back to Jaggers. My heart sunk and all I could think about was another encounter with Bill. My head was still spinning from that hypnotic kiss.

"It was an interesting night, to say the least," Micha sighed quietly from the back seat.

"I'm glad we hung out tonight. Even though it was a strange evening." I admitted. Disbelief had rendered me, not speechless, but close. "Goodnight, I'll call y'all tomorrow," I affirmed as I got out of the car and shut the door.

"Love you, girl. See you soon," Micha hollered loudly through the closed door. I smiled and started to turn towards my house.

"Call me tomorrow," Lizzy screamed as she rolled up the window and drove away. Her voice echoed in the early morning stillness of the black sky.

When I walked in the door I could hear the TV in the family room blaring. I peeked around the corner. Mom was asleep on the couch, curled up in a blanket and Dad was in his big chair, snoring like crazy. I ran upstairs to my room, jumped on my bed, propped my head up with a pillow, and tried to read until I fell asleep. I don't know why, but all I could think about was Bill *if that was even his real name.* And how the heck did he know my real name? Did it come out by accident? I tried to remember the conversations. Going over them in my head, I came to the conclusion my name was not mentioned. Somehow he knew my name. My thoughts about him were overpowering my mind. To think of him and that kiss made every part of my body tingle. Soon I drifted off to sleep.

I know I was asleep, but somehow still felt very awake. *I was standing in the darkness in what looked like my backyard. I sat down in a chair on the deck and looked around to see millions of stars on the ground, and everywhere. Shimmers of light danced on the ground, on lawn chairs, and even on a faded black ceramic panther that stood regally at the end of the deck.*

Suddenly I felt as if I were moving, but I wasn't walking, it was more like gliding. Then I found myself on a beautiful black canopy bed.

I was above myself, looking down. I was asleep and my expressions seemed to be peaceful. Suddenly a big, dark shadow cast over my face and chest. I couldn't move. Something was pushing against me. My body was aching. I had been there before, seen this before, but didn't know where or when.

The next morning I awoke tired even though I had gotten enough sleep. I felt different in a way. There was something different about me, but I didn't have the foggiest idea what. I caught a chill from a breeze and realized my window was open. I ran to close it, locking it. I even tried shaking it loose, then sat back down on my bed puzzled and thinking to myself. *Did I walk in my sleep or was I so wiped out that I was oblivious to the fact that I had opened it.* I was beginning to second guess myself. But I knew I hadn't opened it. "I know I did not leave that window open," I said out loud.

I got dressed very quickly, without even putting my makeup on, and ran downstairs. My mom was sitting in the kitchen drinking her coffee staring out the window. She must have cooked something, there was the smell of pumpkin in the air.

"What's for breakfast, Mom?"

She looked up and said, "It is lunchtime now, Isla," she sighed and shot me a smile decorated with disappointment. I ignored her expression.

I scratched my head and thought, *wow I must have slept along time.* Then I considered that maybe my Mom had opened the window and I hadn't noticed that it was open when I got home early this morning.

"Mom did you leave my window open last night?" I asked while I found something to snack on in the refrigerator.

"No honey, I haven't even been in your room," she confirmed with a questionable expression. I shrugged my shoulders and kept ransacking the fridge and cabinets.

The sliding glass back door opened and dad came in from the back yard holding red roses. I thought, *that's nice, he bought roses for mom.*

Then he turned to me and said, "These were on the back porch, they're for you." He held out the crystal vase full of the most striking red roses I had ever seen. They must of been a new breed. Burgundy wine was the only way I could describe the color of most of them. Some were in full robust blooms and the others were hiding their pollen waiting for tomorrow to blossom.

I stared at him with innocent surprise, and then grabbed the vase and pulled the card. The note read, *Please have dinner with me tonight. Bill?* At first I thought *why so short?* Then I took a whiff of the elegant fragrance of the beautiful roses that glistened with the morning dew and it didn't even matter anymore . It was short, but sweet.

I sat down hastily and almost missed the chair. There were some different roses scattered through out the dozen, that looked like fire with their red and orange swirled designs. They were exotic and alluring. I had never seen anything quite like them before.

Although, I wondered what the question mark meant. I bet he was playing the game, too. I had to find out so I decided to accept, and went upstairs to call Jaggers. I didn't talk to him, but left him a message instead, that I would be waiting. After closing my phone I went to my closet to figure out what to wear. I decided to wear my favorite red and black tie-dyed dress, actually it was gauchos, but it looked like a dress. The purse I picked out was black and had a red dragon down the side in embroidery. I admired myself in the mirror, patting myself on the back for putting together such a stylish ensemble.

A few minutes later my mom yelled up the stairs "There's a black limousine in front of the house." I took a deep breath, picked up my purse, ran downstairs, and out the door before she could ask me who it was, or any questions at all. I had a bit of a stomach ache. The fact that I had no idea where I was going was a bit unnerving, but in a way intensely intriguing.

Walking up to the car, the driver got out, and opened the door for me. He nodded and grinned. I returned the gesture. After getting in, I discovered I was alone. I had half expected him to be in the car waiting for me. More like, hoped.

The bar was lit up with little white lights. There were crystal wine glasses hanging from a dark wooden rack in the ceiling above the bar. The upholstery was a light grey soft leather and the walls of the limo were dark grey velvet. I put my hand out and felt the soft material.

We drove for a long time. I knocked on the privacy window and the driver lowered it. I asked the driver how much longer. He turned to look at me with one corner of his mouth raised and the other down. His facial expression came off as somewhat quirky and laid-back.

Then he returned his eyes in the opposite direction and peered at me through the rearview mirror. "It'll only be a few more minutes. We're almost there. Have some wine and relax. Don't worry, it won't be long."

"Okay, thank you." I was ready for a drink. My tummy was in knots and I was beginning to panic.

"You're welcome, Ms. Van Burren" he replied then turned his attention back to the road. I was astonished that he knew my last name. *Okay, well I guess he knew my last name from the mailbox in front of my house.* I told myself as I leaned over and poured a bottle of red wine into a glass. I brought the glass to my lips to take a sip, and stopped when I got a whiff of it. It smelled really salty. I had never smelled wine with a salty aroma. The smell compared to that of the ocean with out being laced with a stinky fish smell, of course.

I put the glass down as we came to a stop and the driver opened the door. As I step out and my eyes focused I observed that the huge structure before me was a majestic castle.

I couldn't believe my eyes. "Wow! Am I dreaming?" I asked out loud to myself. The front of the castle had a rich, dark, earth tone and the moon shone vividly in each window pane that I could see. The designs and symbols that accented the windows and doors were intricate and mesmerizing, even in the dark. I could have stood and marveled at its exterior for hours.

I was born and raised here in Asheville, North Carolina and never knew this mysterious castle existed. It was so massive, I felt really stupid for not ever knowing of it.

"Where am I?" I asked the driver, hoping he would tell me the name of this amazing place. But when I turned, he was gone. I looked around in surprise and gasped when I realized I was all alone.

"Where did he go?" I asked out loud. I turned and looked all over. There was nothing to hide behind, and nowhere he could have gone that fast. I thought maybe I should get back in the car. Just as I started to turn around, the huge cherry wood double doors opened. I slowly stepped into the foyer and walked over the threshold of the doorway, oblivious to what lied ahead of me. The front room was so monstrous my whole house could have fit inside it. There was an astounding staircase with beautiful Victorian railings and fantastic crystal chandeliers sparkling like diamonds dangling from the extremely tall ceilings. There was an amazing garden room off to my right with red roses trimmed with a fiery orange just like the ones he had sent me. *They were planted in beautiful ceramic pots around a light cream-colored fountain.* There were soft white lilies, purple and pink tulips placed next to the roses. The greenhouse room was shaped like an octagon with a glass cathedral ceiling that went to a point in the middle and had tall, slender palm trees going up the walls in each corner of the room. It was truly breathtaking. I looked for somewhere to sit and noticed a short white chair which looked to be like a lawn chair, but was definitely more sturdy. I had to sit down and take it all in. I gazed down at the shiny dark grey marble floors and saw my reflection. And when I looked back up, Bill was standing in front of me smiling as if he had been watching me the whole time.

"Hello, my sweet," he said, instantly captivating me with his eyes, drawing me in with his satin smooth velvet voice. His gaze was disorienting. It took all I had, to break the stare, to prevent from being sucked in.

"Dinner is being served." I heard from the other side of me. I turned to see where it came from. No one was there.

He took my hand and I spluttered in the air when I felt the shock of his gentle icy hand. I stood up, but tried to cast my eyes in a different direction. And tried to pull myself together... it didn't work. His hand was so cold it caused me to grimace. He had to have noticed, his demeanor changed briefly. He led me into a gigantic room. I swallowed hard, and an echo of it rung out like a door shutting loudly, or maybe it was just in my head. The room had tapestries of colorful dreamy landscapes with people planting flowers and sipping tea in little restaurants along quaint city streets. The one that caught my eye the most was that of a big mysterious looking tree with a figure of a man and a woman lying against the tall textured bark at the base. The roots just beneath them looked like snakes. It was kind of spooky. But what had me pondering was the way the man and woman were positioned. The side of their heads were lightly touching and their hands were entwined, but their bodies were off to either side away from each other. I understood it as how much man and woman were different. One the yin and the other the yang. And finding our soul mates made us whole. We balanced one another. I wondered when I was going to meet my yin or my yang. Maybe---I already had.

In the middle of the room was a long, dark cherry wood table with red velvet upholstered chairs. The deep velvet was woven up the back in an exotic pattern, like vines growing up the middle of the chairs. There were so many chairs, at least fifteen to twenty on both sides. The fire was blazing in not one, but two fireplaces right next to each other. It had one long hearth over the both of them. The painting above it was an enormous ship coming in to dock. There were lights in loops along the sides leading to the very tip of the pier. It was a beautiful black and white picture that made me feel happy and devastated at the same time.

After admiring the amazing art. I returned my attention to Bill.

He held a chair out for me. "Your chair, my sweet," he whispered enticingly. His whisper made my heart race.

I sat down to an empty table, and suddenly there was an appetizing plate of food in front of me. I glanced around to see where it had come from or who set it before me. But I didn't see anyone.

"Eat, my sweet," he insisted, shooting shards of electricity through his eyes to mine. I shook my head trying to make sense of it all. My mind felt a little spacey. I shook my head hoping to rearrange my marbles. To regain my wits about me, like somehow it would all make since.

"You know my name, why don't you use it?" I demanded sternly as I picked up the silver fork and tried to cut through the juicy dark meat. All the while barely breaking our gaze until he circled behind and gravitated to the side of me gently pulling the chair out and sitting down. Our legs were touching. He slid the sole of his shoe up the side of the sole of my black riding boot. I inhaled slow and steady for what seemed like a long time. Then pushed it all out in one sharp breath. I picked up my water glass and guzzled it peering in the glass avoiding his stare.

"If you like, Isla," he responded, noticeably amused.

Hearing my name, it was like the blood retracted away from my heart. I watched him as he got up and walked to the other side of the table and sat down in the chair across from me. I took a bite slowly and looked down at the plate of food averting memorization by his breathtaking eyes. I glanced up quickly and then back down at the plate and continued eating. Now, I'd had chicken and vegetables before, but it never tasted as mouthwatering as it did then.

"Do you like it?" he asked. I thought he was talking about the food. So I responded.

"Yes, it's really good." I tried to swallow without looking nervous.

"No, not the food. Do you like life?" he asked, his voice breathy and deep. My pulse began to race.

"What do you mean?" I asked with my guard up and confusion painting my face.

"Do you like your life?" he repeated in a soft throaty tone. His eyes were fixated on mine.

"Yes, I suppose I do," I answered, my voice shaky and faint. I could barely breathe to speak. My words were stifled by the pounding of my heart.

"What's wrong? Why have you stopped eating?" he asked with a sinful smile as he leaned into my view. I continued staring at the plate of food. Not giving in to his bewitching eyes.

"I need to go home," I demanded abruptly. "I don't even know you. I mean, what is your real name anyway? You're really scaring me." I struggled to get the words out and then I threw my napkin down in a fit.

He paused and then gradually got up. I was nervous as to what he would say or do. "I will tell you in due time, my sweet Isla," he whispered. His breath echoed all around me.

Then suddenly he was behind me pulling my chair out.

"I will have my driver take you home," he mumbled close to my ear. The cold air from his mouth instantly made my ear ache. I could feel his frown. I suddenly felt mean and guilty for turning his lips upside down.

I got up, turned to see him. He was standing very close. I looked up to his staring eyes and sighed, "Thank you for dinner." As I turned to walk away, he grabbed my arm and pulled me close. His lips were about an inch away from my trembling mouth.

"I'll see you again, soon," he promised with a smirk. I suddenly had a sensation of being lost, never to be found.

Then he kissed me, and it was like the world stopped around us. There was nothing, just he and I. He let me go, pushing me away bluntly as if he was afraid he would lose control and never let me go. I felt drugged and would have done anything he wanted me to do after that kiss. I had become a puppet and he was the puppeteer.

He walked me to the corridor and smiled innocently, as he held my hand. After breaking his grasp and turning away I gleamed back at him as the driver opened the front door and escorted me to the car. I got in. My head was wrestling with confusion and desire. I was completely consumed. As I got comfortable in the seat my attention fell on a silver shiny box which had been placed next to my untouched beverage. I could see my reflection in the box as I picked it up and opened it.

When I did I found a beautiful necklace. I immediately took it out and put it on, touching it softly as if I could still feel him there. They were black pearls, that had a purplish tone to them. I started analyzing our conversations, his smile, and the way he held me. His questions puzzled me and I felt highly intoxicated after he kissed me. I was alone with my thoughts of him, for a while, but it seemed like the ride was much shorter that time.

The car stopped; the door opened. The driver never really said much.

He helped me out of the car and said, "Goodnight, Ms. Van Burren."

I smiled politely and went to the door. Before closing the door behind me I turned to look ... the car was gone without a sound. Baffled by what I had seen and felt I headed upstairs to my room.

I could still see his eyes, they burned me like a fire inside, igniting all my desires. I had butterflies; scratch that...I had hawks in my stomach. I got ready for bed and crawled under my big, billowy dark red comforter and prayed until I fell asleep.

Chapter 2
A Trip

J HAD A NIGHTMARE LAST NIGHT ... *I was filling out college applications. I rubbed my eyes, then looked again and in front of me was my death certificate. Freaking out, I tossed it as far away from me as possible. I jumped up shaking it off, running around like a crazy person totally losing it.*

Suddenly I had a feeling I was not alone in the room. Every hair on my body stood up. The terror was real. I didn't breathe for what seemed like a long time. I was afraid to look. All of a sudden I jumped to a loud clicking and rattling sound. Jolting up and realizing it was my phone, I picked it up. It was Lizzy.

"Did I wake you?" she asked sounding excited and anxious.

"Thank God you did!" I screamed quietly.

Then she began to tell me that her parents gave her tickets for two to Amsterdam for getting into Princeton. She had gone to community college to get her grades good enough for Princeton for the last two and a half years.

"That's awesome," I said in an almost jealous way. I had always wanted to go to Amsterdam ... well Europe, in general. Never been anywhere. Born here in Asheville, North Carolina, and I thought for sure I would never get out! Although, it was beautiful in

Asheville, with waterfalls all over the place, and beautiful hillsides. Great nightlife and all the things that went with big cities. But ever since I was a kid, I had wanted to go to Europe.

I think I was about ten when my mom came back after a trip with some friends. She didn't know I was listening, but I overheard her talking to her friends about it. She said she really loved the coffee shops although at that time I had thought it was coffee they served. Though I have been a pretty good girl through the years, but I had flirted with my occasional party favor.

"I wouldn't ask anyone but you to come with me," Lizzy said.

"I have always wanted to go," I said not so softly. I glanced at the clock and realized it was 3:45 in the morning.

"Holy crap!" I yelled.

"What?" she asked, startled by my yelp.

"Lizzy, do you even realize what time it is?" I felt like I had just gone to bed.

"I'm sorry ... just got so excited, I couldn't wait till tomorrow."

"That's alright, I was having a bad nightmare. I'm glad you woke me."

I heard some bumping and wrestling around in another part of the house.

"Oh, Lizzy, I've got to get back to sleep. I think my parents are up," I muttered, staring at my bedroom door waiting for a knock or for it to fly open and either my mom or dad to be standing there pissed.

"Okay girl, I will talk to you in a while," she stammered hoping she didn't instigate anything.

"Call me as soon as you talk to your parents," she said.

Closing my phone and lying back in bed I prayed that my parents weren't really up. Listening very closely, I didn't hear anything more.

I was so ecstatic my heart was beating erratically. I was surprised I fell back to sleep. Later, waking up I realized I would have to talk to my parents to ask permission to go. I also had to ask work; I didn't know which one was worse. It was Saturday morning, what better day to talk to my parents about the trip. I got up, brushed my teeth and then ran down the stairs. My nerves were going haywire.

My mom was in the kitchen cooking breakfast ... eggs, bacon, and biscuits. My tummy was making gurgling noises, yep, definitely hungry. Bill's face came to mind. I pictured his eyes and the feelings rushed back like a fever spreading through my body. His eyes were embedded in my soul.

"Good morning, sweetie," she said softly with a smile as she put a plate on the table. When she spoke it startled me. She was busy so she hadn't seen me jump.

"Good morning," I said groggily.

"What was going on so early this morning? I heard you scream and some talking. Were you having a nightmare? Were you talking in your sleep, again?" She asked concerned as she leaned over me to set a glass of orange juice down on the table. My mind was so foggy recalling the night before, it took me a few minutes before it registered that she had asked me a question.

"Have you heard me talk in my sleep? " I asked with a puzzled expression, hoping she hadn't ever heard me say anything incriminating. Even though I'd been mostly an angel, when you're sleeping you have no control. She did not speak a word. Her mouth formed an impish grin and her hazel eyes squinted with slight scrutiny.

"Yes, I did have a nightmare." I muttered bringing my fingers to my mouth and nervously nibbling on my nails. Barely biting down, but I still had to do something. I was freaking out thinking about that dream. It's strange that Lizzy called and saved me before I saw the date of my own death. Sometimes dreams are curses in disguise.

"Lizzy called to tell me she got into Princeton."

"Oh that is great!" she exclaimed enunciating each syllable.

"Well that's not the only great thing. Her parents gave her tickets to Amsterdam for two. And I figured since my birthday was coming up I would be able to go if that was all I was asking for.

Can I go please? Please!" I handed her my best entreaty. Wanting her to feel my desperate call. I wanted so badly to go.

"Oh, I don't know ... we will have to ask your father," she said smiling thoughtfully, as if she had already decided. She was holding back her enthusiasm to keep me from getting my hopes up, I could see it in her eyes.

"Do you think he will let me go, Mom? I have always wanted to go to Europe," I sighed clasping my hands together begging her for mercy. As I fantasized and hoped that my foreknowledge would invoke a happy outcome. *He will say yes. I know he will.* I told myself, blocking any negative thoughts that tried to enter my mind.

"You know your father leaves today for a week, for work, right?" she reminded me as she sat down with her plate and scooted up to the table.

"I forgot. Do you think I'll have time to talk to him?" I asked, picking up the fork and slicing my fried egg into bite size squares. "Mmmm, what kind of seasoning did you put on this?" I wondered out loud with my mouth half full.

"It's steak seasoning. Do you like it?" she asked staring at me over the rim of her coffee cup.

"Yes! It's really good, with just enough spice." I admitted, taking a few more bites. I muttered, "Hmm steak and eggs without the meat." I sat back in the chair and peered out the window. At nothing really, all the view entailed was some tall, leafy trees. And next to that was the neighbors house. Not much to look at. But you could see a little of the sky especially from where I was sitting at that point in time. "Is dad getting up soon?" I turned to mom and asked.

"I'm sure he'll be up in a little bit," she assured me, she could tell how anxious I was.

"Cool," I said as I finished up my breakfast. I put my plate in the sink and ran upstairs to get dressed. Entering my room, I went straight to my closet to pick my clothes out for the day.

I stood in front of my closet and just stared. Then glanced around my room at all my clothes scattered here and there across my floor. It was no wonder I couldn't figure out what to wear. After rummaging through a basket of clean garments, I picked out black capri's and a pink and black animal print shirt, then slipped into my black clogs. I was scared, exhilarated, and nervous, feeling anticipation about what my dad would say. I brushed my teeth and my hair, but forgot to put makeup on.

I headed back downstairs to the kitchen. My mom was washing dishes. She was so beautiful, even first thing in the morning, with her long brown hair, hazel eyes and a beautiful smile (almost angelic). She was a little petite thing with a big heart and big hair. My parents had been together like forever. Well not really, but since they were eighteen years old. They were only about two months apart in age.

"I hear him," she said, looking at me in anticipation.

I smiled. "Do you think he's in a good mood today?" I asked, hopeful that it would go over smoothly.

"He seemed like he was, we'll see," she said anxiously as she finished up the dishes.

Dad came down the stairs in a tan robe and house slippers. He was handsome and distinguished with dark brown hair and brown eyes. He was very tall and slender. He looked like he would have played basketball in high school, but he didn't. He had his head in a book most of the time. Now he worked as a computer analyst, visiting companies all over the world to help them figure out what they could do to make their jobs easier and more efficient.

"Good morning, ladies," he said, yawning and stretching as he sat down.

"Good morning, Dad," I replied, leaning over to kiss his cheek.

"What was that for?" he asked with wondering eyes.

"Because, I love you," I said, smiling a big enormous smile.

Alright, what do you want? What's going on?" he asked grinning curiously.

"Well ... Lizzy called last night, well actually it was really early this morning, but anyway, she called to tell me she got accepted to Princeton."

"That's great! Is she excited? And where are you planning to go?" he asked, happy for her but disappointed with me because I still hadn't picked a college.

"I haven't decided yet!" I said with no hidden meaning. I did want to go to college. Knowledge is life. If you stop learning you might as well crawl in a hole and pull the dirt over you.

"There is more, honey," mom interjected as she placed his plate in front of him, caressed his shoulder and sat down sipping her coffee and smiling in between each swig.

"Oh?" He looked at her then looked questionably back at me.

I took a deep breath and began to tell him, "Her parents gave her two tickets to Amsterdam as a gift for getting in," I blurted out, waiting for him to yell. I nervously peeked at him through my squinted eyes.

"So she invited you to go, did she?" he asked with a half grin.

"Yes, Dad, can I go? Please! Please!" I begged excitedly.

"Let me think about it. I will let you know before I go on my trip," he said smiling, and then chomped on some bacon.

"What time are you leaving?" I asked, not wanting him to but extremely anxious to hear what his answer would be.

He held his hand up to let me know he was still chewing. "Probably about 4:30," he said after swallowing.

"Okay," I sighed, my shoulders sank some as I got up from the table. "I'm going to go put makeup on so I don't scare anybody," I joked then dashed up stairs.

I could hear my parents laughing and disagreeing that I would scare anybody as I went up the steps to my room. I sat on my bed cross-legged, and poured my makeup bag out. I watched a movie, but listened to *I Want to Be Sedated* by the Ramones. My phone vibrated on the nightstand and before I picked it up I knew it was Lizzy.

"Hey girl!" I answered cheerfully reaching for the volume button so I could hear her.

"So are you going with me?" she asked, hoping the news would be good.

"I will know at 4:30, that's when my dad leaves to go out of town for work. He'll probably say yes. I mean, my birthday is coming up soon and I will be 21. He'll have to let me go. Hope! Hope!"

"What about work?" she asked.

"Oh, I don't know yet, we'll find out Monday. I'm kind of worried about that one, but I'll see what I can do. When do you want to go?"

"We can go the week of your birthday if you want," she suggested lovingly.

"That would be cool," I was exhilarated about finally getting to Europe. "Maybe we can catch a train, and go to Italy. I have always wanted to go to the Van Gogh Museum."

"Oh, me too. I did a paper on him and other impressionists of that era my first year of college, I can't wait!" she said ecstatically and almost breathless.

"I can't wait either!" I yelled in joy.

"I'll talk to you around 4:45," she said, hopeful that the answer would be in our favor.

"Okay, talk to you soon," I responded, then closed my phone. Lying back, to visualize Amsterdam and the fun we would have, I closed my eyes for a second and drifted off. *In this dream I was in a library. It looked like a private library. There were books all the way up the walls on both sides of the room. The ceiling was covered with beautifully painted angels. The furniture wasn't your normal library furniture. Everything was red and black with dark wood. There was a long red velvet couch and on each corner it rolled under, making a swirl It looked so inviting I sat down and felt the material with my finger tips then rubbed it with my whole hand. It was so soft, like lying in a bed of feathery angels. There was a roaring fire in the fireplace and a spiral staircase going up to more books off to the side. Then suddenly I wasn't* alone. *I could hear, and feel heavy breathing right behind me. A piece of my spicy red-brown hair floated out in front of me in the wind of the breath. I tried to move, but felt a heavy weight sitting on my chest. Gasping for air, I felt a horrible pain in my body and neck. Then I was above myself watching. My eyes sprung open in terror in my dream.*

Then I opened them in reality and looked around my room. "Holy crap, what the heck was that?" I exhaled out loud breathing heavily, still unable to catch my breath. I was seriously freaking out. I jumped out of bed, and started pacing around the room.

Now, I have always been a very spiritual person, and emotional too. So I couldn't help but cry. It was a good thing I hadn't put my makeup on yet. I sat down and prayed immediately.

About thirty minutes later my normal breathing had returned, and I felt much better. I looked at the clock and saw it was 4:15.

I was coming down the stairs as my dad was walking towards the door.

He put his bags down, gave me a huge hug, picked me up and spun me around and said sweetly, "I love you, Issy. My little Issy!" He set me down and saw the embarrassment in my eyes.

"Hey Dad, I am almost twenty-one. I'm not little anymore."

"I know, stop growing. Just stop it!" he demanded jokingly. "You will always be our little girl. Don't you know that by now?" he asked not particularly expecting an answer. He smiled and gave me a peck on the cheek.

I shot him a questioning look. His eyes averted as if he wasn't going to satisfy me with an answer. There was joy bouncing in his eyes in the form of a sparkle, "Yes, you can go to Amsterdam," he promised. I screamed and hollered and jumped up and down. I was so thrilled. "Thank you! Thank you so much!

"You're welcome honey. I'm glad you get the chance to go. I'll see you in a week," he said, his happiness bittersweet, because he was leaving.

"Where's Mom?" I asked.

"She's upstairs, you know she can't see me to the door. Your mom is so emotional," he explained.

He hugged me one last time. "I'll be back next Sunday. Be good and help your mother."

"I'll see what I can do. I'll miss you. Love you, Dad," I said as I stood there excited and sad at the same time

"I love you too, Issy," he said as he closed the door behind him.

I ran back up the stairs to my room, threw myself on the bed and rolled around like a teenager. I sat up quickly and grabbed my phone. Just as I picked it up it vibrated. I looked, and of course it was Lizzy. I answered it, "Hey, Lizzy" trying to sound unhappy. I was going to play a little game with her.

"What's the verdict?" she asked hesitantly

"Well," I hemmed and hawed a second or two and then blurted out, "Yes, I can go!"

We both screamed. I jumped around so much, I dropped the phone. It snapped closed hanging up on her. "Oops," I said, quickly calling her back. That was one bad thing about that phone. If you drop it, it either shattered, or closed and hung up.

"Hey girl, sorry about that," I said laughing.

"That's okay, I fell off the bed," she said giggling a bit. We laughed.

"What an adventure it is going to be," she said.

"Yeah we are going to have a great time!" I shouted in delight.

"Hey girl, do you want to go to a party this weekend?" She interrupted my thoughts of our adventures.

"Sure, who's party?"

"This guy named Jee Cee Daine is throwing it at his family's castle. I heard about it through some kids I ran into at the mall. I remembered them from when I was a camp counselor at Camp Pisgah last year. They looked like they needed some sun badly. They were very pale, but anyway," she started rambling.

"It's supposed to be the party of the year!" she exclaimed as if she were coaxed into telling me this.

"Well, okay. Can Micha come, too?" I asked anxiously.

"I'm sure, they told me to bring friends." Lizzy replied.

"Is it Friday or Saturday night?" I asked.

"Saturday night. I'll pick you up. Okay?"

"Sounds great," I squeaked, still so happy about Amsterdam. "I'll call you soon, okay? Love you girl," I said caringly.

"Bye girl, love you too!" She hung up. When I put the phone down it hit me. *I wonder if it's the same castle or palace.* After mulling it over in my head, I realized if it was then I would know his real name, at least last name. The thought of him made me smile picturing his scintillating pale skin, his deep enchanting eyes, and that smile that would turn every head even without a flash or sparkle. He was so dreamy, I felt like I was dreaming when I was with him. Thoughts of him made me feel very warm and cozy. I had had so much going on, I hadn't thought of him very much at all. Suddenly, I felt guilty about that.

I approached my closet. "What do I wear?" I blurted out. As I threw open the door and a shiny flash of light caught my eye. I checked to see what it was. It was the sequins on a dress I had worn to a cocktail party thrown by a friend of my parents' when I was eighteen. I pulled it out quickly and tried it on. It still fit, even better than it had before. I kind of filled it out a little better now. Looking in the mirror I thought, *"Damn, I look hot."*

It was a black dress with silver sequins from the bottom of the bust all the way to the floor. It had spaghetti straps with a real low neckline and a slit up one side. I had forgotten how much I loved that dress. I was happy I could wear it again. I rummaged through my jewelry box looking for a necklace that would go with it. I couldn't find anything that matched.

Ding dong. Just then the doorbell rang.

"I got it," I yelled, running down the stairs.

I opened the door but nobody was there. Looking down as I started to close the door, I saw a package on the front porch. It was a pretty red box. I examined it for a tag or card, but there wasn't one. I carefully pulled off the top and swallowed hard when I saw the same silver box, so shiny I could see my reflection. I knew it was from him. Taking the little box out, I smiled and tears came to my eyes as I opened it. It was the most beautiful necklace I had ever seen. Silver with a big gorgeous black stone, red rubies and diamonds that dazzled like the stars in the sky on the blackest of nights.

I turned to go upstairs and nearly fell as I stepped up. I went to my room, and put it on in the mirror. "It's perfect," I said out loud. I couldn't understand how he knew unless he was listening or reading my mind. After changing and sitting down on my big red fuzzy chair. I began to daydream, imagining that kiss again. My stomach knotted up just thinking about it.

I couldn't wait to see him Saturday night. I knew it was his house. "I am dating one of the Daine brothers," I murmured to myself. I thought about him the rest of the evening, and could feel him pulling me into him. My tummy growled, *I didn't eat much today*, I thought as I drifted off into a deep, deep sleep.

Chapter 3

Just Another Day

*J*WOKE UP FEELING AND HEARING A soft breath blowing by my ear, then heard a deep sweet voice that resonated within me saying, "I'll see you soon, Isla." It was velvety soft and lit my skin on fire. Opening my eyes, I took a deep breath and looked around my room. Glancing at the clock on my bedside table, I saw it was 5:30 a.m. I got up quickly and started getting dressed. "I have to work today," I said out loud.

Anything to get that dream off of my mind. Although it was benevolent, it still got under my skin in an arousing way. It was a turn-on, but frightening too.

I didn't have to be at work until 11:00 a.m. I always took my time getting ready. I went down to the kitchen. My mom was still sleeping, she only cooked breakfast when dad was home or during the weekend.

I picked up a banana then took a handful of mixed nuts and put them in a zip- lock bag. I put a mug of water in the microwave for my hot tea. When the microwave dinged I took my breakfast and headed back upstairs to my room.

Walking in, I noticed that the window was open. I didn't open it. *What if he was there in my room and that was no dream?* Scared yet intrigued, my stomach was beginning to hurt.

I looked out the window, up at the trees and on the ground ... nothing. I closed the window and latched it securely then sat back down on my bed to put my makeup on. I dressed in my long black skirt with zippers all over it with black boots that came to my knees and zipped up the sides. After looking through my closet I decided on a black and red animal print short-sleeve tunic that laced with a thin red ribbon in the front. I wore my hair down and scrunched. Not like eighty's hair, more like a controlled 2007 tousled look. I was ready to go. I was quite pleased with my reflection as I smiled at myself in the mirror. Then I grabbed my stuff and headed downstairs and out the door.

I worked only ten minutes away, and was usually about thirty minutes early. This particular day I was forty-five minutes early. The receptionist Lissa was on the phone when I walked in. I put my stuff under my station and asked Lissa to please print me a sheet of my appointments. Her name was actually Melissa, but we called her Lissa because there were two Melissa's that worked there.

"Oh, by the way, good morning and thank you," I said as I took the piece of paper and went and sat down at my station. Lissa just nodded, she was on the phone. My first appointment was a haircut at 11:00 so I had plenty of time to read.

I sat down in my chair and read some junk mail, most of which was from psychics telling me my time was coming, or that I would have my fortune soon. None of them predicted anything about the party or the mysterious man in my life.

So I crumpled them up and threw them in the trash. I had an itch and scratched my neck, feeling the necklace. I had forgotten that I still had on the beautiful necklace he had just given me. Touching it lightly I drifted off in thought ... about him of course.

The clients I had all day asked what was different about me. They were my regulars since my junior year in high school, so they knew me well.

June, my boss, came in. I told her I needed to talk to her as soon as possible.

"Okay, is now good for you?" she asked me hesitantly.

"Sure, I don't have another appointment for an hour," I said graciously as I followed her to the employee lounge.

We sat there and talked a while. I told her about always wanting to go to Amsterdam. She agreed it was a once in a lifetime adventure.

"If it's for your birthday week, of course, you can have off," she said grinning.

I jumped up to hug her and nearly knocked her over.

"You have to make sure all of your appointments are rescheduled if any are already scheduled at that time," she reminded me.

"I know. Thank you, again," I went back out to the desk to check.

My other co-workers had started coming in. Angel Braiden, then Sandy Gunn. They were great people. I cared deeply for both of them. June too, for that matter. We were all really close.

"What is going on girl?" Angel asked with a mischievous grin. She could tell something was different about me.

I screeched with joy, "I'm going to Amsterdam!"

She screamed and gave me a hug. Then she stopped, stepped back and looked at me.

"That's not all, is it?" She looked into my eyes, trying to read them, her hands clenched firmly around my forearms. "You're in love, aren't you?" She didn't wait for my answer. "That's great, you deserve to be happy, sweetie," she said with a genuine smile.

I fell back into my seat and sat there stunned for a few minutes.

Am I? I asked myself. *Am I really in love?*

I just didn't know. I was confused, having only been with him two times. The first time I was really uncomfortable when he came on so strong; sweet, but strong, gentle, but overpowering. It was almost erotic and scary at the same time.

Remembering how he had gazed into my eyes, I didn't look away no matter what was going on. I just couldn't get that kiss off my mind. That kiss was amazing, exotic, crazy, and spiritual all at the same time. I couldn't wait to kiss him again, to stare into his eyes.

"Isla, your next client is here." Lissa touched my arm to get my attention. I was deep in thought. She saw me jump a little. "You okay girl?" she asked as she snapped her fingers in front of my eyes.

I laughed and turned to go greet my client in the lobby.

"Hello, Mrs. Berham, how are you doing today?" I asked genuinely.

"I'm great except for my back pain, my arthritis; I have a hang nail that hurts badly. I think I have the flu ... ," I tuned her out and went somewhere else in my mind. I just kept saying, "Hmm hmm."

Mrs. Berham always had an ailment. She also repeated everything that was wrong with her every time, but she was a sweet lady and an excellent tipper. So I just smiled and nodded as I finished her hair. She gave me a twenty dollar bill, bought some products and paid her bill.

"Have a great day, Mrs. Berham," I hollered as she walked out the door.

Checking the book, I saw that I had a full day. I was very happy, that meant I could actually pay my car insurance, not to mention saving for Amsterdam. I worked hard and produced some happy clients. I hadn't sat down at all, all day long. My feet hurt terribly; I was ready to go home.

"Isla, your 4:30 is here," Lissa smiled sympathetically as she knew how much my feet were hurting. I did my client's hair; she was very happy when she left. I looked at Angel, she looked at me as though she knew what I was thinking. Angel and I had a real psychic connection. I once had a dream she was going to meet someone special in her life, and I told her the first name of the guy. She had met and was dating him three months later.

When Angel had realized I predicted the truth she was flabbergasted. She was happy and still with him. We were both in tune to our psychic abilities.

"Hey girl, can you do a reading for me?" I asked Angel as she was finishing up a client.

She smiled, nodded, and then went to check out her client. "When do you want to do it?" she asked while sweeping her station.

"What about Friday after work?" I suggested, hoping to get it done before Saturday night.

"We might have time before Friday, we'll see," she added.

I went to grab the broom from her to sweep. Happenin Hair was a cute little salon, the interior was black and white, mostly, with little color accents here and there. It was a great place to work. We were definitely like family. Although, I have always tried to keep people I work with somewhat distant. Even as a little girl my father instilled that in me, don't mix business with pleasure. You can be close to people you work with, but don't get too close. I have always lived by that rule.

It was time to go home for the day. I packed up my stuff.

"Bye, I'll see y'all tomorrow," I said as I walked towards the door.

"Bye Isla," Angel yelled loud enough so everyone knew I was leaving. I walked out the door, through the parking lot, got in my car, and drove home. A few blocks from my house I decide I needed to make a stop. I pulled in to the neighborhood drugstore to get my photo taken for my passport. I was glad I had worn one of my favorite shirts. After that, I stopped at the post office and filled out the paperwork for my passport and mailed it off.

When I got home I went straight up to my room. My window was open again. I gasped and gaped at it for a second or two. This was really beginning to freak me out. I went to my parents' room. My mom was sitting by her window reading.

"Mom, did you open the window in my room?" I wanted answers. It just didn't make sense. I had an uneasy feeling down in my gut.

"No honey, I didn't," she replied with a puzzled look on her face.

"Okay, just wondering." I sighed then went back to my room and closed the window again. I made sure it was locked as tight as I could get it. I took my smock off and counted my tips. It wasn't late, but I was tired. So I prayed, brushed my teeth, laid down, and was out for the count.

Chapter 4

Anticipation

*U*PON WAKING I TRIED TO RECALL MY dreams, but I was drawing a blank. Either I had dreams that my subconscious chose to block out or I hadn't had any dreams at all. I looked around my room and held my breath when I saw my window open again. I ran over and slammed it shut. Panic struck me. I was scared. My eyes filled up and gushed. I searched my room and under my bed. I sat down on my bed and put my head in my hands. My tears were running down my arms I was crying so much. Leaning up against the headboard I began to do some breathing exercises.

I told myself to breathe deeply several times, letting all the air escape from my lungs every time I exhaled. After a few minutes I felt better, but lightheaded. Then he came to my mind. I felt anguish and frustration, wanting to see him, and wondered why I couldn't see him now. I went to the bathroom to wash my face and brush my teeth.

I needed to get ready for work. So I did my usual, put my makeup on, gathered all the essentials I might need for the day, and stuffed them in my bag. I got dressed in a pair of black pants, a long sleeve black somewhat see-through blouse with a red fitted tank top. I styled my hair and headed down the stairs and out the door. I got in my car and started the engine.

Driving to work through the winding countryside roads the sky was a baby blue and the sun was shining bright. "It's such a beautiful day," I muttered. A good song came on the radio. I immediately reached out and rotated the volume knob way up to a deafening level. Nothing like rocking loudly; I had to yell the words to sing along. *Bow Down Before The One You Serve. You're gonna get what you deserve.* I loved Nine Inch Nails. I had performed a rock opera at an independent theatre my junior year, and that song was what I warmed up with. It had a great grungy groove and always got me in the mood to dance.

When I got to work I looked at the appointment book. I saw that I only had a few clients so I sat and read most of the day. Depression was beginning to set in, but I reminded myself I was going to see him soon. The day went by in a blur. Overwhelmed by my eagerness to see him, I couldn't even focus. I guess it was good I didn't have many clients.

It was 5:00 before I knew it. I put my things in my bag, smiled at the girls, and said goodbye.

The drive flew by. I pulled in my driveway, got out of the car, grabbed my bag and started walking towards the door. There was a note on the door. I pulled it off. My name was on the front so I opened it and read ...

Isla,

> *My sweet princess, I think about you every minute of every day. I long to be with you, holding you close. I count the hours till I can taste your lips again. I will see you soon, my sweet, I need you.*

> *Love, Bill?*

Oh, he does care. I can't wait to see him. I thought to myself as I ran up to my room, sat on my bed and wondered what he was doing right then and there. I pictured the castle, the decor, the lights, his smile and his tall firm body. The kiss, that kiss was amazing. Mesmerized by the memory of that kiss I began to close my eyes.

Knock, knock. "Isla are you in there?" Mom asked as she opened the door. I sat up promptly.

"Yeah, Mom, I am here." I sighed and stretched a little.

"Are you alright?" she asked, looking at me attentively.

"Yeah, I'm fine. Why? I'm just tired, it was a long day at work." I sighed shaking my head as I fell back into bed and pulled the blanket up over me.

"Were you busy today?" she asked, elated. It was a shame to let her down.

"No, Mom, I had very few clients today."

"I'm sorry honey, it will be better tomorrow," she promised. I had to concentrate on being positive and thanking God for what I had now. Being grateful is the only way to change things.

I shuddered at the thought that there were two more days until I would see him. I looked around my room at my mess and was instantly frustrated by the disarray I saw.

"Yeah, you're probably right," I agreed, smiling with a facade of happiness.

"I'm going to cook some dinner, are you hungry?" she asked.

I glanced at the clock, it was 7:45. *How long was I asleep?* I asked myself. I hadn't even realized I had fallen asleep.

"Not really mom, I'll eat something later," I replied as my teeth chattered so I curled up in a ball and pulled the blanket up over my shoulders. I was freezing for some odd reason. I laid there thinking a while and dozed off, again.

I was in that library again. It was old looking, but somehow different. I mean it was old before, but it had more dust on the books and furniture. There I was lying on the red velvet couch. My eyes were closed, I could feel something on my chest. Then nothing but pain. I couldn't breath, I was scared to death. I felt something like blood running down the side of my neck and tried to wake up, in the dream and in reality. I couldn't. I screamed, but not a sound. I wasn't alone,

I could feel someone over me. I cried out, "Please! ... Don't! ... No! ... Please don't!

My eyes opened and observed my room. I fixated on my window. It was open again. Disturbed by the odd occurrences, I gasped for air, holding it in so it wouldn't escape in case I wouldn't be able to catch another one.

"I might as well leave it open," I said out loud. Then I staggered to the window and yelled, "My window is open so come on in," in a sincere, but joking manner. I was really furious. Lying back on my bed, I had to get my mind off the phenomenon that was plaguing me. So I picked up a magazine and began thumbing through it. I glanced at the clock; it was 3:45 a.m. I wasn't able to go back to sleep. I grabbed the letter from my bedside table and reread it again and again, not really understanding why. But, maybe, I was searching for hidden messages.

Not really finding anything except the obvious question mark following Bill, I gave up and tried to watch a movie that I had seen before to maybe drift back to sleep. I flipped through the channels, until I finally fell asleep. I didn't have a nightmare, this time. I don't know if I even had a dream.

"Yes!" I woke up saying out load.

It was time to get up and get ready for another day. I did my usual. Showered, got dressed, snacked on mixed nuts, drank my hot tea and put on my makeup. Styled my hair and put my stuff in my bag and headed down the stairs.

"Have a great day," my mom grabbed me and gave me a big hug. "I love you, sweetie," she said peering into my eyes.

"I love you too, Mom," I announced with joy.

I walked out the door got in my car and was on my way.

On the way to work, I was thinking of him as usual. Then it occurred to me why hadn't my mom asked me about the limousine from my date several days before? *That's very strange.* I thought as I exited my car and strolled through the parking lot.

Walking in, I went to check my schedule and I was booked. I knew it would go by fast. That meant only one more day till I would see him.

I ended up doing about three colors and four haircuts. It was a very good day. After paying my car insurance, I could save the rest for Amsterdam.

Just the thought of finally going to Europe got me so electrified. I almost forgot to breathe. The list of things to do was growing. I definitely wanted to go to the Van Gogh Museum. His work was all over my room. I also needed to see the Eiffel Tower, the Louvre, the Rhine River, and to sip vino in Venice. There was so much I wanted to see and do.

"Will a week really be enough?" I asked myself out loud.

"Probably not," I answered. No one noticed me talking to myself which was a good thing.

"What time do you get off?" Angel asked.

"Hmm, what?" I asked startled, and pulled out of my thoughts. "Oh, at 5:00," I replied, still a little out of it.

"Well, I guess you're getting ready to leave then?" she replied, questioning why I wasn't already gone. "It's 5:15 girl," she announced firmly.

"Oh! I guess I was day-dreaming." I quickly began stuffing my things into my bag and cleaned my station.

As I was spraying glass cleaner on my mirror and wiping it clean. Angel asked me, "Were you day-dreaming about Amsterdam or about him?" She could see I was consumed.

There was that psychic connection again. We had been busy and we had hardly spoken three words to each other all day. Somehow she knew I was in awe of someone. I hadn't really told her anything yet. It would only be real to me when I knew his real name. I often wondered what it would be. Would it be fierce and strong, like he looked? Or would it be soft and sensitive, like his voice and heart? I couldn't wait to find out.

"Bye, ladies. See you Monday," I hollered, rushing out the door.

"Bye, Isla," I heard as I closed the door behind me.

I got in my car and raced home. I was in such a daze. The lights on the road were just long stretched streams of light. Blurs of cars darted by, I don't know how I even made it home, my mind was so fuzzy.

When I walked in the door, mom was in the kitchen stirring something in a big silver pot.

"Hey, Mom, what ya doing?" I asked, hanging my coat up and setting my stuff down.

"I'm cooking dinner because your father is coming home early," she said, smiling happily. The steam rolling up in her face made her skin glisten in the bright kitchen light.

"He is? Cool. I can't wait to see him. What ya making?"

"How does spaghetti sound?" she asked, dumping a bunch of noodles into a strainer.

"That sounds great. You made garlic bread, didn't you?" I asked smiling and raising my eyebrows.

"Of course I did," she replied. She crinkled her nose at my question. I knew that was a stupid question. Those two things went together.

"Mom, I'm going up stairs to put my stuff up." I walked into my room, sat my bag down on my bed and noticed my window had been closed. *I know for a fact that I left that open.* I whispered to myself and went back downstairs.

"Mom, did you shut my window?" I asked, wanting to know what was going on.

"No honey, I haven't even been upstairs yet," she said with a look of confusion on her face.

"Did you just get home?" I asked perplexed.

"Yes. Guess what, I sold two houses today," her eyes sparkled happily.

"You did? That's awesome!" I gave her a hug. "So this is a celebration, isn't it?" I asked in utter delight.

She smiled, "Yes, it is. But we'll really celebrate when I get the check."

I laughed and hugged her again. "I'm going to my room for a while." I smiled and gently grazed my mom's shoulder as she headed towards the fridge. Turning on my tip toes, I went up the stairs. I felt a suspicious feeling in the pit of my stomach when I entered my room. Tossing back my black bed skirt to look under the bed, my heart calmed some. But I wasn't completely at ease until I examined the closet to determine that no one was there. It just felt like somebody had been there. I turned my CD player on. I was surprised to hear that it wasn't the Ramones.

"I know I left the Ramones in there," I said out loud, reaching for a breath. The music that began to play was a classical piece I had never heard before; it registered in my memory of sounding a little like Beethoven. I stopped it and pulled it out of the CD player. It was a recorded CD, gold and just had a big C on it. I imagined it stood for Classical or just classics. I gazed at it for a few seconds then set it aside. I put in Nine Inch Nails and hit play.

I needed to straighten my room, it was a mess. There were clothes on the floor and books on my bed. As I put things away I found the letter he left me. I sat down on my bed and read it again. His handwriting was beautiful for a man's.

Rereading it made me want to see him all that much more. The hawks began to circle just thinking about him. Setting the note down, I went to my closet, removed the dress I would wear to the party and hung it on the door. Suddenly I realized I didn't have any shoes to wear with it. I had a pair of black heels, but remembered I broke a heel a few months ago, shopping at an outlet with Micha. It began to rain as we were going to the car. Our arms were overflowing with bags of treasures. We didn't want anything to get wet so we ran. That's when I stumbled and broke my heel.

Crap, I have to go get some shoes. I'll go shopping tomorrow since I'm off. I have to meet Angel tomorrow night after work to get my cards read, I reminded myself.

I heard the front door shut loudly, and I ran downstairs to see mom standing there with a box in her hands.

"It's for you, Isla," she announced, with a puzzled expression. I smiled and took it from her graciously. I turned on my heel and proceeded rapidly upstairs with the unmarked box in my hands. I sort of expected my mom to stop me and ask me who it was from, but she didn't.

"That's really weird," I said out loud as I reached the top of the stairs.

I walked in my room and shut the door. I sat on the bed with the box in front of me, wondering if it was from him. It was a regular brown cardboard box. I took a pen from my nightstand, and ran it through the middle of the tape cutting it open.

There was a red box inside, bigger than last one. I quickly pulled off the top. To my surprise it was a pair of black heels with ankle straps, they weren't that high and they were just my size. They were just what I would have picked out. They were not a name brand I knew, it was French, Lazemie. I pronounced it *lazy me*. Just my style! Recalling the last gift I received from him, I wasn't surprised to find that there was a letter at the bottom of the box. I unfolded it and read...

My Dearest Isla,

> *I miss you so, so much I had to let you know. I thought your outfit would be complete, with these new shoes on your feet. I will hold you close to me all night long. We will dance to every song. I will embrace your body and feel your lips to mine. I will love you till the end of time. I know you're excited and I will have much to explain, but all will be in the open when you know my name.*

Love Bill?

"I knew it! He's so amazing, and he's a beautiful poet," I said out loud as I held the love letter close to my heart. "He's so wonderful," I just couldn't hold back my elated tears. It was then that I truly realized I was in love with what's his name.

Chapter 5

The Outcome

I HAD A GREAT DINNER WITH MY parents, then went to bed.

The next day I woke up around noon..

"Yes! It's Friday. I slept in," I declared somewhat loudly.

Peering up at the window I saw it wasn't open. I got excited and then felt a little sad. I told myself I was an idiot. How silly it was to be sad that my window wasn't open, when I couldn't even understand how or why it had been opened in the first place. Giggling at myself for my absurd feelings, I fell back onto my pillow.

I lounged in bed a while longer and read some letters from psychics and some junk mail, too.

Finally, I got up, got dressed, put my face on and went downstairs. Mom and Dad were on the couch watching a movie. I didn't know what they were watching. I didn't want to disturb them, they looked so cute.

I quietly tiptoed back upstairs after snatching a bag of mixed nuts and a glass of water from the kitchen. I decided to color my hair before tomorrow night; my roots were beginning to show.

Digging through my boxes of color, I examined my selection to see what shades I had to choose from.

"What color do I want to do?" I thought out loud then decided to go with a very spicy brown with blonde highlights. "Yeah, that sounds good," I confirmed to myself.

So I got my mixing bowls out and mixed the color and bleach separately, of course. Applying the color all over my head and then doing some chunky highlights, I waited for the timer to go off and shampooed.

After all of that, and blow drying it with a round brush, I looked in the mirror. It looked so pretty and went well with my hazel eyes. I was very happy. I glanced at the clock, it was 4:30 p.m.

I can't forget to go see Angel to get my cards read, I told myself. I had forgotten what time she got off, so I decided to call her.

"Hey Angel, this is Isla. What time do you get off?"

"What's up, girl?" she sounded happy to hear from me. "You can come see me now if you want," Angel suggested.

"Alright, I will be there in about thirty minutes," I answered with a quick look at the clock above my TV.

"Great, see you then," she said.

"Bye," I said, closing the phone.

Throwing it in my purse along with my wallet, keys, and lipstick, I ran downstairs. I put on my coat and gloves. It was around thirty-one degrees outside, which wasn't that cold. But considering the wind chill factor, it was friggin freezing.

"I'll be back in a little while," I hollered as I gently closed the front door behind me. I practically sprinted to my car, got in and peeled out of my driveway. When I got there, Angel was the only one working besides the receptionist. Angel and I went into the employee lounge. We got comfortable on the comfy couch. She placed the stack of Tarot cards on the table in front of us, tapped it with her non-polished fingers.

"Shuffle the cards and cut them with your left hand," she said, concentrating.

"Okay," I said, shuffling clumsily and then cutting the deck. She dealt ten cards out in an unusual pattern. She knew what she was doing as she began to explain each card.

"The first card is the reason for your question. Optimism with regard of a new venture."

Which basically means; I am excited about my trip to Amsterdam, I thought to myself.

"The second card is the basis of your question: something new is on the horizon, romance is in the air."

"That's true, I am in love," I sighed out loud.

"You're admitting it now, huh? I could see it before you even realized it," she said, smiling as she secretly patted herself on the back.

"I know. When you said that the other day I sat back in the chair in shock, confused that I would feel so strongly so quickly. Is it really possible for me to have fallen in love after only being with him two times?"

"It must have been an amazing kiss. When you know, you know," she replied. "Do you want me to continue?" she asked, motioning to the cards.

"Yes, please do." I shook my head not wanting to inconvenience her. I had gotten sidetracked.

"The third card is your hopes and fears: some sort of debt might be paid. You could meet someone who believes in your talents."

"The fourth card is the birth of something in your life: You will trust love again." I just looked at her and smiled, staring at the card that read death at the bottom of it.

"Why does it read death if it's rebirth?" I asked, baffled as to why it would say one thing and mean the complete opposite.

"It's upside down," she replied.

"Oh, okay. Now I understand," I said as I leaned back and relaxed some.

"The fifth card is what is over you right now: your imagination is very active." She grinned and patted me on the shoulder, insinuating something, I couldn't quite figure out what. She continued as I analyzed her last comment.

The sixth card is your future: you will get irritated on your travels." She looked at me with wide eyes.

"Ouch, I hope I don't get irritated on my trip to Amsterdam," I expressed.

Her phone rang. She got a call from a friend that was too drunk to drive and needed a ride home. So she told me we would have to finish the reading later and went to get her friend. Talk about leaving someone hanging. Oh well, I guessed I would find out the rest later.

I got home and was getting out of the car when my cell phone rang. I reached in my purse to see who it was. Just as I pulled it out it stopped ringing. It was Angel.

I went in the house and up the stairs to my room. I put my stuff down and called her back.

"Hey girl, you just called?" I asked, interested in what she had to say.

"I went ahead and redid the reading. I wrote it down. Do you want me to drop it off or do you just want me to read it to you?" she asked.

"You can read it to me. So this is a new reading?" I asked as I kicked off my shoes.

"Yes, I went to pick up my friend and she wasn't ready to leave yet so I went ahead and reread them while I was waiting for her. Are you ready to hear it?"

"Sure, let me get comfortable," I replied, happy to hear the whole reading.

"Are you ready?" she asked.

"Sure, go ahead."

"Okay your first card is what you were thinking about when you shuffled the deck. Now, keep up. I'm going to read them just as I have written it and kind of quickly because it looks like my friend is wanting to go. But she has made me wait so she can wait a little bit till I'm done." She got quiet for a moment and then said, "Oh, she just ordered another drink. I guess I have time now. Here we go...

The first card I drew was **the sun** *which means new horizons are ahead. Romance is in the air and you will be traveling far away.* The next card was **the fool** *and it was upside down. Which means you need to focus on faith and be optimistic. Expect to travel soon, but be careful and guard yourself from the unexpected.*"

"Interesting," I said. I wanted to keep my comments to a minimum so I would be able to hear the whole reading. She took a breath and then continued.

"The third card I drew was the **ace of was cups.** *This card indicates surprise, prepare to be on a path of amazement. You will have positive development in business, and love life. You will be taking a trip far away.*

You're destined to go on this trip to Amsterdam, that's for sure. But it sounds like... I mean from the looks of things... it seems like you better be careful in what ever you do," she said.

"Uh, yeah," I responded as a strong chill ran up my spine causing me to quiver.

"Should I continue?" she asked.

"Yes! Please!

The three of cups was the forth card I drew. *You shouldn't allow anyone to intimidate you. Be willing to risk failure to get what you want.* The fifth card was **the eight of pentacles.** *There will be a letter arriving or it already has. You will be traveling to a different country, but be careful.* The sixth card was the *four of wands. An old friend, possibly from high school, will call. You'll be traveling soon.*

"Wow! I definitely have to be careful," I said with alarm on my mind. The cards had to be right. They predicted my trip and my new love.

"No kidding!

The seventh card was **the hermit.** *You have a stalker you love. You will be hunted by someone truly evil. Be careful on your travels.*

The eighth card was *the ten of wands. A call or letter from a loved one coming to visit will be delivered in a few days."*

"What, no be careful? That's three times you have said be careful. It looks like I'm going to have to tread cautiously in Amsterdam," I announced and then remembered the comment about a stalker. He had to be stalking me because there was no other explanation of how he knew I needed things for my outfit for Saturday night. Unless he was reading my mind. *Wouldn't reading someone's mind without their permission be construed as stalking?* I thought to myself. Then my thoughts floated off to him. I couldn't wait to see him.

"There is also a letter coming soon," she reminded me.

"Well, I hope it's a letter from Publishers Clearinghouse Sweepstakes," I sighed playfully.

"Girl you're not the only one," she giggled. "Next card?"

"I'm sorry. Continue," I said.

"The ninth card I drew was a very special card You see, several years ago I was visiting my sister in Virginia. My sister Natalie wanted me to do some readings for her and some friends and I lost a card. It was *the night of pentacles.* My car broke down and I had to take the bus home. While I was waiting for my bus a woman approached me. She was tall and thin and had long, silky brown hair. She wore a black hat that shadowed her eyes, plus she kept her head down so I never got a good look at her face. Anyway, to make a long story short, the woman handed me a card and said she had found it and it belonged to me. I looked at it and told her it was an old card, there was no way it was mine. She said it was a magic card. So I shrugged and thanked her. I slipped it in my deck and stuck it in my purse. When I turned to look at her she was gone. It was extremely strange. When I pulled that card for you it vibrated and glowed in my hand. *It said you would go on a trip to another country and to be careful. Don't let yourself get possessed. Also a powerful love would enter your life."*

"Uh ... possessed. Hmm," I sighed befuddled. "It was a magic card? You mean it really glowed and like moved in your hand?" I asked, astounded by what she had just said.

"Yes! I've done plenty of readings and that card has never done that before. Hey, I need to finish this quickly. It looks as though my friend has been cut off."

"Okay, do you need go?"

"There is just one more card. My friend can wait, I've waited on her for a while," she said and giggled loudly.

"Alright, continue."

"The tenth and final card was the **ten of wands**. This one I'm reading in verbatim. *You could lose your soul but gain so much more in return.*"

"What does that mean?" I asked, frightened by her use of the word possess and the fact that I could lose my soul.

"I don't know, girl, this is on the edge of creeping me out," she replied, her voice sounded exhausted.

"Thanks for doing this for me. I appreciate it," I said, grateful but nervous.

"You're welcome. It looks like you have an awful lot to think about. I can't believe we've been on the phone for an hour," she said, sounding tired and worn down.

"It doesn't seem like it's been that long. I guess I do have a lot to think about," I started trailing off. *Apparently I'm going to be possessed, but gain so much more.* I thought to myself.

"Alright, I will see you Monday at work," she said.

"Okay, I'll see you then. Thank you again."

"No problem, see you. Bye," she hung up.

I closed my phone, got up and sat in my big, red, fuzzy chair and thought about all that she had said.

"I need to be careful on my trip, that's for sure. I could lose my soul; what did that mean?" I thought out loud.

I pondered for a few minutes, then turned the TV on, but the cable was out for some reason. I just sat and stared at the snow on the screen. It was very bright and reminded me of energy.

It seemed to me that we were all just energy. Everything was energy. When Bill kissed me I had closed my eyes and could see us both as figures of light, brighter than the sun like veins of white light. The floor was gone and there was nothing, just he and I intertwined in an intense passion. It was like the world around us stopped. I had never felt such peace before---ever.

I was tired, it had been an exhausting day. After I got ready for bed I crawled under my cozy comforter and was out like a light.

Chapter 6

The Castle Party

*W*HEN I OPENED MY EYES IT DAWNED on me that it was Saturday. I was so excited to see him again. The thought of his kisses made me weak in the knees. It was a good thing I was still in bed.

I got out of bed and did some stretches, just felt like exercising. I didn't even bother looking at my window; I had left it open. I was tired of having to shut it all the time.

After exercising for awhile, I brushed my teeth and took a long bath. I got out and put on some lounge pants and a tee shirt. I sat on my bed and did my face. After praying, I realized how hungry I was and went downstairs to microwave a meal out of the freezer, shrimp alfredo. I put a mug of water in the microwave for my hot tea.

When it was ready I took it all upstairs to my room and sat back on my bed. I took a few bites and then gobbled the meal down. It was good, not as good as homemade, but it satisfied my tummy.

I got a little bored waiting for 8:00 to come. I picked up a magazine and flipped through it. I read about more celebrity marriages destroyed by actors falling in love with their co-stars.

Too bad they couldn't be professional and keep their hearts out of on-screen kisses. It had to be extremely hard to kiss without feeling anything, even stage kissing.

It was 5:00 p.m. Three hours before the party. I swallowed hard and took a deep breath. Had hawks in my stomach again; a little anxiety also hit me. I felt like I was going to burst. My head was spinning just a little, it was enough that it made me want to get up and dance, or do something.

I put on some *Violent Femmes* and started dancing all over my room to *Add It Up*. I was really letting go and getting into it. It was a major tension release. Before I knew it, it was time to get ready. I took a shower and did all the things necessary for me to feel beautiful. I didn't do my hair yet, though. That I would save for last.

I went to my closet and put on the dress, then the amazing necklace that went with it. I added diamond stud earrings. The necklace and dress looked as if they had been invented with each other in mind.

"I look awesome and I haven't even done my hair yet," I thought out loud as I gaped at myself in the mirror. I couldn't figure out how I wanted to wear my hair. Up or down, curly or straight? So I put it up with curls all over my head and felt like a queen, without the tiara. I put my new shoes on; they were black with silver stones around the ankle, they were way hot. He had great taste.

The doorbell rang. I took a deep breath and headed downstairs. I opened the door to see Lizzy smiling and then she yelled hysterically, "I can't figure out what to wear" she was almost screaming. "Help me pick which one," she said frantically as we went up to my room.

She held up a number in red satin with lace on top flowing over it ever so lightly.

"You have to wear that one. It's super sexy!"

"What about this one?" Lizzy asked, holding up a cute blue two peice ensemble.

"It's not as hot as the red one, though. No way, you have to wear the red one," I said in a demanding but friendly tone.

"Okay, I'll wear it," she replied getting giddy.

"What time is Micha supposed to be here?" I asked while straightening up my room. I grabbed some cups and headed down the stairs and was almost to the bottom of the stairs when the doorbell rang. I opened up the door and there it was, the same long, shiny black limousine, with the driver waiting by the open door. *He'll just have to wait*, I thought to myself.

Just then Micha pulled up in her white VW Jetta. She got out and started walking to the door. She kept motioning to the limo. "Whose is that?" she asked enthusiastically.

"That's our ride," I replied, smiling big.

"What? Are you kidding?" Micha asked, taking off upstairs; I followed.

"Lizzy, guess what we're riding in," Micha yelled with eyes wide in excitement.

"What do you mean?" Lizzy asked puzzled as she zipped up her dress.

"Peek out that window," I said.

Lizzy ran to the window, "We're riding in style," she screeched.

"Whose is it?" Micha asked really interested.

I laughed and replied, "It's my man's!"

"What man?" Lizzy and Micha asked at the same time, trying to squeeze information out of me.

"You'll see," I answered, smiling. "Let's go girls," I motioned for them to hurry up. "I don't want our driver to wait too long. Are we ready?" I asked, getting my clutch.

Micha looked beautiful. She had on a white dress with pink satin designs against a silky white linen, it went to the floor, but in no way would be considered a wedding dress. We all ran downstairs. I shut the door behind us.

"Good evening, Ms. Van Burren."

"Just call me by my first name, please," I said touching his arm.

He nodded and said, "I'm Calvin." He held his hand out to shake mine.

"Nice to meet you, Calvin." I shook it and looked him in the eyes smiling. He had cold hands, too. I raised my eyebrows mystified that his touch was similar. Well, at least in temperature. Bill's touch set me on fire.

"What about your friends?" he asked as he motioned to both of them.

"This is Lizzy and Micha," I pointed to them, as we got in the car.

"Very nice to meet you," he said, smiling at them both. They returned the gesture as he closed the door behind us.

"This is so awesome," Lizzy squealed.

"This one is a lot nicer than the ones I've ridden in," Micha said, touching the soft grey leather upholstery.

Lizzy was already getting some soda with some ice from the bar. I wanted something a little stronger. I picked up a vodka bottle, took a whiff, and poured it in a glass with some ice.

"Is there anything to mix with this?" I asked.

"There's cranberry juice," Lizzy said as she checked the refrigerator's contents. I held my hand out and she handed me a small bottle. I checked to make sure the seal hadn't been broken. Not sure why; guess I was raised that way. I opened it up and poured it into my glass then drank it in about five swallows.

"Are you thirsty, or just nervous?" Lizzy asked, patting me softly on the back.

"Girl, we're going to have so much fun tonight," I said, wiping my mouth with a napkin from the bar. Lizzy hugged me tightly.

"I want some rum," Micha muttered as she made herself a rum and coke.

"Awe heck, I'll have a rum and coke, too," Lizzy said as she poured some rum in her coke. "I mean, it's not like we're driving."

"Alright you talked me into it. I'll take a rum and coke, too." I fixed myself another drink.

We all raised our glasses in a toast.

"Here's to an incredible night," I announced. We clicked our crystal glasses lightly.

It wasn't long before the car stopped.

"We're here," I said exhilarated, looking out the dark tinted window to see the lights of the mansion. Then Calvin opened the door and we all got out. Their mouths dropped when they saw where we were.

"Oh my God," Micha said thunderstruck as she gaped at the mansion and all around.

"Cool, this is going to be fun!" Lizzy said with her eyes sparkling, staring at the beautiful architecture. We walked up to the humongous door. It opened by itself, or so it seemed. There was a tall, white-haired man standing just inside the door. He just nodded as we passed.

We followed the sound. A young guy, about fifteen or so, took my hand. I smiled, not knowing what was going on. He led us into a big, beautiful ballroom. There were glamorously happy people everywhere. Everyone was smiling. My heart skipped a beat the second I saw him. He came straight over to me. I was completely fixated on him, so much so I hadn't even noticed Lizzy and Micha weren't behind me anymore.

"Isla, my sweet," he called out as he approached, reaching for me.

I dropped my hand that I had extended to him just before he had a chance to grab it. "I need to know your full name, please," I demanded, staring him in the eyes.

He chuckled a little and said, "I'm Johnathon Daine."

"Johnathon," I repeated it in a breathy, dreamy way.

"May I have this dance?" he asked, shooting me a dynamic smile. His teeth were so white they were blinding.

"Yes," I answered, reaching my hand out to him. He took it and we were off. He spun me, dipped me, threw me into the air and caught me miles away. It was definitely not a dream. I was really living this.

He held me so tight it felt as if he was going to pull me in so far I would become him. I felt like a princess, and barely noticed anyone else there, except for Micha and Lizzy who were sitting at a table talking to some guys. They looked content from what I could see. I turned quickly back to him and gazed in his eyes. I was lost. He picked me up and swung me around like a doll. I was having the time of my life.

The song came to an end. He put me down softly. We stood there staring at each other. The music began again, but this was different. We both glanced up. There was a man playing piano; he was good-looking from what I could see, with long black hair pulled in a ponytail at the nape. As he played, all the women in the ballroom started walking towards him. I saw that even Micha and Lizzy were mesmerized and going towards him. The men just stood there not knowing what was going on.

Who is that? I wondered to myself.

"That's my brother, Sigrid Daine," he said, like he'd heard me.

We looked at each other. He touched my cheek gently. His hands were so cold, it caused me to yelp quietly as I felt his icy touch. I saw his hand move towards my cheek, but it still startled me.

"I missed you, Isla," he whispered, pulling me closer.

"I missed you," I replied with longing in my voice.

The music stopped abruptly. We didn't look away to see why. Then I felt a tap on my shoulder. I turned to see what it was, but no one was there. I looked at Sigrid on the piano. He was staring at me; I felt paralyzed. I was terrified and immobilized by the decay of his glare. It was like he saw through to the core of my soul.

"I want to be alone with you, Isla," Johnathon sighed, pulling me to him and out of his brother's trap.

I was spacey and felt violated. "Okay," was all I could say. He picked me up in his arms and carried me out of the room.

We came to a door and it opened automatically as if it had heard him say so in his mind. We entered a room with gorgeous tapestries hanging from the ceiling to the floor. They were of beautiful landscapes. One was of a roaring waterfall surrounded by leafless winter trees. It was ominous looking. I hated feeling that way about it, that something so breathtaking could look dead or evil.

He stood there holding me. He could tell I was taking everything in. Then he broke the silence.

"This is my room," he said, setting me down on a black canopy bed with black and red chiffon curtains. *This is exactly what I plan on having when I finally move out,* I thought to myself. He went to light a candle.

"So when are you moving out?" he asked, diving on me playfully.

"I knew you were reading my mind," I sighed in a scornful tone.

"Those look perfect with that dress," he said, touching my ankle softly as he unbuckled the strap of my shoes. *You look amazing in your black suit with red satin collar, but you always look incredible,* I thought to myself, admiring him.

"You changed the subject," I sighed, then grinned and glared at him.

"Isla, I have waited for this moment."

"I have dreamt of this moment too," I said confirming the feeling.

He pulled me to his lips and kissed me as he laid down next to me. I had wanted that to happen since I first saw him. We kissed a long time. The passion was intense and way deeper than my fantasies had ever grazed. We got a little crazy, really going at it. I loved kissing him.

"Ouch!" I yelled, "That hurt," I yelped raising my hand to my mouth. He stopped and looked at me with sympathy in his eyes and my blood dripping down his chin. He turned away.

"You bit me," I shouted, wiping blood from my lip.

He wasn't next to me anymore. Looking across the room I could see his eyes in the shadows of the candlelight reflecting off the windowpane.

"You don't want to be with me, Isla. I'll hurt you. I'm a monster."

"What do you mean?" I gasped, holding back my tears, not understanding why he would say that. In my heart he was no monster.

"I would rather die than hurt you," he breathed.

"It's okay, it's not hurting anymore; the blood is drying up," I whispered reassuringly as I held out my hand. He suddenly shot towards me. I gasped when all of a sudden he was on top of me.

"It's out of my control when there is intimacy," he growled, low and scary. My heart was beating so hard I thought it might jump out of my chest. I sat up and held my knees and then cradled my head in my hands. He squatted on one foot and a knee at the foot of the bed and looked at me with compassion.

"I don't understand. Why are you doing this to me?" I could barely say anything, because my emotions were getting the best of me.

"I love you, Isla," he whispered, touching my face with the side of his arctic hand. My heart stopped and then sped up. I was scared to say anything. I covered my mouth with both hands, one on top of the other as tears streamed down my face. My breath was stifled by my elevated emotions.

"Don't you love me?" he sighed, with pain in his voice that I did not return his sentiment. I wondered to myself *How is it possible to fall so intensely in love, in such a short time. Is this love or is this lust?* While I was questioning my fervency, he moved to the side of the bed.

"I will leave you then," he murmured, standing at the foot of the bed and then turning to walk towards the door. I felt his anguish and it tortured my insides.

"Wait! Don't go!" I cried out.

He paused at the door, but didn't turn around.

"If I tell you I love you, you must tell me the truth. Why did you bite me? Why you think you would hurt me? And why do you think you're a monster?" He glared at me; I could see he was mad that he had to explain himself. But I could also see that he wanted to share with me, in every way possible.

"Well, do you?" he sighed, almost growling.

I closed my eyes tightly and when I opened them he was closer, kneeling beside the bed. It startled me. I looked away, preventing him from seeing the confusion and trepidation that was hanging over me.

"Do you love me?" he whispered, his breath echoing all around me. He waited a minute or two and then spoke again. "Obviously I was wrong, I thought you cared. But, now I see." He stood and headed for the door again. My heart felt like it was going to burst.

"Yes!" I had never said it to anyone, in that way. I tried to catch my breath as I cupped my hands back over mouth. Then it erupted out of me, spilling out. "Yes, I love you. You're all I think about. I dream of you every night, and long to be with you always. But I don't understand all of this."

In a flash he was beside me again. "Do you ever see me during the day?" he asked, his voice soft and satisfied.

"No!" I shook my head, confused by his change of direction. "But I haven't seen much of you, at all," I cried. "Now, why did you bite me?" My lip was throbbing as if it had it's own heartbeat.

"I got lost in the intense passion and wanted so badly to taste you," he whispered and it was painted with a deep growl, as he leaned into me and looked me square in the eyes. I couldn't look away.

"We were kissing, you were tasting me," I gasped. I still couldn't catch my breath. But my tears had calmed down some.

"I wanted to taste your blood," he echoed, turning his head in the opposite direction. I froze. Even if I wanted to move, all I could do was rock back and forth. My saliva felt like sharp rocks tumbling down my parched throat.

My heart stopped and then pounded so hard it felt like an earthquake in me. Then it happened, I started hyperventilating. Everything was spinning. I tried to laugh it off and blurted out.

"Why, are you a vampire or something?" I asked, making a joke.

"Yes," he said and gazed straight through me. The word yes replayed over and over again in my head. I started gasping and wheezing for air. The thoughts in my head were spinning, making me feel dizzy.

When I was able to speak I took a deep breath and let it gush, "Oh my God, you're a vampire?" I swallowed my breath. My tears were flowing like white water rapids down my face. I was barely breathing. He wrapped his arms around me and whispered in my ear. I couldn't move.

"Please don't be afraid, Isla. I would never hurt you," the air from his mouth froze my ear causing a sharp pain, then it went numb. I thought it was strange that his skin and his breath were cold, but his kisses were warm. Another thing that was strange, I believed him. But I wondered how much control he really had. I brought my hand up to wipe my eyes and noticed it had a remnant of mascara on it.

I wish there was an on and off switch for these salty drops of emotion, because I know I've cried all my makeup off. I need a tissue, I thought to myself.

"Here you go," he replied sweetly, handing me one.

I shot him a surprised expression laced with slight annoyance. "How could we truly love each other in an intimate way?" I gasped, wanting him so. But trepidation had my throat and was squeezing the air out of me.

"We couldn't, unless you were one, too," he whispered, and my mouth went dry, dryer than it already was. I gaped at him with wide eyes, swallowed several times and tried to say something.

"What, a vampire?" I questioned breathlessly, feeling bewildered and somewhat disturbed. His eyes saddened by my expressionless face. I was stunned to say the least. I said to myself, *The man I love feeds on blood.* "I don't know," I gulped like I was swallowing a brick. *I want to be with him no matter what that entails, but a vampire? I* thought. "I have to think about that," I sighed, feeling obligated, but scared out of my wits.

He bowed his head and slowly turned away. His back was facing me. "You should probably forget about me and go on with your life as if we'd never met," he uttered with his head hung low as if he had accepted the inevitable.

"I have to know more," I replied with my head up and breathing better. "I don't want to be in the dark, so to speak. Do you take innocent lives?"

"No. I'm a counselor and a part-time warden at the prison. I read their files and if an inmate has murdered, raped or pillaged, taking their lives is my duty. I don't make them vampires," he said with his mouth in a line, straight and tight.

"You mean you actually rid the world of its filth?" I asked, really interested as I observed him in a different light. It was like the candlelight had been turned up. I really admired how he used his hunger for the greater good. "I thought if a person gets bitten, they automatically become a vampire."

"That's a myth," he sighed, turning around and pulling me closer to him. I looked at him differently now. I saw a glimpse of a soul when I gazed in his eyes. Or maybe I had put it there. I didn't know, all I did know was that I loved him.

I was beginning to relax a little.

"You see, when I bite someone, if the blood is drained completely from their body, they die. If I leave any blood in the body, they become a vampire. The change is excruciating."

"What do you mean by excruciating?" I asked, running my finger down his arm.

"It's an agonizing death. The body dies, but not without a terrible war first. Blood still runs through, but it's not enough for the human body to survive on. So the body dies and a vampire is born, starving and trying to fill the void. But I must warn you, it feels like knives slicing you up, from the inside and then fire when you feel like you're getting used to it. Then you spend an eternity feeding on what you've lost."

"So how do you choose who to kill and who to turn into a vampire?" I asked.

"I read their minds. If they're remorseful of the crimes they've committed, we work on rehabilitation. I have a code to follow. I shall never kill an innocent person in cold blood."

"What if you do, not meaning to?" I asked hesitantly.

"I'll tell you another time, my love, it's almost 3:00 am."

"What? I have to go! I'm already late!" I hollered frantically. I quickly put my shoes back on and started to get up. He pulled me close and held my face with both hands. He gazed deeply in my eyes.

"I love you, Isla. We will make it work," he sighed so breathily that his deep growl of glacial wind chapped my skin. Not to mention that my flesh was freezing into ice under his delicate fingers.

Then with one last kiss, he grabbed my heart and ripped it out of my body and carried it with him from every moment on. I could never be swayed even if he broke the code.

"I love you, Johnathon," I whispered, leaving all of me with him. I was so happy to say his beautiful name.

I gazed in his eyes and said softly, "It just occurred to me you're actually saving the taxpayers money." I smiled, picked up my clutch off the bed, and started for the door.

"Wait, Isla! I'll walk you to the car," he commanded as he snickered under his breath.

"Okay, let's go, I've got to get home," I replied, quickly walking two steps in front of him.

"Isla, slow down, you're already late," he shouted, pulling my arm back. I knew he could have been a mile ahead of me, but for some reason he was lagging behind.

I stopped. He twisted my other arm around my back, holding both of them behind me in a firm, but painless way. Then he put his lips on my neck, the sensation of his ice cold lips sent razor sharp shivers down my spine. I wanted him to ravish me, right then and there. *Go ahead, bite me. I want you to,* I said to myself.

He kissed my neck then turned me around and said, "You forget I can read your thoughts." Then he laughed loudly, kissed me again and hugged me tightly. "My driver is waiting for you," he whispered smiling and handing me my clutch. He walked me to the door and opened it, without using his hands of course. Calvin was standing right outside the door.

"Isla, I'll see you *soon*," Johnathon whispered and sighed deeply emphasizing the soon. It literally took my breath away.

I turned and slowly stepped towards the car. After two steps I turned to wave. He was gone. Getting sad immediately, I got in and Calvin shut the door behind me. I leaned back against the soft leather. Already missing him but smiling, to keep my tears at bay.

The whole ride home my heartstrings were being torn and yanked on. I felt numb, almost like I wasn't even there. *When would soon be? Would it be tomorrow, or a few days later?* I didn't know, and it was driving me insane.

But I was happier than I'd ever been. I had found my yin or yang. The whole ride I just kicked back and contemplated everything. To me, this was reaffirming that there was a Santa Clause. There probably were aliens, because I knew we weren't the only ones here. I had to believe in anything and everything now. I was in love with a vampire.

It was right about that time when the car came to a stop. Calvin opened the door. I got out slowly and almost lost my balance. He stopped me from falling.

"Thank you. I must have gotten up too fast," I remarked. He smiled as he made sure I was on my feet and then let go of my arm.

"Goodnight, Ms. Van Burren," he said as he shut the door to the car and then stood there looking at me. I thought, *Aren't we on first name basis, by now? Why was he still calling by my last name?*

"Have a good evening," I replied, smiling genuinely.

I turned and walked up to my door. When I opened it and pivoted back

around; the car was gone, without a sound. Walking in I noticed all the lights were off. I went up to my room closed the door and fell on my bed feeling full, yet empty. It was a strange feeling, like a part of me was missing. My meandering thoughts did huge circles in my mind. Taking a quick glance around the room, I noticed it.

The window was closed. I had left it open. I had given up closing it.

My mom must have shut it, I told myself. *Or…perhaps I didn't know all that Johnathon could do. Maybe, just maybe, he was here right now,* I thought to myself. Then my closet door began to leisurely creep open.

I held my breath, hoping it was him then I nearly jumped out of my skin when he appeared right on top of me in the blink of an eye. I hugged him a long time. Our bodies ignited with fire and ice to become explosions, hugging him was heaven. I couldn't believe he was there! Suddenly I knew what I had subconsciously suspected all along.

"It was you, you have been in my room every night since that night at Jaggers," I growled in a furiously playful way while poking him in the chest. I really was mad though, but was glad it was him.

"Yes Isla, I have been visiting you," he sighed in an extremely laid back, almost nonchalant way. He was grinning like he was blushing, but there wasn't much pink to his pale face.

"A visit is when someone knows you are coming and can plan, you know, clean up," I shouted, stepping away from him and motioning to my room.

"I love your mess, Isla," he smiled and pulled me close kissing me, practically devouring me then quickly pushing me away, and falling on my bed.

"You need to sleep, Isla," he said, lying back on my bed, with his long, curly, dark brown hair cascading lightly over my pillow.

He looked so good on my bed. I laid back in his arms, and thought to myself, *I could die right now, and it would be okay.*

"I want to know more about you," I sighed softly, gazing in his dark brown eyes.

"Sleep, Isla," he grinned, gently pushing my head down on his chest.

"Do I have to? I asked. He said nothing but gently started running his icy fingers lightly above my eyebrows back in forth to my hairline till my eyelids got heavy. "Okay," my eyes closed and it wasn't long before I was dreaming.

There was a beautiful courtyard with flowers and huge trees. I walked along a sidewalk and came to a tree that was as big as a house. I looked up to the sky, staring in awe at this tree that kept going and going. I climbed the tree as high as it went, and there was a bed. It was beautiful and inviting. I realized it was Johnathon's bed. I got excited jumping up and down, looking around the room in anticipation. Where was he? I saw a dark shadow off in the distance.

Suddenly an uneasy feeling came over me like a fever. I was burning up.

"Johnathon, is that you?" I cried out, into the touchable clouds.

I could hardly move or speak. Then he came into my vision. He glared at me, then crept over me like a black cloud edging slowly over my head. In a jolt of lightening, flashes of his face at the castle party came to my mind. It was him, Johnathon's brother, Sigrid Daine.

All of a sudden he was behind me holding me so tightly it was hurting from the inside, like being cut by millions of knives. I felt the most intense fear. Suddenly, I woke up screaming and thrashing around.

"Isla, are you okay?" Johnathon asked, pulling me close. I broke away from him and sat up hastily, trying to breathe.

"Isla, Isla, what's the matter?" Johnathon asked in a worried tone. I got one breath in and then everything went black.

Chapter 7
Darkness Over Me

I WOKE UP TO HIM KISSING ME. There was a knock at the door. I shot up like a spring and opened it, not even thinking or looking to see where he was.

"Isla, what time did you get home last night?" Mom asked me sternly with harsh undertones. My eyes were subtlety combing the room to see where he might have hidden, even though I knew he could just disappear.

"I don't remember, Mom, I just woke up. I was having a nightmare," I said, trying to change the subject.

"Are you okay?" she responded lovingly, but still unhappy with me.

"Yeah, Mom, I will be down in a little while," I replied, trying to get her out the door.

"Okay," she said. I closed the door, and listened for her footsteps as she went down the stairs.

"She's gone, although I have a feeling I'm in trouble," I whispered.

He came out as if he was already in plain view.

"That was close," he murmured as he swept me up and laid me down on the bed. He was lying on top of me, kissing me, his fingers soft, but cold, running along my neck. It felt like ice, causing a tingling feeling all through my body. Not holding back, I wanted him to taste me again.

I flipped us over so I was on top, still kissing him passionately. I slid my hand under his shirt and touched his belly. He grabbed my hand and pushed me away.

"You drive me insane," he moaned, holding his head with both hands, and sitting up in bed.

"I'm sorry, but I can't control myself either," I admitted as my eyes and my heart got emotional. Trying to suppress my hormones only made matters worse. I was losing my mind in his enchanting dreamy eyes.

"This is only going to get harder," he replied, squeezing my hand. I glanced down and giggled as I bit my lower lip thinking to myself, *Our emotions will be the least of our worries.*

"You're probably right," he agreed, as if I had said it out loud. He stood up. I caught a glimpse of the clock, it was 1:45 p.m.

"I have to go downstairs now," I said reluctantly. My body ached at the thought of being apart from him.

"Yeah, I need to get to work," he murmured, smiling and pulling me up to him. He wrapped his beautiful cold limbs around me.

"I'll see you tonight," I sighed, hugging him tightly, not wanting to ever let go. And afraid if I did, he would disappear.

"Yes you will, my sweet. I hope you have a great day. I love you, Isla," he whispered low and breathily, touching my cheek and kissing my lips.

When my eyes opened he was gone. That was what frustrated me more than anything, the fact that I never saw him leave. *Oh, but he will be back* I reminded myself.

After he vanished I decided to sit down and write a song for him. I had not written a song or poem in a long time. It was time.

Twisted Dream, Dead Moon
Take my heart
Take my soul

Take all that leaves me whole

Take my dreams
Take my moon
Take my breath, the time will come soon
For my twisted dream, dead moon

Take my life
For it's nothing without you
Take my blood
For in my vein it's blue

Too many souls out dancing in the night
For your love I give up the fight
Take my smile
Take my pain
For only you I remain the same

Take my finger
Wrap it in gold
You're the only one I will forever hold
Close to my heart
We will always be
Forever and eternity

I had just finished it and put it on the table when I heard, "Isla, are you ever coming down?" My mom was screaming up from the bottom of the stairs.

"Yeah, I'll be down in a minute," I yelled back. I went to my closet to figure out what I wanted to wear. Choosing a long red silky dress, I quickly changed my clothes. Although, I wanted to stay in the dress from the night before, it was so comfortable and I felt beautiful in it.

"I wonder if I'll ever get to wear it again?" I thought out loud as I put it in a bag with the rest of my dry cleaning..

I brushed my teeth and my hair, then curled my crimson hair around my face. When I went downstairs, my mom was in the kitchen cooking something. It smelled odd, I couldn't tell what it was. The aroma kind of made me feel nauseous.

"Mom, what are you cooking?" I asked with a sour look on my face. She looked at me with an expression of astonishment.

"Eggs and bacon, it's your favorite. I know it's not breakfast time anymore, but think of it as brunch," she said, making a plate for me.

Suddenly, I felt sick and ran to the bathroom. I was very lucky there was a bathroom downstairs. I barely made it.

"Isla, I hope you're not getting sick," mom hollered from the other room.

"Oh, I don't know. It just hit me all of a sudden. I'm feeling a little bit better now," I said, coming out of the bathroom wiping my mouth with a paper towel.

I went and sat on the couch and curled up with a blanket. I didn't know why I was sick. Maybe subconsciously I was rebelling against food because I knew I was eventually going to have to give it up for love. Although, I believed there was always something in life you would have to sacrifice for love at some point, food wasn't on my list.

"Your plate's on the table," mom announced, unsure if I would be able to eat. I got up and went into the kitchen. I sat down and looked at the plate of food. I tried to eat a bite or two, but wasn't hungry and that worried me.

I fixed a cup of hot tea and sat back down. Mom was eating really quickly.

"Are you in a hurry?" I asked smiling, while turning my nose up at the smell in front of me.

"I have to show a house in twenty minutes," she explained as she got up from the table and went to the sink.

"Wash your dish, okay?" she ordered, kissing me on the forehead then grabbed her coat and purse and headed for the door.

"See you later, honey," she said and then pulled the door closed.

"Bye," I said with my mouth full, trying my hardest to swallow without getting sick, again.

Maybe I am coming down with something, I thought as I tried to eat a couple more bites. But I couldn't, so I dumped the rest in the waste basket, washed my plate and put it in the rack. I grabbed my tea and went upstairs. Setting it down on my bedside table, I noticed a folded piece of paper and opened it.

My Dearest Isla,

> *You are the most precious gift this world has ever given me. I cherish every second we are together. I miss you like crazy when we are apart. I love you with all my heart.*

> *Forever and an eternity,*
> *Johnathon*

I sat there on my bed thinking...thinking about what all I would have to give up and what I would gain. I picked up my pen, and paper and began to write. I wrote out a list of the pros and cons of becoming a vampire. The list was much more lengthy on the pros side. And at the top of my list I wrote *Johnathon* and next to it the word *forever.* I circled them both and suddenly the rest of the list didn't even matter anymore.

Then Sigrid's face popped in my head and once again I was haunted by evil. I was still in a writing mode so I continued as I recalled the unusual nightmare I had had earlier that morning. Remembering the darkness over me, I began to write ...

Darkness over Me

I climbed up a huge tree
I went as high as I could see
Up in the clouds

No one could look down on me

Saw something familiar
Something close to my heart
Thinking of you
Not to ever part

Then a dark cloud rolled in and paralyzed me darkness,
Darkness over me
It took hold and ripped me in shreds, scraping all
of me, darkness,
Darkness over me
Your power had a strong grip on me, tore me up
so deeply, darkness,
Darkness over me

Let the sun shine
Let the fear die
So much so deep, he could read a lie
He breathed in my last breath as he edged so closely

So closely he took my soul
He took over everything in me
He breathed so close to my ear, and now
I am consumed.
By nothing but fear

The time got away from me; looking at the clock I realized it was 6:00 pm. I had no idea where the time went. *Soon, I'll see him, I can't wait.*

Should I introduce him to my parents? The question ran through my head. I might be able to see him more if I did. I just didn't know how that would go over. My parents would be surprised if I introduced him to them because I had never introduced a boy to them before. I had dated, but nobody worthy of meeting them.

What if they didn't like him? They would make it hard for me. How could they not like him, he was completely irresistible ... to me anyway. Time was going by too slowly. I missed him terribly. I sat there eying the clock, waiting. The old adage about a watched pot not boiling was true. I needed to make time go by faster.

"I need to clean before he gets here," I told myself out loud, examining my room. I put on some loose fitting faded black jeans and a tight black tank top lacy and see through. I picked my clothes up off the floor and took some dishes down to the kitchen. After washing the dishes I cleaned the kitchen, then straightened up the living room. After doing all of that I went back up to my room, and continued to spruce it up. I leaned over to pick up something in my closet and when I stood back up.

"Ahhhhhh," I screamed. "You scared me," I yelled, popping him in the chest playfully with my hand and then jumping in his arms.

"Isla, I couldn't wait any longer. I had to see you. Sorry, I frightened you though." We kissed and kissed some more. I could tell he actually missed me as much as I missed him.

"My heart has returned," I whispered as he hugged me.

"Do you want to go do something?" he smiled, and wiped a smear of lipstick around the edge of my lips. My face reddened with embarrassment.

"If I had known that you were going to be here this early I would have put a lipstick on that didn't smear." I sighed and scowled at him.

"You didn't answer my question," he sighed, chuckling low and melodically. "Do you want to go do something?" he repeated, holding my arms out in front of me, intertwining his chilled fingers in and out of mine. He yanked me closer giving me a questioning look.

"Sure! Where do you want to go?" I asked, so lost in his eyes I almost forgot he had even asked me that question, again. I was also mesmerized by his mouth; his big pouty lips, yum.

"How about my house?" he suggested, playing with my necklace. My face went white and my heart tore up my chest with loud, rapid beating.

Terror came at me like a freight train. I went to the window and put my head out.

"I can't...breathe," I murmured, that was all I could get out.

"What's wrong, Isla? There is no one there; it will only be you and me, well, and the staff, but you'll hardly see them," he affirmed, trying to ease my anxiety some. "What are you afraid of?" he asked, leaning into me and intensely gazing in my eyes. I glared at him, my expression showing my irritation that he was playing dumb.

"Who? Sigrid? He isn't there," he announced.

"His omen eyes get under my skin, what can I say?" I sighed, looking away. I breathed an enormous sigh of relief, my panic began to subsided.

"You went white, you were even paler than me," he snickered.

"Funny," I said, poking him in the stomach.

"Are you ready?" he asked running his cold fingers across my chest. It gave me shivers like lightening shooting up my spine. Strange that it felt good.

"You want to meet my mom tonight?" I asked.

"Some other night, my sweet," he replied, hurrying me up.

He handed me my purse. I put the strap over my shoulder. "I'm ready," I announced, reluctantly.

He opened the door without touching it and we headed down the stairs. He opened the front door and closed it behind us with his mind; I observed with amazement.

The long stretch limo was waiting. Calvin opened the door and we got in.

"This is the first time we have ridden in a car together," I murmured, smiling and moving closer to him. "I don't like riding alone," I whispered.

He smiled and kissed me. "I won't let you ride alone anymore."

"Good," I said and flashed him a big grin.

He leaned in to kiss me. I pulled away teasingly. His lips were within centimeters of my trembling lips and once again I tormented him. He grunted in frustration and attacked me. For a moment I actually forgot where we were going and who might be waiting in the shadows. He slowly ran his icy lips down my neck. I closed my eyes when he paused and held position with his arctic lips lightly on my skin. I opened my eyes and looked at the dark grey car ceiling anticipating something.

"Are you paying me back?" I asked annoyed and somewhat defeated.

He brought his head up and looked at me, "Maybe...how does it feel...does it drive you crazy? Should I stop?" he sighed kissing me in between every few words. He grinned and chuckled faintly when he saw how bothered I was.

"No. I want you to start." I whispered looking up at him. He was laying on top of me and it was causing me to breathe shallow. He scooted to the side of me when he felt my chest halt for a moment. He was about six foot four and two hundred and forty pounds. A big guy. I was incapable of fighting him off. He won.

When the car stopped Calvin opened the door and it caught us off guard. My head was near the door and when he opened the door my head fell back. I looked up at Calvin who was upside down to me and smiled. Johnathon took my hand and pulled me up. I fixed myself up as Johnathon got out. He took my hand and helped me out.

"Whose car is that?" I asked apprehensively, pointing at a red sports car, worried at what the answer would be.

"My brother's," he sighed, annoyed and apologetic. I stopped and couldn't move. My heart was pounding so loud, it was in stereo in my ears. "Don't worry, I'm keeping you all to myself," he breathed, pulling me to him.

"Okay," I sighed and took a deep breath. "I don't want to see anybody else though," I demanded with a shaky voice.

"It'll be okay, Isla. You're safe with me. You're not going to faint again are you?"

"Faint?" I grabbed his arm and peered up at him. "When did I faint?" I asked, startled by the notion.

"You had a nightmare early this morning, remember? I think you hyperventilated."

"I did? I...don't remember that, but I definitely remember the nightmare," I murmured, bleakly, astounded by what he had just said.

We walked around to a different door, not the front door. I wasn't as tense anymore. Relaxation was beginning to wash over me. He opened the door without touching it as usual.

"After you, my sweet," he said lusciously with that smooth voice. I stepped in and was speechless. The walls were lined with gold, and textured with exotic woodcarvings. The furniture was old and exquisite. The room was decorated with rich browns and a dark red burgundy color. There were enormous blooms of roses and other flowers on the wall paper. The colors and every detail were so vivid and bright it was fantasy-like.

"Do you want to go to my room?" he asked, standing in front of me, rubbing my back suggestively with an impish grin.

"Yes, but that's going to make it even harder. We might lose control again," I replied, hoping to finally push him over the edge.

"I know, I just want to lay back and hold you," he murmured and then smiled warmly, gazing in my eyes.

The place was so big I was astonished by how quickly we were in his room. I had pretty much stared at him the whole way. In fact, I don't even remember walking at all. I must have been gliding backwards. He carried me, he must have. His bedroom door was closed when we reached it. He opened it without touching the brass knob. We entered his room and he immediately pulled back the canopy curtains and laid back on his bed.

"I'm still tired," I sighed as I kicked my shoes off, and climbed up to lie back into his chilling arms.

"Well, go to sleep!" he suggested, softly brushing my hair away from my face. His icy fingers running along my fiery flesh at the top of my shoulder, back and forth to the crease of the hollow of my neck.

"I can't, I have to work tomorrow. I've got to go home soon."

"Please stay with me, stay the night," he smiled and kissed me. "Please!" he begged so sweetly it made it brutal to say no.

"I would have to say I was staying the night with Lizzy. Oh crap, I forgot to call Lizzy. She probably thinks that I'm dead, kidnapped or worse."

"What's worse than dead or kidnapped?" he asked being funny. I ignored his antics.

"I have to call her right now," I insisted, picking up my purse and fumbling through searching for my phone. "There it is," I said out loud, as I pulled it out and dialed Lizzy.

"Hey girl, what's up? I know, I know, I'm fine. Yes, I'm with Johnathon. Yes, very much so; more than I thought was ever possible. Hey, could you please say that I am staying with you tonight? I know. I'll owe you. Okay. Thank you, girl. Love ya, too. Bye." I closed my phone and then opened it back up to call my mom.

As I dialed the hawks in my stomach were fluttering. I had a hard time lying to my mom.

"Hey mom, is it cool if I stay with Lizzy? She will drop me off at work tomorrow. Thank you. I love you, too. I'll see you tomorrow night." I closed the phone, threw it in my purse, and set it on the floor next to the bed.

"That was easy enough, wasn't it?" he asked, flipping through a book standing at the end of the bed with one foot propped up on the bed frame.

"I'm yours, but I don't have a change of clothes or anything to sleep in."

"I can take care of that!" He went to a tall, dark cherry wood chest of drawers.

He pulled out a shirt and tossed it to me. I held it up and shouted, "Oh my God, you like the Violent Femmes!" in a high pitched tone.

"They're one of my favorite bands," he replied, jumping on the bed.

"Can we listen to them?" I asked, getting eager. I screamed *"Add It Up."* He got up and went to a big black file cabinet, pulled out a drawer that seemed to go on forever. He had quite a collection.

"Wow! You have everything," I gasped as my eyes bulged out of my head, observing the CD labels as I leaned over his shoulder. You name it he had it.

"This is just my collection I keep in my room. I have a bookshelf full in another room. The bathroom is through there if you want to change." He pointed, paying attention only to the assortment of music in front of him.

"Okay, I'll be right back," I whispered, kissing his cheek.

I cautiously made my way down an extremely long hallway. I looked in doorways, but didn't see a bathroom. I kept walking, peeking in every room, still no bathroom.

I walked around a corner and saw a dark shadow race by. Suddenly I was taken by fear. I turned around and walked back. I still hadn't found a bathroom. Now, I was scared and had to pee, bad combination.

I saw movement out of the corner of my eye and stopped frozen, just standing there. Somehow I knew it was him, Sigrid Daine. Suddenly I felt a polar hand clench my throat and before I could scream he jerked me back furiously. Then a door slammed. I opened my eyes and gasped when I realized what was happening to me. I thought about pinching myself. *This is a nightmare and any minute I'm going to wake up,* I told myself clamping my eyes together, praying that I would awake and Johnathon would be lying next to me, and all would be well. No such luck. When I peeked, I was in hell and being held hostage by the devil himself.

It was dark, I couldn't see much of anything. Except for his pale face in my peripheral view. I was choking to death from his painful grip around my neck while his sharp nail scraped across my skin. I felt the tightness of the rope as he coiled it around my wrists. All the while clenching my neck with the other hand. I screamed and it came out muddled and gurgled.

I cried out again, but he held my throat so tight I couldn't make a sound loud enough for Johnathon to hear me. My feet were dangling in the air as he hoisted me up effortlessly. The music was blaring in the distance. My eyes were pouring. I was so terrified. *I had always wondered how I would meet my demise, but this never came to mind. Was this it?* I thought to myself.

"Do you love my brother?" he whispered and even his whisper oozed of evil. He was still behind me and could kill me any second, if that was his intention. My stomach hurt thinking about not seeing Johnathon, ever again.

"Well do you?" he interrogated with snarling, dripping words.

"Y...es," I tried to get it out, but my words were smothered. I felt my feet touch the ground. I wanted to collapse on the floor. My legs were shaking, even if I wanted to stand I couldn't. He looked bothered that I was so weak. Then he savagely pushed me down into a rock hard wooden chair. It felt as if it had splintered into my lower back. It caused me to shriek.

"Isla!" He snapped his dead fingers in front of my face. "Now pay attention! I'm going to give you a choice. I will take your life, your heart or your soul... you choose!" He reached out again and grabbed my throat squeezing it tighter and tighter in a twisting motion as he walked around to face me. When he did he dug the heel of his tall black boot into the middle of my bare foot. I wailed and bit my lower lip.

I didn't understand how he could maintain such a secure hold on my throat when he was moving around so much. He let go for a brief moment. I coughed and wheezed trying to get oxygen to my lungs. *He's a vampire, that's how,* I told myself.

"Joh…." I tried to scream, but it barely came out. He came more into focus as my tears slowed. Then he stood back, smiled wickedly. I was coughing and hacking as I tried to get oxygen which seemed to be extremely difficult. He stood there and glared at me with his long, black, shiny hair. The black around his face made his skin that much more vividly white. His skin was almost glowing.

"Sig…" my words were suppressed and my breath was caught in my throat. He didn't have a hold of my throat anymore, but it still felt like he did. He glared at me exposing his long pointy teeth. He was so pale it was blinding, it was like staring at the snow in the bright sunlight. I tried to put my hand up to block the light of his face, but my hands were tied.

"I'm waiting," he snarled at me. His piercing eyes cut through to my very soul. His words sliced through to my core.

I wheezed and gasped for the air that had been cut off from me. Then I was finally able to speak. "What do you mean?" I asked, thrilled that I could breathe and speak again.

"I mean I will go after everyone you know and love. You can die, or you can become what I am. DECIDE!!!" His words echoed in my head.

"Alright…then make me a vampire," I conceded. Then it hit me what I had just said. I closed my eyes and could feel him coming closer. He was the dark cloud hanging over me. But I would do anything to protect the people I knew and loved.

Tear upon tear kept falling. He walked behind me. I swallowed hard because I knew it was coming. He grabbed my throat, cutting off my air again. His nail dug into my skin. I felt tremendous pain in my head, neck, and then my heart. I held my breath. My eyes were rolling back in my head. My light was dimming.

Then I heard what sounded like a door open.

"GET AWAY FROM HER!" a voice shattered the terrifying silence. It was Johnathon. They began growling like huge monster trucks, revving their engines. Sigrid let go of my throat. The chair tumbled over and I hit the floor. I tried to hold back my tears. But it was so loud it made me cry harder and I was afraid to look up, because of the ear bleeding noises of thrashing, tearing, and smashing. Then suddenly it stopped. I held my breath and squeezed my eyes tightly, fearful of what was next. I saw a blurry figure coming at me and then I slipped into unconsciousness.

I came two when I felt cold hands touching me. I started to struggle until my eyes adjusted and I heard a sweet voice.

"Isla, are you okay?" Johnathon asked, then untied my hands and picked me up. He swiftly carried me out of the room. The wind of us moving dried my eyes and the blood on my neck. He locked the door to his room and laid me down on the bed.

"I'm so sorry, Isla. No one will ever hurt you again," he breathed. I wanted to believe him, but I knew it wasn't over.

He began to cry, resting his head on my chest. I was very unresponsive and in shock from the terror I had just faced. I shook and cried uncontrollably. He held me firmly to control my convulsing body. He embraced me a long time. When I calmed down he looked at me and smiled, sweetly.

"Can I get you anything?" he asked, still regretting that he brought me there. Staring at the ceiling, his cold hand startled me when he softly brushed the blood-coated locks away from my face. I screamed and shook from the shock of his Alaskan fingers as I pictured Sigrid's face.

"Isla, it's me, Johnathon," he whispered with a low growl. He threw his arms around me and held me for a while longer. I sobbed in his arms and felt a slow release as I came back to me. "I'm so sorry Isla." He repeated again and again. "What can I do to make it up to you? Do you need anything?" he asked, feeling somewhat responsible.

"It's not your fault. I'll be okay. But, I'm hungry and I still have to pee," I answered, still not feeling quite normal yet. He picked me up and carried me to a bathroom. We were in front of the door so fast it made me lightheaded.

"I'll wait right here," he promised, kissing me gently and setting me down on my feet. As he set me down I tilted my head back and felt something wet running down my neck. Johnathon's jaw tightened and his eyes went black as he gazed at me. He turned his head quickly and closed his eyes. I raised my hand and wiped the blood. He motioned for me to go, so I stumbled through the door and closed it behind me. When the mirror came into view and I looked at my reflection. I was horrified by the two inch bleeding gash on my neck from his nail slicing my skin. I wiped my eyes and washed the blood from my hands. I gathered myself, did my business and opened the door. He was standing there with a silver tray in his hands. He lifted the cover revealing spaghetti and garlic bread.

"You're so sweet," I whispered and smiled. "I need a bandage," I stated, holding my hand to my throat hiding the cut.

I heard a noise somewhere in the house and went pale, I couldn't move.

"Don't worry, he's not here anymore. He's gone home," he assured me.

"Are you sure?" I asked, still not satisfied.

"Isla, don't worry. I won't let you out of my sight," he promised as he held me. "I think there are some bandages in the medicine cabinet, let me see. He stepped past me and went into the bathroom.

"What about home or work?" I sighed as I peered in every direction while he was in there.

"Don't worry, Isla. Nothing will hurt you, I promise." He set the tray down and took the bandage out of the package. I looked at him questionably.

"Are you sure? I can put it on," I suggested as I watched his eyes carefully.

"I got it. It has stopped bleeding. I'll be okay," he assured me. He went to put it on. His icy fingers barely touched my skin and it caused me to jump.

I was still freaking out; anybody would be after such an ordeal. I just couldn't calm down. He didn't say another word. He just picked me up and carried me to bed. He laid me down and handed me the tee-shirt to put on. He turned around so I could change.

But, I caught him trying to peek. I giggled quietly and then jumped in bed pulling the covers up.

"I'll be back in five seconds. You can count if you want," he grinned boyishly, like he knew that I noticed him sneaking a peek.

I nodded and attempted to look at my non-existent watch. He looked like he was getting ready to take off. Then he was gone and all I saw was a tracer of his silhouette, then he was back. He set the tray on my lap and I sat up quickly.

"Do you want anything to drink?" he asked, being hospitable.

"Maybe some hot tea or ice water," I replied smiling.

He leaned over pressed a button and said, "I would like some hot tea and ice water, please." He sat down next to me on the bed.

"Yes, sir, it will be sent up in five minutes," the voice on the intercom said.

Five minutes later he opened a compartment on the wall and pulled out a tray. I was already eating. I was famished from not eating anything at all, since this morning. And that hadn't been much, considering I had thrown it up.

"Thank you, you're so good to me," I expressed with my mouth half-full.

He chuckled and wiped the side of my cheek with a napkin. I sipped my tea and finished every bite. "That was good," I said, beginning to feel fairly.

"Are you full?" he asked, taking away the tray.

"Yes, I am. I feel a lot better now," I replied, yawning, "Thank you again," I couldn't thank him enough. "You're amazing. You saved my life," I smiled and gazed at him, gratefully. "I thought he was going to make me into a vampire, not kill me. I was okay with that."

"My brother doesn't work that way. He would have taken your life, and then said, 'Oops, I didn't mean to do that,' as he dropped your body to the floor."

"You sound like you have already experienced that," I sighed, wanting to hear more.

"It was centuries ago," he said glowering, not wanting to go there. I could see he had some pent up hostility with that subject. I let it go and didn't pry.

"Tell me about your Mom and Dad," I demanded, rolling over on my side and adjusting the pillow.

"I was told my Dad died of a fatal disease before I was born. My Mom was bitten when she was pregnant with me, by a vampire named Neco Diallia, a member of the S.P.I., Society of Powerful Immortals. He bit her, changed her, and then after I was born he put a steak through her heart and took her head."

"I'm so sorry. Who raised you?" I asked, water built in my eyes, but I was too tired to really feel.

"His name is Jaymen Daine. He is a member of S.P.I. He lives in Hungary. I haven't seen or heard from him in centuries. He denied the code."

I yawned a few times, not meaning to be rude, but I couldn't help it. Exhaustion had taken its toll.

"You're tired, Isla. Sleep." he ordered as he crawled up on the bed and laid down. He put his lips to my forehead and whispered, "I just don't know what I would've done if he had killed you." His cool cheek brushed against mine as he held me tightly. A piece of his long curly hair tickled me as it slid up under my chin. I lifted my shoulders as a chill moved through me.

"What? Are you cold?" He picked his head up and looked at me when he felt me shake. I was, but I would gladly freeze to be next to him.

"No, your hair tickled my chin."

He gazed in my eyes, kissed me and said, "Liar."

I smiled and nestled my head in the hollow of his neck. He cuddled up closer, as if that was possible.

"Sleep, baby," he whispered.

"Okay," I replied too tired to fight him, feeling aloof. He held me all night. I slept peacefully.

Chapter 8

Desperation

*W*HEN I WOKE UP IT WAS HARD to tell if it was night or day, it was so dark in his room. Johnathon was still curled up next to me the same way he was before I fell asleep.

"Crap! I'm late for work," I yelled, looking at the clock.

"Baby, you had a rough night. Why don't you just call in sick?" he suggested, pulling me back down to him.

Well I'm already late, I thought in my head. "Okay," I needed to sleep some more. I started to lay back down.

"I better call, though," I reached for my purse, pulling my phone out and dialing work.

"Hi Lissa, I'm sick today. Can you reschedule all my appointments for Wednesday? Thank you, I hope I do too." I closed my phone and tossed it into my purse on the floor beside the bed. I laid back down and cuddled up next to my love. He fell back to sleep and so did I.

In my dream I was running, scared and alone. Someone was chasing me, I didn't know who, but I had the feeling he was very powerful and fierce. I was running down a dark alley off a street somewhere, it didn't look like Asheville. I glanced back to see if anyone was behind me, and when I turned back around, he was right in front of me. I let out a blood-curdling scream and tried to run. But he caught me before I could get away. He was tall with short, spiky, white-blonde hair. He had white or pink eyes, it was hard to tell it was so dark.

"Hm, hm, what do we have here? hm, hm, hm. So this is Johnathon's love hm, hm, hm, hm," he talked with a hum, it was like he was humming a song in between his words.

Then two others stepped out into view. It was a man and a woman. The woman had long, black hair hanging down past her waist. She was tall, toned, and beautiful. She looked to be about twenty-eight or thirty. She was dressed like a sophisticated cat burglar. The other man was not that tall. He had short brown hair, dark eyes,, and was good looking. He was dressed in a long black trench coat with high boots and silver chains all over his pants.

The woman spoke. "How will we torture her?" she asked as she sauntered up to me and hissed.

I cried out, "Johnathon! Johnathon!" I was scared and hoped he would hear me. The blond-haired man had both of my arms around my back, very tightly. I was in a lot of pain.

"Hm, hm, he can't hear you, we're blocking your frequency, hm hm hm."

He got up so close to my ear I could feel his cold breath. It made my ear hurt. It felt like I had been in eighteen degree weather all day without earmuffs. My tears began to fall. I tried to hold them back, but couldn't. The woman was glaring at me. She was so close her breath froze my tears. I

watched a few fall to the ground, and shatter like glass. But, when it shattered it was a loud smash and an explosion. After I observed that strange phenomenon, I thought to myself, **This is a dream, anything can happen.**

I closed my eyes tightly saying Johnathon over and over again in my head, praying he would hear me.

"Hm, hm, I told you he can't read your thoughts. Besides, if he does by chance, hm, hm, hear you it will be too late."

I swallowed hard, then tried to break free from his grasp.

"Hm, hm, you're not strong enough my dear, hm, hm," he said, humming in a tormenting tone.

"Neco, may I have the first taste?" the woman asked with hungry eyes and sharp spiky teeth, ready to pounce on me any second.

"Hm, hm, not yet, Dezi, in due time my dear, hm, hm. Myriad might want the first taste, hm."

The other man, Myriad, stepped forward and lunged at me with the force of a jet engine. I was slammed up against the building; hitting my head hard, I could feel the cold blood running down my forehead. I brought my hand up to feel my head then held it out to see the blood dripping from my fingers. I grimaced from the pain as I raised my head. Suddenly all I could see was three sets of fangs sparkling in the moonlight all of them coming for me. Then I awoke screaming and gasping for air.

"Isla! Isla! Are you okay?" Johnathon asked, kind of shaking me.

Stunned and paralyzed I came to the realization that my dreams seemed to be coming true. *I wonder if Johnathon can read my dreams.* I contemplated.

"Oh my!" I breathed, cupping my hand over my mouth. "Neco, his name was Neco," I blurted out loudly.

"What about Neco?" he growled and then really shook me.

I stared blankly across the room. "Can you read my dreams?" I mumbled then stared him in the eyes. He looked at me and got quiet, then looked away.

"No," he sighed, flatly. His shoulders dropped in slight shame.

"What if when I'm awake and I'm thinking about the dreams I've had?"

"Dreams are sacred. That is something that all vampires have in common. If they can read minds, that is. We can't read dreams, even if the person is going over the dream in their head while they're awake. He turned to look at me. His eyes hard and full of vengeance. "Now, what about Neco?" he growled.

That name sent daggers of sharp shivers up my spine. *I can't even imagine what it did to him,* I thought to myself.

"Neco was in my dream; he captured me. He held my arms behind my back. I was scared and in a lot of pain. His intentions were very obvious, that they planned on killing me, not converting me. I say they, because there were two others, Dezi and Myriad. Neco was ripping my arms out of the sockets, well it felt like it anyway." I swallowed sharp as I continued. "He hummed while he talked. Then Myriad lunged at me, throwing me up against a building in a back alley somewhere. I busted my head open, there was blood all over me. The last thing I remember before I awoke, was seeing three sets of fangs sparkling brightly in the moonlight and all of them coming for me." My voice was low and monotone as I explained.

"What did Neco look like?" he asked, very edgy and wanting to hear more. I got nervous when his jaw became rigid and his fists tightened revealing every vein in his pale hands.

"Calm down baby," I whispered, caressing his back attentively.

"What...did... he...look like?" he roared carefully pronouncing each syllable and his mouth straight lined in furry. It gave me chills to see him like that. But, I knew it was restitution he sought.

"Uhh... he had short, spiky, white-blond hair. He was tall and I think he had pink eyes, they were almost white in the dark, like an albino's."

"I can't let you out of my sight. Ever!" he announced, worried and upset, with avenge in his eyes. *That sounds good to me,* I thought.

"It was a dream, but I had a dream about Sigrid before he attacked me. I think my psychic abilities are in my dreams," I explained, as the truth was revealed. "So if it's not some fluke and I have been blessed with this gift, I will be seeing Neco soon," I whispered. My mouth was dry and panic was beginning to set in.

Johnathon disappeared beside me and with in a second he reappeared across the room putting his tall, black biker boots on.

It never really mattered how much I saw it, seeing his magic was always a shock to me. A breathtaking shock, literally.

"Not if I kill him first," he snarled, looking away, his neck muscles were tight and his veins were bluish, showing through his skin. "I have to go find him," he stated in a horrible growl.

"No! I would die if anything happened to you," I yelled, jumping out of bed terrified by thought of something happening to him. I grabbed his arm in a loving, pleading gesture. I started to feel an absence of my heart. I realized I was standing there in his black Violent Femmes tee-shirt and my panties. "I have to change clothes," I announced as I picked up my jeans and slipped them on. I looked all over for my black lacy top and couldn't find it.

"So would I, if something happened to you and you are way more vulnerable than I am," he replied, protectively throwing his arms around me. "I'll take you home," he murmured as he clenched both of my arms and held me out in front of him to look at my eyes.

"He might kill you like he did your mom." He let go and grabbed his long, black trench coat that was draped over the end of the black velvety couch next to the bed. "I would crawl in a hole and die if he took you from me."

"Nothing is going to happen to me," he murmured.

"How do you know that, your not invincible. If you die I will throw myself in front of a freight train. No! No! I would let him kill me, too. I would put myself up for sacrifice to the council," I promised as the salt water slid from my eyes.

He pulled me into him. "You must not think like that, Isla. I will kill him, and come back to you," he promised in a low whisper. "Do you mind if I have my driver take you home?" he asked as he squeezed me. Then he kissed me, before I had a chance to say anything. That kiss! The way he held my face with both hands. I loved kissing him. Each kiss was like a vacation from reality, a trip I never wanted to end. I couldn't stand being away from him.

"No! I shouted, then gazed into his deep chocolate eyes. "You swore you would never let me ride alone," I whispered, reminding him. Our lips were an inch apart. I could feel his breathing against my chest moving me. My heartbeat was loud and vibrated throughout my body. "You also promised me...you would stay with me and protect me," I murmured turning my eyes down in despair.

"To protect you I have to kill Neco," he growled pushing me away.

I stood there, stunned that he pushed me. I couldn't believe that he would do that. It pissed me off, so I hastily grabbed my purse and walked out of the room as fast as I could.

"Wait! Isla," he demanded, smiling slyly. He was already waiting for me in the hall. Standing leisurely leaning up against the wall. "I'm sorry, my sweet," he sighed, pulling me close. "I will ride with you. Isla, I have to protect you," he explained, trying to get me to look him in the eyes. I didn't plan on giving in. But he was so beautiful and alluring as he put his glacial fingers under my chin directing my vision to his eyes. He was so strong, winning was not an option for me.

"You know, all of this would be over if you would just make me a vampire," I sighed with exasperation.

"Isla, I don't want that for you," he whispered while trying to hug me. I pushed him away, but of course he won. He was way too powerful. He kissed me. I resisted and then melted into his encompassing embrace. His lips softly grazed mine and then he teased by pulling away slightly when I reached for more. I got tired of his torture and engulfed him in my flames. Just when I had him wrapped, I stopped.

"Okay, I'm ready to go home. But, I couldn't find my top." I announced.

"Keep the shirt, it looks sexy on you," he demanded and then kissed me soft and slowly. I was lost in his eyes and every kiss we shared. He walked me to the car, Calvin opened the door. We both got in; Johnathon held my hand and kissed me the whole ride home. I even felt him kind of let go a little. I did get a little nervous when he was kissing my neck though. I wanted him so...badly, it hurt. I wasn't sexually frustrated, just painfully frustrated. There was a small part of me that was beginning to go a wee bit crazy.

There were spurts of profound devotion and then instantly our passion was faced with encumbrance, as usual. And then the car came to a stop. Johnathon took my hand as I exited the car. I looked to see if my mom's Bronco was in the driveway, *nope just my car*, I assured myself.

"Isla, I'll be back soon. You can believe that. I love you, my sweet," he promised as he cradled me in his arms.

We kissed one last time and before my eyes opened he was in the limo and gone, without a sound, as always.

I went up to my room and fell on my bed, the minute I was inside. I laid there for a while, pining. Later, I was startled by my phone ringing in my purse, and thought it might be him. Pulling it out I saw it was a number I didn't recognize.

"Hello," I answered with slight hesitation.

"This is Preston Hill, from high school. Do you remember me?"

"Yes, how are you?" I asked, interested as to what he had to say. I had had a crush on him my freshman and sophomore years. But, he never gave me the time of day. He was a big football jock, the best looking guy in high school. I was puzzled as to why he was even calling me. He only dated cheerleaders. Granted, I was a cheerleader for a very short period my junior year til I told them all to go to hell over the intercom during a pep rally. And that was the end of my cheerleading career. Even then he didn't pay any attention to me. Why now?

"I'm doing well; I'll be in town for a few weeks, and I'm throwing a party and wanted to invite people from high school. Kind of like a reunion," he paused saying something to someone in the background. He must have covered the receiver with his hand, I couldn't hear what he had said. "Anyway, I was wondering if you would like to come? Jolie Jameson, Betsey Cain, Michael Williams, just to name a few, will all be there."

"I guess. When is it?" I inquired, still wondering why after all this time.

"This Friday night," he replied, sounding excited.

"Okay, what's the address?" I asked as I reached for a pen and paper from the top drawer of my nightstand.

"It's 2451 Sweeten Creek Road. It's in Valley Springs. Do you know where that is?"

"I think so. That's close to where Jolie lives, right?"

"Yep, she's about three or four blocks up the road from me," he said.

I had been to a slumber party at Jolie's in the tenth grade. She's really cool, and we were pretty close, I missed her.

"It starts at 7:30," he said.

"Okay, I'll be there," I promised, still not knowing what was up.

"See you then. I'm looking forward to seeing you, Isla," he replied in a suggestive way. Then he hung up.

I closed my phone and sat back on my bed.

"That was interesting," I thought out loud. My thoughts quickly drifted to Johnathon and I imagined him lying on my bed, his muscular body and his long, curly, dark hair cascading over my pillow. I thought about our first kiss at Jaggers; how it was like the floor dropped out from under us. I could almost see us as figures of energy like lightening stick figures.

Ding Dong, my doorbell rang. I flew down the stairs hoping it was him, although I knew he would come in the window. I opened the door. Nobody was there, but there was a letter taped to the door. My name was on the front. I opened it, and read ...

Isla, my sweet,

> *I can't stand being away from you. I love you and long to be with you. Please meet me Thursday night at Looking Glass*

Falls in Transylvania County in the Pisgah Forest Cradle Forestry at 7:30 pm.

Also if I ever call or write you and use the word "captivate" in any text … disregard everything. It's a trap. Calvin will pick you up. If he does not show, don't go anywhere. By the way, Calvin can take you to Preston Hill's house Friday if you like. You forgot I read your thoughts didn't you?

Isla, I can't wait to hold, and kiss you. Don't forget our secret word. One other thing, if you want to write me, just call out to Calvin Walker, my driver, to come pick it up. Tape it underneath your mailbox. He will deliver it to me.

> *I love you, want you and need you. I'll see you Thursday.*
> *Love forever and an eternity,*
> *Johnathon*

I was ecstatic and couldn't wait to see him. But three days was a long time. It was going to be difficult to be away from him so long. I had forgotten he was reading my thoughts though. I decided to write back.

Johnathon my love,

I can't wait to see you. I miss you so. I want you to lose control when you kiss me. I don't care if you bite my lip again. I long to be in your arms forever.

I want you to know that if you ever get a letter from me telling you I don't love you and don't want to be with you, it's not from me. Just in case he gets to me first. Just know I will forever love you and hold you close to my heart always. I want you! See you soon.

> *Love forever and an eternity,*
> *Isla M. Van Burren*

I wrote Johnathon Daine on the front. On the way down stairs I grabbed some scotch tape and ran outside to the mailbox, taping it underneath. I went back in, started back up the stairs then noticed my mom wasn't home yet. It was almost 9:00 pm. "Where is she?" I blurted out. *If she doesn't get home soon I'll call her cell phone*, I told myself.

When I walked in my room I realized I hadn't asked Calvin to pick it up.

"Calvin Walker, come pick up a letter, please." I said out loud.

I turned on some music and laid back on my bed. *Something* by the Beatles was playing. I sang with it, changing the words a little.

Something in the way he moves, instead of she. *Something in the way he moves me, attracts me like no other lover.* He really attracted me like no other, even though we weren't lovers, yet. He was the love of my life. He made me want to give up my soul, just to be close to him. To truly be intimate. I would have to give up my life for him. I was scared, but happy.

I was beginning to get tired. But I noticed it was almost 11:00 pm, and I still hadn't heard my mom come in, yet. I decided to call her. I picked up my phone and dialed her cell number. It rang a few times and then went to voice mail.

"Mom, I am worried about you, please let me know if you're okay," I sighed, letting her know I was concerned. After closing my phone I laid back on my bed. I was extremely worried on so many different levels, but tired so I drifted off.

Chapter 9

So Deeply

MY FIRST THOUGHT WHEN I AWOKE, WAS if my mom was home. I stretched a little, got up, and opened the door to my parents' room. The bed was made and everything looked as though she hadn't even been there. I went back to my room and called her again. Again it went right to the voice mail. I quickly dialed my Dad's cell, thankfully he answered.

"Hello, Sweetie," he said, sounding happy to hear from me.

"Have you talked to mom?" I asked nervously.

"I talked to her yesterday. She said she was going out with friends and might stay the night with her friend Gwen," he explained in a reassuring tone.

"Oh, thank God. I was worried," I breathed a sigh of relief.

"She's fine, I'm sure she'll be home soon. Don't worry your pretty little head," his words comforted me.

"When will you be home? I miss you, Dad."

"Tomorrow night, probably late. Are you off today?" he asked.

"Yes, its Tuesday. I am always off on Tuesdays."

"Oh yeah, I forget. What are you going to do today?

I thought about it for a moment or two and then replied, "I don't know--- nothing. Maybe I'll hang out with Micha and Lizzy."

"Well, have fun. I'll see you soon. Love you Isla."

"I love you, Dad, bye."

We hung up. I felt so relieved, I had all kinds of scenarios going on in my head. First I thought for sure Neco had somehow captured her. That scared me to death. And Sigrid was a threat, too. Even though dad told me she was safe, I had a weird feeling that I needed to pray anyway. My gut was in knots and I just couldn't shake the feeling something was wrong.

She is fine, I convinced myself and then prayed some more.

"I need to do something," I said out loud. *I know, call Lizzy. No, better yet I'll text her instead. I told myself.*

"Whatz happenin hot stuff?" I sent her.

She texted me back,

"Wanna go eat? Micha and I are coming by to get you."

I texted back, "Where?"

"We'll figure that out when we get there," Lizzy texted.

"Ok!" I sent back.

I went to my closet, put some black pants on, then picked out a beautiful aquamarine shirt with black lace on the collar and the bottom of the shirt.

I looked good, but needed a necklace. I went to my jewelry box and pulled out that shiny, silver box and opened it. I put on the most beautiful necklace in the world. To me. It was my most precious treasure. *What earrings do I wear with it?* I wondered. After rummaging through my jewelry box I couldn't find anything to match. And I didn't feel like wearing diamond studs.

The doorbell rang. I ran downstairs and opened the door. There was no one there, but there was a red box on the porch. As I picked it up, Lizzy and Micha pulled up in the driveway.

"Hey!" I hollered and waved as they got out of the car.

"Hey girl," Lizzy shouted. I set the box down on the ledge of the wooden porch railing, and gave her hug.

"Hi Isla, I've missed you," Micha announced as she gave me a hug.

"Did you get a present?" Lizzy asked.

I smiled and replied, "Yes!"

I must of been blushing, too, because Micha teased, "It looks like someone's in love." She drew it out with a funny accent. I grinned.

"Well open it," Lizzy demanded, rushing to help me. "What is it?" she asked as I pulled off the lid.

I pulled out the same beautiful silver box and quickly opened it.

"Oh my," I breathed, holding my hand to my mouth.

They were earrings, white gold encrusted with diamonds and a medium black onyx stone dangling from them. I wondered if they would be too heavy for my ears.

"Wow! They're gorgeous," Lizzy said. I took them out and put them on. "They must be like three carets," Lizzy commented. I closed the door behind us and went to the nearest mirror to see. To me it didn't matter whether they were cubic zirconia or crystals. It was a gift from my beloved and it meant the world to me that he liked showering me with precious treasures.

"Do they match that necklace?" Micha asked, eying both the necklace and earrings.

"They do! They're awesome girl," Lizzy said grinning.

"Isn't he amazing? I'm completely consumed," I sighed, closing my eyes and touching my necklace. I stood there staring at my reflection in the mirror. "I didn't think a love like this existed anywhere. Let alone that I would experience it," I breathed.

"Where are we going to eat?" Lizzy asked, changing the subject. She was a little uncomfortable with love, right now.

"I don't know, maybe Billy Bob Barbeque," I suggested.

"Yeah! That sounds great!" Micha agreed enthusiastically.

"Okay, let's go," Lizzy said.

"Wait let me get my stuff and put this upstairs," I said gathering the boxes and stacking them together.

They followed me upstairs, I grabbed my purse and made sure my phone was in it. Remembering that there might be a letter at the bottom of the box, I took a look and sure enough there was. I took it out and put it in my purse.

"I'll read it later," I whispered to myself as we headed down stairs. I closed the door behind us. We got in Lizzy's car and drove off down the road.

Half way down the road I realized I still hadn't heard from or seen my mom.

"*Where is she?*" I said to myself. I was still worried. I sat in the back seat this time. Micha rode shotgun. Micha and Lizzy talked back and forth. I tried to jump in on the conversation a little here and there, but I didn't feel that sociable for some reason. When we got to Billy Bob's Barbeque we went in and sat at a booth. The waiter came over. He had short, light brown hair and a nice smile and was of average height.

"How are you ladies doing?" he asked.

"We're good, how are you?" Lizzy answered for us.

"I'm good! What can I get you?" he smiled and handed us our menus.

"I'll have water," I said not knowing what to order. Lizzy and Micha ordered iced tea.

"I'll be back with your drinks," he said, as he walked away.

Lizzy was texting somebody.

"Why don't we get a sampler platter?" I suggested.

We all agreed that would be a good idea.

"So, what happened to you the night of the party?" Micha asked, playfully poking me in the shoulder.

"Johnathon wanted to be alone. We went to his room, kissed and talked all night. It was very romantic. Before we knew it was 3:00 a.m."

I didn't tell them he bit my lip or that he was a blood-sucking vampire. That didn't matter to me. They did not need to know all of that anyway.

"I'm really sorry you had to go home alone, though!" I said, looking at both of them.

"That's okay, we noticed the fire between you two and kind of figured you would be staying the night," Lizzy explained as she drank a fake drink. "Where are our drinks?" she asked.

"His tip is getting smaller," Micha announced jokingly, but she meant it.

"What about the guys you were sitting with?" I asked, interested in how their night went.

"Well" Lizzy said as they both looked at each other. "The guys that were sitting with us were strange. I think their names were Forest and Chad, we never got their last names. They kept sniffing us all night, it was really beginning to freak us out. They never really said much though," Lizzy said, looking around for the waiter.

"I didn't even see the ones who invited us," Lizzy said crinkling her nose and glancing up at us from her phone.

"How did y'all get home?" I asked.

"The driver took us home. He was waiting for us after it was over," Lizzy said, glaring around the room. The place looked like your ordinary diner with plastic tablecloths over metal tables and hard wooden chairs. The booths were the same except with oval looking benches. It wasn't very clean.

Twenty minutes must have gone by and we still didn't have our drinks. I looked around at the sparse restaurant and was confused as to why the drinks were taking so long. How long could it take to fill glasses, anyway?

"This is ridiculous!" Lizzy sighed, beyond pissed off.

"I know, maybe we should go somewhere else," Micha suggested.

"Yeah," I agreed, picking up my purse and putting my jacket on.

We all got up and started walking towards the door. A woman standing behind the desk could see we were very unhappy.

"Is everything okay?" the woman asked. She was tall and lanky with light brown hair.

"Twenty minutes for drinks, I think not," Micha said.

"We won't be back," Lizzy yelled furiously.

We slammed the door behind us and headed towards the car.

"Why don't we go to Jaggers?" Micha suggested.

My heart dropped, but I was so hungry and thirsty it sounded good.

"Okay, sounds good," Lizzy agreed.

We got in the car and took off. The tires squealed as we left the parking lot.

"That was absurd. He only had two other tables. He must have been drinking in the back or something. He didn't look drunk did he?" Lizzy asked.

"His eyes were a little blood shot," Micha replied.

Hearing the word blood in any text made my heart pound harder. "Obviously we were not supposed to eat there," I admitted, with fate on my mind.

They both agreed. Micha was changing the radio station looking for something good to listen to.

"Go back, please!" I yelped, touching Micha's shoulder.

"What, this one?" she asked, stopping on the song. I nodded. It was *Add It Up* by the Violent Femmes. I sang along and started to think about that night and the fact that I never got to hear the song, being attacked by Sigrid and all. Thinking about it made me feel ill. I held my hand up to my throat, and water began building in my eyes. Flashes of that horrible night came to mind. I got chills picturing Sigrid's face.

We pulled into the parking lot. There were not that many cars there. We didn't care, we were hungry. We parked the car and went in. When we walked in, everyone, which was about ten to twelve people, stared at me as if they knew who I was. One of the waitresses I had seen at the party ran to the back when she saw us. We sat down, the same waitress came over. She had long, dark brown hair with red highlights.

"Hello, Miss Van Burren," she said politely as she handed us our menus. "Anything you want, it's on the house," she said, looking at me.

I smiled and said, "Thank You!"

"I will have a Strawberry Daiquiri," Micha said.

Lizzy glanced up from her phone and said, "I want a White Russian."

"I'll take a Buttery Nipple," I said grinning.

"My name is Sarah, I will be your waitress. Are you sure you don't want to order your food now?"

"My name is Isla, and this is Lizzy and Micha."

She nodded to all of us.

"Nice to meet you. Is there a Jaggers sampler platter?" Micha asked.

Sarah stood there in black pants and a hot pink and black shirt with her collar up writing on a pad. She smiled warmly and then asked, "Are you sure that's what you want or would you like to hear the specials?"

"No, thank you. We will just have the sampler," I said, we all shook our heads in agreement.

She took our menus, then looked at me questionably.

"Johnathon wants to know why you haven't read the letter?"

I was speechless, then asked, "Is he here?"

"No, but he says to read the letter, it's important."

"Okay," I sighed, my heart sped up and pounded as I reached for my purse and pulled out the letter. Sarah walked away. I began reading ...

My dear Isla,

> *I have found him. There is a problem though, he has your mom. Don't worry I will get her away from him before anything happens. Please, Isla, don't worry. She'll be okay. I only knew it was her because he said he had a Van Burren. I knew you were okay, I could feel it.*

*I guess she will meet me sooner than later. I love you, Isla!
I won't let anything happen to her. See you Thursday night
unless something happens.*

Love forever and an eternity,
Johnathon Daine

I could barely finish reading it, I started to cry. I was so
scared.

"Isla, is everything okay?" Lizzy asked, getting up and
comforting me.

Micha joined her. The waitress came over with the food and
our drinks. I drank mine in two swallows. I couldn't speak or eat,
though.

"What is going on?" Lizzy asked, getting kind of upset. Micha
grabbed the letter from me and began reading.

"Oh my God, who has your mom?" Micha asked, sitting back
in her chair.

"Neco!" That was all I could say.

"Who is Neco and why does he have your mom?" Lizzy asked
getting more and more exasperated.

Sarah came back to our table.

"He's on the phone in the back, he wants to talk to you."

"Why didn't he call my cell?" I asked. Sarah shrugged her
shoulders and said nothing. I took my phone out of my purse and
saw there were two missed phone calls. I had forgotten to turn my
ringer volume up so there was a chance one of them was him. Both
numbers were unfamiliar, he probably called from a pay phone or
something.

I got up and went to the back. Sarah showed me where the
phone was and handed it to me kindly.

"Hello," I said as calmly as I could.

"Isla, she's okay! I have her." I was so relieved to hear that she
was alright. It was good to hear his velvet voice, again.

"She's not hurt is she?" I asked, shaky and nervous.

"She has a few bumps and bruises, but other than that Simone is fine."

"Thank you. Did you kill him?" I asked hoping to hear good news.

"No, he got away, but I know where he's going. I will find him. I love you and can't wait to see you Thursday night."

"Where is my mom? How did you introduce yourself?"

"I told her I was your boyfriend. She just hugged me and thanked me over and over again. It was really close. When I found her, he was just about to bite her," he said, still comforting me.

"Does she know?" I asked in a hushed tone.

"No! She was blindfolded and gagged. I am sure she heard us fighting though."

"Oh my God, is she okay?" I remembered the loud roar of their fighting and how frightening it was for me. I got emotional.

"She is fine, Isla. It's alright I will take her home. I'll find Neco," he promised.

"So you won't wait for me to get there? I miss you so much," I cried out, I was suffering badly inside.

"I can't! I have to find him before he finds you or someone else you love."

"I understand, but I don't have to like it do I?" I asked, hurt and sulking.

"No, my sweet, see you Thursday night. I love you, Isla."

"Can't wait, I love you, too. Bye," I said, not wanting to hang up. I paused.

"Bye," he replied and then hung up. I hung up the phone and went back to the table.

"Are you okay? How is your mom?" Lizzy asked.

"Is your mom okay?" Micha asked.

"Yes, Johnathon rescued her and is taking her home. I need to get home."

"We were worried. Do you want to eat something first?" Micha asked, pointing to the food left.

Sarah came over and gave us a to-go container. She had a bag in her hand.

"Here, Johnathon told me you and your mom might get hungry later," she said smiling, as she set it on the table.

"Thank you," I replied, picking up my purse and the bag from the table.

"He is so sweet," Micha said, putting her arm around me.

Lizzy picked up the to-go container saying, "Well, that was fun." She sighed with a hint of sarcasm.

I laughed a little, Lizzy put her arm around me. "We can't take you anywhere," she joked.

We walked out the door, got in the car and headed to my house.

"Are y'all mad at me?" I questioned, feeling like I was an inconvenience.

"No! Why would you think that?" Micha stared at me in confusion.

"I just seem to cause so many problems for you both."

"Stop, Isla. We love you, you're never a problem," Lizzy assured me.

"Are you kidding? You keep it exciting." Micha grinned.

"Are ya'll coming in?"

"No girl, your mom needs you," Lizzy replied.

"I know, love y'all, call me tomorrow," I said, placing my purse strap over my shoulder as I got out.

Micha handed me the bag of take-out.

I closed the car door, ran up to the front door and opened it swiftly.

"Mom!" I hollered then threw my purse down, set the bag of food on the counter, and ran up the stairs. I opened her door and saw her lying on the bed. She had scrapes and bruises on her face, to see her like that made me immediately start crying.

"Mom, are you okay?" I could barely get it out.

"Yes, I'm just a little bruised and shook up."

"What happened?" I asked, sitting down next to her on the bed.

"I got a call to show a house. He was a strange looking fellow. While walking him around the house he started asking me questions. The next thing I knew my back was against the wall, and I couldn't get past him. His humming while he talked got on my nerves. I tried to leave. He threw me up against the wall, hit me, tied me up and blindfolded me. I just knew I was going to die. Just when I had accepted my demise I heard another voice; it was soft and captivating. He told me his name was Johnathon Daine and that he was your boyfriend, whom I knew nothing about, by the way, "she said frowning. "How come you never told us about him? He is such a charming young man."

"I don't know, Mom," I answered, regretting everything. *Mom if you only knew. I said to myself.*

"Anyway, they fought. I couldn't see anything, but heard this loud roaring and things smashing and breaking. Suddenly it got quiet and I felt my hands being untied. He told me everything was going to be okay. He took the blindfold off and told me everything."

"He told you everything?" I asked, alarmed and afraid of the real truth getting out.

"Well, about you and him. How much he loved you and would do anything for you."

My heart gushed. I missed him terribly and could hardly wait to see him.

"Do you need anything?" I asked.

"Will you make me some of your hot tea?" she asked, with a pitiful look on her face.

"Sure, Mom. I'll be right back."

I went downstairs to the kitchen, and put a mug of water in the microwave.

While that was heating up, I did some dishes and cleaned up. The microwave dinged, I put a tea bag in the mug and two teaspoons of sweetener, just the way she liked. I wanted to bring her something to snack on, too, I grabbed a bag of mixed nuts that we could snack on. I put them on a tray, and slowly walked back up stairs.

"Here you go Mom," I said placing the tray across her lap.

"Thank you, sweetie," she said then looked at the mixed nuts and frowned. "I'm really hungry, maybe we can order out."

"No! I forgot Johnathon gave us some take out from Jaggers. Let me run down and get it." I ran down stairs, took the two entrees out of the bag and nibbled on a little to test the temperature to see if it needed to be reheated.

"Mmmm, lasagna," it was still very warm and tasty. It was hard to eat just two bites. I gobbled down a little more, closed the container, and put them both in the bag and headed back upstairs.

After mom and I ate our tasty entrees, I noticed the clock. It was so late. *Wow, time really flew by today. I can't believe I have to work tomorrow.* I thought.

"Mom, I need to go to bed. I love you and I'm so glad you are okay."

"I love you too, sweetie. I'll be okay. You go to bed," she sighed. I kissed her on the cheek, said goodnight, and went to my room.

Walking in my room and I noticed my window was open, but I couldn't remember if I had shut it or not. Looking around the room I noticed something on my pillow. It was one red rose with a letter tied to it like a scroll. The rose was blood red and picture perfect with a few drops of moisture on the silk petals. As I opened the letter, I got comfortable on my bed and read …

My Dearest Isla,

You are my sweet love. I can't wait to see you at Looking Glass Falls. Yes, you closed the window. I opened it just to give you a sign that I was here. Well, besides the letter and the rose. You're a lot like your mom, soft and sweet, with a pure soul. I am not at all nervous about meeting your dad if he is anything like the two of you.

I've been eating a lot of filth to build up my strength so I can attack you without biting your lip again.

> *I can't wait to hold you, kiss you and lose control.*
> *Love forever and an eternity,*
> *Johnathon Daine*

As I laid there reading it, I started to fall asleep. The letter came to an end and I was out.

Chapter X

Take Me In The Sky

*H*E WAS STARING RIGHT AT ME WHEN I opened my eyes. No, it wasn't Johnathon, it was Sigrid. I froze and couldn't move. *Should I try to run?* I whispered to myself.

"He's not my real brother, you see, and I know I can have you," he growled with ferociousness. In his eyes I saw the devil waving back at me.

"Why would you do that to him?" I asked, trying to get answers.

"I don't care about him. I don't believe in the code and he does. You see I have the power now."

His last words rang out in my mind echoing over and over again. Then I woke up sharply, sitting up and sucking all the air in I could, so much so I fell back on the pillow. I laid there a minute then got up. *I'm going to see Sigrid again*, I thought. I was terrified, but somehow changed by all that had happened in the last few weeks.

"I have to get ready for work!" I sighed out loud. While I showered and got dressed I thought about the dream and wondered how exactly it would play out in reality. I was scared, but in a way amused. It freaked me out a little. I was sitting there putting my face on and realized I could die soon. I was strangely calm. I went down stairs got my tea and mixed nuts. I discovered that being late might be in the cards today as I glanced at the clock on the microwave.

I had ten minutes to get out the door. I drank my tea down, stuck the bag of nuts in my purse and ran back upstairs. I closed my window, picked up some magazines off my bed, and headed downstairs quietly so I wouldn't wake mom. I put my jacket on, walked out the door, got in the car and was on my way.

When I got to work Lissa was on the phone. She nodded at me and went back to working on the computer. I put my purse under my station and looked at my schedule. "I'm busy today," I said, excited. I still had to save up for my trip to Amsterdam and it was going to be hard.

The day was going great. I had some great clients and awesome tips. Everybody was busy. I went to lunch in the employee lounge. Luckily I had some leftovers in the fridge from a few days before; it was meatloaf and vegetables mom made. I smelled it and took a bite. It tasted fine so I heated it in the microwave, shoved it down in less than ten minutes then threw my trash away as I headed back to my station.

Angel stopped me, "You have a walk-in request. He's sitting in your chair."

"Okay, thank you." I replied as she walked passed me to take her client to put her under the dryer.

I tried to see if I recognized him, but I couldn't see him. It seemed like all the women in the room were gathering around my chair. Either that or there were a lot of girls standing around the station next to mine. It was difficult to tell

I ran to the bathroom quickly before walking towards my station. Bad feelings started stirring deep in my stomach or I had just eaten some bad food, one or the other.

As I walked up to my chair some of the ladies stepped aside and I saw him as he spun around in the chair and glared at me. My next client was Sigrid.

Okay, so this is how it's going to go down, I told myself in my head.

"How did you think it would happen?" he asked. He leisurely sat back in my chair in his faded black jeans and a crisp white, untucked long sleeve shirt.

"I had no idea, I kind of figured a dark room somewhere, like last time," I sighed with attitude. I was getting tired of being his doormat. Although I knew my strength wouldn't even compare to his. I swallowed painfully, recalling the torture he had unleashed on me, just a few days before.

"That can be arranged," he replied wickedly dry, without an ounce remorse in his body. "Get your stuff and follow me," he commanded.

"Why would I do that?" I asked, thinking about how delusional he was.

"If you don't, I'll kill my brother, Johnathon," he rumbled.

That got my attention. My heart sank. My life would be nothing without him. I wouldn't want to live anymore.

"Okay, let me get my stuff," I sighed, giving in. I got my purse from under my station, and glanced at Angel. She was completely oblivious of what was happening right next to her. It was as if there was a wall around her chair, she was continualy in her own little world. I stared at her as he followed me to the door. She didn't notice. I was curious if anyone else saw. I guess our psychic connection was broken.

"Now, walk to my car. It's the red sports car," he roared as he opened the door of the salon.

"I know what it looks like," I growled back at him.

I hope he doesn't ruin my chance to see him, I thought to myself.

He opened the passenger door to his crimson car and shoved me in. He was already in the front seat with the car started in less time than seemed possible.

Where are you taking me?" I asked hoping Johnathon was reading my mind or his.

"You won't find out until we get there," he murmured in an abysmal tone.

Johnathon, if you can read my thoughts, Sigrid has me. I have no idea where he's taking me. I love you and pray that we'll be together soon.

"He can't read your thoughts, I put a block around you ... us."

I couldn't see much, everything looked like tracers of light flashing by at what must have been two hundred miles an hour.

"Just sit back, Isla. You know, none of this would have happened if you had been attracted to me, instead of my brother. You invited this in."

"You're not my type at all ... anyway why do you call him that? You don't like, love, or even care about him. You're evil and he is good."

I was trying to piss him off so he would just get it over with. He reached a hand over, and barely touched a spot on my throat and everything went black.

When I came to, I heard voices. This time I was blindfolded, and all I could see was the grass I was sitting on, and the winding roots of the tree I was tied to. It was getting dark. But it was already dark for me. I could hear water running in the near distance. But I had no idea where I was.

I was jolted to reality when I heard a familiar voice, feeling those sharp knives from the inside again. Even though I couldn't see him, the voice was unmistakably familiar, it was Neco.

Great! Sigrid and Neco, working together. This can't be, I said to myself.

"She is waking up," a woman's voice came out of the dark. I was sitting on the ground tied to a tree with a black scarf covering my eyes. I knew it was a black scarf, I recognized the patterns on it, because it was mine. Sigrid obviously found it in my purse. She crouched down next to me but I could only see her jet black boots in my lower peripheral view. "It's almost time," she said in a pestilent whisper.

"Time for what?" I asked.

"It is almost hm, hm, hm, 7:30 hm, he will be here soon hm, hm. He'll watch you die, hm hm."

Yep, it was Neco, I know that hum. Could I have slept all night? I wondered what work thought, my car was still in the parking lot and I didn't show.

"Sorry to interrupt your thoughts my dear, you have bigger things to worry about than work," Sigrid said, his voice painted with an undertone of sarcasm as he stood over me.

He walked away. I suddenly had an overwhelming, irrational desire to sing. Having been in choir all through high school, I always felt better when I sang.

"Black bird singing in the dead of night take these broken wings and learn to fly. All your life you were only waiting for this moment to arise. Black bird fly." I sang high and as quiet as I could. I could hear their mumbling in my head, but I blocked it out to sing. The wind picked up quite briskly, I could hear a loud roar in the distance, and it got louder. It sounded like a freight train coming towards us. Closing my eyes I began to sing louder. My eyes had dried of all the tears, and some damp strands of hair were stuck to my face. The wind was blowing hard.

I felt pain in both arms and realized someone was behind me pulling me in two different directions. I felt my body being torn in half and my arms scraping against the sharp bark. Then the pulling stopped and I heard a loud bang behind me like something or somebody had been thrown up against the tree. Suddenly my arms were free. The wind was still blowing, the roar was so loud and I was afraid to move. My arms hurt so bad. Confusion set in like a virus. I removed the blindfold.

Run, ran through my head. But I had no idea what was going on. I didn't know if they were fighting in the midst of the storm or if they were the storm. I just knew I had to get away. My eyes focused and I ran like the wind.

Taking off into the wilderness, I began to follow the sound of the water. I walked around some skyscraper trees to see an amazing rushing waterfall. It was beautiful and serene in the moonlight. I hid behind a tree and fell down in exhaustion. I hoped Johnathon was okay. I sat there trying to regain my strength. The inside of my arms were scraped and bloody and stung badly.

"Are you okay?" a voice came from behind the tree sounding so sweet and comforting. The second I heard that suave velvet voice I closed my eyes knowing I was safe. He stepped in front of me and sat down. My heart sped up drastically.

"I heard you singing. What brought that on?" he sighed as he reached out and lightly picked up my hand and saw the blood on my arms.

"I don't know. It makes me relax," I replied, grunting from pain. He quickly turned his head away. I knew why he had looked away when I saw the blood dripping down my arms.

"It was beautiful and calming, it almost made it hard for me to kill," he muttered, breathing heavily as he gently moved me into his lap. I wrapped my legs tightly around his waist.

"Ouch, my arms hurt," I cried out in pain when the sleeve of his black tee-shirt grazed up against one of my arms as I straddled him.

"Should I take you to the doctor?" he asked, breathily and calmingly as he held my arms while he gazed in my eyes.

"Ooo, we should get some bandages on these cuts," he suggested, not breaking eye contact in fear of his overwhelming hunger taking over. He softly laid his arms across mine and the cold of his hands and arms made the pain subside some.

"Did you kill them?" I whispered. I prayed it was all over, that there would be no more conflict. But before he answered my question I knew it wasn't going to be that easy.

"Sigrid got away. The woman was hurt pretty bad, but still got away. Myriad and Neco are dead." I leaned into him resting my head in the hollow of his neck.

We hugged, well kind of--- he hugged me. My arms didn't quite work. It did not matter, it was so good to be in his arms again. It was where I felt peace. It did not matter where we were. Wherever he was, was home to me.

He softly brushed the hair from my face so caringly. We kissed passionately. All I could see were flashes of the brightest light I had ever seen. I closed my eyes and pictured us as lightening entwining and when we touched our lights combined and became this shining explosion. It was a very spiritual moment for me. We didn't talk for a long time. Our passion grew beyond immortality; it was universal. There was no one in the world except us, we had our own little universe. I named it Islathon.

"That's an interesting name," he stopped kissing me, and said.

"When you're reading my crazy thoughts, don't you just want to laugh your ass off at my ridiculous ideas?"

"What's crazy is that sometimes I have the same thoughts before I hear yours. Sometimes!" he sighed softly, caressing my arm while still staring in my eyes. . His frigid fingers felt so good.

"Okay, so what do you think of the name Islathon?" I asked, motioning to the waterfall.

"I like it, it's our own little world. So if I write to you to meet me in Islathon, you'll know exactly where to go!" he replied as he pulled me closer to his chest.

"Sounds good but I was referring to anywhere we are as long as we're together," I whispered.

"I understand what you mean. But baby, this is our Islathon," he sighed drawing me in even deeper. It sounded even dreamier when he said it, he made it sound like a truly magical place.

"Isla, I need to get you home," he murmured.

I held my breath and thought to myself, *that was a record screeching to a halt, and a smack down back to reality. I exhaled knowing he was right as I recalled the storm that had just blown through.* "Okay! There should've been some kind of warning about that tornado, though. That was quite a storm."

He just laughed. "Isla---that was not a tornado; that was me," he said, only lifting one corner of his mouth. Even his crooked smile was charming and seductive.

"That was you? Wow! You're extremely powerful," I replied, my eyes wide with surprise.

"You do that to me. It's our love, the love I have for you that makes me so powerful, well that and being a vampire," he shrugged in a smug way and then snickered at his smugness.

"You're already that powerful," I whispered. I felt immensely grateful and adored his amazing attributes. I leaned into lay my head on his shoulder.

"You make me strong. I have to be to protect you. Our problems aren't over. The woman Dezi has gone back to gather more force and other majestic predators from the S.P.I. She'll be back," he concluded regretfully.

"Not again. It's hard enough knowing that Sigrid knows where I work and live. Now I have to deal with that, too," I hollered towards the sky as I wrapped my arms around his neck. My holler came from way down inside me. It was mostly pain and weariness that had crippled me.

"Sigrid knows where you work?" he growled. The vibration of his rumble shook my heart.

"He came to my work Wednesday. He forced me to leave with him. He knocked me out by touching a place on my throat. I was awake and then I wasn't. When I woke up, I was tied to a tree. Then you came and rescued me," I whispered, gently squeezing him to my chest.

"You know I would do anything for you. I hurt when I'm away from you. I should probably get you home now. It's getting late." He slowly rose to his feet with my legs still around him and swung my legs around cradling me like a baby. He kissed me and the wind began to blow hard. We were still kissing. I stopped and opened my eyes, we weren't on the ground, we were in the air.

I gasped as I caught a glimpse of the ground far below us.

"It's okay, Isla, just keep kissing me," he whispered. With my eyes closed I took a deep breath and continued kissing him. We were in the air for a long time. I hugged him and peeked over his shoulder at the incredible view.

"The world looks so peaceful from up here," I whispered.

I felt truly free. The wind blew through his dark brown hair and he was completely breathtaking. The lights of Asheville were so spectacular, and the few cars that were on the roads looked like ants with lights for eyes. The mysterious and beautiful mountains were gray and black shadows.

"Can't we just stay up here?" I asked, not wanting this to ever end.

"I wish we could, my sweet. It sure would make things easier," he sighed and kissed me. I teased him by slowly pulling away. He pulled me closer. And I could feel the sharpness of his teeth on my tongue as they grew. His nails were digging into the top of my spine underneath my auburn hair, causing a burning pain. I turned the sensation around in my head and told myself, *Don't stop him this is what you want.* I nibbled on his earlobe and licked down his neck. At first I kissed and licked it. Then I bit down hard.

"Isla, what are you doing?" If you don't stop, I'll take you right here in the sky," he growled vastly.

"Take me in the sky! Besides wouldn't it be easier for us to *be together* if I was a vampire," I whispered, gazing in his black eyes, my breathing became almost wheezing at that altitude.

"Isla, you know how I feel about causing you an undying misery. I'm trying to spare you the pain. Not now! Not yet! End of subject," he whispered, staring me in the eyes.

My heart was beating so hard it felt like something was pounding from the inside of my throat.

"Yet? You mean, you will do it someday, but when?" I asked as I tried to catch my breath.

"I'll surprise you some day. There's no doubt that I will eventually have to change you. But I will decide when," he sighed sternly.

"Well, that doesn't mean I'm going to give up," I said bluntly and then wrapped my teeth around his flesh and bit him a little harder.

"Isla, we're here," he tightened his jaw and murmured low and breathy. I could feel him wanting to give in.

We landed in my back yard. When my feet touched the ground I felt a slight sense of relief. It was a good feeling to be on the ground, again. He held my hand gently as we walked around to the front door. Reaching for the door knob I hesitated and looked at him. I knew he was reading my mind because the door flew open. I grinned at him as we stepped through the doorway. My dad stood and greeted us when we walked into the living room.

"This must be Johnathon," he said, reaching out to shake his hand. I was holding my arms across my chest. I didn't want him to see my wounds.

"It's nice to meet you, Mr. Van Burren," Johnathon replied as he shook his hand.

Dad looked at him a little strangely, then said, "You can call me James or Mr. Van Burren, it's up to you. Have a seat. Stay a while.

"Okay, Mr. Van Burren. You have a lovely home," Johnathon uttered, grinning at me as he went to sit down. I thought in my head, *Honey you're sounding silly.* Johnathon shot me a weird look. I just smiled and then walked away. I went to the kitchen and made a cup of tea. While I waited for the microwave to ding I thought about just talking to him instead. It would be one sided of course. At least until he answered my questions later. *There is no way that you could live in a beautiful castle like yours and think that this house is lovely. But, sweet of you to say so,* I said to him in my head. I grabbed my tea and headed back into the living room. When I entered the room him and dad were watching football. Johnathon stood when he saw me.

I could tell my dad approved. They looked like they were getting along famously.

"Thank you for rescuing my wife, Simone," he said as he stood, too.

"Of course," Johnathon replied smiling warmly.

"I try to watch over them both, but I am out of town with work so much. And I don't have much time to spend with them. It makes me feel better knowing Isla has you," Dad sighed. He looked as though he had been beating himself up about it.

"I love Isla and would do anything for her," he announced, looking my dad in the eyes. He never kept that to himself. He would shout it from the tallest building around and he could. I loved that about him. Just then I dropped my arms, not thinking.

"Oh, my God, Isla, what happened? Are you hurt?" dad hollered and ran to the downstairs bathroom.

"You need to put bandages on those scrapes! What happened?" dad asked, waiting for an answer as he came back into the room and started pulling stuff out of a first aid kit.

"Well, Dad, Johnathon rescued me, too. That's all I can tell you."

"What have you gotten yourself into, Isla?" he asked with a worried expression. I just shrugged. There was no way I could tell him the truth, although I wanted to.

"Well I have to call the cops so we can find this kidnapper. Was it the same guy that attacked your mom?

Dad got up and went for the phone. I looked at Johnathon with wide eyes. He took his hand and waved it in front of my dad's face, very quickly. Dad set the phone down and walked back over to me. He turned to Johnathon and said.

"Thank you, again. It looks like we are going to need a bigger first aid kit," he said laughing.

We all chuckled a bit. I breathed a sigh of relief as he bandaged me up.

"James, I need you!" mom yelled from upstairs.

"I'll be right there honey! I'll be right back. Johnathon, keep an eye on my girls," he said with a grin as he got up.

"We're going to my room, dad," I announced before he headed up the stairs.

"Okay, it's late and you have to work tomorrow," dad said.

If I still have a job, I didn't call or show yesterday, I thought to myself.. We went up to my room. Johnathon jumped on my bed and laid back.

"Do you think your dad could tell I wasn't like you all?" he asked, looking at me attentively.

"Probably not, he liked you, I could tell. That was really close. I thank God that you have that ability, otherwise it could have gotten really sticky." I sighed, pouncing on top of him.

"Don't forget to call work. And to your comment you made while you were in the kitchen, every home has character," he said as he kissed me on the forehead.

I giggled and smiled. Okay, I'll call them in the morning." I started looking around for my purse. "Oh no, I left my purse somewhere. Where did I leave it?" I thought out loud.

"Maybe it is still in Islathon," he said, smiling a childish grin. "I will go back and see if it's there." he promised. He started to get up, but I laid on top of him.

"You don't have to go now do you?" I whispered. We began kissing. I ran my fingers through his long curly hair. I got up on my knees, pulled his shirt up and kissed his belly.

"Isla! Isla! Stop!" he growled and pulled me back up to kiss him more.

"You're going to push it aren't you?" he asked as he slowly rolled over on top of me.

"How long are you going to make me wait?" I sighed in frustration.

"You'll just have to be patient, my sweet," he answered.

"Patient! I don't like patience!" I rumbled, getting angry as I sat up at the end of the bed away from him.

"Isla, we'll be together forever and for that to happen you will eventually have to become a vampire," he growled and whispered at the same time.

"Good, but when?"

"Stop asking me. I will surprise you!" He moved behind me and hugged me, jerking me back to him. I lied back down with my head on his chest. As I got comfortable with my head resting in just the right place on his chest. My eyes got heavy and I began to yawn.

"You're tired, go to sleep, my sweet," he whispered, softly running his icy fingers from my cheek to my ear and back and forth. It felt good, but gave me chills.

"Okay, good night. I'm cold," I murmured. He noticed my body trembling and pulled the black furry blanket up from the end of my bed and tucked it around me. He laid down wrapped his icy arms around me.

"Cozy now?" he asked.

"Perfect," I breathed then closed my eyes.

Chapter 11
Captured In A Dream

*C*APTURED IN A DREAM, I COULDN'T WAKE up. Instead I decided to face my fear and examine it. My dream began in a restaurant. There were candles on the tables, and a soft band was playing on stage. Johnathon and I were sitting at a table, cozy and close, staring into each others eyes. There was an aroma of good food cooking in the air. We were sitting next to the door and there was only one other table of people in that part of the club. I kept seeing the wait staff walk through to another part of the restaurant, so I realized we were in the back room. A woman walked past our table and turned and look at us. She walked up to our table and bent down, in front of Johnathon. She put her hand gently under his chin and invited him up enticingly. She pulled him closer, he didn't resist.

"My name is Jeziaka. I am the daughter of a Hecate, one of the higher providences of the S.P.I. My father is Vladimir Novgor, he has requested that you appear before the council," she grinned then looked my way.

"What?" I yelled as I stood up.

Johnathon was under some kind of spell; he wouldn't even look at me. My tears began to fall.

"*Johnathon! I love you! It's me Isla.*" *I jumped in front of him, but saw nothing in his eyes.*

He wasn't himself; he only looked at her. She was pretty, but not amazing looking or anything. She was of average height with wavy brown hair to her shoulders. I took his hands and repeated his name over and over. I even shook him a little hoping he would snap out of it. He glanced my way briefly and then back at her. My heart was breaking.

"*Snap out of it!*" *I yelled at him. Jeziaka barely even pushed me and I slammed up against the wall. Pieces of wood splintered and shot all around the room. I held my hand up and felt the back of my head. It was wet with blood when I looked. I slowly pulled myself up and stood. I tried to pull him away from her one last time, but I had no strength because I was losing blood. I bent over trying to breathe. The loss of blood caused extreme dizziness. I fell to the floor when I tried to take a step.*

She led him out of the club and there was nothing I could do.

"*No! No! Please! Don't leave me now,*" *I tried one last time, screaming from the floor.*

Then I awoke and sat up. I gasped, inhaling all of the air in that I possibly could. It was saturated with despair.

"Isla, why are you shaking?" Johnathon asked, trying to comfort me.

I couldn't say anything. He hugged me tight. I held him, scared of it being the last time.

"Tell me! What was the dream about?"

It took me a few minutes to gather myself. I was searching for air and coming up empty. I didn't let go of him for a long time. My eyes filled to capacity and then flowed.

"We were in a club somewhere. We were sitting at a table staring into each other's eyes when this woman came in, walked past us looked at you and put you under some kind of spell. She introduced herself. She said her name was Jeziaka and that her dad wanted you to appear before the council. I tried to get you to snap out of it, but she had you. She pushed me hard into the wall and took you away from me and led you right out of the restaurant."

"Did she say what her father's name was?"

"Yes, I think it was something like Vladimir Novgor, something like that anyway, that's all I can remember." He went white, even whiter than he already was. "Why? What, do you know him or something?"

"Yes! Isla, I have to go to work," he replied in a dry tone.

"You're not going to leave me are you?"

"I have to go to work," he said sharply.

"Okay, will I see you tonight?" I sighed. I was feeling like my insides were being ripped out. I knew my dreams were my future.

"Aren't you going to Preston Hill's party?"

"Oh, I forgot all about it!" I answered.

"You should go. I'll see you tomorrow." He kissed me, but it was colder than normal. No feeling whatsoever. His eyes were glazed over. I didn't know what to do. I sprinted to the window, catching his arm just before he flew out.

"Please don't let this dream come true."

He stopped, turned to me and gazed into my watery eyes. "Isla, don't worry. I will go face the council and I will come back. I love you more than the universe, more than the blood I need to survive, and all the galaxies in space rolled into one. I'll be at the party tonight."

"What, you're coming to the party with me?" I asked, hoping it was true.

"No. Calvin will give you a ride. I might even be there to ride with you. Then I'll be outside watching."

"Oh, my own personal stalker," I said, laughing to get a rise out of him.

"I love you, my sweet," he replied with a low chuckle. Then he kissed me. It was back. Our love ignited and exploded like a fiery volcano all over again. I was consumed. When I opened my eyes, he was gone.

After he left, I sat on my bed in a daze. So much so, that I was late for work. I saw that it was 11:00 am, and I was supposed to be at work by that time. I wanted to call work, but I didn't have my phone. Out of the corner of my eye I saw my purse. I picked it up and quickly dug through it to find my phone. I pulled it out and dialed work. *I guess he had picked my purse up after all*, I thought to myself.

"Good morning, Happenin Hair, this is Lissa how may I help you?"

"Hey Lissa, this is Isla. I'm running late."

"That's okay, you don't have anyone till 1:00 pm. Where have you been, are you alright? We were all so worried that something terrible had happened to you."

"No, I'm fine. I just had something unexpected happen to me yesterday. It's personal."

"Well, we were worried. This is not something you do ... ever."

"I know. We can talk more when I get there," I said.

"Okay. See you at 1:00."

"Okay." I closed my phone and plugged it in to the charger. I ran to the bathroom, turned the bath water on, brushed my teeth, took my clothes off, got in the tub. Lying there I pictured us in Islathon, in my mind we were finally able to show our love to each other fully. It was a delicious daydream.

Coming back to reality, I got out, got dressed, put my makeup on, picked up my purse and headed downstairs.

"Good morning, Mom. I got to go!"

"Hello honey. Okay. See you later," she said looking up while washing the dishes.

"Love you. Have a good day."

"Love you too, Mom." I closed the door behind me and was completely surprised to see that long stretched limo waiting on me. I had totally forgotten that I didn't have my car.

"Good morning, Miss Van Burren," Calvin said, opening the door for me.

"Good morning Calvin, is it okay if I call you Calvin? I asked.

"Yes, Miss Van Burren," he smiled.

"Isla! Please call me Isla." I got in, he shut the door behind me and we were off. When we got to the salon he pulled up right in front and opened the door for me. "Thank you, Calvin. See you tonight," I said as I exited the car.

"Would you like me to pick you up at your house, Ms. Va … Isla?" He asked, shaking his head.

"Yes, that would be great, Calvin." He opened the door to the salon for me.

I could get used to this, I thought to myself as I walked in. Lissa looked at me warmly.

"Hello Isla" she said as she picked up the phone. I went to my station and put my purse away.

"Isla, your first client is here," Angel said as she darted by me to go to the back to mix color. She stopped.

"Hey girl! I'll talk to you after my client," Angel said rushing to the back.

I took care of my client. She asked me how my life was treating me, I responded in only highly positive tones, although I was feeling quite numb. That dream truly disturbed me. After I finished her hair and she left, Angel and I had time to talk.

"What happened to you on Wednesday?" she asked with concern in her eyes.

"That man made me go with him. He told me he would kill my boyfriend."

"What? Your boyfriend, you haven't told me anything about him!" she said, pushing me for details. She wouldn't leave it alone so I told her.

"His name is Johnathon Daine, he is amazing and beautiful. What can I say? Love is an awesome thing."

"So let me get this straight, you were kidnapped by a man," she said.

"His brother!" I added.

"His brother, why would he do that?" she asked, her eyes wide in confusion.

"Because he wants me to want him, and I don't."

"Wait! Is that Johnathon Daine, as in the Castle Le Daine?"

"Yes! So you know it?" I asked surprised.

"I definitely know of it. It's a huge friggin castle."

I didn't want to tell her that I was the stupid idiot that didn't know about it til I was dating him.

"I had never seen it, or I just never paid attention. It's a magical place, but I have had bad things happen there, too."

"What kind of bad things? If you and Johnathon get married, you will live there, right?"

"I hope to, I don't know when that might happen. Do you have another client soon?" I asked, trying to change the subject. "Do you want to smoke a cigarette before your next client?" I suggested, digging for some cigarettes that I had put in a pocket in my bag. They weren't in a pack they were just randomly floating around and some were broken.

"I don't have a client for a while, so yes, let's go smoke," she said.

I'm not really a smoker, just a social smoker. We went outside, smoked and came back in. I sat down and began reading through some mail that I had forgotten about. I had a few more clients as the day went on. It was a fairly good day.

I was beginning to feel hawks in my tummy about the party. I hadn't seen those people in a while. Some were good and some of them were just down right mean. Before I knew it, it was time to go home. I cleaned up my station and got my stuff together. I said bye to the girls.

"See you, Isla," Angel shouted as I walked out the door. I opened my car door, got in, started it and drove off down the road. I didn't get far from the shop before I got caught in major traffic jam.

Something by the Beatles was playing in the CD player. I put it on repeat. I listened to that song a lot. It made me sad, but in a good way.

When I got home both my parents' cars were gone. I parked my car in the street. I walked in the front door and went upstairs to my room. I jumped in the shower, styled my hair, got dressed in a black mini skirt, black and red patterned button up shirt, and the black heels that Johnathon had given me. I looked in the mirror.

"Gosh darnet, I am hot," I told myself and laughed a little at my foolishness.

I changed purses to a cute red and black one that matched. I went down the stairs and fixed myself some hot tea then snacked on some apples and peanut butter. It was 7:10, and the party didn't start till 7:30. So I took my time and relaxed while sipping my hot tea. I definitely did not want to be early.

I washed the few dishes that were in the sink and ran back up to brush my teeth. I headed back down stairs and opened the door. Calvin was standing there with the door open to the limo.

"Good evening, Isla," he said professionally.

"Good evening, Calvin," I said as I jumped in, to find that I was alone. I couldn't help but wonder where he was. I had hoped he would be there for the ride. We rode for a while then I noticed that Calvin was pulling off the side of the road after we crossed a big bridge. I had no idea where we were as I looked out the heavily tinted windows. When we stopped, the door opened. Calvin was still behind the wheel. I slowly peeked around the edge of the door. Then Johnathon rushed in.

"Hello baby," he yelled, with a big smile. I nearly jumped through the roof.

"Oh my gosh, you scared me," I threw my arms around him and gave him hugs and kisses. We made out the whole ride there. He didn't hold back much at all. I teased him at first by pulling back and turning my head when he'd try to kiss me, just to make him want more. I tried to push him over the edge so he would get it over with. He must have eaten past full stage. It became obvious when he began kissing my neck and then wrapped his razor sharp teeth around my fiery flesh. I held my breath and thought. *Is this it? Is he really going to do it?* And then he kissed my neck and moved to my lips. It was always such a let down. But this time he kissed my belly and many other unmentionables. It was incredible! The car came to a stop sooner than I'd hoped or expected.

Calvin didn't open the door. Instead he rolled down the privacy window just a wee bit.

"Sorry to interrupt, but I need the exact address," he said.

It is…. hold on," I pulled the paper out of my purse, while fixing myself up. "Okay, it is 2451 Sweeten Creek Road."

"Thank you," Calvin said and then closed the privacy window back up and began to drive.

"Isla, you look beautiful tonight," Johnathon said as he grabbed me passionately and began kissing my neck.

"Stop baby, I need to fix myself up before we get there."

"That's a switch," he replied.

We both adjusted our clothes a little. I put on some more war paint. Not really. I just put on some gloss. It was weird though, I did kind of feel like I was going into battle, seeing all these people from high school. I had no idea what to expect.

The car stopped again. Calvin opened the door.

"I'll be around," Johnathon promised as he kissed my forehead, my cheek, then my lips.

When I got out of the limo everybody was standing outside watching. They observed me curiously until I walked towards them and they recognized me. It was kind of cool, I felt like royalty.

"It's Isla," somebody shouted from the porch as I walked down the chain link fence and through the iron gate.

"Oh my God, girl, how are you?" Brandy asked, happy and smelling of booze. I could tell she was three sheets to the wind, and feeling no pain. In high school she was always a heavy partier. She threw her arm over my shoulder and leaned into me. I almost lost my balance.

"You haven't changed a bit, girl," she said loudly in my ear. She was funny and I had missed her. Brandy was definitely a friend through high school, we had just been out of touch. I went through a phase of partying but it had left me as quickly as it had come. And so did the friends that went with it.

"Isla, I am so glad you could come," a voice said from the doorway. I knew that voice well, that was Preston Hill. He walked up to me and hugged me genuinely. His big buff arms were just about swallowing me whole. Brandy saw some other friends to talk to and wandered off.

"Brandy wait!" I yelled as I reached my hand out in the direction she headed. I turned back to see Preston standing two inches away, in his white and green long sleeved shirt and tight jeans. He ran his hand through his dirty blonde conservative short cut. I wanted to giggle at his sly move.

"Hi Preston, thank you for inviting me," I sighed cheerfully but was a little upset that Brandy had left me alone with him. My stalker might have gotten pissed watching me talk to him alone.

"Isla, I have missed you," he said with passion in his voice. I was really freaking out. I stared at him in disbelief.

"You hardly even talked to me in high school," I scowled, wondering what the heck was going on.

"Oh, but you've obviously forgotten about that one time at Jolie's, playing spin the bottle," he joked as he poked me with his finger in my belly.

"Oh yeah, I do remember that, you spun, it pointed to me and we had to kiss. You leaned over to kiss me, leaned too far and fell on Shawna and dated her through high school. Yes! I think that's just the way it went," I concluded with a bit of attitude, shaking my head and pointing my finger.

His face went red and he placed his arm over my shoulder and whispered in my ear. "I would really like to make that up to you." It felt like he was sticking his tongue in my ear and I turned around and knocked his arm off of me. In the nicest way possible, of course. I hadn't the foggiest idea why I had had such a crush on him back then. He was not attractive at all, now.

"Hey, Isla," I heard from behind me. I turned to see Jolie Kenya who was my best friend in school. We had lost touch. She was tall and slender with short straight red hair. She wore glasses and was cute as a button, just like she had been in high school.

"Jolie, hey girl. I've missed you." I said as we hugged.

"Sorry Preston, but I need to steal her away for a few," she said, laughing as she dragged me away. Although I was happy to go, I didn't want to be rude.

"Okay, promise you'll dance with me before you leave," Preston insisted.

"Sure," I replied back reluctantly. I didn't feel like it, and I was so happy Jolie had saved me. I didn't know if I could dance with him anyway. I had a stalker.

"Come on girl," Jolie put her arm around me and we headed inside the house. From the outside it looked like your normal red brick rancher That was the front of the house. The back of the house was two story. I could see it from where I was when I got out of the car. The street was at a higher elevation. It was a lot bigger inside than it appeared on the outside. There was a magnificent entertainment center. With a seventy two inch flat screen TV and recording equipment that would make anyone involved in music salivate. I had seen this kind of equipment in a studio I had recorded a CD in. It was for a rock opera I had performed the year I graduated. But this was quite impressive to see in a residence.

Jolie and I walked around talking to everybody. The people I saw looked different, but the same. I don't know how to explain it. I saw Michael Williams, Ambrosia Simpson, Betsy Cain, Rosy Mason, Terry Miller, Tatumina Orion, and Stephanie, I couldn't remember her last name. That was just to name a few. They were all people I remembered well. First time I ever skipped class off campus was with a bunch of people including Ambrosia, Tatumina, Craig, Jolie, and Stephanie. We all went to hang out at Stephanie's house and didn't do much of anything. We got expelled the following week. Busted! And we didn't even do anything worth getting busted for.

We were all standing around chatting when Preston spoke up.

"So Isla, who are you dating? Do you have a boyfriend?" he asked it so loud everyone stopped talking and looked at me, patiently waiting for my answer.

"Yes, I do have a boyfriend," I replied.

"Well … who is it?" Jolie asked, getting excited.

"It's Johnathon Daine." The room got so quiet you could hear a pin drop. Everyone just stared at me. My hands began to sweat because everyone was staring at me.

"Oh, I think I need to leave," I mumbled as my face turned red.

"No, Isla, here's a drink. It's a margarita on the rocks," Jolie said, handing me the drink. I grabbed it and took three huge gulps. When I looked around they were all talking and mingling again. Thank God, the pressure had dissipated.

I walked over to a table and as I passed by a window, I glanced out and saw his face. I wanted so much to be out there with him. I just stood there, smiling and drinking my drink, staring out at him. Jolie came back over and told me to put my purse down in the room around the corner. I was tired of carrying it, so I walked down a hallway, opened the door, went in and put my purse on the floor behind a speaker. Out of sight out of mind, I always say. Looking around the room I realized I was in Preston's parent's room, at least judging from the pictures of his parents in compromising positions lying in bed, but covered by sheets. I thought to myself *Hmm, I wonder who took those pictures.*

Feeling a little tipsy I sat down on the bed. I was just getting up, when Preston came in and shut the door behind him.

"What are you doing, Preston?" I slurred just a little.

"I wanted to be alone with you. You need another drink?" he suggested, as he slyly switched my old drink for a new one.

"This is a party! Drink up!" he yelled. Being thirsty and tipsy I drank some more. The room began to spin causing a fever of dizziness to rush through my body. I fell back on the bed, and couldn't move. He crawled on top of me. I felt his hands on my chest as he started to unbutton my blouse. I tried to move, but I couldn't. I tried to tell him to get off me, but I could barely speak. His hands were all over me and I was screaming on the inside as tears rolled out of the corner of my eyes..

"No! Stop! Get off me!" I cried. I was surprised that I was able to say anything. I didn't have much power behind my words. It was only loud enough for him to hear. But he didn't listen and then he put his hand up my skirt. Suddenly I heard a loud smash; glass went flying everywhere, but I still couldn't move. Preston flew off of me and slammed up against the wall, smashing his head, then he fell to the floor. I felt myself move, but I wasn't doing it. I kept slipping in out of consciousness. Then I gazed into his dark chocolate eyes.

"Johnathon," I could barely say his name. I looked in his eyes for a second then was out.

Chapter 12

In Heaven With You

*A*S EVERYTHING CAME INTO VISION, I looked around to see where I was. It was Johnathon's room, and he was next to me. I curled up to him and put my arm around his waist.

"Baby, you're awake, I was so worried. I had no idea what he had given you," he said as he rolled over to face me.

"What, what do you mean?" I asked, still a little out of it.

"You don't remember?" he asked in amazement. He put his arctic fingers on my cheek and softly swept my hair away from my eye.

"I remember going to the party, seeing some old friends, then it's all foggy after that. I remember staring at you out the window as I stood there drinking my margarita on the rocks. But that is about it."

"Preston Hill drugged you, and if I hadn't smashed in the window he would have raped you," he bluntly said and then pulled me closer to him and surrounded me with his body as I broke down. I let it go, and cried on his shoulder for a long time.

I gazed back in his eyes and whispered, "Johnathon you are always saving me, you are my hero. You're so amazing." I hugged him and then our lips touched lightly.

"Why are you shaking?" he asked.

"I'm just worried I guess, terrified about that dream coming true. Can't live with out you, you know."

"You have done fine for twenty years before I came along," he whispered.

"Yes, but I was never truly alive." I didn't know how to explain how much more awake I felt since he came into my life.

"Funny how meeting someone dead can make you feel alive," he said sarcastically as he snickered.

"Yeah, funny," I said, pushing him off the bed. But instead of hitting the floor he hovered in the air.

"You know what's really amazing to me is that I feel like I'm in heaven with you. It doesn't matter how much bad happens to me because I've already been there. I could die tomorrow and it would be okay."

"You are not going to die, not if I can stop it," he muttered, taking hold of my hand as he stood up.

"Don't you have to leave though, to go in front of the council?" I asked as he brought me to my feet.

"Yes, but I'll be back." he promised.

"It doesn't matter, I'm not afraid anymore," I replied as I wiped my tears with my fingers.

"Before I leave we'll go to Islathon," he said, pulling me into him.

"Okay, when?" I asked, excited to be alone with him in our own little world.

"Tonight. I will have to go to work today so I can ravish you later."

"Well, bon appétit!" I blurted out in my best French accent.

He laughed then threw me on the bed. We rolled around kissing for a while.

"Promise me something," I said, sitting up on top of him and straddling his waist.

"What? You know I'd do anything for you," he whispered, gazing up at me.

"If Jeziaka takes you away, somehow, someday you will return to me."

"I promise she won't put me under some spell and take me away from you," he sighed.

"You can't promise that, in my dream she had you so deeply spellbound no matter what I did you wouldn't snap out of it, besides what about the council? What are they going to do to you?"

"I don't know, but I have to go," he replied, lifting me off of him and lying me back on the bed. He jumped off the bed.

"Just stay away from Jeziaka, please," I begged as I propped my head up with a pillow.

"I will do my best," he sighed. "I got to go to work. Do you work today?" he asked.

"No, I'm thinking about calling up some of my friends and just hanging out at my house." He stood on the end of the bed looking down at me. I looked up at him and grinned and then he dropped suddenly his body parallel to mine. I flinched, but he hovered in the air above me and didn't touch me at all. My body yearned for him. His long, dark, curly hair swayed from my heavy breathing. *You teaser*, I thought in my head knowing very well that he was dipping into my mind.

"Please do not put your self in danger today," he said, kissing the tip of my nose and then like magic he was back on his feet, standing next to the bed.

"I'll see what I can do," I said as I rolled over on my side and watched him as he turned and walked away.

"Come back here," I reached up catching his arm. Hindered, he returned my gaze. I put one hand over the other slowly crawling up his arm to him. "I want a real kiss," I begged, pulling him to my lips.

When he kissed me this time he picked me up off the bed, if I had had

socks on they would have shot off like in a cartoon. When he set me down I was light headed, I nearly fell over.

"Whoa ... be careful Isla," he replied, catching me before I tumbled off the bed.

I sat down on the bed "I need to go to the bathroom," I said, standing up slowly.

"I'll take you," he replied, knowing I was scared of walking through that castle, because of what had happened. I was terrified of having any encounter with Sigrid or anybody else that might cause me harm.

As we walked down the hall, he held my hand and I stayed close to him. He stopped suddenly.

"What is it? Why are we stopping? I have to pee!"

"We should go back! There is another bathroom at the other end," he suggested, turning me around immediately. We were walking so fast it felt like we were flying.

We finally got to the bathroom. I went in and shut the door behind me. Did my business, checked my hair and when I opened the door, he wasn't there. My heart sped up and pounded so loudly it sounded like it was in my ear.

"Johnathon," I cried quietly as I peaked around the corner. "Where did he go?" I whispered loudly.

I started walking back to his room. As I got closer I heard two voices. Not recognizing the voice I figured it was safe. I crept into the room slowly. The creaking from the ancient hard wood floors gave my presence away.

"Isla ... I want you to meet my other brother Jee Cee, he is the cool one," Johnathon murmured as he drew me to him by taking my arm.

"Hello Isla, it is very nice to meet you," Jee Cee said politely. I shook his hand. It was the same cold, but it didn't feel the same as Johnathon's hand.

"Nice to meet you, too," I said relieved. He was of average height with short, dark brown, curly hair, brown eyes and a short trimmed goatee.

"So this is Isla. This is your true love," he stated to Johnathon as he looked me up and down like he was examining the merchandise.

"Yes, this is my Isla," Johnathon agreed, wrapping his arms around me holding me from behind.

"Hey, how's the music going?" Johnathon asked Jee Cee.

"The band broke up. I'm trying to get another one together. My band members fought like cats and demons," Jee Cee explained.

"What do you play?" I asked interested.

"Guitar and a little bass, but not like Johnathon though. No way man, he wails on the bass."

He could tell that I didn't even know he played.

"You play bass?" I turned and looked at him, puzzled and perplexed at the notion that he hadn't told me.

"Yes ... hey maybe we could start a band, she sings," Johnathon suggested, standing behind me playfully tickling my belly. The thought of doing music again was exhilarating. It made me feel as though I had ice in my shoes.

"Okay, yes I sing. I was in all state choir two years in a row." I bragged a bit. I was really proud of my accomplishments. I had a great voice and I would love to sing again.

"Cool, maybe we can get Harris on drums," Jee Cee suggested to Johnathon.

"He'd be into that...well I don't know, he might be a little too intense for our band," Johnathon scowled holding my wrists then spinning me around so he could see my eyes, his chilling arms encompassed my body.

"What would we name the band?" Jee Cee asked.

We stood there in deep thought for a few minutes then Johnathon broke the silence.

"I know, *Isla and The Bloodsuckers*," Johnathon replied smiling.

"That's Good!" Jee Cee agreed, chuckling under his breath.

"That is good!" I said, seeing the name in lights in big venues all over the world, something my dreams had been built on since I was a little girl singing in my room. "Where would we practice?" I asked, immediately feeling like a numb skull.

They both snickered. Of course there would be a music room or studio in a castle owned by musicians. I felt stupid.

"Here of course," Johnathon said shooting me a puzzled look, then grabbing me tightly around my waist.

"I know that was a stupid question, I know you have a huge studio somewhere in this house."

"Yep, it's in the west wing," Johnathon replied behind me in my ear. His cool breath burned my ear red instantly.

"Would you like to see it?" Jee Cee asked in an enticing way.

"Definitely," I declared excited. I knew it had to put any studio I had seen to shame.

"Well follow me," Jee Cee commanded holding his hand out and moving his pointer finger back and forth wanting us to follow him.

Johnathon let go of me so I could follow him. When we began to walk to the door I hesitated and Johnathon took my hand.

"It's okay. Sigrid isn't here," Johnathan assured me.

"Did Sigrid do something?" Jee Cee asked, like he knew he was evil. He could see I was a little scared.

"Yes, he kidnapped her and was going to kill or turn her," Johnathon explained, drawing me in to him.

"Obviously you saved her," Jee Cee replied smiling at us.

"Yeah, but it was close. It's been close quite a few times," Johnathon sighed.

"He saves me over and over again, I am so lucky." I kissed him quickly on the lips. "I keep telling him that he wouldn't have to save me so much if he would just make me a vampire," I sighed as I stared into Johnathon's eyes

Jee Cee smiled. "But he, won't will he?"

"No! Not yet," I replied, nudging Johnathon in the shoulder.

"I don't want her to go through the pain," Johnathon explained, squeezing me so tight I could hardly breathe.

"I love her ... I can't stand seeing her in pain." Johnathon announced to Jee Cee.

"Well, I am so happy to see you in love, big brother. You deserve to be happy." Jee Cee said, motioning for us to get going.

"Oh sorry, we must have gotten sidetracked," I apologized.

We started walking through the magnificent house. His ice cold fingers running softly up and down my fingers as he held my hand.

We walked past a large open door. I glanced in and stopped.

"What? What's wrong?" Johnathon asked, gripping my hand tighter.

"What is that room?" I asked in an uneasy tone. I continued looking down at the floor. I squeezed my eyes shut waiting for his answer.

"That's the library," Johnathon answered dryly. I felt an instant pain in my stomach the second the word left his cherry lips.

"Can I see?" I asked, having a strange feeling in my gut. My mouth was dry and I couldn't do anything but continue swallowing which made it dryer.

"Sure," Johnathon said with a slight hesitation, not knowing what I was thinking.

When I walked in the room a chill stretched through my body and didn't end. My eyes filled with water just realizing that the place was real and it was in my boyfriend's house.

"I have been here before in a recurring dream," I explained, staring blankly at the floor.

"Are you okay?" Johnathon asked pulling me to him for a quick embrace and then holding my arms out in front of me as he took a good look at my face. "You're really pale. Do you need to sit down?" Johnathon asked with concern. I was beginning to hyperventilate. I leaned over gasping for air.

"Is she alright?" Jee Cee asked, with worry in his eyes.

"Just get me out of here," I whispered.

Johnathon took my hand again. I looked up at him and then collapsed. He caught me before I hit the floor, and picked me up in his arms. He carried me back to his room and placed me lovingly on his bed.

"Can I get her something?" Jee Cee asked.

"No, she'll be fine. I think I know what the problem is. "Have you eaten today?" Johnathon asked me while reading my eyes.

"I don't think so," I replied groggily.

"I keep forgetting that you need to eat," he admitted, leaning over to the intercom and pushing a button.

"I need some spaghetti and hot tea, Thank you."

The voice on the intercom responded. "Yes sir, right away."

"Thank you. I forget to eat when I'm with you. I feel like I don't need to. You are my food," I whispered and he smirked.

"Isla you have to eat to keep up your strength," he softly brushed my hair away from my eye and just held his hand next to my cheek softly stroking my skin.

"Please remind me from time to time," I commanded, seriously, while gazing vastly in his eyes.

"I will. Speaking of eating, I need to feed soon, too." His eyes launched into dilation as I watched. I had forgotten his hunger, that was building. Now I could see it in his eyes. The waves were beginning to smash furiously.

"I know, will you take me home?" I asked as I sat up and started to get off the bed. His hands hindered me from doing so. He made sure I laid back down.

"After you eat. Of course, I'll take you home. You don't have to ask," he said, waiting for the light on the dumbwaiter. He was gritting his teeth and swallowing a lot and he kept squinting his eyes every time he looked at me.

When it dinged he reached in and pulled out the platter and when he turned around his teeth were long and pointy and his eyes wide and black. I was scared but actually thought maybe I'd use this to my advantage. I sat up quickly as he placed the tray on my lap. I tilted my head back nonchalantly exposing my pulsating vein. I heard him grunt faintly then he stood and averted his eyes.

"I am completely famished," I announced picking up the fork and digging in. After I took a few bites I asked him, "Do you miss food at all?" I continued eating as I awaited his response.

"I was born a vampire, remember?" he replied, still staring off to the opposite side of the room.

"Oh yeah ... so how old are you?" I asked in between bites.

"I was born January 8th 1906, which means I am a hundred and two years old," he explained. His voice was bleak and monotone.

"So wait, I thought when you became a vampire you stayed that age for ever."

"Usually that's the case if your twenty five and up. Otherwise a vampire that is bitten at the age of twenty four and under, ages to twenty five and then stops."

"Cool. Please don't wait till I am twenty five to bite me." I replied, laying my fork down. The thought of having to wait that long, made my stomach turn.

"I've already bitten you once, remember?" he reminded me as if I'd be satisfied and not desire to become one anymore.

"You know what I mean," I replied scowling at him. "Wait! Why didn't I turn into a vampire?"

"I only tasted you. I would have to consume a lot more to change you," he said breathily as he leered at me. His teeth had gone back to normal, and his eyes were golden brown with red peaking out around the pupil.

"Okay, so when will I be a vampire?" I asked, sipping my hot tea and drinking in his eyes. They seemed different, or maybe I was just finally seeing his phases of hunger. I wanted so badly to be like him, to be with him forever.

"I told you it would be a surprise," he replied firmly. I sensed an edge to his voice. But I wasn't ready to stop.

"Alright!--- I just want to know when? So I can prepare myself."

"Don't think about it now. Just finish eating," he demanded, grinning as he observed me taking several more bites of my spaghetti.

"I'm full. Thank you, it was delicious," I sighed as I blotted my lips with my napkin.

He took the tray from my lap and placed it in the dumbwaiter and pushed a button.

"Are you ready to go home?" he asked, standing up and offering me his hand.

I got up feeling better. Having some nourishment helped. I acted like I was getting up and then I charged him knocking him over on the bed. We hugged and kissed and kissed some more. I wanted him so bad it was agonizing. Then all of a sudden he was across the room.

Stunned and shell shocked by the abrupt ending, I shoved my head down into the bed. I pulled the pillow over my head gripping, both sides tightly and screamed, "I CAN'T TAKE THIS!" I tried to muffle the sound, some. I removed the pillow and rolled over on my back. I turned to look at him, his teeth had grown and his eyes vibrated of death. He diverted his eyes from mine.

"Get your purse, I will ride with you," he growled softly.

"My purse!" I looked around frantically. "I must have left it at the party."

"No, I picked it up before we flew out the window," he replied, handing it to me.

"You are so awesome. Thank you. I want you more than I could have ever imagined," I announced as I slowly stood and draped the strap of my purse over my shoulder. I took his hand and peered at him.

"I need you, and want you more than I crave blood. I wish I didn't need it to keep breathing," he whispered in a low and sultry tone as he gazed in my eyes.

"Yeah, me too. It seems to take you away from me too much," I whispered in his ear.

He smiled without showing any teeth. "Lets go!"

We kissed on the way to the car. At one point we passed through the sunlight, I could feel him, but couldn't see him. It was weird. Calvin opened the door, we got in and got comfortable.

"Now, tell me about this dream," Johnathon said, gently running his frigid fingers across the top of my shoulder.

Who knew chills could feel so good?

"Alright. In short, I went into a library, your library. I knew it was a private place, but I never imagined it was yours. I saw that red velvet couch and laid down, or sat down, I don't remember. Then I was above myself watching as a dark cloud came over me. I felt a horrible pain in my whole body. Then there was someone breathing in my ear. After that I woke up."

"Are you sure it was my library?" he asked puzzled.

"Positive, not a doubt in my mind. That's why I collapsed, well that and not eating anything."

He scratched his head in curiosity. "Well, I will make sure to keep you out of there. I really can't leave you alone at all, can I?" he asked, moving me into his lap and surrounding me with his arms and body. He squeezed me tight and even though I couldn't get any air into my lungs, it was heaven to me. He didn't know his own strength, at times.

"Honey ... I ... can't breathe."

"Oh, I'm sorry baby, are you okay?" he asked, letting loose just a hair.

"Yeah --- thank you," I really couldn't breathe. "Now, what were you saying about not being able to leave me alone at all, ever?"

"Isla, I have to go feed, but I will see you tonight in Islathon. Calvin will pick you up. Don't worry when I leave, you will be watched over."

"By who?" I asked, fascinated by who he would choose.

"My brother, Jee Cee," he replied, grazing his cheek against mine.

"He doesn't know me the way you do." Water was already filling to its full capacity in my eyes.

"I know, and he better not know you that way," he answered, turning me around to face him swiftly.

"Oh---do I detect a hint of jealousy?" I asked playfully, through my now falling salty drops.

"Maybe--- yes, only because he will be here and I won't," he replied blankly.

I knew it was way deeper than that. It sounded as if he was referring to a past experience. I wasn't going to pry. After he changed me I would have forever to learn about his splendid life times.

"How long are you going to be gone?" I asked as the tears kept pouring out of the windows to my soul.

"I have no idea, but it won't be too long," he replied as he looked away.

"What if they lock you up, or God forbid, kill you?" I asked, praying that the events I'd seen in my head would not come to pass.

"That won't happen. I live by the code and have only killed for love. I would never take an innocent life, only bad vampires and the rotten scum of the earth."

"They might not understand the vampire killing," I replied, terrified of what the council would unleash on him. I looked into a small corner of the long, stretched windows. And just stared. I couldn't get my eye off that spot. I thought if I concentrated on something else I could make the tears stop, the pain of feeling like my insides were being turned inside out.

"Isla don't get yourself all worked up. I will explain it to them, they will understand. The S.P.I. has always commended me for following the code," he explained and then kissed me.

"I hope so," I whispered, kissing him some more. My tears became frozen pellets sitting on his Alaskan skin.

When the car came to a stop my heart sank into a deep black hole at the thought of not seeing him again.

"I need to get to work, I will see you tonight in Islathon," he promised with waves crashing in his eyes and hunger on his lips.

Kissing me one last time I could feel his razor sharp teeth scraping against my tongue. It was a major turn-on.

"What time should I expect Calvin tonight?" I asked, wiping the left over salty residue around my eyes with my fingers.

"He will be in front of your house at 7:30," Johnathon whispered, smiling with little drops of saliva running down his fangs. He wiped the drool from the corner of his mouth with the side of his pale wrist.

"Okay. I'll be counting the minutes till you're back in my loving arms," I said as I edged my way to the door. He moved closer kissing and hugging me.

"See you tonight," he replied.

I started to get out then turned back around and jumped back in his arms Johnathon chuckled, "Isla, you're amazing." We kissed even more. He was losing control. I didn't care. That was what I wanted.

"I have to go, see you tonight my sweet," he growled and turned away.

As I got out of the car, Calvin stood by the door.

"See you tonight, Calvin." I nodded to him as he shut the door behind me.

I went in my front door. The TV was on but I hadn't noticed if there were any cars in the driveway besides mine. I headed upstairs to my room and set my stuff down and flipped through some CD's looking for something that would relax me. I saw Pink Floyd *Dark Side Of the Moon*. I put it in and hit play and laid back on my bed. Halfway through the album I fell asleep. When I awoke I glanced at the clock and saw it was 6:30. I got up, took a quick bath and got dressed in evening attire. I put on a long black flowing dress, but felt like it needed some color. Digging through my drawers and looking at some scarves. I came upon a red one that caught my eye. It had a black Chita pattern on it. I tied it around my neck and put on the black shoes he had given me. I observed my reflection and was pleased. But I was still sad, thinking about the what ifs.

I sat on my bed and did my makeup. I turned my TV on and began channel surfing. I landed on a news channel first. I never watched the news. It was always so depressing. I was about to turn the channel when a bulletin in bold black going across the screen caught my attention. It read ...

Mysterious Deaths in
Asheville Prison!

I dropped my mascara wand when I read it. My heart started pounding hard and fast. I needed to hear more, but of course they cut to a commercial. If this information leaked out, it could bring on terrible repercussions.

The news came back on and a woman with dirty blonde hair, and blue eyes was telling all. Maggie Phillips looked a little like my mom, or maybe it was her mannerisms.

"Asheville prison has been experiencing a slew of mysterious deaths. They don't know the exact cause of death, but it seems to be an absence of blood in all of the victims bodies. Yes folks, we may have a case of real, live, vampirism. It is now under investigation. This is Maggie Phillips reporting from R.M.S. Channel forty-five out of Asheville. Thank you and goodnight," she reported, smiling as they cut to another commercial.

It was probably good that he was leaving town. If the deaths stopped maybe, the investigation would fall by the wayside.

Glancing at the clock on the night stand, I saw that it was now 7:15 p.m. I turned off the TV, got my purse and ran downstairs. I opened the door to find Calvin standing at the limo with the door open waiting for me. I shut the door behind me and walked to the car.

"Good evening, Calvin," I said.

"Hello, Isla. You look lovely this evening. Special occasion?" he asked with a big grin.

I just smiled and got in the car. I sat back and melted into the plush leather. I could not get that news report off my mind. *What could they do about it?* I questioned in my head.

It was definitely a good thing he was leaving town. Oh, but my heart was breaking at the thought of him going away. The once hawks in my stomach were now vultures gnawing at my insides. But I knew he had to disappear, to go feed on filth somewhere else. It was killing me.

I knocked on the privacy window. Calvin rolled it down.

"Yes, Miss Van Burren?" he asked, looking straight at me while he was driving. He hardly looked at the road, the car seemed to be on auto pilot.

"Please call me Isla. How much longer is the ride going to be?"

"Sorry habit I guess. About twenty more minutes," he said, turning his attention back to the road, but only briefly.

"How long have you worked for the Daine's?" I asked.

"Eighty-five years, they are a wonderful family, minus a few exceptions."

"What do you mean?" I asked, already knowing the answer. I just wanted to see if he said what I was thinking.

"Sigrid doesn't live by the code," he replied, eying me through the rearview.

"You don't mind me asking questions do you?" I asked, reassuring myself I wasn't stepping over any boundaries.

"No, not at all. I'm just glad to have someone to talk to," he said, smiling warmly at me through the rearview mirror.

"Where is the S.P.I. located?" When I asked that question his facial expression changed, it was lined with apprehensive fear. I became nervous awaiting the answer.

He finally spoke after a long, drawn-out lull in the conversation. "They change locations from time to time, but mostly they're in Hungary."

"Where else? Is there some place else that they meet?" I continued.

"I think Amsterdam," he said, looking at me with compassion in his eyes.

Telling me he thought it was there wasn't entirely true; he knew that was where the headquarters were. I could tell by the way he was holding his mouth, his eyes were saying one thing, but his mouth was a tight, straight line.

This realization sprung at me like a frightened cat.

I leaned back, in the seat thinking. *Maybe Johnathon should wait and go to Amsterdam when Lizzy and I go. What if Jeziaka comes to get him sooner? I will lose him forever if she has a chance to bewitch him.*

"We're here, Isla," Calvin announced, peering at me through the rearview.

"Okay, thank you for answering my questions Calvin."

"No problem, anytime Isla," he replied, looking at me and then quickly turning away.

The car stopped and the door opened. Calvin was still lounging in the front seat. I got out slowly. Johnathon took my hand as I exited the car. He drew me in to him and said, "I've missed you, my sweet." He smiled and rested his head on my shoulder.

I felt happiness glistening over my face, shining like the sun itself.

I could barely contain myself in the excitement of being alone with him. "I have missed you." I breathed. We kissed passionately. After a long embrace I stepped back to gaze at both of us. "We match," I announced.

He had on a black collared shirt and black pants. His black belt was decorated in red flames, and he had shoes to match. He looked so incredibly hot it made my teeth sweat.

"You're right! You look amazing, Isla," he replied with a serious smile, stepping back to take a look.

"Would you like to dance?" he asked and then bowed to me.

Without a second thought I said, "Sure, but don't we need music?" I looked around at the trees and the waterfall. Just as I finished the word music I could hear *Something*, by the Beatles. I couldn't tell where it was coming from. It was everywhere.

"How did you know this is one of my favorite songs?" I asked, smiling gloriously. His answer was so quiet. I didn't hear what he said. But I didn't ask again.

He escorted me over to an enormously big rock that had a nice flat surface. It was dark, but we were guided by the light of the full moon. Luckily it was full otherwise we might not have seen very much at all, well *I* might not have been able to see. My vampire could see everything, except for my dreams, or nightmares.

"Are you ready?" he asked, stretching his arm out to spin me. I grinned then swallowed because I knew that he was powerful and would lead amazingly well. Spinning me out and then back in again, picking me up he twirled me like we had been ballroom dancing professionally for years. He threw me in the air and caught me, and as I slid down into his arms our lips met and our tongues played. Soft and gentle, yet overpoweringly in control, he led me. And what a leader he was. *I could die now because nothing could ever surpass this*, I said to myself.

That thought led me to thinking about the one thing that would be the end of all of my existence: to have all of him in me. Blushing at the thought, his face mirrored mine as he read my mind. As much as he could blush, anyway. It struck me as funny how loving someone so mysteriously desirable, and of the living dead, could make me feel so alive almost as if I had been dead all along.

The music came to an end. "Follow me," he politely commanded as he took my hand, never letting go of my body. He was all over me and I loved every second of it. We walked over to the tree where we had rested after he had saved me from Neco and Sigrid.

There was a big, red blanket on the ground with a picnic basket on top.

"Oh, you are so romantic," I sighed, kissing him.

"Love is something that you can never take for granted," he replied, as I sat down and got comfortable. I looked around at the elegant setting he had prepared.

It was no ordinary basket. It was made of dark cherry wood with silver utensils in the lid, and lined with red satin. There were two wine glasses sitting on a small table that came out of the side of the basket. A bottle of vintage wine was next to them, one of the glasses was full the other empty. Taking the empty glass he poured the dark red liquid to the middle of the glass and handed it to me. First, I took a whiff then a small sip and let it roll around in my mouth. Then I took a big gulp. My eyes were wide with delight as I eyed the red liquid rolling around in my glass.

"I can tell by your eyes that you're pleased," he said.

"It is exquisite, this is the best wine I have ever tasted," I announced, still examining the flavor. It tasted of soft fruit, elegant lavender with an after taste of vanilla. I finished my glass and held it out for more.

"May I have some more, please?" He filled it to the rim. "That's good."

"Did you look in the basket?" he asked.

I peered in and saw something wrapped in a smaller basket, I pulled back the stark white napkin and saw it was garlic bread. So I knew that the rest was spaghetti. Upon inspecting the contents of the basket, I found a tall, silver thermos. I removed the lid; it was hot water so I figured there must be tea bags, too.

"You remember everything don't you?" I asked, leaping into his arms, surprising him. I actually startled him, which puzzled me. We kissed a long time and I put my hand under his shirt, lightly touching his frosty abs. He jerked and his eyes went blacker than the night. There were rivers of wild winds and waves smashing in them. It was mesmerizing.

"Are you hungry?" he asked, pushing me away, blocking me from seeing his face.

"How about some more wine? I can't get enough of it," I sighed as I grinned at him. He picked up the bottle and poured it into my empty glass. I looked at the bottle intently.

"Tell me about the wine," I said.

"If you like. This bottle of wine is very old. This is an 1823 Avenglavendar. It is from a vineyard in Venice."

"Wow," I was speechless.

He put down the bottle. I finished my last swallow and he took the glass from me and set them down. He stood up then reached for me, drawing me into him. I thought maybe he wanted to dance some more. A serious expression came over his face, then he dropped to one knee taking a little box out of his pants pocket. Water instantly filled my eyes and began to fall, when I realized what was happening. He gazed up at me took my hand and smiled.

"Isla Michelle Van Burren, will you marry me?" he asked his voice was breathy and sensual.

This was truly the most amazing date any girl could ever dream of. I jumped in his arms and we fell down, rolling around kissing. He stopped abruptly.

"You didn't give me an answer." he sighed, awaiting it with anticipation.

"Yes! Yes! Yes! I love you and want to be with you forever," I breathed, throwing my arms around him passionately. We rolled around getting hot and bothered for a while longer. He sat up suddenly slanting forward, blocking his face. Then he looked like he was searching for something. He quickly turned to me.

"You didn't even see the ring. You jumped on me before I even had a chance to give it to you," he sighed, sounding sadly stunned.

"Well, show it to me," I replied, wiping the tears from my eyes so my makeup would not run.

"I want you to stand up, let's do this right," he commanded as he gently offered his hand to help me to my feet. He took my hand and slipped it on my finger. It fit perfect. We fit perfect. *I can't believe I'm getting married*, I said to myself, screaming for joy in my head. I felt beyond happy, I felt AMAZING.

We kissed some more and it got a little out of hand. We rolled over the garlic bread. It was still edible, though. We also knocked over the bottle of wine. But thank God it was empty. I didn't want to waste a drop of it. He was getting hungry, I could tell. The first sign was his nails beginning to dig in my skin. It hurt, but in a good way. He, of course, stopped suddenly. I sat up, out of breath and wanting oh so much more, but as usual he slammed on the brakes.

"So when? How long are you going to make me wait?" I asked with a little attitude.

He looked in the direction of the waterfall and said, "How about April 25th of next year, exactly one year from tonight?"

"Yes, that sounds fantastic," I sighed, placing my arms around his neck and kissing his lips. "This night should be our anniversary," I remarked, with a slight slur. After all, I had consumed a whole bottle of wine by myself.

"I can't wait!" I yelled as I jumped on him again. We fell down kissing and both of us began to lose control. I wanted him to give in. He sat up quickly and turned away. I laid back down. "I don't think I can take this anymore! I want you so bad," I yelled, as I tried to get a hold of myself.

"Isla, I want you so badly it hurts, literally. But it's not time."

"When? When will you finally do it? Will it be our wedding night or what?" I asked, beginning to get irritated and somewhat pissed off.

"Yes, that is perfect! I will change you then!" he stated, like he wanted to change the subject.

"Isla, you need to eat," he ordered in a nurturing tone. I was hungry so I looked in the basket and pulled out a long, wide container and removed the lid. An appetizing smell rolled out as I broke the seal.

"OOoo Spaghetti and meatballs. Yum!" I replied, then took a fork out of the basket lid and ate a few bites. Then I realized I hadn't told him about the news report.

"Johnathon I almost forgot to tell you about a news report. I saw it before I left to come here tonight."

He looked very intrigued. "What was it about?" he asked curiously.

"You mean you don't know?" I asked, not understanding why he couldn't read my mind all of a sudden. He shook his head.

"It was about mysterious deaths in Asheville prison," I blurted out loudly.

"Really?" he asked in a low growl.

"So it is probably a good idea that you go to Amsterdam to see the S.P.I. You can hit prisons in other areas and in another country for a while," I sighed, secretly praying he would stay.

"Yeah, it is probably a very good idea," he glared in another direction quietly thinking for a second or two. "By the way how did you know that the S.P.I. met in Amsterdam?" he asked.

"I asked Calvin. I just don't think I can take being away from you. The thought of it makes me sick, but I know you have to go. Just know if I don't hear from you by my birthday I will be in Amsterdam looking for you," I promised with tears developing on my lower eyelashes.

"You will?" he asked, surprised.

"Yeah, I'm going there for my birthday with Lizzy. Well, it was actually a gift for Lizzy from her parents for getting in to Princeton. She invited me. Hey, how come you don't know about the trip?"

"You haven't thought about it when I was reading your thoughts," he stated. I shook my head and thought *Yeah, I had only been thinking about my nightmares, my dreams and him.* Then I pictured Jeziaka luring my man away.

"If I come up there and that bitch has her claws in you, you can bet I will kill her by driving a steak into her heart," I promised.

"Calm down, Isla," he replied, consoling me as he chuckled under his breath.

"Are we staying the night?" I asked, attempting to change the mood.

"Would you like to stay the night?" he asked, running his arctic fingers over the side of my cheek, pushing hair away from eyes. He cupped his cool fingers under my chin and kissed me tenderly.

"Are you leaving in the morning?" I asked, with my eyes watering at the dreaded answer I knew was coming.

"Yes, I have to leave in the morning. But we have tonight,"

My heart sank when he answered and my eyes dropped from his. I thought to myself. *What will I do with my time while he is gone? How will I stay sane? to strive to maintain a healthy mental capacity, which at that time seemed totally impossible.*

"Isla, you will be fine. Jee Cee will watch over you," he sighed with a serious expression of duty in his face.

"I guess I will work on songs for our band," I replied, leaning into see further in his eyes, and memorizing them just in case I never gazed in them again.

"That is a great idea. When I get back we will start working on them," he replied, placing me in his lap and throwing his arms around me.

"I'm kind of cold," I said shivering. Having his polar arms across my chest wasn't helping, but I would gladly freeze to feel him all over me.

"There's a blanket in the car, I'll get it," he got up and instantly appeared at the car like magic. He got in the front seat for a few minutes then stepped out, and was instantly back by my side with a silly smirk knowing that I had watched in amazement.

Calvin drove down the road and disappeared. Lying back I began counting the stars, and planets. He did the same. I could feel the cold from his body without even touching him. He felt me shake from the movement of the blanket we were on, so he tucked the big billowy black blanket he had retrieved, around my body.

"Are you crying?" he whispered in a low mumble. I rolled over from my back to my side, hiding myself in shame. This amazing mythological creature holding my mind, my body, and my soul so tightly, truly wanted to marry me. I was overjoyed. Then quickly struck by sadness thinking about his absence.

"I can't help it. I will be held hostage by misery while you're away." I glared at the waterfall wishing my flesh blue so I could go with him.

"Want to know why they call it Looking Glass Falls?" His wintry breath sent little shockwaves pulsating through my body as the air caused pain to my ear. Maybe I was a glutton for punishment, no matter how much the frost bite burned me I always wanted more.

"Sure. Why?" I asked, sniffling as the light of the moon reflected off the waterfall, penetrating the blackness of the night. *I wish I had a tissue*, I thought to myself. Within seconds he was handing me one over my shoulder.

"Thank you," I murmured quietly, taking it from his chilled hand.

"It comes from looking glass rock where the water freezes on its sides in the winter and glistens in the sunlight like a mirror or looking glass."

"It is so peaceful here. I just wish we could stay here in Islathon forever," I sighed, grievingly missing him so, and he hadn't even left yet.

"I know. We will always have Islathon. Now turn back around so I can kiss you," he commanded in that sweet velvet voice. With the flick of his wrist I was spun around staring in his eyes. I hid mine when I realized he had flipped me over. I didn't need a mirror to know smudges of black invaded my face.

Our lips ignited and my worries of traces of makeup on my face dissipated and faded away. We kissed all night with an occasional halt or two for his hunger to calm, then went back to the throws of deep love. Making out continuously all night, it was the most incredible night of my life, so far. I couldn't wait to become Isla Michelle Daine.

Chapter 13

You Took My heart

J WOKE UP TO BIRDS CHIRPING AND whistling in the tree above me. Rolling over slightly, I could feel nothing. He was already gone. My eyes were pouring again and I was completely numb. As I got up and folded the blanket, I stared out into the woods. I realized I was totally alone. Despair ran over me like a big rig. I took a few deep breaths and tried to regain my composure. Then I picked up the basket that Johnathon had packed back up for me. He was so considerate. He must of known what a wreck I would be, to take the burden off of me. As I came up with basket in hand, I saw the limo was there and Calvin was standing by the door waiting. I picked up the blankets and sadly began walking towards the car. I just couldn't stop the leak in my eyes.

"Are you okay, Isla?" Calvin asked, taking the basket and blankets from me. He put them in the car. I shook my head, completely speechless as I got in and he shut the door behind me. The whole ride home I felt so empty and numb.

My cell phone rang in my purse. I dug around, pulling it out just in time. It read Lizzy across the tiny screen, so I answered.

"Hey Lizzy, how are you?" I asked in dead monotone. She asked if I was okay but the answer never came to my mind. "Not really, can I call you when I.

get off work tonight?" I asked dryly, not wanting to rehash. I could tell she knew something was wrong. "Okay, I'll call you later, bye," I said then closed the phone. Melting back into the seat, I realized that I had to work today. How was I going to do that?

I wiped my tears and felt the ring scrape across my nose. I held my hand out to look at it. It was hard to believe I was engaged, and to a vampire no less. The ring was amazing. It must have been four carats, but I would give it up to have him here now.

The car came to a stop. I couldn't move. Calvin opened the door.

"Isla, are you okay?" he asked. I sat there still and barely breathing as he got in to check on me. Tears invaded my eyes continuously and my breath had walked away from me. Or I had forgotten how to breathe.

"Isla, he'll be back soon. He proposed, right?" Calvin reminded me. I nodded as a few whimpers escaped me, I was trying my best to hold my sobbing in.

"I just feel like he took my heart with him, like I'm an empty shell," I sighed, my chest feeling truly heartless.

"Well, you have his. I've never seen him this happy before, in all the time that I have known him. He laughs more. I've even heard him hum now and then since he met you. You belong together."

"You're just saying that," I replied, looking down at the ring on my hand.

"No! You are the love of his life, and now you have a wedding to plan. So cheer up and focus on the wedding," he suggested as he put his arm on my shoulder.

"I know you're right, but at this point in time I could care less about wedding plans," I sighed blankly as I ran my finger under the corner of my eye, wiping away any of the mascara that might still be on my skin. I thought for sure I had cried it all off, by now.

I wanted to pull a mirror out of my purse, but I just didn't have the energy.

As I got out of the car I noticed my mom's Bronco in the driveway. I didn't really want to talk to anyone, but I knew she was up and it was inevitable.

"Thank you, Calvin," I replied, grateful for his concern. I looked down hiding my face. I didn't want him to see me like that.

"If you need anything, just say my name out loud, and I'll be there," he said, handing me my purse. I was so undone I had almost left it behind in the limo.

"Okay." I took it. I could barely talk. I felt so weak and numb.

When I walked in the house Mom threw her arms around me. "Where have you been and why are you so upset?" she asked, hugging me tighter and then holding me out in front of her to really look at me.

"I was with Johnathon." I replied. She relaxed a little.

"Crazy ideas went through my head I was so worried when you didn't come home last night. I have called everyone. Lizzy, Micha, and I even called all the hospitals."

"Sorry, Mom. Can we talk about it later?" I asked annoyed. It figured she would freak after only one night.

"Yes, but we do need to talk," she demanded, taking my hand. When she did, the light through the window caught the diamond causing it to shine a blinding ray right in her eye.

"Oh my God, did he propose?" she hollered and gasped as she got a better look at it. "It looks to be like three or four carats, is it real?

"Mom!" I shouted, bothered that she had the audacity.

"Sorry, I'm sure it is," she said and smiled a little crookedly with an apology in her expression.

"What did you say?" she asked. I wanted to say duh, I'm wearing the ring.

"Mom, I love Johnathon more than life itself. I said yes otherwise I wouldn't be wearing the ring," I announced. She was excited, but reserved.

"Why are you crying? You should be happy," she asked, touching my shoulder lovingly.

"I know." I really did want to be happy, but it seemed entirely too far fetched at the time.

"Where is he? I would like to talk to him." Mom stated, looking around as if he was hiding. Like I was kidding or something.

"He had to go away for a while. I am going to miss him so much." The tears just kept coming. I was dizzy from not being able to get any air.

"Where did he go?" she asked, anxious to congratulate the both of us together.

"I don't know, somewhere in Europe I think," I replied, staring off into space.

"Did you choose a wedding date?" she asked curiously.

"Yes, April 25th next year. Exactly one year from last night," I responded, appearing to be happy for a minute while inside diving off a skyscraper hoping to die before I hit the ground. I was so afraid that last night was the last time I would ever see him.

"It must have been an amazing night!" she proclaimed, wanting to hear more.

But I wasn't comfortable talking about it. "Yes, it was the most incredible night of my life. I want to be alone now mom," I announced bleakly.

She sat there in silence with one of her eyebrows raised and a peculiar look on her face. As I got up thinking the conversation was over she asked. "You aren't pregnant, are you? I mean the other day you got sick for no apparent reason. I just can't push safe sex enough."

I stopped dead in my tracks and turned around briskly standing at the bottom of the stairs. "No Mom, you have to have sex to get pregnant."

"You mean you haven't?" she asked, puzzled but proud. I wanted to yell 'Yeah, he won't give it to me Mom,' but, of course I was talking about his teeth in me sucking me into life. But I obviously couldn't say that.

"No, we do not have sex," I replied. She looked relieved. All that would have changed bitterly if she had known that he wanted my blood and that I was going to marry a vampire. I sat back down next to her on the earth-toned couch in our living room.

She hugged me tightly.

"I'm so proud that you're waiting, honey." She smiled warmly and then hugged me, again.

That's a major understatement, I thought to myself.

"Do you work today?" she asked, looking at the clock.

"Yes, at 11:00. I need to go get ready."

"Okay, go on sweetie," she conceded as she got up and went to the kitchen.

I got up and went up to my room to take a bath and get ready. I put on some black capri's, a black shirt with thin white stripes and black shoes. I sat on my bed and put my makeup on. I was just going through the motions, not really wanting to move or go anywhere.

I put my arm through the strap of my purse and headed down stairs.

"Isla, have a good day," I heard mom say as I closed the door behind me. I got in my car and started the engine, the first song I heard when the CD player kicked on was *Something* by The Beatles. I listened to it over and over again crying the whole way there. I cried so hard I knew by the time I got to work there would be black running down my face. I didn't care much, I was still so numb.

When I got to work, I went straight to my station and didn't do much talking throughout the day. I was busy, so I did not have much time to think about it. I switched hands with the ring because it would have hurt too much to talk about it. I tried my hardest to avoid it, even in my mind.

Angel was busy, we both were. We didn't even have time for a cigarette, the day flew by so fast. I smiled but the tears were always on the verge of coming down. I pulled my cell phone out of my smock to see the time. I was relieved to see it was 5:00, time to go.

I cleaned up my station, packed up my stuff and waved goodbye as I walked out the door.

When I got in the car I turned the CD player off for the ride home.

Home at last, I went straight up to my room. I decided to take the pain and use it. There were some lyrics coming quickly in my head so I got comfortable on my bed with my notebook and pen and began writing.

So Deeply
I never thought that I would feel so vulnerable
I never thought that being without you would be
so unbearable
I never thought that I would sacrifice so much of me
I never thought that I could love so deeply
So deeply, it hurt me so deeply
To not have you with me
So deeply, I cried out so deeply
It felt like knives inside me

Now I feel every drop of rain
Every ray of sun
I know you are the one

The one to ease my pain
And cause the same
Love hurts that is true, but I'd rather die
than live without you
So deeply, I know in my head, so deeply
Even though your flesh is dead
You have awakened something in me, so deeply
Everyone is after me to get to you
I'll take it gladly for you are all I see
And all that will ever be love to me
You have already drank me in

No way could our love be sin, for me
My heart is wrapped in you, I love you so deeply
After writing, lying back on my bed I fell asleep holding it. *In my dream I was in a forest. It didn't look familiar but it could have been Pisgah Forest which was close to Islathon (Looking Glass Falls). I was running, cold and scared, wandering through the woods stumbling on rocks and limbs. Breathing so heavy the mist from my breath became clouds, I ran through. I saw a shadow out of the corner of my eye, and froze. I didn't know which way to go. Keeping on a path of sorts I came around a huge tree. I screamed when someone was right in front of me. It was Dezi, she had one hand. I guess Johnathon had taken her other one in their last fight.*

She thrust forward clenching my throat.

"We meet again, Isla," she smiled, making sure I saw her sharp white teeth.

A voice came out of the darkness, wet with sin. It was Sigrid.

"Isla you won't get away this time, I know my brother is nowhere near." I could barely breathe.

"Let go Dezi, it's my turn," Sigrid ordered, shoving her aside. I started coughing, trying to get some air. I looked up slowly and he backhanded me into a tree. Being hit by a normal person was way different than the same impact by a vampire. I couldn't get up. Then he picked me up by my throat and hit me again. I landed on a rock, felt my body smash and crack. Trying to get up again, I wiped my lip and saw the blood on my hand. I was coming to terms with the fact that I was about to die. My pain was so vivid.

"Just kill me now. I can't take much more of this," I thought to myself.

Suddenly another voice came out of the skeletal blackness of the forest.

"Get away from her!" I didn't recognize the voice but knew he was going to save me. Before I could see his face I woke up. Looking around my room in a panic, I realized I was safe. I was lying there with my eyes wide open, analyzing everything very carefully in my head. Who saved me if it wasn't Johnathon? Like a light bulb

flashing over my head it struck me. "Oh, it was Jee Cee," I said out loud and then jumped up out of bed, never even looking at the clock. It was early in the morning. I glanced out my window and saw it was still dark with an early morning haze.

I got dressed, brushed my teeth, put on my tall black boots to match my all black outfit. I wore one of my favorite shirts, it was a black baby doll shirt with Beatles on the front in rhinestones.

I caught a glimpse of the clock it was 3:45 a.m.

"What made me get up so early?" I asked myself out loud. Knowing that my dreams seemed to be coming true, I guess I just wanted to face it head on. It may not happen exactly like that, but I was definitely going to see my enemies soon.

"Calvin, come pick me up," I commanded out loud. After I said that I peeked out the window and he was already there. Realizing that they were coming for me, I knew I had to keep them away from the people I loved.

I picked up my purse, wrapped it around my body and quietly headed downstairs. I opened the door and closed it behind me, careful not to make much noise.

As I walked out to the car I had a terrible feeling I couldn't shake.

"Isla, is everything alright?" Calvin asked as he held the door.

"We will talk in the car," I replied, getting in.

He shut the door lightly and before I even sat down he was in front rolling down the privacy window.

"Okay, talk," he said, totally interested and intrigued by the early morning urgency.

"Here is the low down," I explained, getting serious. "Just recently, I have discovered that my psychic abilities are in my dreams. They don't happen in the exact way, but the struggle is always the same. Tonight, or this morning, was different. Sigrid did not give me a choice, this time he just beat me up. So I need to know a vampire's weaknesses and what causes the worst damage the fastest."

"Well, Johnathon would be disappointed with me if I helped you, because he told me to keep you out of harm's way. But I would feel horrible if I didn't arm you. So that being said, any kind of water be it holy, spring, or tap, is a necessary weapon. If a victim eats garlic it does something to the blood, tastes disgusting, but it's poison to a vampire. They die not too long after consuming it. Every vampire knows that, though, and can smell it. Therefore they stay away," he warned, staring at me.

"So, garlic is deadly. What does the water do?" I asked curiously.

"It burns like fire," he replied in a low, breathy voice that made it sound like it was hard for him to talk about this.

"Have you been burned?" I asked, leaning over the back of the seat.

"Yes," he sighed as he pulled back his sleeve and showed me his arm.

"Ouch, that looks like it hurt," I gasped, looking away. His skin was melted and a bit disfigured. I had the idea that a vampire healed. But I guess I was wrong.

"Where am I taking you?" he asked, rolling his sleeve back down and starting the car.

"I need to see Jee Cee," I answered. His eye brows rose. "I want him to show me some self defense, so I can fight back."

"You are getting ballsy," he stated, smiling in the rearview.

I laughed. "Yeah, I'm not going to take it lying down anymore. This time I'll be ready."

It wasn't long before the car came to a stop. "We're here," he announced in a low, nonchalant voice. I gulped as I looked out the window for that dreaded car. "Will you take me to see him?" I asked hesitantly. I didn't want to inconvenience him anymore than I already had, but I was terrified of Sigrid.

"Don't worry, Sigrid's not here."

"Is Jee Cee here?" I asked.

"Yes, that's his car," he held his arm up pointing. "That's his blue Maserati." The knots in my gut loosened a little as I scanned the castle grounds and saw only one car.

"Good," I replied, at ease some.

"He knows you're coming. He's expecting you."

"How does he know?" I asked. I temporarily blanked on the whole mind reading thing.

"He is reading my thoughts. He's also somewhat in tune to yours," he explained with a comforting grin.

"Wow! We haven't even spent any time together. How can he read my mind?" I asked as I scooted my way towards the car door.

"He is watching over you for Johnathon, remember?" Calvin reminded me.

"Oh yeah! It's just weird being here without him."

He got out of the car and opened the door. I got out, feeling slightly reluctant to be in the castle without Johnathon there. Calvin could see that I was determined, but edgy. Calvin held my wrist and at first it startled me. I hadn't felt the frigidness of a vampire's touch in a few days. I only wished it was Johnathon instead.

He led me around to the back of the house through the green grass and around bushes and giant trees to a tall, gray iron door. Calvin waved his hand in front of a red light. It turned blue and opened. Ah...yes it's red then he waves his cold hands over it and then it's cold, so it's blue. What an epiphany that was. When the door opened it made a spooky sound. I gulped nervously.

"Go ahead, after you," Calvin insisted, he put out his hand, motioning for me to go first.

My first thought was *Are you insane?* But, only for a brief moment.

"You're not coming with me?" I asked. As I stepped forward I kept my eyes on Calvin and wasn't paying attention as I walked smack into Jee Cee. He cleared his throat with humor.

"Isla, it's nice to see you again," he greeted me with a bit of a chuckle. I stepped back a little to get off his toes.

"It's good to see you again. I'm sorry," I apologized genuinely as my face went a soft shade of scarlet.

"I know why you've come, follow me," Jee Cee announced. I turned to look at Calvin, but he was gone.

Jee Cee led me into a huge gym. Jee Cee had me kicking a punching bag for a while until I was sore. After I was warmed up he suggested kicking the bag. Jee Cee had a calm, laid back personality. We got along great. Then he taught me some self-defense. He told me to punch him. I did, but he was so fast I saw tracers of his body when he moved. I never even came close.

"Now, a vampire's power is stronger than any human being's, so you have to think one thing and do the other to catch them off guard. They will read your thoughts to know what you will do next," he explained.

"That sounds difficult," I replied, a bit confused.

"With practice you will be able to. Let's try it," he suggested, moving in front of me. "Now think in your mind you're going to punch me, then do something completely different," he commanded.

I took a step back from him. I thought to myself, *I'm going to punch him.* Then I kicked my right leg out and swept both of his legs out from underneath him. He landed on the floor with a stunned expression on his face. He stood and dusted his blue and black sweats off like he had fallen in the dirt.

"Wow, I wasn't expecting that. You're better at this than I thought you would be," he sighed. "I don't think we need to practice that anymore," he stated with chagrin.

"Sorry, did I hurt you?" I asked, knowing there was no way I could have affected a vampire with my human abilities.

He let out a roaring laugh. "No.... you surprised me," he admitted, pressing his lips together and scratching his goatee.

"You seem surprised that I could do that." I replied, puzzled.

"Yes, it usually takes special powers, or a vampire, to do that. You're not a vampire though, so you must have special powers on your own."

"Well I have always had some psychic attributes, but only because I was never told I couldn't do it. When I was about nine my mom didn't come home. She was showing a house on the outskirts of town. We had no idea where. So without even thinking about it I sat down and meditated. I saw her with two flat tires on a highway somewhere. I saw the sign that was right up from her car and told my dad where she was. He picked her up exactly where I had said she was.

"That's definitely a psychic ability. I think you're a vampire, you just haven't been bit yet," he replied.

I wanted to shout out 'Yes I have!' But it didn't change me so it didn't matter. "You think so?" I asked, excited to become one. "Do you think you could show me how to master that power?" I asked. I knew after one training session I would still be a human weakling compared to the undeniable strength of a vampire.

"Take every bit of love you have for my brother, your family and friends and throw it at them full force. I think you already have it in you."

"I do," I replied, knowing he was right, but still painted with doubt. Lack of confidence was the hurdle I had to get over.

"Now, I want to talk about something else," he said, changing the subject. "What about this band?" he asked as his eyes sparkled with the talk of music.

"Oh yeah, I almost forgot." I reached into my purse and handed him a paper.

"What is this?" he asked as he opened it up and proceeded to read it. I watched his eyes get wide and his facial expression change to enthusiasm.

"Twisted Dream Dead Moon, I like the name. This is good," he said, still eying the paper.

"It needs music. I had hoped that Johnathon would help in the writing of the music, but he is not here." My mouth went dry and I had an ache in my heart when I said his name.

"I'll see what I can do, so *Isla and the Bloodsuckers*, is it?"

"It's a great name," I admitted, placing my purse strap over my shoulder. "I need to get going. Thank you for your help. I'll talk to you soon." I started walking back towards the door I came in. Jee Cee walked beside me and directed me through the many halls of that amazing house.

"What sound do you want it to have?" he asked still reading it.

"I think it should be dark and sweet, the way I like my chocolate and my man for that matter," I replied smiling.

He smiled and walked me to the big iron door. "See you, Isla," he promised as the door opened. I waved to him as it closed.

I cautiously walked around to the front of the house to see Calvin standing by the car with the door ajar, waiting for me.

"Did he help?" he asked.

"Yes, more than I had hoped." I replied as I got in.

On the ride home my phone rang, as I looked for it in my purse I thought maybe, just maybe, it would be him. The phone number looked familiar but I didn't recognize it right off the bat.

"Hello," I answered.

"Oh, hey Jolie how are you doing?--- Sure, what movie are we going to see?---Okay, that sounds great. And Betsy's coming too? Cool! When? Friday night, I'm there. No, that's okay I have a ride. Why don't y'all come ride with me in the limo? I know isn't it? I get off of work at 5:00 maybe we could go get something to eat first. Yes, I still live off of Haywood. Okay, I will see you at 6:00, bye." Closing my phone I tossed it in my purse. I hadn't hung out with them in so long. What if something happened before, like my dream becoming reality?

I noticed the car wasn't moving anymore, it was such a smooth ride it was hard to tell. Calvin opened the door for me. I wrapped my purse strap around my shoulder and got out.

"Isla you know what to do if you need me," he reiterated.

"Yes. Would you mind driving me and some friends to the movies Friday night?"

"Not at all. I told you, anytime," he replied, shutting the car door.

"Please let me know if Johnathon contacts you," I sighed as my eyes filled again.

"Of course! Don't worry. He's fine. He is checking in on you through my thoughts and Jee Cee's."

"He is?" I asked as one single tear slid down my cheek, then more followed.

"Isla don't cry, you are stronger than that. Don't forget what Jee Cee taught you," he reminded me as he wiped my tears with a tissue from his pocket.

"Believe me, I wish the tears would stay away, but it just hurts so much. I'll talk to you soon." I sighed, bowed my head and turned to walk away. I took two steps then looked back, he was gone.

"Figures," I sighed under my breath as I opened the front door and went in. Before shutting it I glanced at the driveway to see what cars were there. My car was the only one, *all alone*, I whispered to myself as I took the steps up to my room. I set my purse down, the clock caught my eye, it was 10:00 p.m. I couldn't believe where the day went, it flew by. I had the yawns, they were coming continuously. I was so tired from training and working out. I fell on the bed and my head soaked into the pillow.

"Johnathon, I love you and miss you," I breathed, praying he heard me. My eyes won the fight and I drifted off.

Chapter 14

The Fight Back

THE NEXT MORNING I GOT READY FOR work as usual and was putting my makeup on when the door bell rang. I put the mascara wand in the container and yelled, "Mom, can you get it?" I listened to see if she heard me, but heard nothing---maybe she had already left. It rang again. I got up and ran downstairs to answer the door. I opened it to find Micha standing there with a smile and a look of relief in her eyes when she saw me.

"Hey girl, Lizzy told me to come by and check on you. She was really worried; she said you sounded depressed and upset," Micha explained.

I motioned for her to come in. "Yes, I am depressed. Johnathon had to leave unexpectedly and I'm falling apart. I love him so much," the tears visited again. I couldn't think about him with out crying.

"Oh! I almost forgot . . . this note was on the door," she blurted as she handed it to me, excited to see what it was. Looking at my name on the front I knew it wasn't his handwriting, but I still opened it with urgency and began to read.

Isla,

> *I wanted to warn you, Sigrid is in town and he has two others with him. Don't worry, just be prepared for anything. Practice what Jee Cee taught you. Jee Cee wants you to meet his girlfriend, Lexi Kennington. She wants to meet you, too. She is someone that can help you.*

> *Sincerely,*
> *Calvin*

I must have had a weird look on my face because Micha looked at me with a puzzled expression.

"Is it from Johnathon?" she asked curiously. I lowered my head.

"No, it's from Calvin, my driver." I murmured. When I heard myself say that, I giggled at the thought. Even though he was my friend I never wanted to take advantage of his services, but he was my driver at least while Johnathon was away.

"Is everything okay?" Micha asked. She smiled and patted me on the back when she saw the water building in my eyes.

"Yes. I don't really want to talk about it right now. How have you been?" I asked, getting the focus off of me. And doing whatever I could to get my mind off of my ripping heart.

"Did something happen?

"A lot! More than I can believe," I replied, staring off in space, replaying every moment Johnathon and I had shared in my head. All the way back to our first kiss at Jaggers.

Her eyes were heavy on me, wondering what was going on. Shaking her head and mumbling, "Whatever. Are you okay?" She gripped my arms lightly and made me look he in the eyes.

"I'm sorry, I'm so out of it. It'll be okay," I responded with a bit of enthusiasm, just so we could change the subject. She shot me a crooked smile then let go of my arms and eyed the floor. I was holding my breath that the subject wouldn't arise again.

She turned away, peering around the room aimlessly. Suddenly she blurted out. "Lizzy's gone," as if she were reminding me.

"What do you mean, gone?" I muttered.

"She went to Vegas last weekend and she's not back yet. I talked to her yesterday and she seemed a little out of it. She did talk about you; she said she was scared for you. " Micha explained and then sat down in the tall dark wood chair by the front door.

"What did she mean by scared?" I asked, perplexed by the fact that she could sense it from Las Vegas. Maybe Lizzy could just hear it in my voice. She had caught me at a wretched time. I was a ship that had broken in two and was sinking fast.

"I don't know, she was just worried about you. Let's just hope *she* doesn't do anything crazy while she's in Vegas." Micha said, insinuating that she might be in some kind of trouble or do something stupid. *Lizzy, nah,* I thought sarcastically in my head. If there was jeopardy to be had Lizzy was usually in the middle conducting. She didn't invite it, or egg it on, it just seemed to find her.

"Well, you know Lizzy. Anything goes," I replied, then glanced at the clock. "Crap! I've got to get to work, Micha," I shouted, and then tried to hurry her out the door without being rude.

"Oh, I'm sorry. I didn't mean to hold you up," she replied as she got up and slowly backed towards the door.

"That's okay. I love ya, but I got to get going," I sighed, giving her a hug. I missed her and wished that we could hang out longer. *But duty calls,* I said in my head.

"Bye, call me," Micha muttered as she walked out the door.

"I will. Bye," I replied then waved as she walked down my driveway to her car.

I shut the door and ran upstairs praying that somehow June wouldn't be there when I got to work. I was pretty much ready to go. I brushed my teeth threw my hair up in a high ponytail, grabbed my purse and ran back down stairs and out the door. I got in my car and as I backed out I looked in the rearview mirror at my face. It captured my attention that I had only put mascara on one eye. "Oops! Oh well," I commented out loud.

I wondered what was going on with Lizzy. She was a bit on the wild side and would try anything. I mean I was wild too, but she could be a little over the top at times. Things that happen in Vegas don't always stay there, they follow you.

While I was driving our song came on. But, I couldn't listen to it. I took the CD out of the player and put it in the CD holder in the visor. *I don't have time to cry today.* I told myself.

When I got to work June wasn't there yet, luckily. Checking my schedule I noticed that my first appointment would be at 1:00. I thought maybe this would be my window of opportunity to get to the store, because I hoped that I would be busy all day and wouldn't have another chance.

"Lissa, I'll be back in thirty minutes," I spoke quietly as to not bring attention to myself. The girls that had been there longer had more rights and could leave to go to the store, no problem. But I hadn't been there that long and the only reason I was able to leave was because June wasn't there.

"Okay, see you then," she replied, smiling as she answered the phone.

I took my purse from my station and walked out the door. I got in my car and drove about seven miles up the road to the *Stop and Shop.* I went in and picked up lots of garlic, some balloons and some spearmint gum. I paid for it and headed back to the shop.

When I got back, Lissa told me my client was waiting. She was a teenage girl, a little younger than me, who wanted a highlight and low light. When I finished her hair she loved the color and haircut and told me she would send me all her friends; she was a cheerleader so I knew I would be expecting the whole squad. She tipped well, too. The rest of the day went by really fast. I did a lot of hair cuts and styles.

Angel was busy most of the day so we didn't get much time to talk. 5:00 came fast and I cleaned my station and went home.

When I got home my mom was there. She was in the kitchen when I walked in. I threw my stuff down in exhaustion as I fell back into a chair and rested my elbows on the sand colored table.

"Hey mom, how was your day?" I mumbled.

"It was okay, I drove around showing houses most of the day, and the

couple still didn't find a house they liked," she sighed, sounding frustrated and her body language showing fatigue as she slid into the chair across from me.

"How was your day, what did the girls think about the news, and your ring?" she asked, slurping her coffee with sparkling eyes, happy that I had found someone.

"I didn't tell anybody, it just hurt to much to talk about it," I replied, hoping that the conversation would cease, after my comment.

"I thought for sure you would be excited and giddy with your girlfriends. Does anyone know besides me?" she asked as she got up and filled her mug a second time.

"No! I just don't want to talk about it right now," I replied in a huff.

"Honey, he'll be back soon. And you'll have a beautiful wedding. I don't know how much we can help on the wedding though," she sighed, nervous about how much it would all cost. She patted my hand and held it there.

"You don't have to do or pay anything. I'm sure that Johnathon will take care of everything," I told her as my head fell low, just thinking about him.

"The planning too?" she asked, wanting to help in some way.

"You can help me if you want." I really didn't want to talk about it. *Oh great, here they come.* Once again that wet emotion was building and was about to flow.

"Of course, you probably want to work on the guest list first," she suggested. She sounded excited. Quite the opposite of how I was feeling. I mean, don't get me wrong I was ecstatic about being engaged, but missing him was overriding it big time.

"I just want to wait til he gets home," I sighed, way beyond ready to end the discussion.

"Do you know when he will be home?" she asked. Which was the wrong question, because I had not an inkling of his scheduled home coming. Not knowing was driving me insane.

"No!" Tears were running down my face, and my reaction cut her off, but I just couldn't talk about it anymore. That question was plaguing me.

"I'm going to my room," I mumbled hastily, but as I turned around she caught my arm.

"He'll be home before you know it," she reminded me in a comforting tone. I hugged her and went upstairs. As I walked up the steps I hoped my window would be open and he would be there. But, no such luck. It was closed when I entered the room. Sad and upset I changed into a long black silky night gown, and dry-brushed my teeth; a dentist once told me that was a good thing to do, so I did it from time to time. My mind was playing movies of terrifying things happening to Johnathon. I had to find a way to stop the projectors from rolling. I shook it off and climbed on my bed. Sitting cross-legged I dumped my purse on the bed. My phone needed charged so I plugged it into the charger. It was early, but I was totally wiped out. I sat on my bed going through my stuff. Then I saw the letter from Calvin. After reading it again I decided to go see Jee Cee and meet Lexi. I got a second wind.

"Calvin come pick me up," I said out loud. I put my phone with what little charge it had, in my purse, picked up a few more things, tossed them in and went downstairs. Mom was in the kitchen, sitting at the table typing away on her laptop.

"I'm going out for a while, be back later," I announced as I threw a long thin black jacket over my arm just in case the weather man had predicted right.

"Okay, have fun," she replied as I opened the door. Calvin was already there. I stopped before closing the door. I ran back up stairs to my room and picked up a grocery bag then headed back downstairs and closed the door behind me.

"Good evening, Isla," he greeted me smiling as he opened the car door.

"How are you, Calvin?"

"Good, let's talk in the car," he suggested, motioning for me to get in.

"Okay." He was sitting in the front seat and had already rolled down the privacy window, before I even got settled. It was amazing how fast they were.

"Sigrid is at the house, so I don't think it's a good idea for you to go there. Jee Cee wants you to go to Lexi's house. She's expecting you," he said, which baffled me. How could she be expecting me on such short notice?

"Okay, sounds good," I replied, getting comfortable. "About how long is the ride?"

"About thirty minutes," he muttered, eying me through the rearview mirror.

"Alright, do you mind if I take a nap?" I asked, fluffing up a black body pillow that I had never noticed before.

"Not at all. I'll wake you when we get there," he replied.

I was beginning to lie down and get comfortable when a strange feeling came over me. I sprung back up, and blurted loudly, "Calvin, stop at a convenience store, please." I had a jolting sensation that I was about to walk into a trap.

"Sure, there's one up here through this light." He motioned with his eyes and a little head bob. A few minutes went by, then the car stopped and he opened the door. I jumped out.

"I'll be right back," I said running in. I immediately noticed there was a deli. I decided to order some garlic mashed potatoes and shrimp in garlic sauce. While they were getting that ready for me I picked up two gallons of water. "How much longer will it be?" I asked the dark haired, older man behind the counter.

"It will be a few more minutes ma'am," he answered in a thick Indian accent.

"Okay, thank you." I paid for the water and went to put it in the car.

"Thirsty?" Calvin asked as I approached the car nearly dropping one jug. I was able to balance it on my knee until Calvin caught it and then handed it back to me.

"Nope, they're weapons," I grunted as I lifted both jugs and placed them on the floorboard of the car.

He looked a little puzzled at first then nodded his head in agreement. Calvin was standing outside by the open car door. I was sitting in the seat with my legs hanging out.

"Calvin, Sigrid is reading my mind, right?" I asked, even though I knew the answer.

"Yes, he probably is," he replied with his arm holding the door so it wouldn't close on me.

"I'm not taking any chances this could be a trap," I explained. I could tell by his nod that he concurred with me. Going there without being armed in some way would be like crawling into the lion's mouth itself.

"Ready?" he asked.

"Not quite, I ordered some food. I'll be right back," I replied, getting up and going back in. Walking in I realized I was thirsty, and not for water, so I decided to get a V8. As I passed the candy aisle the chocolate reached out and grabbed me. So I picked up a candy bar and thought, *Would I really be able to give up chocolate?*

"Thank you, have a great day ma'am," the man behind the counter said after I paid him. He handed me my food and I walked back out to the car.

"Now I'm ready," I murmured as I jumped in and immediatly began preparing for the mission that was about to unfold.

I took about six cloves of garlic and broke them up in both dishes. I was

going to consume as much garlic as possible. I was famished so I ate every morsel, drank my V8, and started filling up the balloons with water. It was tremendously hard to do without a funnel, but I did it, and didn't make too bad of a mess. I tied them up and put them in my purse. My stomach started hurting. Probably nerves, either that or all the garlic.

"Have you heard from Johnathon?" I asked, hoping to hear good news.

"No, not a thing," he sighed, focusing on the road.

"Can you read his mind?" I asked, grasping on to any leg of hope.

"I can try, but I don't know where he is," he replied, squinting his eyes at me in the rearview.

"Will you try? Please! I have to know that he is okay," I pleaded with him.

"I'll try while you're visiting with Lexi," he promised, like it was a chore, but I knew he really didn't mind.

"Okay, thank you so much. Is Jee Cee going to be there too?" I asked, looking down at my wrist and admiring the glare of my big silver bracelet.

"Maybe later he'll show up," he answered, stopping the car and turning around to look at me.

"We are here," he replied as he got out and opened the door for me. When I got out I was surprised, to see we were in front a book store.

"She lives above the book store," he explained and grinned when he observed my expression.

"Oh, how do I get up there?" I asked, looking up at the tall building.

"You go right through there and up the stairs," he said as he pointed.

"Let me ask you something. If by chance you were able to read his mind, could he read yours at the same time?"

"I'm sure he could," he answered.

"I'll be back," I said as I turned to walk away. I walked down a short dark alley lined with tall trees and bushes until I came to a set of stairs. The steps were fairly steep. I kept my hand in my purse, just in case. I was ready for anything as I made my way slowly up the concrete stairs to a narrow, red lacquered door and knocked. It opened and there she stood. She was tall, toned, and beautiful, with long golden brown hair. She was about the same age as me.

"Isla, I'm so glad you could come," she greeted me, inviting me in with such a gleam of innocence in her light brown eyes.

"It is very nice to meet you, Lexi."

"Come on in and sit down," she muttered, indicating the couch.

The living room was small and quaint with a big red-brown paisley couch and a magnifying fish tank coffee table. There was a poster of Casablanca hanging up above the couch.

"I like your coffee table and your apartment, it's really cute."

"Thank you, it's not much, but it's mine," she said as she moved closer to me on the couch. I was taken back by her overly friendly behavior.

"So, I hear you need help fighting the bad undead," she looked at me and grinned with a twinkle in her eye.

"Yes, that would be great, Sigrid is always trying to kill or change me," I admitted sheepishly.

"Oh, Sigrid, he used to be that way with me too, but he eventually gave up when he couldn't have my heart. A few years ago it seemed like all I did was fight to not become a vampire. Now I want it so bad, and it seems like no one will do It," she said with morosity.

"You mean you're not one either?" I asked, a little surprised. But after all Jee Cee was Johnathon's brother and they went by the code.

"No! Jee Cee won't do it, he gets mad when I try to push him," she replied with her head hung low.

"Johnathon gets mad, too. He says the pain is unbearable."

"What's unbearable is growing old and watching him stay the same," she mumbled with a glaze of sadness clouding her eyes.

"How old are you?" I asked, hoping I didn't offend her.

"Twenty three, I think he is going to wait either til we get married or til I am twenty five."

"Well, I already know when Johnathon will change me. It will be April twenty-fifth next year, on our wedding day," I announced. She jumped up and hugged me.

"So you're engaged? Congratulations!"

It did feel good to tell someone who knew what I was going through. I held my hand out to show her the ring.

"Wow! That's amazing. Put it away you're blinding me," she shouted, holding her hands over her eyes, joking around. "Jee Cee hasn't asked yet. Sometimes I wonder if he ever will," she sighed kind of solemnly.

"I'm sure he will. How long have you two been dating?"

"About two years, he might be waiting for my birthday, which is next month."

"Mine too. I'll be twenty one on May twenty-fifth."

"Are you kidding? My birthday is on the twenty-sixth," she screeched, exhilarated and amazed. "That's cool, we need to celebrate together," she suggested, touching my arm softly.

"Actually, I'll be in Amsterdam on my birthday," I replied, thrilled about going to Europe. I was excited about our birthdays, too.

"Really, that's cool maybe we can all go?" she suggested, just kind of throwing it out there.

"That would be cool. Start saving now, it's expensive. The only way I can afford to go is because one of my best friends invited me to go. Her parents gave her two tickets as a reward for getting in to Princeton."

"I have been saving some money for a car for a long time," she said, in deep thought, staring off into another part of her apartment.

"Is Johnathon going too?" she asked, not even looking at me.

"I don't know. I might actually have to go get him, rescue him for a change." I waved my hand in front of her eyes. She turned her attention back to me.

"Oh sorry, I didn't mean to space out on you. From who or what?" she asked, highly curious.

"Jeziaka and her love spell. I'm psychic in my dreams and I had a dream she put him under a spell and took him away from me. I told him that if she takes him away I will hunt her down and kill her."

"You sound fierce. I'd probably do the same thing if someone tried to take Jee Cee away from me," Lexi sighed.

I pulled my phone out of my purse to see the time. Opening it I saw that Lizzy had called. I needed to get home and call her. I stood up.

"It's 10:30, I really need to get home. It was wonderful to meet you," I announced, placing my purse strap over my arm.

"You too, maybe we can hang out again soon," she suggested as she hugged me.

We definitely had a lot in common. I felt really comfortable with her. So we exchanged cell phone numbers and I walked to the door.

"Have a good night! Talk to you soon."

"Have a great night; I will call you this weekend," she replied.

"Cool" I shouted as I walked out the door and she closed it behind me. As I walked down the stairs I hesitated on each step. I felt uneasy and stopped, stiff from apprehension in the middle of the stairs. "Calvin come get me," I whispered out loud, but still quietly enough so no one could here me.

I was just about ready to take the next step down, but I froze when I heard, "Isla, run!" I didn't question it I just turned around and went back up the steps, quickly. I knocked hard on Lexi's door and she opened it, letting me in. She could see the fright in my eyes.

"What's wrong?" she asked, gripping my arm trying to calm me down.

"I was walking down the steps and someone yelled 'Run, Isla.' I think it was Calvin. A creepy feeling crawled up my spine as I walked down the steps. Even though I am armed, I thought I better listen."

"What do you mean, you're armed?" she asked with her eyes big as she stepped away from me. "Let me see," she demanded, looking excited. So I obliged her by opening my bag and showing her my balloons of water and all the garlic.

"I wondered why you smelled like garlic," she replied, turning her nose up and fanning her arms.

"Sorry, I ate a lot before I got here, too," I admitted, grinning and laughing at her expression.

"It's okay, it smells good, I like garlic," she admitted, with a half smirk.

"Well, you won't when you're a vampire. It will kill you slowly to consume it or drink blood of someone who has eaten it."

There was a knock at the door. We both were struck by a nervous chill as she looked through the peep hole.

"It's Calvin," she sighed, relieved as she opened it.

"Hey Calvin, is it safe?" I asked tense, tired and ready to go home. I thought Lexi was super cool, but it was just time to get home.

"Thank you for opening the door so quickly," I uttered to Lexi as we walked to the door.

"You're welcome. Have a good night, Isla. You too, Calvin," she called as we were walking out. She shut the door behind us.

"Calvin, was it Sigrid?" I asked as we took the steps back down.

"Yes, I told him to leave you alone. He said if you'll have dinner with him he'll forsake your soul." He smiled as if he knew what my reaction would be.

"Is he insane? He would torture, beat and then kill me. Besides, what does that mean *forsake my soul?* He thinks he's all high and mighty, doesn't he?" I vented. There was just no telling what he would do to me. I don't think he had an ounce of mercy in his coldhearted body.

"Wait!" he growled, blocking me from going any further with his arm out in front of me. He took to the path swiftly. Out in the street he looked around and called "Okay, it's safe." He waved his arms trying to get me to the car fast.

He opened the door and I jumped in quickly. He rolled down the privacy window and turned around to face me.

"Alright, here's the scoop. I talked to him." he announced, leaning over the seat some.

"Tell me, is he okay? When is he coming home?"

"Whoa! Slow down, Isla. He is going before the council tomorrow. He said he's proud of you. He's very happy you have met Lexi and he hasn't run into Jeziaka yet, but he will do his best to steer clear of her. He misses you and can't wait to get back to Islathon. He loves you and misses you more than the sun loves the day, and that was direct quote." Calvin then turned around and started to drive.

"Johnathon," I whispered, as tears began to fall. "I miss you so much," I breathed quietly as Calvin raised the window back up. He could tell I needed some time. I sat back and imagined him next to me. His breath on my skin and the way it felt when he held me. It was as if his body surrounded me from every angle. I couldn't stop thinking about the other night when he proposed, his ancient scent, his breathtaking eyes, his perfectly proportioned lips, and his scintillating skin. I had to catch my breath just to ponder. I closed my eyes to picture him kissing my neck. It always sent chills through my body, in so many ways. With my eyes closed to visualize him there with me, I began to drift off. I hadn't even realized I was asleep until Calvin was waking me up.

"Isla, you're home," he announced, shaking me lightly.

"Huh? Oh! Thank you," I sighed, wiping my eyes and slowly getting out of the limo with my stuff in hand. "Thank you for being such a good friend."

"You're very welcome. I'm glad to have you as a friend, so thank you," he replied, giving me a hug. "Call me if you need me," he murmured as he smiled and closed the door.

"You know I will! See you later!" I spun around and headed to my front door and opened it quietly. I snuck up stairs and went to my room, put my stuff down and threw myself on the bed. I tossed and turned awhile, praying and thinking about my sweet

Johnathon, asking God to protect him and bring him home soon. *Please Lord don't take him away from me.* My teary eyes began to close and it wasn't long before I was in a dream.

I was back in high school except it was different, the people were the same, but I felt Johnathon in my life. Some friends and I were sitting on a bench. Looking up I thought I saw Johnathon walking in the distance. Without thinking I shot to my feet and ran to him. As I got close to him he disappeared, I looked around dismayed and confused. Students were scattered everywhere. I began to question whether seeing him was in my mind as I walked back over to my friends still on the bench.

"Where did you go?" Jolie asked.

"I thought I saw someone," I replied. *Then she waved her hand in front of my eyes because I was in a daze, scanning through people walking by, seeking to see him again.*

"Who did you see?"

"My boyfriend Johnathon. I mean my fiancé."

"Your what? When did you get engaged? I thought you were dating William."

"We broke up years ago." *I replied. She stared at me like I was crazy. I was still searching the school yard, but could feel her stare. I saw him again and this time I sprinted towards him shouting his name.*

"Johnathon, it's me, Isla, Johnathon," *he stopped, looked straight at me and then poof like a cloud of smoke he was gone again.* I woke up with my heart aching, deadened by hollow trails of emptiness. "I don't think I can handle this much longer," I whispered to myself. I was so tired of crying. I dug my head into my pillow. One thing for sure, that dream wouldn't happen, at least not in a school yard.

Maybe he just vanished because of the sunlight. Or, maybe I would never see him again. *No! No! Stop thinking like that,* I told myself.

Closing my eyes, I could see him lying on my bed reaching out to me. Then I saw him on his knee proposing, and remembered the joy and delight I felt at that moment. The pain of being without him was unbearable. My eyes got heavy so I gave in. Every time

I started to dream I woke myself up. With widened eyes peering across the room and staring at my closed window I fought the slumber for hours. His eyes were engraved on the inside of my eyelids. First I envisioned his eyes as they were before they dilated and his craving for blood grew. I was reliving every kiss and touch in my mind and felt every sensation. My hallucinations became more authentic and vivid as I pictured him lying on top of me. His teeth entered my flesh and my eyes rolled back in my head. Then he raised his head with blood dripping out of the corners of his mouth and down his chin. I wanted so badly to be with him that I fantasized about it coming true. I felt myself being drawn vastly into an entrancing state. My struggle was over and I dozed.

Chapter 15

My Awakening

*I*T WAS, MY DAY OFF. I SLEPT in til about 10:30, and couldn't remember if I had anything planned that day. Then it came to me. I was supposed to go shopping with Jolie and Betsy that night. I had been saving my money for Amsterdam, but maybe I had a little to spend. I'd just be able to buy one thing. Paying for the movie, popcorn, and whatever else was expensive enough. "I wish I had more money," I whispered to myself.

Suddenly the doorbell rang. "Surely, it couldn't be," I murmured out loud then jumped up and ran downstairs to find out who it was. I opened the door in my pink panther pajamas to see Lizzy standing there grinning.

"Lizzy, I was worried about you!" I sighed as I hugged her.

"I'm back," she replied with anxiety in her voice.

"How was your trip? I had no idea you were even going to Las Vegas."

"Yep! Spontaneous! I was given a ticket as a tip at my new job."

"New job, where are you working?"

"Jaggers!" she replied excitedly. "I made awesome tips on Friday night."

"So what you're telling me is you're working for my boyfriend!"

"Oh that's right! I guess I am!" She hadn't even put two and two together.

"This was on your door," she muttered, handing me a letter. Who do you know in Amsterdam?" she inquired. My heart pounded like a bass drum.

I snatched the letter out of her hand quickly and opened it. It read . . .

My Sweet Isla,

> *I can't take being away from you much longer. The pain is worse than turning. I thought you could use this. Please go out, have some fun and celebrate because I'm coming home soon.*

My heart stopped and then sped up so rapidly I thought it was going to vibrate right out of my chest. "He's coming home!" I yelled and started jumping around.

"Who, Johnathon?" she asked, puzzled as to why he was gone in the first place, but happy for me.

"Yes! Yes!" I waved the letter in the air flinging my arms in eagerness and excitement. Lizzy leaned over to pick up something up off the floor. But I was so ecstatic I barely noticed.

"Oh, you dropped this," she announced holding out a sealed envelope. I put it under my arm and kept reading.

> *I miss you and love you with every bit of breath or blood I consume. You are my only true love and next year on April 25th you will be my wife and so much more.*

> *Love forever and an eternity,*
> *Johnathon Daine*

I opened the other envelope. I pulled out the paper and opened it and nearly fainted. Lizzy caught me, but barely, we both fell against the couch.

"Whoa, are you okay? What is it?" She took it from my hand.

"Twenty five thousand dollars!" she screamed and gawked at it with her mouth open, completely speechless for a short time.

So was I.

"OH MY GOD! He's so amazing!" I could barely talk through the tears.

I thought loving him was all I could ever hope for but the anguish was so powerful and my heart was breaking without him.

"He's very cool---hey, and he's my boss. He obviously loves you girl," she stated, handing me the check back. When I tried to take it from her grip she wouldn't give it up. She played keep away from me for a few seconds. We giggled and wrestled around before she gave it back.

"Now let me tell you what happened to me," she sighed, looking serious all of a sudden and sitting up straight and still on the couch.

"What happened?" I asked, still in shock about the gift, but curious as to what was going on with her.

"Okay the tip I got, the ticket, was given to me by a rich and powerful man who comes into the club regularly. So I went and he introduced me to some very important people. I wore a different cocktail dress every night. I was there for a week and didn't even spend any of my own money. Then one night, I saw too much. I walked in on a murder. This guy, the one that tipped me, shot this other guy in the head, point blank. I was freaking out, but I acted like it never happened. That night I was wined and dined as usual then I woke up with this on my finger."

She had a look of disgust on her face as she held up her hand displaying the ring.

"Now I am married to a mob boss who just blew somebody's brains out of the back of his head. So I'm scared and I don't know what to do. He would kill me if he had to."

I just sat there, stunned.

"Where is he now?" I asked, trying to let it all penetrate.

"He is at the new house that he bought two days ago." She turned away and hung her head low.

"Where is this house?" I asked, grabbing her hand to get her attention..

"It's over off of Sweeten Creek in the Forest Lake district," she announced as water built up in her eyes.

That's where Preston Hill lives. I thought to myself. A chill shot through me as I recalled that terrifying night. What I could remember of it, anyway.

"Where does he think you are?" I asked, hoping he had no idea.

"He was shopping with his big stupid bouncer body guards and I ditched them. But it won't be long before he starts hunting for me."

"Crap! Now I'm going to have to get a gun," I declared, smacking the couch, making a low popping noise. "Do you want to stay here?" I asked, knowing she had nowhere else to go, and doing what I knew she would do, if the roles were reversed.

"Yes! Please. He can't trace me to you. But---Do we have to get a gun?" she sighed. I thought she was frightened by the thought of him catching up to her. She was very skittish and jittery. She sat in silence, shaking and staring at her hands. I watched tear drops fall and slide along her fingertips on the way down.

"Yes, of course you can stay here, but what about work?" I asked, putting my arm over her shoulder.

"You're right, he does know where I work," she admitted, trembling as she clenched my arm tighter with one hand, then ran her fingers under her eyes catching the tears with the other.

"What are we going to do?" I asked, spacing out and casting my eyes across the room, thinking intensely. "I know---we can take this money and go to Amsterdam sooner! We will leave next Friday. Until then we will get a hotel room somewhere far away from here. I just hope Johnathon gets home sooner so he can go with us, and keep us safe. Either way, we will protect you or I will have to get a friggin gun. You know what they say, it's better to have a gun and not need it then to need a gun and not have it. It looks like we are going to have to make a stop on the way to a hotel," I continued, thinking about where I could get one. *Oh yeah, Michael, I could definitely get a gun from him,* I thought to myself. Looking over at Lizzy I saw she was having a full-blown attack. Sweat was pouring from her forehead and she was breathing heavily.

"It'll be okay. Don't worry. Johnathon will be here soon and he will protect us." I slumped over and stared in her downward eyes and smiled til her attention raised and I was able to sit up tall.

She whimpered, "Where are we going?"

I sat tall and replied, "We're going to Amsterdam, baby!" I said it with posh, widened my eyes and smiled big. She smiled back as she ran her deep-purple polished fingers under her eyes to wipe her tears. "And also we have to stop somewhere, on the way to the hotel. A friend's house, his name is Michael Williams. He's a gun dealer, amongst other things.

"Let's go!" I chirped, walking towards the door. Glancing down I realized that I was so caught up in all that was going on, I almost left in my pajamas. "Wait, I need to change." I sputtered. "Let me put a little makeup on too. I won't take long." I murmured, taking the stairs to my room. She followed.

As we got to the top of the stairs I asked, "What is your new husband's name?"

We walked in my room and she immediately started helping me pack.

"Christian Steele, but he goes by Christophe," she replied as she bent over, gathering clean clothes out of a basket on my floor. She got clothes that she would like to wear, because she didn't have anything with her except her purse. I watched her try to shove a lot of things in a little bag. It was funny.

"You might need a bigger bag," I suggested, giggling at her as I dashed to my closet. I pulled out a huge black suitcase, and we packed if full. "Lizzy, go get my Bialage shampoo and conditioner from the bathroom." She did as I asked and threw in some other beauty products that we might need, while I put on some makeup. I finished a light touch up and then put my makeup in my purse.

"Let's get going," I said, dragging the suitcase down the stairs to the door. We loaded it in the car. "I forgot my purse," I yelled and then ran back inside to get it. Looking around to make sure I didn't forget anything important, I laid my eyes on my phone charger, "I can't leave without that," I reminded myself as I reached down and picked it up. As I walked back down the stairs, and went to the car I had a strong feeling I was forgetting something, but I couldn't think of what it was. I got in the car. Lizzy was patiently waiting and with a turn of the key we were off.

"By the way Mrs. Steele, you want to compare rings?" I asked grinning ear to ear as I held my left arm across my chest to show her.

"Can I see it?" she asked, then tried to take it off and I pulled my arm back. "You see with your eyes not your hands," I replied, grinning and watching the road. Her lips turned down at the corners.

I took a quick peek at her pouting face while trying to keep my eyes on the road "I'm just joshing ya. Go ahead," I sighed, smiling and holding my hand out again.

I nodded and she took it off. I swallowed hard as the ring left my finger.

"I like yours better, yours isn't as big and bulky as mine," she replied with a sour expression. "How did he do it?" she asked as she slid it back on and peered out the window in front of us observing the scenery. The trees were vibrant and bright as we headed down the back country roads into Transylvania County. The winding roads were causing me to feel a bit woozy. My problem was I hadn't eaten anything yet and motion sickness had always been an issue for me.

"What?" I asked as I rolled the window down trying to get some air.

"How did he propose to you?" she asked curiously. She wasn't panicking anymore.

"Oh that. I'm sorry, I just had a wave of nauseousness come over me." I took a deep breath in and held my head out the window.

"Are you okay? Do you need something to snack on? I think I have a bag of chips in my purse," she said as she picked her bag up off the floorboard and handed the chips to me. I opened the bag without a word and popped several in my mouth. With my mouth full of the dry potato chips I thought *Now I need something to wash this down.*

The feeling subsided some so I was able to tell her about the proposal. "We danced and kissed then he got on one knee and proposed. It was the most incredible night of my life," I sighed, keeping it short because of the way I felt. I smiled and drifted into a fantasy world. It was hard to concentrate on the road, so it was good that we were going to Michael's first. My mind was sort of spacey, not to mention the fact that I still felt like I could hurl..

"Feel any better?" she asked rubbing my arm softly. I shoved a few more chips in my mouth and nodded. "Where were ya'll?" she asked, leaning into my gaze, but conscious of not blocking my view.

"We were in Islathon," I replied, keeping my eyes on the road.

"Where is that?" she inquired with her head tilted to one side like a puppy.

"It's our own little world," I sighed as my thoughts began to drift off again.

"You're not going to tell me?" she asked sounding disappointed. She crinkled her nose and pierced her pucker, as she turned to look out the passenger window.

"If I tell you I will have to kill you," I replied with a straight face, but unable to hold it, I busted out laughing.

"Funny, come on tell me," she begged, sitting up in her seat and turning her whole body to face me.

"Okay, okay, Looking Glass Falls in Transylvania County."

"I have always wanted to go there," she admitted, slouching back in her seat.

"It's beautiful. There's a waterfall about sixty feet high. Purple flowers as big as saucers. White lilies and pink tulips around the waterfall. A perfect flat rock to dance on. A huge tree excellent for a picnic under it, and the best wine I have ever tasted, ever." I took a deep breath and sighed thinking about that night.

"Wow! That sounds amazing," she replied, staring ahead in awe as she pictured the place in her head.

"It was a magical evening," I replied, smiling through the tears developing on my pupils.

"So how is the intimacy, is he big?" she asked, seriously curious.

"The what?" I stammered and swallowed hard. "Oh, the sex, we don't have sex. He can't lose control too much," I sighed, not wanting to say too much more. Besides, she couldn't handle the truth.

"You have not had sex yet?" she asked surprised and baffled.

"No, there is only so much he can do. We have been to the brink of it many times, but not past that," I explained sadly, rubbing my eyes with one hand and steering with the other. The tears always caused my makeup to burn my retina. I can't find mascara that doesn't irritate my eyes.

"Why is he ill? Does he have some kind of disease that keeps him from doing it?" Lizzy asked mystified, placing her hand on my shoulder to comfort me.

"Not exactly, but it's driving me insane," I admitted, reliving the misery in my mind. "I want him so . . . so . . . so . . . bad." I sighed as the rush of our love barreled over me again and again. Once you have been bitten by love, YOU ARE NEVER THE SAME!

We pulled up to a black house with a red door and red shutters. I had not seen this house since my freshman year of high school. I went to some crazy parties in that house. I thought about all the times the cops had been called there as I threw the door open and got out of the car.

"Come on, you get to meet Michael Williams," I announced, motioning for her to come in with me. She sat in the car frozen. "Lizzy, what are you doing? Get out of the car and come in with me." She did, reluctantly and we walked up the driveway between several fancy cars to the wide, candy apple red door. I barely even tapped on the door and it opened by itself.

I yelled, "Hello, Michael." I stepped in and Lizzy followed, squeezing my arm and keeping very close to me. I peered around looking at the disarray of the place. There was trash scattered about like he hadn't cleaned up from his last two parties. It was a disaster. Then suddenly the lights went off and we were both slammed up against the wall. The lights came back on and there were guns held to both of our heads. The barrel of the gun was pushing mercilessly on my temple. It felt like it was going to make a permanent indention.

"Oh—I know you. How have you been, Isla?" Michael asked after recognizing me.

Michael was a cool kid gone bad. He had a buzz cut; he stood about six one. He barely had any fat on his body. He appeared as though he hadn't eaten in a while.

We had dated for a while in high school. But he had changed over night. Let's just say that the guns went to his head and our relationship went sour. We used to be head-bangers. Metallica nuts through and through, total metal heads. But now he teetered on the edge of just plain psycho. Also, he was a paranoid gun or drug dealer, depending on your preference. Back then he had dressed in tight jeans and a black concert shirts.

"Down," he motioned to the two men holding us. They let us go, and went to stand by the door. If looks could kill we would have been dead from their evil stares.

"I haven't seen you in years," he commented, looking me up and down licking his lips and then his teeth.

"You can say that again. You look completely different," I stated, making it obvious that I was checking him out. When we hung out before, he had long brown hair, and now he had a shaved head. He was more muscular than he used to be.

We hugged. He went to kiss me on the lips, but I turned my head.

"Hey, is that all I get," he asked, jerking my arm back. His cold hands shocked me.

"Yes!" I replied, pulling away from his grasp.

"Hey buddy those lips belong to someone else now. She's engaged," Lizzy hollered, pulling me towards her. I looked at her and smiled, touched by how protective she was of me.

"Really, who are you engaged to?" he asked, trying to look all tough like he was going to fight him or something.

"Johnathon Daine," I replied, rubbing my hand a long the back of my arms to get rid of the pain from being man-handled. The two bodyguards weren't saying anything. But they glared at us like panthers waiting to dive on their prey. The guy that had clutched my arms was wearing an entirely too small black tee shirt with white letters that read GOT GUN?. Talk about advertizing. Michael went pale at the mention of Johnathon's name, well even paler than he already was.

I could tell he knew of him.

"I know Johnathon very well," he admitted. As he looked at me I could see his eyes going jet black. He turned away when he saw me examining them.

"Michael, I need your help, I need a gun," I said, troubled, but trying not to look too desperate to him. Inside I was going completely out of my mind.

"It's Mikeal now," he enunciated, sounding almost barbaric.

"Okay, Mikeal, will you please give me a gun?" I asked, scared of him now because I knew what he really was.

"Sure, but it won't do you any good," he replied, turning away and walking over to a book shelf. He pulled a big white book out just a little bit and then stepped back, and stared at the wall, waiting for something."

Suddenly the wall opened up to a huge room. We walked into a room with walls covered in guns; machine guns, handguns, pistols. I wasn't an expert so I had no idea all the names, I just knew any weapon you wanted he had it.

A dagger caught my eye. It was silver with black onyx stones on the handle.

"How much for the dagger?" I asked, taking it off the wall. Holding it made me feel powerful. I displayed the dagger to Lizzy who seemed to be slipping back into panic. 'Are you okay?' I mouthed to Lizzy. She was shaking, crying, and standing on the other side of the room. I knew if I started focusing on her this deal might not go down, so I smiled at her giving her a caring expression and continued the conversation.

"It's around one-forty," he replied, watching my every move. He was still leering at me like he wanted to jump my bones. I was suddenly worried about Lizzy.

"Why so much?" I asked curiously and with a hint of attitude.

He leaned into me and said, "It's a very special dagger." He leered into my eyes. I couldn't look away, our stare was frozen.

We had a short telepathic moment. I knew what he was. But more importantly he knew who my fiancé was, so he began to hit on Lizzy. She started moaning and sobbing as he went near her.

"Back off!" I stepped in front of her with the dagger in my hand pointed at Michael's heart. His eyes glazed over like a foggy dark night. I could actually see clouds in them. It was like he had suddenly gone under a spell. I certainly didn't understand what was going on. Usually I'm the one in tears or freaking out.

He backed off from Lizzy. She looked relieved, and stopped moaning, turning it down to a faint whimper.

She leaned her head forward, "Get the gun... and let's get... out of here," she whispered in my ear. I only understood the 'out of here' part because she was blubbering so badly.

"Alright, how much is this gun?" I pointed to a medium sized black thirty two.

"I'll give it to you, pay me later," he said in a daze, almost like it wasn't him talking at all, like there was some other force he was obeying.

"I'll need some bullets," I announced, taking the gun off the wall and placing it in my purse. He handed me bullets, like he was on autopilot.

"Let me load it for you," he offered, taking my purse away. I got nervous. He took the gun out handing the purse back to me. I shook my head in disbelief. *Yep! He's definitely under a spell*, I thought to myself as I observed his mannerisms. I was fortunate that I had changed purses. Otherwise he might have seen my weapons and it would have ruined the whole deal. He loaded the gun and gave me a case of bullets and a carrying bag for the dagger and the gun. He snapped both weapons into the case. It was weird that the case was made for those two weapons. Very strange.

He handed it to me and I put it in my bag. He threw a case to Lizzy. She caught it, not meaning to. She cried hard and handed it to me like it was on fire. Lizzy had been standing in between a big tan chair and the wall since we got there. After tossing the case to me she went back to her cubbyhole.

I opened the charcoal grey case to see a small silver twenty two.

"Thank you!" I said, stunned. At that point I wasn't going to question anything. Knowing something else was in control of him made me relax a bit. "Thank you, Mikeal." I hugged him and said goodbye. I grabbed Lizzy and pulled her out of the corner and we headed towards the door. The two goons by the door weren't even there anymore. We walked out the door and got in my car. Lizzy was beginning to calm down some. She laid down in the back seat.

I know that both of our hearts were thumping hard. I felt a sense of power I had never felt before as we drove off.

"First, we need to go to the bank," I sighed as we pulled in the parking lot of my bank. I was lucky there was one out in that area.

I signed the check, put it in the box and pushed it up a chute with my drivers license and account number.

"Hello, Miss Van Burren, do you want to cash or deposit this?" the slightly bald man in the window asked.

"I'll deposit twenty-thousand. Go ahead and give me five-thousand of it," I replied, leaning my head out the window.

The man said, "I'm sending a slip through for you to sign." I took it out and signed it, put it back in the box and sent it up the chute.

"Have a great day, Miss Van Burren," the man said with a smile.

He sent it back through the chute. I pulled it out of the envelope, counted it and stuck my driver's license back in my wallet.

"Do you think five-thousand is enough for us both?" I asked Lizzy, glancing over the back seat at her.

"Maybe--- no I'm sure that's fine," she sighed, grinning as she continued wiping her tears. I had no idea what her major malfunction was. I pulled into a parking spot behind the bank.

"Now, we aren't going anywhere until you tell me what the heck is going on with you," I said assertively, getting up on my knees in the seat, turning my whole body towards her leaning up against it.

Lizzy had her hand over her mouth and tears still rolling out of her eyes. "I'M DEATHLY AFRAID OF GUNS!" she screamed, throwing her body into it.

"Oh! Why didn't you tell me? You know we need one though, right?"

She nodded as she sat up. "Ever since I was a little girl I have had a phobia of guns. I break out in sweats, cry and shake and I have literally no idea why. It must ...be something I'm blocking out.

Something I don't want to remember. So now you know." She sat there slumped over, staring at her hands for a minute or two. Then she reared up and whispered, but then got louder and louder with each word. "Would you please PUT THOSE WEAPONS IN THE VERY BACK! PLEASE!" She was screaming and it made my hair blow back from the power of her shouting air.

"I can do that!" I mumbled as I opened my door with my purse in hand. I pulled the handle up and opened the very back of my cruiser. I set my purse down and took the cases out and put them in a special compartment. I had never seen her so upset, so I decided it was better not to push the subject. *Let it be*, I told myself.

"What hotel should we go to?" I asked as I got back in the drivers seat, started the engine and slowly pulled out on to the road. She had moved from the back seat to the front when I got in.

"Let's stay at the Hyatt. I hear they have a good reputation," she replied calmly and then opened the glove compartment to get the map out.

"I would like to be near Islathon. I mean, Looking Glass Falls," I remarked while keeping my eye on the road.

"Is that in Transylvania County?" she asked, unfolding the map to find out which highway we should be on. "I'll call information and ask for a Hyatt near or off US two seventy-six by the Blue Ridge Parkway."

"Sounds Good," I replied, concentrating on the road. "Choose a lane, idiot," I yelled when the car in front of me cut me off and then just couldn't decide what lane he or she wanted to be in.

"I need a pen," she said.

"There's one in the glove compartment," I responded.

She looked and found it.

"Is there a Hyatt on U.S. two seventy-six or Blue Ridge Parkway?" she asked the operator on the phone. "Okay, can I get the address, please?" she asked. "Yes, I'm ready." She said it out loud as she wrote it, "6245 U.S. two seventy-six, two miles before the

Parkway. Okay, thank you," she closed her phone and put it down by her side. "Got it, it's right off the two seventy-six."

"Great! Oh no, I forgot to call Calvin and Jolie, and I forgot to leave a note for my mom. That's what I forgot," I realized as if a light bulb had flashed over my head.

"Calvin if you can hear me I am at the Hyatt in Transylvania County," I said out loud. Lizzy shot me a look of confusion. I acted like I hadn't seen it.

I grinned and asked, "Can you hand me my phone from my bag?"

I motioned to Lizzy that it had fallen behind my seat on the floor board.

She handed it to me. I saw that Jolie had called, so I called her back. Her voicemail picked up after the second ring. "Hey Jolie, I'm going to either have to take a rain check for tonight or you have to come to us. My friend Lizzy and I are staying at the Hyatt off two seventy-six. I'll get back to you in a few hours, talk to you soon. Bye," I closed my phone and set it in the console. "It all depends whether Calvin comes to the Hyatt, or not," I said.

"Why? Is Calvin coming shopping with us?" she asked.

"No, but he will protect us and drive us there if we want," I replied, facing forward.

"Well...are you going to call him and let him know?" she asked.

"I already did," I answered. She looked at me perplexed, but looked the other way when she saw how serious I was.

"Okay, whatever. Are we almost there?" she asked, getting irritated.

"Yes, we will get to two seventy-six in a few minutes." I only new that because I had seen a sign a little ways back that read seventeen miles to the exit for U.S. two seventy-six.

"When is your fiancé coming home?" she asked, smiling as she and observed the road and the signs passing.

"I don't know, he just said soon. It could be today or next week. I miss him so bad. I have a constant ache in my stomach. What was that address again?" I asked, changing the subject because my eyes were filling up with water and getting heavy. Plus we had just come off the exit.

"It's 6245 two seventy-six," she said, holding a section of the map in her hand with a bunch of writing on it.

"There it is," she pointed. The sign for the Hyatt stood out like a sore thumb. I noticed it at the same time she did. We pulled up to the front.

"So, do you want a suite or honeymoon suite?" I asked her as I dug in my purse for my wallet. I got out of the car and opened the back to pull out the suitcase.

"Whichever one you want," she yelled so I could hear her. She picked up her purse and got out.

"The valet will park the car," I announced, and just as I spoke a guy walked up in a dark maroon uniform.

"How are you ladies doing?" he asked, taking our bag.

"Good," we said in unison. I handed him a tip as we walked in. He was heading back out to move my car. He smiled when he saw the twenty in his hand. I lived on my tips so I knew how to tip very well, plus it didn't hurt that I had all that money now thanks to my beloved Johnathon.

When we walked in I thought *Man this place is nice.* The lobby was huge with plush black and grey striped couches to perch on while you waited. There was an enormous fountain in the middle. In the center was a sculpture of a beautiful woman holding a vase sideways, pouring water into it. We walked up to a shiny black marble counter. "We would like a suite for a week, with two bedrooms please," I said as I nodded and smiled graciously.

"Do you want a balcony room?" Again I nodded, but this time with my eyes. How will you be paying for that?" the dark haired lady asked.

"We'll be paying cash," I replied happily.

The lady shot me a disapproving expression. "We need to get a credit card and driver's license number please." I wrote my license number down on a form she provided and slid the form and a credit card across the counter..

"Can we put the room under a different name?" I asked, leery of anyone that might be eavesdropping.

"Sure, what name?" the woman asked with a staged smile on her face.

"Mrs. Smith---wait are there any people staying here now with that name?"

"Let me look." She typed in something on the computer.

"It would probably be better to put a first name, too," she suggested, sounding annoyed.

"You're right. Make it Sarah Smith?" I replied, putting my wallet back in my purse.

"Just Sarah Smith or Mrs. Sarah Smith?"

"Sarah Smith is fine. Thank you." I smiled and counted the wad of money I was holding in my hand.

"Okay, that will be nineteen hundred, please."

"Here you go," I replied, looking around as I pushed the money to her.

"Do you have a pool and what time does it close at night?" Lizzy asked, eying the front lobby.

"Yes, and it doesn't close. But we clean it about 4:30 every morning." After I had given her the money she became a lot warmer.

"Okay, thank you," I replied appreciatively.

"Here are your keys." She handed them to me; of course they were cards, not too many hotels have actual keys for rooms anymore.

"Go up the elevator to the eighth floor, your room will be a few doors down on the left," she said, pointing to the elevator.

"I want to go swimming, but we didn't get suits did we?" Lizzy asked as we walked to the elevator.

A tall fair-haired man overheard us. "There is an excellent gift shop here," he didn't take his eyes off Lizzy. I had never stayed at a hotel that had a gift shop.

"He was alright looking," she commented and crinkled her nose as we got on the elevator.

We went up to the eighth floor, got off the elevator and went to room eight oh four. I stuck the card in, pulled it out and the door opened.

"Wow, this is awesome," I said as we walked in and the door shut behind us. The two-bedroom suite was huge. The sitting area had a big red and dark tan couch and the kitchen had a balcony. As I was checking out our new pad, there was a knock at the door. I went to get it and looked through the peephole. I saw it was the doorman with our bag. I opened the door and he came in.

"Thank you." I smiled, giving him a tip.

"Thank you, ma'am," he said as he exited the room. When I closed the door. Lizzy was already on the couch watching TV.

"So, what's on?" I asked, jumping on the couch next to her.

"I don't know. What time is it anyway?" Lizzy asked, flipping through the channels.

I picked up my purse and pulled out my phone. I had three missed calls. Jolie, Mom and a number I did not recognize.

"It's 5:30. Should we go get some swimsuits, if they have any in the gift shop?"

"Yeah, that sounds good," Lizzy replied, excited about going swimming and anxious to go do something.

As we left the room we made sure we had a key and that the door shut all the way. I put the key in my purse. When we got on the elevator we saw there were two men already on it. They stared at us for a few seconds then introduced themselves.

"Hey, how are you ladies doing? My name is T-Bone and this is Marty. Where are you ladies going?" T-bone asked with a sinister grin. T-Bone had light brown hair, dark hazel eyes and must have been like six ten. I got a crick in my neck looking up at him. At the time we were talking to them all I could think about was Johnathon. T-Bone smiled at me, showing his perfectly white teeth and causing a chill to come over me. I moved away from him holding Lizzy's arm. She looked at me and could tell I was very uncomfortable.

Marty was of average height with dark brown hair, dark brown eyes and pale skin. As I began to figure out what they were, I started looking at the numbers getting anxious. When the elevator stopped, the door opened and they followed us off.

"Can we come with you?" T-Bone asked, following not far behind.

We walked faster and faster. Lizzy took my arm, "The pool is right there, let's hide in the women's locker room," Lizzy suggested as she pulled me in the door.

We entered the locker room and the door swung to behind us.

"Maybe we can swim in our clothes," Lizzy replied.

"I don't know if I want to swim. They might be out there," I said, scared and extremely jumpy.

"They definitely gave me the willies," Lizzy admitted.

"Maybe there's a back way out of here," I said.

I don't know what it was, but I was attracting more of them. Do I have a sign on my forehead that says *Vampire Wanna Be?* Or maybe they've been right in front of me all along. I must have been marked because Johnathon bit my lip.

"Let's go this way," Lizzy ordered, tugging on my arm.

"Okay," I followed her and she led us to a door leading outside. We opened it and went out, walked around the building and back to the front door and straight to the elevator. We hid behind the ice machine so when the elevator door opened we could check it out before getting in. It opened and the elevator was empty so we made a run for it. *Hurry door, close, close.* An elevator door just can't close fast enough when some blood thirsty non-humans might be after you.

We made it to our room without running into anybody. I put the key in quickly and opened the door, closing it behind us. I pulled my phone from my bag and called Jolie.

"Hey girl, what's up?" I asked. "Well, I don't know if we're going to be able to go with y'all." Just when I said that there was a knock at the door. "Jolie there's someone at the door. I'll call you right back. Okay. Bye." I closed my phone and tossed it on the couch.

Lizzy looked at me with her eyes wide and her mouth scrunched together. I walked to the door and looked through the peep hole.

"It's Calvin," I said, opening the door.

"Hi Isla, I have some news that is going to make you scream," Calvin said with a half grin, on the edge of a straight face.

"What?" Worry hit me hard, and then I told myself I was being neurotic to be nervous about *good* news. He paused and didn't say anything for a few seconds. "Please be good news," I whispered. "Well, tell me!" I shouted, almost coming out of my skin.

"I talked to Johnathon and he's on his way home." As soon as he said that he flinched. He knew I would scream.

"AAAAAH Yes! My man is coming home!" I screamed so loud everyone in the hotel must have heard me. I ran and jumped on Lizzy, who was now sitting on the couch.

"He's coming home! I am so excited," I screeched shaking Lizzy and jumping.

"That's great! I am so happy for you," Lizzy replied, rolling off the couch and on to the floor with me.

"So, when? When will he be here?" I asked Calvin as we got up off the floor.

"He'll probably be home by Wednesday night," he said with a smirk. I hugged him jumping all around.

"Do you still want to go shopping with your friends?" he asked. His words brought my head out of the clouds. My smile was a permanent fixture on my face.

"Sure, do you mind taking us?" I asked, trying to tone down my enthusiasm. But, I couldn't contain myself.

"Of course not, that's why I'm here," he replied as he scanned the room.

"Thank you!" I yelled and jumped up and kissed him on the cheek. "Let us change and get ready." Lizzy and I both went to the bedroom to get dressed.

"I know, can I wear your black jeans with that blue top you wore that night we went to Jaggers?" Lizzy asked, yanking stuff out of the suitcase with gusto.

"Sure, I'll wear my black capri's and red shirt with the tie on the shoulder." I announced as I found them in the pile of clothes. We both got dressed and refreshed our makeup and hair.

"I'm ready," I said, throwing the strap of my black bag of weapons over my head and pulling it snugly to my body.

"Let's go!" Lizzy hollered, grabbing her purse.

Calvin opened the door and we all walked out. We got on the elevator and before the door shut T-Bone and Marty stepped on. I felt safe because Calvin was there.

"Hey it's you two, where did you ladies go?" T-Bone asked. Calvin stepped protectively in front of us, staring him in the eyes. In that brief time of silence many thoughts were zooming through my head. *What's going to happen? What is he saying to them? When would Johnathon be home?* Well, whatever he said to him in mind conversation, it made both of them get off at the next floor without a word.

"So what did you say to them?" I asked Calvin as we exited the elevator.

Lizzy had stopped at the gift shop to look at something. Calvin turned to me and replied, "I told him you were both marked and you were the fiancé of Johnathon Daine. They knew who he was, so they left."

"Thank you so much, those guys scared us earlier. I don't know what it is, but I seem to be running into them more often now."

"You have always run into them, *us*. You just never believed or could see the signs."

"It's strange, though. I feel like I have a stamp on my forehead that reads *Vampire Wannabe*. Does it say that?" I asked with a smirk on my face.

"No, but you do wear a mark. You have been bitten haven't you?"

"Yes, he bit me on my lip a while back," I sighed as I pictured the castle, the party, that amazing night that I learned that he was an immortal. My breath caught when I thought of him standing in front of me and holding me tight.

"There's your mark," he replied, peering in my eyes sincerely.

"Hey Isla, you have to see this," Lizzy yelped and then drug me off to the gift shop. I grinned at Calvin and shrugged my shoulders as she pulled me away.

"What? Oh, I love it!" I yelled, picking up a Beatles shirt. On the front was the picture of them walking across Abbey Road, a classic. Definitely a must have. As I was going to the checkout a black shirt with red writing caught my eye. *Love at First Bite.*

I picked it up and bought them both along with some things Lizzy wanted.

"Girl, I'm going to owe you so much money before this is over with.

"Don't worry about it. You get by with a little help from your friends," I began to sing.

"You get high with a little help from your friends." we began to sing and in harmony. It sounded great. Everyone in the store just stared at us.

Calvin came in, "Isla aren't you supposed to meet your friends in thirty minutes? We better get going."

The older lady from behind the counter handed us our bags and replied "I like that song, too."

I giggled a little and replied, "Have a good night," as we walked out. I checked out a few more items on our way towards the door. But there was nothing else I had to have.

We walked out of the hotel to the limo sitting right in front. Calvin opened the door.

"Thank you Calvin," I grinned getting in after Lizzy.

"No problem, Isla," he replied, shutting the door behind us.

"Where are we going?" Lizzy asked as I settled in the seat.

"Well, we haven't really decided yet, maybe the Sky Club or Flying Frog

Café. I better call Jolie, so we can figure this out." I pulled out my phone and hit send since she was the last person I had talked to. "Hey girl did we decide on the Flying Frog or the Sky Club? The Sky Club, that sounds good. Are we still going to the movies too? Okay, we'll just cross that bridge if we get to it. Hey, why don't we go shopping first," I suggested. "Cool we'll meet y'all there. Okay bye." I closed the phone and sat back to relax a bit. Then it struck me that I didn't know where we were meeting if we were going to shop first. I was a little confused. Maybe she didn't comprehend what I said. Oh well, we'll go to the club first.

Melting into the seat, I closed my eyes and my head soaked into the soft leather and my mind wandered. The feelings I crossed before Johnathon swooped down and carried me away were not really feelings at all. But a mere glimpse of the light that would capture me. I felt like ever since Johnathon came into my life I had been awakened. Awestruck. Sometimes I felt like I had been asleep for the first nineteen years of my life and now suddenly my eyes were wide open. Then there were times I felt like I couldn't catch my breath, like any minute I would suffocate.

Chapter 16

My Returned Heart

*W*E PULLED UP TO THE SKY CLUB since we hadn't discussed where to meet for shopping.

We sat there comfortably, peering through the dark tinted windows out at the crowd that was watching our limo with interest. There was a packed patio and every face was turned in our direction.

"Hold on, Calvin. We'll wait here for a few more minutes," I murmured, observing the stretched necks of the patrons in front. We were attracting a lot of attention from the people standing outside waiting to get in. They were trying to see what celebrity was going to step out.

"Okay, I think we're ready," I announced with a little gesture to Lizzy who just shot me a thumbs up. Calvin got out and opened the door. Lizzy and I both fluffed our hair and checked our make-up. We weren't dressed to the nines, but we thought we looked pretty cute.

A funny thing happened when we exited the car. People began taking pictures. We posed and smiled for the camera it was kind of fun. I guess they thought we were supermodels or something.

Whatever or whoever they thought we were, we strutted our stuff.

When we opened the door to the club Jolie was standing there to greet us, enjoying the show. "So that was pretty cool. Who did they think you were?" Jolie asked and then gave me a hug. "I'm so glad you could come. It's been too long, girl.

"It's great to see you, too. I don't know who they thought we were. Maybe they thought we were models. We just decided to eat it up."

"I saw. How did it feel?" she smiled and placed her arms across her chest.

"It was pretty amazing actually," I answered. "Oh, this is Lizzy," I motioned with a sway of my head.

"Nice to meet you!" Jolie replied, shaking Lizzy's hand. They both smiled warmly at each other. "We're sitting up here, follow me," Jolie said as she turned and walked up a long spiral staircase to a balcony table where we could see the lights of downtown Asheville. The city lights were gorgeous from that height. The square wooden railings were decorated with little white lights. There were tall trees in big round pots sporadically spread out on the roof top.

As we approached the table Betsy saw me and stood.

"Isla! I haven't talked to you in so long. How have you been?" Betsy asked as she hugged me.

"I'm good. It has been a long time. Are you still doing art?" I asked as I sat down in the green and white striped, padded wooden chair and scooted up to the table.

"Yes, three of my paintings are hanging on the wall in the Asheville Art Museum, you will have to go and see them." Betsy suggested.

"Love too; I am so proud of you. Do you think you might want to help me with my CD cover?"

"What? You're doing a CD? It figures that you'd be doing something in music. I remember in high school you had a beautiful voice," she commented.

"Well, thank you. I hope I still do." I laughed a little and then went on, "We'll be working on the CD by the end of the year, hopefully."

"Do you have a band?" Betsy asked as she took a sip of her soda.

"Kind of, we're just starting it up. Well, we are talking about it anyway. I know it will happen, soon." I rolled my eyes at myself for explaining so little and so much.

"What's the name of your band?" she asked, staring at me intently.

"Isla and the Bloodsuckers," I replied, waiting for mixed reactions. Betsy's eyes brightened and she started quietly giggling and then went into a full laugh.

"That's cool, who came up with that?" she asked, giggling.

"It was Johnathon, my fiancée," I sighed, flashing my ring. "God, that felt good to say," I admitted, delighted that I could say it with dry eyes.

"Oh my God! That's beautiful! When do we get to meet him?" Betsy asked, excited to hear more as she ran her fingers through her dark brown hair with flecks of gold throughout.

"What happened to you at the party?" Jolie chimed in, after coming back from the restroom.

I looked at her then looked at Betsy.

"Soon you'll meet him. I need a drink of water my mouth is dry," I replied, changing the subject.

"So, what did I miss?" Jolie asked, sitting back down.

"Isla is starting a band," Betsy replied smiling and patting me on the back.

"You are, and the name is?" Jolie asked.

"Isla and the Bloodsuckers, isn't that cool?" Betsy replied.

"Why did you name it that?" Jolie asked, looking at me perplexed.

"My fiancé named it. He just thought it was cool, I guess." *If they knew why they would all be scared*, I thought to myself.

"Your fiancé? When did you get engaged?" Jolie asked in amazement.

"Last Saturday, April the 25th. Or was it a Sunday? I can't remember. But we are to get married on April 25th of next year. He's my dream come true. I'm so in love," I sighed, missing Johnathon something terrible.

"Where is he? Why isn't he here with you?" Betsy asked.

"He is out of town but he'll be back by Friday, or sooner hopefully. I can't wait!"

"Are you even going to introduce me?" Lizzy asked.

"Oh my! I am so sorry, Lizzy. I feel like a fool." I apologized, hoping she wasn't mad at me. "Betsy, this is Lizzy Phoenix," I sighed feeling awful that I had completely ignored her for so long. Lizzy shook her hand as Betsy introduced herself to her. "We haven't really talked since high school. Again, I am so sorry, Lizzy."

"It's okay; I know you were just caught up in the conversation," Lizzy replied, standing up. "I am going to the restroom. Be right back," she announced.

"Where is the waitress? Have you all already ordered?" I asked, having hunger pangs. I couldn't remember the last time I had eaten.

The waitress finally came over.

"Have y'all decided?" the tall blonde waitress asked.

"Yes, I'll have your chicken fingers basket with honey mustard and a salad," she had looked at me first so I ordered.

"What dressing do you want on your salad?" the pretty blonde waitress asked.

"Just four slices of lemon, please," I replied.

She looked at me strangely.

"I've never heard of anybody eating it that way," the waitress said.

"It actually brings out the real flavor of the salad without all the calories. Oh, and can I have a huge glass of tea?" I asked.

"I'll have the turkey club on wheat," Betsy chimed in, sipping her soda.

"How are your fried mushrooms and jalapeno poppers," Jolie asked.

"They're really good," the waitress said.

"Okay, I'll have both of those," Jolie leaned over to pick up her purse that fell on the floor.

"I'll have a mushroom burger with fries and a side salad," Lizzy said, pulling her chair out after returning from the restroom.

"What dressing do you want on your salad?" the waitress asked.

"Ranch would be good, thank you, oh and a large tea please," Lizzy replied as she tried to scoot her chair up so the waitress could get by.

After we ate and visited it was time to go shopping. When the bill came I took it and said, "I'll take care of the check." I always wanted to say that, if felt so good. I handed the waitress my card and drank up the last of my tea.

"You don't have to do that," Jolie and Betsy expressed in unison.

"I want to, it feels so good, plus I have never been able to before."

"Well, at least let us pay the tip," Jolie replied, digging in her purse.

"No, it is taken care of," I said, signing the receipt that the waitress had just laid down in front of me.

"So, where to now?" Betsy asked.

"How about Bellagio's Everyday," I suggested.

"That sounds great; I think they are having a sale today," Betsy agreed and Jolie nodded her head in approval.

"I've never been there before," Lizzy admitted, and then finished her tea.

"You haven't? They have great clothes and incredible prices," Jolie explained, looking at something across the room as we were walking towards the door. Preston was standing in the entranceway, waiting for us. He had some gashes on his face, but other than that he looked fairly unscathed. *If he only knew how lucky he really was,* I thought to myself.

"What is he doing here?" I asked with an expression of disapproval and a feeling of uneasiness.

"I invited him to come along," Jolie said smiling at me.

"What? I don't want to be anywhere near you," I yelled, poking him in the chest.

"Ouch! Why, what did I do?" he asked, feigning surprise.

I stomped to the door grabbing Lizzy's hand, taking her with me.

"Why do you hate him so much?" Lizzy asked.

"Because he drugged me and tried to rape me," I screamed loud enough so Jolie, Betsy and Preston heard. They all just stood there stunned. Lizzy hugged me and tried to calm me down.

"Johnathon saved me just like he always does," I cried. I began to get pissed that the water was filling my eyes. I stepped around Lizzy and walked straight for the car. Calvin was already standing outside of it holding the door for us.

"Hey, Calvin," I sighed as we were getting in the car. He could tell I was angry. Lizzy got in behind me and put her arm over my shoulder. I looked down and cried. My nerves were getting the best of me, because I began to shake.

"Lizzy, go ask Betsy and Jolie if they want to ride with us," I commanded in a low monotone. She got out of the car and I sat there trying to recall the night he attacked me. I was drawing a blank. All I could recollect was going to put my purse down in a room at the party.

Lizzy came back and said they are talking to Preston, but they would be right over. I was fuming but it began to dissipate as I thought of Johnathon.

Betsy got in saying, "He said you came on to him and he turned you down." When I heard her say that, the steam of anger rolled out of my eyes and ears.

"Oh! You believe him? If you believe him then we'll go alone," I growled.

"No, I don't believe him. He drugged one of my friends at a party in the tenth grade," Betsy admitted, leaning back in the seat. "So, I don't doubt he did it. He lied to everyone and my friend got a bad reputation," Betsy explained.

I wiped my nose and the tears that escaped the corner of my eyes.

Jolie got in. "Okay, let's go!"

"Do you believe me?" I asked Jolie.

"Yes! Absolutely! He's a bastard," she replied as Calvin shut the door.

"Good!" I peered up at her and smiled. "Let's go shopping," I replied, changing the subject.

Calvin rolled down the black tinted privacy shield. "Where to next?" he asked with a grin.

"Bellagio's Everyday," I answered. The girls nodded in agreement.

Calvin grinned at me through the rearview as he started to drive.

We drove down the road a ways then stopped. "We're here," Jolie announced, looking out the window. Calvin opened the door and we got out.

"Wow, this place is huge," Lizzy remarked as we got out of the car and slowly entered the store. When we walked in, there was a tall slender faceless mannequin wearing a gorgeous ankle-length candy apple red dress with a sheer chiffon material with sparkles all over it and a red scarf that matched. I pictured myself in that very dress in Islathon with Johnathon. I stood and stared at it in awe. A lady with long curly red hair approached me.

"Would you like to try it on?" the lady asked smiling as she took the exact dress off the rack and held it up.

"Yes! I would love to," I replied. She handed it to me and I went into the dressing room. I put it on and it fit my hourglass figure like it had been made with me in mind. I did something I had never done before. I didn't look at the price tag and continued shopping. It was an amazing feeling.

I ventured over to the jean section and tried on a few pairs. But didn't like the way any of them fit. As I walked by the dressing room I saw Lizzy come out after trying on a black pair of pants with zippers all over them and a hot pink shirt that tied on one shoulder.

"You should definitely get that," I commented. She hadn't noticed me standing there until I spoke.

"I would if I could, but I have no money, remember?" she explained as she changed back into her clothes. She came out of the dressing room empty handed.

"Aren't you forgetting something," I said, looking at her with a smile.

"What do you mean?"

"I mean, get it. It's on me."

"Are you sure? You don't have to do that," she replied. Her eyes got glossy as I grabbed them from the dressing room. She threw her arms around me and held me tightly.

"Thank you! You're such an awesome friend," she announced with a sniffle as she wiped her eyes with her wrist.

"You're welcome! I love spending money on my friends. When I have it, that is. We caught back up to Jolie and Betsy who were already in the checkout line. I think all I bought was red and black. I also bought a long black straight skirt with a red satin corset with black designs in a lace pattern. Jolie got a few pale blue shirts with white pants and a few pairs of jeans. Betsy bought a few multicolored poet blouses and some pants. It was definitely fun to shop because I had the money to splurge for myself and a little on Lizzy. We paid for our stuff, got all our bags and headed for the door. I did feel a little guilty that I hadn't purchased anything for Betsy or Jolie. But they had their own money.

Calvin greeted us, as we walked out. He took all of our bags and put them in the car for us.

"Thank you, Calvin," I said as I got in.

"He's so cool. How did you end up with a driver and a limo anyway?" Jolie asked, getting comfortable in the seat.

"He works for my fiancé and he's a good friend of mine," I replied as I got cozy.

"What did you think about those jeans I got?" Betsy asked.

"Which ones? I only saw the navy blue dress pants you bought," Jolie replied. "Oh, I remember which ones, the jeans with the zipper up the ankle, they were so cute," Jolie answered.

I was in a fantasy world as I looked at my dress and imagined myself wearing it and dancing in the moonlight with Johnathon. The hawks were back just thinking about it. I had not felt them in a long time, not since we first started seeing each other.

"I'm tired," Lizzy announced as she laid down on the long couch-like seat and closed her eyes.

"Oh, are we keeping you up?" I asked, joking around.

"Shut up!" she yelled and then kicked me playfully.

"Lizzy, ouch, stop!" We were just playing with each other trying to get a rise out of one another.

"Hey, y'all want to hear a joke?" Jolie asked, already kind of giggling as she thought of it.

I nodded and Betsy said, "Sure, I'd love to hear one."

"There are these two older ladies that work at a hospital. They both smoke, but they have to go outside to smoke. One day it was raining and one of the ladies pulls out a condom, cuts off the end of it and puts it over her cigarette so it wouldn't get wet. The other lady says, 'That's cool, where did you get that?' The lady replies, 'At any drugstore.' So the next day the lady goes to the drugstore and asked the pharmacist for condoms. He asks 'What size?' She says, 'Oh I don't know, anything that fits a camel!'

"That's funny," Betsy laughed.

"Isn't it?" Jolie asked, cracking up.

Lizzy and I laughed so hard we couldn't say anything. We all just sat there and snickered a while.

"So, where do y'all want us to drop you off?" I asked.

"At the Sky Club. That's where my car is," Jolie replied.

"Okay." I knocked on the privacy window. Calvin rolled it down.

"Calvin we need to drop Jolie and Betsy off at the Sky Club."

"Sure, are you positive you don't want to go somewhere else?" Calvin asked.

"I'm sure, I'm tired. Thank you, though," I responded.

Jolie and Betsy were talking about going out somewhere else, but Lizzy and I were wiped out.

We pulled up in front of the Sky Club.

"I had a lot of fun. Thank you for dinner. Call me so we can hang out again soon," Jolie said as she hugged me and got her bags together.

"I'll call you soon. You're welcome. It was great seeing both of you again," I added and looked at Jolie and Betsy.

"Hey girl, call me about the CD soon, so I can start working on it," Betsy reminded me as she hugged me.

"You know I will. I have missed you, so don't be a stranger, okay," I responded, smiling.

"I won't. I'll call you soon," she promised as she gathered her bags and got out.

"Bye," I said.

Jolie popped her head back in and murmured quietly, "Tell Lizzy it was nice to meet her."

"I will. See you soon," I whispered so as not to wake Lizzy. I put my head back and closed my eyes.

Suddenly Calvin said, "Hey, I think he'll be here sooner."

"Really, when?" I sat up, wide awake at the news. "How do you know?"

"I read his mind. He's closer than I thought," Calvin announced, grinning.

"I can't wait to see him!"

"See who?" Lizzy awoke, groggy and stretching her legs.

"Johnathon is coming home sooner than Friday! I am so excited!" I yelled, almost reaching for my breath.

"That's great! Is he going to stay at the Hyatt with us?"

"I don't know, maybe if he wants to. What am I saying? Wherever I am he will be. I don't plan on letting him out of my sight," I declared. Calvin and Lizzy laughed.

"Isla, what am I going to do? I know he is probably looking for me." Lizzy asked with terror seeping through her eyes.

"It will be okay, we'll hide out for a while," I replied, consoling her. "Does he know where your parents live?"

"No, I don't think so," she murmured, looking through her bag of purchases.

"What if he looks up your last name in the phone book?" I asked.

"He can't. I lied about my last name. I told him it was Munson."

I shot her a strange look and asked, "What made you do that?"

"I don't know. I felt like I needed to," she sighed as she bit her lower lip.

"Good thing you did. Otherwise he would be at your parent's house. How did you get on a plane without showing your ID? What about work could he get your last name by calling and saying he was someone else?"

"It was a private plane so I never had to show an ID. Surely they wouldn't give out that kind of information over the phone. I mean places of employment aren't supposed to do that," she gasped with panic in her eyes.

"You better call work and tell them to not give your information out to anybody," I insisted caringly.

"Yeah, I guess I should," she agreed, pulling her phone out of her purse.

"What's going on?" Calvin asked from the front, hiding the fact that he knew she was running from someone.

"Is it okay to tell him?" I asked Lizzy.

"Sure," she replied, waiting to talk to her manager on the phone.

"Okay, here's the scoop. Lizzy went to Vegas and was forced to marry someone. He's in the mafia and we're pretty sure he's looking for her right now. That's why we're staying at the Hyatt."

"I was wondering why I picked you up there," Calvin sighed, looking at me through the rearview.

Lizzy closed her phone and sat back in her seat, breathing a sigh of relief. "It's cool, somebody did call earlier today and asked a lot of questions, but they wouldn't tell him a thing," Lizzy reported.

"That's good. I was worried," I replied yawning.

"Do you think Johnathon will be home tomorrow?" I asked Calvin.

"Let me check, I'll let you know by the time we get to the Hotel."

"Okay, thank you, again. Calvin, you're a really good friend."

"What does he mean by he'll check. Does he have his number, why can't you call him?" Lizzy asked with a perplexed expression.

"No, not really it's kind of a psychic thing," I muttered.

"Really? That's cool. Do you have any psychic abilities?" Lizzy asked curiously.

"Yes, but only in my dreams. When I dream something it usually comes true. Maybe not quite the way it happens in my dream, but it resembles my dream closely."

"How come I'm just finding this out? We've been friends, best friends, for so long," she asked, disappointed with amazement in her wide eyes.

"I've just recently noticed or acquired this gift. Since that first night at Jaggers when Johnathon came into my life."

"He must be psychic, too. That explains how he knew your real name," she declared.

"Yes, from that first kiss, my life has been sent in a whirlwind and I'm doing my best to ride the wave."

"That's cool, I'm ecstatic you have found true love, you deserve to be happy," she replied, putting her arm around me and her head on my shoulder.

"You will too, honey. Someone wonderful will come along and snatch you up before you know it."

"Hope so, someone's got to get me out of this predicament I'm in," she sighed, holding her head in her hands.

"Maybe, you'll find you a young handsome lawyer to help you through this," I replied, softly stroking her hair.

"Good idea, I'll make a call," she joked as she looked up at me smiling.

It wasn't long after that that the car stopped. "We're at the Hyatt," Calvin announced.

"Thank you for driving us, Calvin. I appreciate it."

"You're welcome, Isla, anytime."

We got our bags together and put our purses on our arms. Calvin opened the door and we got out. Lizzy walked to the door.

"Do you have your key?" I hollered to her.

"Yes," she yelled. She could tell I needed to talk to Calvin. "I'll go up to the room. Thank you, Calvin. I'll see you around," she called with a smile then turned around and walked in the tall glass automatic door.

"So, what's happening? Is he close?"

"He'll be here late tonight," Calvin replied.

I immediately got giddy. My heart began to race. And then Calvin looked up from the ground and gazed at me with a serious expression and grabbed me by the shoulders. I winced when I felt his icy touch.

"There is something else, though," he said and looked back down at the curb, and still held on to me. He peered back up at me with concern written in his eyes. "He got called to go before the council again, so he has to go back," Calvin divulged with hesitancy.

"What? I thought he already went in front of the council!" I blurted out in shock.

"He did, but they have changed their minds."

"What do you mean changed their minds? What does that mean?" I was starting to freak out.

"I'm not quite sure. You'll have to talk to him about that." I could tell he was nervous about it, and he could sense my tears were on the verge of pouring down.

It was weird to be happy and scared to death at the same time.

"What should I do?" I began to cry.

"Go back up to the room, rest up, and he'll be here late tonight," he responded comforting me. His smile softened my anxiety some. But, I still felt like I was going to hyperventilate.

"Breathe, Isla. Don't get yourself all worked up when you don't know what's going to happen," he asserted, giving me a hug trying to calm me down. "Go up, order room service, relax, he'll be here soon," he added with a playful smirk.

"Okay, thanks! What time do you think he will be here?"

"About 12:30 maybe," he estimated. "Now go in and relax," he ordered cordially.

"Alright, thank you again," I sighed as the door automatically closed. I turned and headed to the elevator hoping no one would see me. I was trying to hide my eyes, which I knew by now were black and smeared.

I set my bags down and pulled my purse strap up tighter on my shoulder then pressed the number eight on the elevator wall and the door began to close. Then it stopped and I felt a sense of dread. T-Bone got on and he was all alone. The door closed and I stood there nervously fidgeting, not knowing how to react. He smiled and had a kind of haughty air about him. Suddenly he reached over and hit the stop button. I freaked out. I swallowed so hard I thought my tongue might have gone down my throat.

He got up right in my face. "I'll turn you if you like?" he asked in a deep, throaty growl. It made my heart shake it was so low. Not knowing what to do, but remembering what Jee Cee had taught me, I thought *sweep his feet out from underneath him*. So I punched him in the chest with all the power and love I had in me. The force of the blow slammed him into the wall and the elevator started up again. And before he could get up the doors opened on my floor. I slipped my arm in the handle of my bags. There was a *Wet Floor* sign by the door. I picked it up and threw it at him hard. He deflected it back at me, but the door closed in time.

Sprinting to my room, I dropped my bags and stuck the card in quickly. The light turned green so I opened it. I hastily picked up my stuff and managed to squeeze in before it closed. I heard it click as it locked behind me.

Wow, that was close, but why did I fight? I should have said okay. No, I would never want any other vampire's teeth on me, except Johnathon's. If and when I die it will be in oceans of passion no other way, only swept up by the waves in his eyes.

Lizzy was asleep on the couch. I tiptoed past her on the way to my room careful to not wake her. As I entered my temporary room I realized I was beginning to miss my real room and my parents.

Remembering I needed to call my mom before it got too late, I picked up my purse and fumbled for my phone. I dialed it and it rang twice before going to her voicemail.

"Mom, I'm okay. I'm staying with a friend. I'll be away awhile, and will explain later. Love you, Isla."

I know it was vague, but it kind of had to be just in case anyone intercepted her messages.

"Dear Lord, please protect my mom and dad and keep them as far away from this chaos as possible," I prayed out loud. In my head I was pessimistic, seeing only treacherous things unfolding. In my heart I was positive that God would guard me and protect the ones I loved. My head and heart were quarreling profusely.

I fell back on the bed, staring at a clock on the wall. Was it time yet? I thought about the old saying *a watched pot doesn't boil.* I needed to do something.

Sitting on the side of the bed I pulled the drawer of the bedside table open and took out a hotel notepad and a pen. I began to write.

My Returned Heart
My heart is not in view
I am so lost. I don't know what to do
When would my heart be back
Feeling nothing but emptiness and lack

I see the light even in the night
When you're holding me oh so tight
But it seems so long ago you cradled me in your arms
You're not here to caress and protect me from harm

Anguished and torn waiting for my returned heart
To come home, but where was my home, anywhere you
are and where we can be alone

Desperate for that feeling once again
Never wanting it to end
The tingles, the hawks deep down inside
Praying that you would always be by my side

After writing it I looked at the clock and saw that it was midnight. Where was he? My heart yearned for him and I was fighting to stay awake. What if I fell asleep and didn't hear the door? *I can't go to sleep,* I told myself sternly, and went into the living room.

Lizzy wasn't on the couch anymore, she must have gone to bed. I went into the kitchen put a mug of water in the microwave. I hit 2:19, just like I did at home. I looked around for tea bags, and couldn't find any, so I picked up the phone and dialed the front desk.

"Front desk, how may I help you?"

"Hello this is Sarah Smith in 804, could you please send up some tea bags?"

"What kind would you like?" he asked in a raspy monotone voice.

"Do you have any Chinese tea?" I asked, waiting for the inevitable answer, no.

"Yes ma'am, Wu-Yin tea, it is a very popular tea with our lady staff and guests."

"You're kidding. That's the tea I drink at home," I replied, completely surprised.

"That is great, is that what you would like or do you want to hear other teas we have?" the man asked.

"No, thank you, that'll be perfect," I answered glancing often at the clock on the coffee maker. It was 12:32 and even though he was only two minutes late my heart beat slowed and became faint.

I had been thinking awful things, like what if he changed his mind about me, or what if he was being held against his will by his so-called brother Sigrid? What if - what if, every crazy idea that popped in my head was more far-fetched than the last.

I was startled by a knock on the door.

"Yes! He's here!" I shrieked and skipped to the door and opened it without even looking through the peephole, which was completely idiotic considering the dilemma we were in.

"You're here!" I jumped into his arms, straddling his waist. He kissed me. Everything disappeared, we were in Islathon again, standing by the waterfall with the flowers in full bloom and the smell of white lilies permeating the air.

"Did you order tea bags?" a man in a uniform asked as he cleared his throat to announce his presence.

"Yes," I answered, climbing down Johnathon.

"Here you go ma'am," the short squatty man said.

He handed me the box, then grinned a little. He looked at us both twice and turned around and walked off.

"Thank you," I called, hoping he heard me.

"How could you ever think I would change my mind about you?" he asked, picking me up like he was carrying me over the threshold. He kissed me and the door opened by itself. He carried me in and the door closed behind us. Staring in his eyes, I knew I was home. My heart had returned.

"I love you, Isla. I have missed you terribly," he sighed, his voice breathy and sultry as he gazed into my eyes.

"Please don't ever leave me again," I pleaded with tears of joy rolling down my face. "I feel dead without you, being away from you hurt beyond pain," I revealed as I explored the waves crashing in his eyes.

He set me down on my feet and pulled me close against his cool body. His body was so cold the sensation burned, or maybe that was the fire building in us. He kissed me and slowly moved down my neck. I didn't flinch like I used to. I leaned my head back as he kissed down my neck to my chest then kissed my neck again. I felt him let go, like he was going to lose control at any minute. He would finally do it, or so I thought.

He stopped abruptly, looked at me and whispered, "I have control. I told you when it would be that I would suck life into you," he breathed in a vast whisper. He gazed at me and I could feel my blood boiling over so he could drink me in. His voice and breath were enough to turn me into vapors.

"Is Lizzy asleep?" he asked, his voice alluringly arousing.

"Yes," I took his hand and led him into the bedroom.

As we walked in I thought about what Jee Cee had taught me. So thinking about lying down on the bed I took his hand like I was leading, then I threw him on the bed and jumped on top of him.

"Whoa, you have been practicing," he grinned and I saw a reflection of myself, swimming in his eyes. It mesmerized me breathless.

"It worked in the elevator earlier, too," I sighed.

"What?" he asked.

"Yeah, this guy T-Bone stopped the elevator and told me he would turn me if I really wanted him to. I thought I would sweep his feet out from under him and then I punched him in the chest as hard as I could. He hit the wall hard and I got away."

"That's good. So he was in the elevator tonight?" he asked, his jaw tightened and his eyes narrowed as he became edgy.

"It's okay, you're here. I'm so happy, the anguish was unbearable," I gasped, leaning down to kiss him. In one instant he was on top of me. He overpowered me and I let him. We kissed a lot more until I laid my head on his chest. Right before I closed my eyes I thanked God for my returned heart.

Chapter 17

Dream Dragon

THE MORNING LIGHT STREAMING IN THE balcony bay window shone down on both of us. I woke up blocking my eyes, and sitting up a little, I noticed he was gone. But, I could still feel him. Sunlight was filling up the room, visiting every corner.

"Johnathon, are you there?" I called out, bewildered. The sound of his voice startled me.

"I'm here," he sighed. I gulped when I felt his icy hand on my arm.

"Where? I can't see you," I breathed, not knowing what part of him I was touching.

"It's what happens in the sunlight," he whispered.

"I feel you, but I can't see you ...this is weird. Kiss me," I demanded. Closing my eyes and feeling his soft chilled lips on mine electrified me. When I opened my eyes we had moved into a shadow, but I could see only half of his face.

I jumped up quickly and ran to the balcony window and pulled the drapes closed. It was dark again, so I leapt back into the bed.

"Good idea," he sighed, and then he started kissing my hot skin with his freezing lips, sliding lightly up my arm from my wrist to my shoulder and then my neck.

"There you are! My prince has returned," I whispered, and caught a glimpse of the waves in his eyes, erupting.

"I always wondered what would happen in the sunlight," I confided.

"Well, now you know," he replied, not knowing whether to be proud or ashamed.

"That's a cool thing though, being invisible. It doesn't help in the dark, though. I mean if you're trying to sneak up on somebody you usually do it in the dark, right? Or is it something you can control, but you can't control it in the sunlight?"

"Something like that. Now stop talking and kiss me," he sighed.

"K" I breathed, lying back down.

"Now where were we?" he asked, licking my naked earlobe. It made me giggle.

"Even though you haven't really bitten me all the way and drank my blood, every time we're together you drink me in til I'm consumed," I uttered in a raspy whisper.

"I want to consume you, to have you in me always. I've never wanted anyone as much as I want you. Not in my whole existence," he avowed, gazing deeply in my eyes.

"I'm ready, bite me now, don't make me wait any longer," I begged, wanting it more than anything in my life, ever.

"No, I told you when it'll happen, you have to wait." He was upset, but understood my yearning and frustration.

"I will taste you again," he whispered and growled at the same time, overpowering me like a freight train. He kissed me hard and long, and then I wrapped my teeth around his skin and bit down, but not enough to break the skin. He tried to pull away then kissed me aggressively. The sharp pain in my lip moved through my body as blood ran down my chin. I didn't struggle like I had before. He began to pull away and I pulled him closer to me, hindering him from letting go. Suddenly he jumped up, his eyes piercing black, blacker than space without stars. He paced around the room.

"You need to get something to eat," I said, wiping the blood from my lip.

"Yes, I suppose I do," he growled.

"You can't work at prisons anymore, can you?" I asked.

"Yes, or maybe I'll just go over to the bad parts of town and when someone gets murdered I'll feed on the killer," Johnathon sighed sharply, then smiled with his long pointy teeth exposed and traces of my blood still on them. To see him like that just made me want him that much more.

"That's a good idea. But, not now! I want you to stay with me."

He took my arm and threaded me up to him and licked the blood on my neck that I had missed, licking all the way up to my lips. I closed my eyes as he kissed me again. I could feel him wanting more and then he turned his head and rested it on my shoulder.

"I want you, Isla," he affirmed, in a husky, vastly dark tone.

"I need you, Johnathon, with everything that I am."

Just then there was a knock on the bedroom door. I opened it.

"Hey guys, I'm not disturbing you, am I?" Lizzy asked, knowing she was. Her eyes were wide in shock.

"Good morning Lizzy." I said, as I hugged Johnathon tight.

"Hello Lizzy, it's good to see you again," he greeted her.

"Isla, why are you bleeding?" Lizzy asked, protectively.

"Oh, I bit my lip badly," I explained as I put my hand to my lip and wiped the blood. "I was sure it would have stopped by now," I mentioned in a blasé tone, like it was no big deal.

"I'll call the front desk and get some bandaids," Lizzy stated, picking up the phone in my room.

"No, I'm sure it will stop. Besides what would I look like with a big bandaid on my lip? Don't worry about it," I said nonchalantly.

"Okay." She stared at me in disbelief.

Johnathon went into the bathroom, got a wash rag and brought it to me.

"It's a good thing the towel is red," I observed as I applied it to my lip.

He giggled and Lizzy just shut the door hastily.

"Speaking of food, you need to eat some breakfast," he suggested, picking up a menu on the dresser by the door and handing it to me. I rushed him knocking him on the bed. Sitting on top of him, I opened the menu.

"I'll have a Johnathon on a platter please with some Johnathon on the side," I said jokingly.

He chuckled a boyish laugh and replied, "Isla, you're too much." He took the menu away from me and threw it across the room.

"Your wish is my command!" he promised, pulling me down to him. In a flash he was on top of me, kissing my neck and the top of my chest.

"Your wish is my command? What does that mean? If that were so I would already be a vampire," I sighed, with a hint of anger.

"Isla, stop. The time will come.î

"If you don't make it soon somebody out there might get to me first," I reminded. "I don't want just any vampire to bite me. Besides, they could just kill me."

"Stop being so melodramatic. I'm here to protect you," he asserted.

"And when your not? What will happen then?" I yelled.

"It looks like you have done a pretty good job so far. Jee Cee says you have a natural magical spirit and with a little more training you would be unstoppable."

"He said that?" I asked astonished as I sat up away from him.

"Yes he did! But, it was something I had seen the first time I gazed in your eyes at Jaggers. I knew you had a magnetically charged mystical aura around you and that was what drew me to you."

"I felt the same way about you, but I felt that it was bad to feel that, like taking a forbidden drug. I even heard a loud, daunting voice in my head that told me to get the heck out."

"Do you feel like you should have listened?" he asked, pulling me back into his arms.

"Yes," I replied with a straight face.

A look of shock flashed across his eyes.

"I'm just joking! I didn't live until you came along. I love you," I whispered, kissing his chest, his neck, and then his lips. When I closed my eyes, I could see us as stick figures of light getting brighter when we touched.

"I wish we could lie here forever and kiss, and just let the world go on without us," I sighed as he began kissing my neck again.

"That would be incredible," he replied, pulling my red shirt up and kissing my belly.

"You're torturing me," I whispered, but I was screaming in my head. I looked down at him and pulled him back to my lips.

"You don't know what torture is. That's what I'm trying to keep you from," he sighed.

I rolled my eyes.

"Don't roll your eyes at me," he mumbled, running his lips up my arm.

It gave me goose bumps. He didn't even look at my eyes to know that I rolled them.

"I'm hungry and I need some hot tea," I said, getting up.

"Well, I guess I better go feed. It probably won't take long to catch me a killer," he said, sitting up on the edge of the bed and putting his shoes on. Which seemed to be the only piece of clothing either one of us ever took off.

"I'm going to the kitchen," I announced as I opened the bedroom door. Lizzy was sitting on the couch watching TV and looked at me with a concerned expression..

"Is he hurting you? Did he hit you? Is that why you were bleeding?" Lizzy asked lovingly. I kind of giggled.

"No, you know I would never let anyone do that to me."

"Do what to you?" he asked, walking into the living room. I put a mug of water in the microwave and started it. Johnathon came up behind me and wrapped his arms around my waist.

"Hit me," I replied with a grin.

"Oh, she thinks I hit you?" he whispered as he leaned in and gently kissed my neck. I turned around quickly to kiss him.

"Yeah, she just loves me and doesn't want to see me get hurt," I explained as I looked around him at Lizzy. She smiled.

"Lizzy do you want to order room service?" I asked.

"Sure, that sounds good. Where is the menu?" She got up to look for it and found one sitting on the counter.

"It's almost 11:00. Do you think they're still serving breakfast?" she asked as she stood there reading the menu.

"I don't know, call them and ask. If so, just order me two eggs sunny side up, and a lot of bacon," I ordered as I fixed my tea. Johnathon turned me around.

"Baby, I need to get going. I'll see you in a while."

"Please be careful," I whispered in his ear and slid my lips down his neck. He kissed me and his lips lingered with mine. I wrapped my legs around his waist.

"You two need to go back to the bedroom," Lizzy remarked as she gawked at us. I tried to get down, but we were stuck, the button on my pajamas got caught on his belt buckle. We started laughing while we were kissing which just made us laugh more.

He gazed in my eyes and I didn't want him to go.

"What time will you be back?" My heart was already aching at the thought of his absence.

"Probably around 2:00 if everything goes well," he replied, staring at my lips and eyes. "Maybe we can do something tonight," he suggested, playing with my necklace. "Where is the necklace I got you?" he asked with a staged pout.

I was so lost in his eyes I didn't even realize he'd asked me a question.

"Isla, you do still have it, don't you?"

"Yes, what? Yes, I still have it," I answered starry eyed, and feeling scattered.

He smiled at me, laughed a little then kissed me on my forehead and then my lips and whispered, "I need to get going." He rested his forehead on mine and gently held his hand under my chin directing my eyes to his.

"Okay, I'll see you soon," I sighed, not letting go of his waist.

"Isla, I have to go, so I can attack you later tonight," he whispered in my ear.

I just stood there, lost in a fantastic daze as I looked up at him and grinned ear to ear. He peered past me at Lizzy.

"Lizzy, take care of my girl. I sure hope the both you have some fun today," he expressed, turning around to walk towards the door.

"Yeah, I'll see you," Lizzy replied trying not to get distracted from her task of ordering room service.

As he got to the door he turned and stared at me and mouthed "I love you." I whispered it back and he opened the door without touching it as usual, and closed it behind him. Lizzy was to busy talking on the phone to notice his phenomenal ways. Every time I saw it I inhaled in awe of his gracefulness.

"Do you want some orange juice?" Lizzy asked, talking on the phone.

"Sure, that sounds good," I murmured. I continued staring at the door in a daze. I took a deep breath and put my hot tea back in the microwave because it had gotten cold.

"The food will be here in twenty minutes or sooner," Lizzy told me as she came over to the light sand-colored kitchen bar. She pulled the tall black stool up to it which made an annoying screeching noise as she moved it. I was stirring my tea and had to stop until the noise did. The sound got to me like someone had ran their nails down a chalkboard.

"You two look so in love. Y'all look good together, too." Lizzy gazed at me. I could see a twinge of sadness in her eyes. She wanted the kind of love that Johnathon and I shared. She definitely didn't want to be running for her life.

"Thank you. We're beyond in love. By the way, will you be my maid of honor?"

"Yes! I would love too," she hollered gloriously as she came around the counter and hugged me. "What color do you think our dresses will be?" she inquired.

"I'm thinking black with a white and red corset."

"That sounds beautiful. Do you mean a black skirt and white blouse with a red corset?"

"Something like that," I murmured as I sat down and sipped my tea.

There was a knock at the door and we both stared at each other with wide eyes, even though we knew it was probably room service. Lizzy got up, went to the door and looked out the peephole. "It's room service," she announced, opening the door. I went to the door with her.

"Breakfast is here!" A tall, skinny man with blue eyes wheeled a cart into the room. I went to Lizzy's side.

"Come on in. I am starved," I murmured, standing aside to make room for the cart.

Lizzy eyed the cart and agreed, "Me too."

He sat the platters on the bar and said, "You ladies have a great day."

As he pushed the cart towards the door I handed him a tip. "Here you go, thank you," I said.

He glanced down at it. His expression changed dramatically and his voice was decorated with sarcasm as he said, "Thank you." Then closed the door behind him.

"Well, I guess that wasn't a good enough tip," I observed and laughed and shrugged my shoulders as I sat back down.

"How much did you give him?" Lizzy asked, pulling the chair out to join me.

"I gave him a twenty."

"WHAT! I'm sure he didn't give you attitude over twenty dollars. That's ridiculous. I'd be grateful to get a twenty dollar tip from a table of three or four, plus I'll bet he just pushes the cart, he probably didn't make the food." Lizzy got a little upset because of his cockiness.

"It doesn't matter, let's just eat," I sighed, picking up my fork and digging in. For the next twenty minutes we didn't say much except yum and mm. It was a great breakfast. I sat there thinking about whether or not I would miss food. I came to the decision that I would, but knew that I had trouble remembering to eat as it was, so I couldn't miss it that bad.

"What do we do with the trays?" Lizzy asked.

We both got up and went to sit down on the couch.

"I'll put them outside the door in a bit. I'm just too full to move from this spot." I muttered, as I got comfortable. My head was on one side and Lizzy's on the other and our feet met in the middle. It was a big couch.

"This is what they call comfortably numb," Lizzy sighed.

"No, we will really experience that in Amsterdam." I took a deep breath, melting into the couch.

"Your right. It'll be so awesome! I can't wait," she agreed. I had no idea what we were watching on the TV. We were falling out, and soon we were both asleep.

I began to dream. *I was hiding behind some big boxes in a warehouse, feeling scared of what they would do if they caught us. Where is Lizzy? I thought. I couldn't see much because there were no lights on. The only light in the room was from a sky light, but I couldn't tell if it was dark out or if the light that shown through was from a street light.*

"Lizzy," I whispered. I heard nothing.

A light came on in the distance, toward the front of the warehouse. I heard voices, three different voices speaking English with thick Italian accents. mixed. They kept switching back and forth, but even their English, I couldn't understand.

"Lizzy, where are you?" one of the men shouted as he cocked his shot gun. My heart was beating so loud in my ear, I just knew they could hear it. At least they didn't have Lizzy, I thought. I needed to find her quickly, before they did. Turning around, I headed to the back of the warehouse, hiding behind huge boxes, crates, furniture in clear plastic, and stacks of lumber tied with red rope. My wrists hurt and I could see indentions from rope engraved in my skin. From the looks of things, we had somehow gotten away.

"Lizzy, can you hear me?" I whispered sharply, but as quietly as I could.

"Yes, I'm here," she replied softly, but with gusto. I promptly followed the sound of her voice.

I looked everywhere, behind chairs, and columns of boxes and in empty crates. I still couldn't find her.

"Lizzy, where are you?" I shouted as quietly as I could.

"Shush! I'm up here!"

Looking up and to the side of the warehouse I saw some stairs. I spotted her hand waving at me, sticking out of a small hole the size a tea cup Chihuahua could fit through at the bottom of the door. I ran as fast as I could, trying to be silent as I climbed the stairs. I clenched her hand, letting her know I was there.

"Go back down the stairs and just before you reach the bottom on your left is a doorway. Go through there and then up the spiral staircase, hurry," Lizzy ordered, with confidence in her voice now that I was there. I did exactly what she said. When I got there I found her on the floor on her back with her hands in the air tied to a long metal pole. She could not get to the end of the pole because there were boxes piled high. To make matters worse there was a samurai sword dangling from the ceiling, about to impale straight through her head. By the looks of things she had tried to knock the boxes over and had hit the sword, which was now hanging by a very thin string at the end of the handle.

"Untie me quickly," Lizzy demanded franticly. I urgently pulled at the knot, it wouldn't budge.

"Lizzy, I'm going to have to cut it," I sighed, searching for something sharp.

"Hurry," Lizzy cried with tears rolling down the side of face and into her ear and hair. The place looked to be a beat up tool shed. I located some big wire cutters, hanging on the wall. I took them down from the hook.

"Hurry, the sword is moving," Lizzy cried, knowing any second that thing would pelt into her skull. I stuck the sharp edge of the cutters in between her skin and the rope.

"Do it!" she commanded squinting her eyes.

"I might cut you," I gasped.

"I don't care, just get me out of here," she ordered, terrified and exhausted.

"Okay," I squeezed on the two wooden bars and heard a deep snap.

"AAAWWW," she screamed. It did cut her, and it was bleeding pretty badly. I pulled and pried at the rope til finally it loosened around her wrists and hands. I jerked her out of the line of fire as the sword plummeted down and slashed through the badly painted hard wood floor where her head had been. She hugged me tightly and I put my hand on her cut accidentally, but was it an accident? I couldn't even be sure that cutting her wasn't something I meant to do.

As I held my hand out in front of me staring at the deep red blood dripping from my hand, I had the unbelievable desire to taste it. Lizzy jumped up and started wrapping her wrist with some dark towels she found stacked in the corner of the room. I made sure she wasn't looking, and slowly moved my hand to my mouth and stuck out my tongue, licking life. Closing my eyes I could feel that one drop coursing through my body, causing me to feel lightheaded. I really did like the way it tasted.

Peering up I noticed Lizzy staring at me. "What are you doing? Let's get out of here!" Lizzy demanded, disoriented and dizzy.

"Nothing, I just got woozy from all the blood," I explained, pushing off the wall that I was leaning up against.

"Great, don't you pass out on me. I've lost a lot of blood, I don't think I could carry you. Let's go. Follow me," she commanded, having no idea which direction to go. She looked in all directions and then shook her head like the room was spinning.

We risked a glance out a window that overlooked the rest of the warehouse. We didn't see or hear anything.

"Come on," I said, taking her arm. We set out down the stairs to the back wall and ran back and forth, both of us going in different directions. The warehouse was huge.

Bang! Bang! Bang! Shots were being fired at our heads. We ran back to each other and found a tall white door. We pushed down on the handle but it wouldn't open.

"Please open," Lizzy cried, gasping for air and freaking out. I stepped back about two feet and took a running start and kicked the handle. It opened.

"Thank God," she sighed, sprinting outside. I shadowed her swiftness. Turning a corner we ran directly into three angry mafia men holding guns that seemed to be matching their size. They just stood there sneering at us. We had come to the realization that every breath we took could be our last..

Suddenly my eyes flew open and I fell off the couch. Lizzy was still sawing logs. I got up off the floor and went to the kitchen. I caught a glimpse of the time on the microwave. It read 4:30. "Holy crap, did we sleep for 4 hours?" I said out loud to myself. Where was he, why hadn't he returned yet? A million thoughts were zooming through my head, none of them good. I went into the bedroom to change out of my pajamas. I pulled my clothes out of the suitcase and placed them in drawers and on hangers. After trying on several tops, I went with a red satin, short-sleeved shirt and some black Capri's. I put my hair up in a ponytail then changed my mind and took it down. I decided to curl it and then sat on the bed to do my makeup.

Glancing up, I saw a shadow on the balcony. I jumped up and moved the curtain to see Johnathon leaning up against the railing. It was a covered balcony, so he was in the shade.

"How long have you been out there?" I asked, opening the sliding glass door.

"I have been watching you awhile," he replied, wrapping his body around me, and kissing me sweetly. "I've missed you Issy," he whispered, kissing me on the tip of my nose. I had been called Issy on and off throughout my teenage years, but it never sounded as sensuous as that. We kissed and played for a few hours with the occasional halts here and there. I wanted so badly to get past those invisible boundaries. I got a little crazy trying to push him over the edge. I wrapped my teeth around his icy skin and clamped down. He overtook me, kissing me madly.

Chapter 18
Don't Leave Me Now

WE NEED TO GET OUT OF HERE and go do something," he sighed, jumping up and blocking his face.

"Johnathon, just do it already, I'm ready now," I demanded as I observed the blood on my hand from my lip. It didn't hurt as much, this time. What did hurt was the gut wrenching yearning of wanting to be with him forever, and the fact that he wouldn't follow through with it.

"No, I can't. Now get up and let's go do something. I know Lizzy is edgy to get out," he mumbled, still facing the other direction. I was furious, and the tears began to swell in my eyes. "Come in the living room," he murmured, shutting the door behind him. He quickly returned and said, "Clean up and come out here," he murmured then closed the door again.

Lying there crying, I held my hand in front of me. Blood was dripping; it was a lot more than last time. I had an urge to taste it, so I did and before I knew it I had licked my hand clean and hungered for more. I could feel the blood coursing through my body, like I had in my dream, but it was my own so it wasn't the same feeling. Or was it? I got up and went into the bathroom.

Looking in the mirror I noticed my lip wasn't bleeding any more, but I still had blood on my teeth. I shrugged it off, thinking it was from my lip, then I cleaned up and pulled off my red shirt that had been spotted with blood. It was a good thing it was red. I replaced it with a black lace shirt with a white camisole under it. As I reached for the door knob a sharp pain hit me like a Mac truck. My knees buckled and I fell to the floor, writhing in pain. The torture of my insides felt as if there was a chainsaw slicing me from the inside out. Johnathon must have heard me hit the floor, because he opened the door.

"Isla, are you okay?" he asked, shutting it behind him so as not to alarm Lizzy. He scooped me up and placed me on the bed. As he did the collar of his black shirt moved and I saw my teeth marks. I had definitely broken the skin. It was his blood on my teeth.

"Did I hurt you?" I asked as the pain shot through my body like fiery lightening burning my cells from the inside. "AAAhh! Ow! Ouch, this really hurts," I cried, breathing heavily trying to block the pain. I had never felt labor pains before, but imagined them to be a lot like this. But, I couldn't imagine a mother going through this pain more than once. This had to be worse.

"No, Isla, but you did swallow some of my blood," he said, softly brushing the hair out of my eyes as I lay there, still til the next sharp cripplingly pain scraped through me.

"Finally, I will be a vampire," I gasped, through my tears.

"Not too fast. I still have to bite you, and you have to make your first kill to become what I am," he grimaced while I screamed as quietly as I could. I didn't want Lizzy to be startled.

"You mean…that wasn't enough? I still have to wait?" I breathed as the salty translucent liquid over flowed and ran like a waterfall down my empty face.

"Yes, I'm afraid so. The pain you feel is your blood fighting my blood, like a war."

"How long will it last?" I asked, out of breath from the agony.

"Just a little longer," he replied, lying down next to me.

"I'm sorry I bit you," I sighed, hardly able to speak.

"No, you're not, but that's okay," he whispered, squeezing me tightly.

"I'm so afraid of losing you, I thought if I could push you to attack me then there would be nothing Jeziaka or anyone could do and you would be mine forever."

"I am yours forever," he breathed, holding me, his body was glued snugly to mine, the pain subsided some. I couldn't breathe as I gasped to inhale. But, the pain was fading and the difficulty of breath didn't matter anymore. He read my thoughts, because I felt his embrace loosen. I took a few heavy breaths, now that I could.

"Don't let go. I'm starting to feel better," I sighed, taking in only shallow breaths. Can we---just lie here...and never go anywhere?" I breathed focusing, on every word that left my mouth. His icy hand was resting on my chest just below my neck. I pulled it in to me and slid my fingers in between his. He was spooning me and I could feel the cold from his body all the way down mine.

"Eventually the hotel will kick us out," he whispered, chuckling quietly as he leaned his head over my shoulder.

"I know-but I'm tired of fighting with the world," I moaned, letting go of his hand and doubling over with my head in my hands faintly sobbing.

He was silent for a second or two. I listened to my whimpers and cried hard as another paralyzing torment shot through me.

"Maybe... I should go away...and let your life return to the way it used to be before I came along," he sputtered, sitting up and facing away from me.

"No! No! Don't you dare!" I roared in agony. His mention of abandoning me hurt worse than the pain I was experiencing. "Now that you're here I could never go on without you." I sat up on my knees and threw my arms around him and rested my head in the hollow of his neck as I yanked him back to me. "I'm tired, but I would fight for you forever," I cried, crawling on top of him.

"You're so beautiful and amazing, Isla." he whispered, lifting his hand up to gently caress my cheek. It never failed, no matter how many times his ice blue hands touched my scorching skin, I melted into butter. In the time before him something cold touching my skin would have caused me to recoil or yelp. So much had changed.

"Are you feeling better? Is the pain still coming?" he asked, kissing me on the forehead as I leaned down to him.

"Yes, the pain is fading," I sighed, as I began to relax.

"If the pain is going away why are you still shedding tears?"

"I don't know," I sniffled. "I guess the thought that you would actually leave me is more gut wrenching than the pain itself. Just please don't ever say that again. I would fall apart," I sighed and then wiped my eyes with the side of my hand.

"I would love to say that I would never leave your side. But the truth is *Oh be still my heart,* I thought as I swallowed hard hanging on his every word, but wanting to tune him out if he was about to say something I didn't want to hear. "I have to go to work sometime," he sighed and I gasped. *Breathe Isla,* I told myself.

A fever of relief washed through me and I buried my head in his chest as he wrapped his arms around me..

"I must warn you," he breathed. My eyes opened wide and I held my breath as I thought in the back of my mind, *He also has to go before the council, again.* I stared at him, waiting. "You'll see and feel changes in the days to come," he explained, gazing in my eyes. His voice was breathy and hypnotic. I stared so far in his eyes that the future became the past. I could see an eternity of him and I, together. But, I didn't know if it was my mind playing tricks on me or my destiny unfolding before my very eyes.

"What kind of changes?" I asked as I gently touched the back of his cool hand with my fingertips, drawing invisible designs in his skin.

"Your vision will become very vivid. You'll see colors around everything and everyone," he whispered staring in my eyes. After all I had seen in his eyes I wondered what he could see in mine. We laid down next to each other on our backs holding hands. I blinked my eyes, and when I opened them he was on his side looking down at me. Without warning of any movement he ran his chilly fingers lightly across the inside of my arm. It sent little splinters of shock shooting throughout my body. It was electrifying and made me want him, terribly.

"Do you mean like auras?" I asked, kissing him sweetly. The sensation of his voluptuous, cold, wet lips to mine was pure ecstasy. I wanted to crawl up inside him and hide from the world.

"Yes, have you ever done any ecstasy?" he asked, smiling big. He read my mind and threw out the same word I had just thought. I squinted my eyes and gaped at him profoundly.

"Yeah, I think---I did my junior year at a party."

"Do you remember anything about it?" he asked, playing with the lace fabric of my blouse and flashing his beautiful white teeth.

"I recall rainbows and tracers around everything. I also felt euphoric when my own hair grazed my skin," I sighed breathing deeply as I laid back looking up at the white textured ceiling.

He grinned mischievously and said, "That is how you'll begin to see things. Your hearing will become more intense, too.

"You mean, I will hear birds and dogs from miles away?" I asked, rolling over on my side to gaze at him. He put his hand on my back under my shirt. I jerked and screamed in shock then giggled. I was feeling giddy from his cool touch. Especially when he touched me where I was the warmest.

"Yes, it gets to you at first then it will become second nature," he whispered as he snickered at my reaction to his touch. "Your dreams will morph into airy hallucinations so vivid that you will feel like you're awake but you'll be dreaming," he explained.

I thought for a moment, then peered around the room in silence. I laid my head on his chest. "So, when will I see, feel, and hear so intensely?" I asked, nervously fidgeting with my hands as I lay there curled up to him.

"Probably by tomorrow, but it could come sooner. It all depends on how fast my blood works its way through your body. And judging by the beat of your heart, it could be soon," he commented nonchalantly. I laid back on my side and he put his hand on my chest to feel my heartbeat. I put my hand over his and held it close. I was scared and excited all at the same time, kind of the way I felt when he kissed me that first time at Jaggers. Petrified and thrilled!

"I'll be right here to help you through it," he promised, enfolding his glacial arms around my body, flipping me over so he was looking down at me.

"Promise?" I cried, gazing up at him taking in every inch of his milky skin and exploring every mile of his eyes.

"I promise," he replied as he cupped his fingers under my chin and kissed me. "By the way, Jee Cee and Lexi want us to do something with them this weekend. Jee Cee is chopping at the bit to work on music, and Lexi just wants to hangout with you.

I opened my eyes, "Okay," I cleared my throat. "Sounds great, I'm anxious to get *Isla and the Bloodsuckers* going."

"Me, too. We need to get out of here. Let's go do something," he suggested, standing up. I got up on my knees on the edge of the bed and jerked his arm back, catching him off guard.

"Why? I want you all to myself," I sighed in a playfully whiny voice, kissing him passionately, trying to persuade him otherwise.

"Baby, we'll go to Islathon tomorrow night and you will have me all to yourself," he promised.

"Alright---I have a hot new dress to wear." I smiled suggestively, shaking my shoulders from side to side.

"OOoo," he breathed and his eyes widened and sparkled. "I can't wait to see it," he said, pulling me up to him, up onto my feet. We kissed and then went into the living room. Lizzy was on the phone and she looked mad. She slammed the phone down.

"They're going to fire me if I don't go into work tonight! And I can't because Christian might be there looking for me," Lizzy shouted.

He smiled calmly, "Call them back," Johnathon said sternly. Lizzy hit redial.

"Let me have the phone," he demanded as he grabbed it from her hand. She felt the coldness of his skin, and shot him a strange look. Then she looked at me with a baffled expression and a crooked smile.

"This is Johnathon Daine, Lizzy will be out until further notice and she will *not* be fired. Thank you." He hung up. "That's that!" he said, smiling at her.

"Thank you, Johnathon," Lizzy smiled back, genuinely relieved.

"Don't worry, you'll have a job there when we get all of this cleared up," he said, standing behind me with his chilled arms entwined in mine.

"I don't see how this will ever be over, unless they are dead, or God forbid, they kill me.

"No need to worry, Johnathon will protect us," I promised, turning to face him with my arms all over his body. He returned my affection.

"How? They have guns, big guns," she said with deathly fear written in her eyes, twisting the phone cord around her finger so tightly it was turning a bluish purple color. She stared off into another part of the room as if a part of her, had predestined her own doom.

"You'll see," he said, with ominous undertones, giving us that award winning smile I loved so much.

"Now, where do you ladies want to go this evening?" he asked, raising his eye brows in an enticing way. He held me and looked at Lizzy. Then he gazed in my eyes. I was lost. I felt week in the knees as I sat down in a chair behind me at the kitchen bar.

"Why don't we go to the Flying Frog Cafe? I've heard they have great food and entertainment," Lizzy suggested, thrilled that we were going somewhere.

"Sounds like a plan, Calvin will be here in about twenty minutes." Johnathon agreed, bending down to kiss me, his freezing hand sliding to my nape under my curly auburn hair, giving me a chill.

I hopped up from the chair. "I need to go fix my makeup," I announced, realizing that I had cried it all off.

"Me, too. Can I wear that navy blue skirt and the shirt that matches?" Lizzy asked.

"Sure, I think I'll wear my new black pencil skirt, and... I'll see what to wear with it," I spouted.

"You two go get ready," he said, leaning into give me a big, sweet kiss and smacking me on the butt as we walked away.

"Ow," I yelped because it caught me completely off guard, and it hurt. There's that vampire strength again.

We got all fixed up and pretty, and went into the living room. Calvin and Johnathon were waiting for us patiently.

I guess Calvin had brought him a change of clothes because he was wearing a deep red long sleeve button up shirt with black pants. He looked so hot standing there, his long dark brown curly hair gently falling over the collar. I threw my arms around his neck and kissed him. Then I turned to face Calvin.

"Hi Calvin. You look nice," I said, giving him a hug. He was wearing a sapphire blue long sleeved shirt and dark blue jeans.

"Hey, Isla. How have you been?" Calvin smiled and then turned his attention to Lizzy.

I put my arms around Johnathon's waist and said, "Better now that my man is home." Calvin and Lizzy smiled at me.

"You look beautiful, my sweet," Johnathon whispered, pulling me up off my feet to kiss me.

"Once again we match." I observed as he set me down. I was wearing a deep red blouse that hung off of one shoulder and a black skirt. Oddly enough Calvin and Lizzy also matched, both wearing royal blue.

"You look lovely, Lizzy," Calvin said, kissing her hand. She looked at him mesmerized by his brown eyes. Johnathon and I watched them for a few seconds then looked back at each other. We could see sparks igniting between the two of them.

"Let's get out of here," Lizzy said, feeling a bit stir crazy and cooped up. As we walked through the hallway to the elevator, Calvin had his hand on the

small of her back. Johnathon held me close when the elevator door opened and he saw my facial expression change drastically when I saw Marti and T-Bone standing there. Johnathon strapped his arms tightly around me, as he read my mind and knew who they were. Marti and T-Bone didn't even glance our way and then they got off on the next floor.

When the door closed we all laughed.

"OOoo," Lizzy trembled shaking her shoulders and head. "Those guys give me the creeps," she announced

"That was T-Bone wasn't it?" Johnathon asked, covering up the fact that he already knew, so Lizzy wouldn't be suspicious.

"Yes, did you see that cut on his nose? I did that," I bragged. I was proud of myself and the fact that I didn't fall down and cry. As terrified as I was my head was quite clear during that whole incident. But, I was surprised that I was able to fight him off.

"Good job, baby," Johnathon said, kissing me.

"Yeah good job, Isla." Lizzy said and Calvin nodded his head and agreed. They were standing close together. If anybody was worthy of my best friend it was indeed, Calvin. I was anxious to see them hook up.

When we got to the car Calvin held the door and Lizzy's hand delicately as she got in, their eyes were fixated on each other. Just before I got in Johnathon swept me up in his arms and kissed me long, so long that Calvin got in, but not in the front seat.

I was lost again, every kiss led to a magical trip. Closing my eyes I could see galaxies, black holes, and other universes. It was incredible. Everything was heightened and illuminated. I felt like I was on cloud nine, scratch that cloud nine million. Then something began to change, the illuminations became tracers of rainbows. Dizziness rushed me and I began to fall, seeing it in front of me, everything in slow motion. I would have crumpled to the ground if Johnathon hadn't embraced me. The movie played out as I lived it and watched it at the same time, so vivid I felt intoxicated.

We hadn't noticed the crowd forming outside in front of the hotel, everyone was staring at us when I glanced over. I could read their minds. "A forty-something year old lady was thinking *Wow, what romance*. A man getting out of a cab with his tongue hanging out was thinking, *He's going to get some tonight*.

A young teenage boy with his mom and dad was getting out of a Lexus. The parents averted their son's eyes, but dad got into it, thinking of his mistress. That was all in one quick glance. We gave them a show for sure. When we got in the limo we must have caught Calvin and Lizzy off guard, they were intimate. I was just pleased to see the both of them happy.

"I have to go drive now," Calvin sighed, sad to leave her side.

"Keep the privacy window down," Lizzy said to him as he got out. Calvin began driving, but kept staring at her through the rearview. It's a good thing that Calvin's a vampire; otherwise we would have probably crashed. He was definitely on auto-pilot.

When we arrived at the restaurant it seemed like Calvin was in the backseat before the car came to a complete stop. He got in and sat next to her. I could tell she had been consumed by him in the same amount of time it took for me to be lured by Johnathon. It was almost instantly and all it took was one kiss.

Johnathon kissed me, distracting me from what they were doing. "Lets go in and give them some privacy," he whispered, but he didn't need to I had already read his mind, and was getting my purse.

"Lizzy, y'all come in when you're ready," I said as we were making our way out of the limo. She nodded, never taking her eyes off of Calvin.

"He lives by the code, doesn't he?" I asked when we got out.

"Yes, he wouldn't hurt her," he replied, taking my hand leading me to the door of the restaurant then holding it open for me. He could have opened the door with his mind but he didn't want to display his powers to everybody. I had never been to the Flying

Frog before, it wasn't what I expected. It was actually quite quaint. In a weird way it felt familiar. A dark haired lady with a welcoming smile took us to a lovely corner table with candle light. Johnathon pulled out my chair and we both sat down. He held my hand in his, gazing deep in my eyes, while I looked at the menu.

"I'm going to have the grilled chicken salad with their house dressing," I announced.

"Sounds good," he sighed, not really meaning it. I grinned because I knew he was just saying that for my benefit.

"Have you ever had food?"

"Yes, it was bland and it didn't satisfy me at all," he said, getting up. My eyes followed him wondering where he was going. He circled the table and came back around to face me holding his hand out. "Would you like to dance?" he asked suggestively.

"I would love to, but do you think they are going to come in while we're dancing and not know where we're sitting?" I asked, slowly standing up.

"They'll be fine," he sighed, taking my hand and leading me to the dance floor. When we got out there they were playing club music I'd never heard before. The song ended. The next song I knew very well. He wrapped his arms around me as we moved to the music. We were dirty dancing to *Head Like A whole* by Nine Inch Nails. It was so hot. Then a wave hit me of rainbow lights and beats getting louder and louder. I closed my eyes and went with it. Our moves were so fluid it was hypnotic. He dipped me, kissed my neck, and then licked all the way back to my lips, kissing me erotically while we danced. I wanted him so bad it hurt. The song ended and I couldn't catch my breath. We headed back to the table. He pulled my chair out and I sat down, but felt as if I was going to pass out. My vision was entirely too vivid, causing everything to spin. It was extremely unnerving.

"Are you okay?" he asked, knowing what I was going through.

"Yes, it's just too much," I said, holding my forehead with my hand and looking down at the table, trying to make sense of it .

"You'll get used to it," he whispered, still standing over me.

"By the time I get use to it I'll be a vampire, right?" I sighed peering up at him squinting my eyes from the bright rainbow lights.

"Maybe," he replied, smiling slyly.

"What do you mean by maybe?" I asked, my voice edgy and sharp.

"Its okay baby, I just meant you might be used to it by then," he said staring at me intensely as he sat down in the chair across from me.

"Alright," I sighed. "I thought---" That was all I got out, Calvin and Lizzy walked up to the table.

"Did you already order?" Lizzy asked as Calvin pulled the chair out for her and she sat next to me.

"No! We were dancing," I replied, looking at her with a funny expression on my face as I fixed her hair in the back. Calvin smiled at me mischievously when he saw me playing with her hair.

"We thought we were going to have to come get you two," I said, eying them both playfully.

Lizzy whispered in my ear to go to the ladies room with her. We got up, Johnathon and Calvin stood. The way a gentleman should do, but something that was very rare these days. Johnathon hugged me tightly and kissed my cheek then my lips.

"I'll order for you, baby," he said.

"Lizzy, what do you want to eat?" Calvin asked, leaning in to kiss her.

"I'll have what she is having and a glass of merlot," Lizzy announced, grabbing my arm.

"Merlot for me, too, please," I said as we walked away.

Lizzy told me of their romance in the car and how he kept pushing her away or stopping in the middle of making out. I just smiled and didn't say anything.

"I really like him a lot. Is that weird?" she asked, smiling big and squeezing my hand.

"No, not at all. Calvin's a great guy. I think you two look great together," I said through the bathroom stall.

We both did our business, then washed our hands and checked our faces. I fluffed my hair and ran my finger under my eyes to wipe away any makeup that was smeared.

"What if it ends badly? It would be awkward for me to hang out with you and Johnathon," she stated, seriously. She gritted her teeth in excitement.

"Don't worry. I don't think it will, I have a feeling about you two. This will be perfect. We'll all hang out together. We'll have an amazing life," I expressed, reassuring her.

"You think so?" she asked as she opened the door. I was seeing major rainbows of light, and her voice was blaring. My heart was pounding so hard it caused me to hold my ears. Boy, when it came in waves it was ferocious. All of that and a sense of power, but I was scared to venture there. We got back to the table and sat down to our food. I just loved coming back from the restroom to find my food waiting for me. I was very hungry so I picked up the fork and started chowing down.

After we ate Calvin asked Lizzy to go talk. They went off somewhere.

Johnathon leaned into me and whispered in a breathy and sultry voice. "I love you, my sweet. Why don't you move over here closer to me?"

"How about I move into your lap?" I said in a joking manner, but not joking at all. I got up and sat as snugly to him as possible. The waves in his eyes crashed over me again.

Then the D.J. played a song that sounded so familiar it made me feel ill. All of a sudden flashes of that terrible nightmare came splashing over me like intense white water rapids smashing me around violently. I knew right then and there that Jeziaka was there, and going to walk in any minute.

"Johnathon this is my dream I told you about. Jeziaka's here right now and she's not alone," I revealed trembling.

"I know, it's a good thing I ordered both of your meals," he announced. I gazed at him. My expression changed to baffled by his comment. I probably could have read his mind sooner and known that he had done that, but I had too many other voices in my head. It was hard to decipher what was what.

"Garlic. Your salads were loaded with garlic," he said, grinning slyly.

"Oh, I thought that was just the way their salads came, but thank you," I sighed, and kissed him and meandered there. "How come I can kiss you, isn't it on my breath?" I asked in amazement.

"The wine actually cleanses the pallet so I can't taste it, I can smell it on you, seeping through your pores, which at this point in time is just keeping me from attacking you.

"Please don't let her take you away from me?" I begged knowing deep down that he would have no control over it. My emotions got the best of me, as usual those salty drops of emotion showed their ugly faces.

"Isla, don't cry. I love you more than I could ever show you," he expressed with his ice cold limbs encompassing me. If I had had the power to freeze that moment forever, I would have. Well, there were other trice's I would've liked too suspend, also. I had locked away every twinkle.

"You have shown me. But, please don't leave me. I love you and I will fight for you till death," I said, gazing in his eyes.

"Isla, whatever happens I'll always return to you, remember that." We kissed long and sweetly as if we both knew it could be our last goodbye kiss. Tears raced down my face, and kept refilling in my eyes. I was living my nightmare, only I couldn't wake up. I couldn't do anything to change it.

Inevitably, the door flew open. There was a big gust of wind and stuff started flying around. Johnathon just stared in my eyes. He mouthed, "I love you" repeatedly.

An attractive brunette strode into the room, eyes black with hunger, emanating power. To me she was the devil, here to take my love away. There were two others not far behind her.

The last patrons ducked out the door behind them when they saw the storm building. Johnathon stood, pulling me up with him and holding me tight. As she approached he put me behind him blocking me from every angle.

Jeziaka came towards us casually. "Johnathon, it's very nice to finally meet you. I'm Jeziaka, the daughter of Hecate one of the higher providences of the S.P.I. My father is Vladimir Novgor and Neco was my brother," she said, smiling and licking one of her fangs.

"Neco killed my mother," Johnathon growled.

"That doesn't matter to me, you killed Neco. Therefore you will be mine in slavery," she hissed as she stretched out her arm and leisurely placed her hand under Johnathon's chin and stared in his eyes. Then she kissed him vengefully. My heart fell out and shattered on the floor.

"No! Those lips belong to me! Johnathon! " I cried loudly, reaching out to jerk his arm, but neither one of them paid me any mind. They stopped kissing, but she still had her hand under his chin. He gaped at her, without even a glance in my direction.

"Johnathon, please come back to me. I love you, please." I yanked on his arm, but his eyes were glued to her. I was dying inside, my heart bloody with entrails of tissue dragging behind him, as she bewitched him away.

"Derak, Zane, get her! Kill her!" Jeziaka ordered. I spun around to see them both foaming at the mouth. Their bloodthirsty eyes on my every move.

Oh this is bad, I thought to myself. Then it must have been Derak that lunged at me full force, with his long blonde hair shooting out around his head like daggers, and his long teeth shining from the overhead light of the room. He slammed me up against the wall savagely. He was lying across my body, eying the throbbing veins in my neck and chest. I could sense his arctic core generating ice on my bare skin, causing me to shiver. He then gripped my throat, catapulting me into a table which shattered beneath me. I shook my head trying to stay conscious. When my vision cleared I saw that he was on top of me again. Cocking his head back just about to sink his teeth in, he stopped dead in his tracks and repelled.

"Well---I said kill her," Jeziaka growled, wrapping her arm over Johnathon's shoulders. Derak glared at her in silence. They looked as if they were having a telepathic conversation. "Garlic!" Jeziaka hissed, then looked at Johnathon and seductively ran her long red shiny nails across his face. Her nails sliced his skin and then she *glared at me.* My heart stopped. She then turned back around and licked the blood from Johnathon face. He didn't even react he was so catatonic. "Leave her! We have what we came for!" she growled. I could see her fury when she discovered my resourcefulness.

Derak was still on top of me snarling. His hands were shackling my wrists above my head. My back hurt so badly I could hardly breathe. It was at that very moment a wave hit me, stronger than it had been before. I was furious therefore it was feeding off my adrenaline. I squeezed my eyes tightly and shoved him away with all my might. He flew across the room hitting the wall ferociously. The shattering wood sent splinters shooting out in all directions. He fell to the floor. When it sank in what I had just done, that I had power, I jumped to my feet. The pain in my back was gone.

"I don't have time for this. We have him, that's all we came for," Jeziaka murmured, brushing me off like I was nothing, even though I had defeated one of her own. Johnathon never looked away from her. His eyes were vacant, like a boarded up shack.

"Say goodbye to your precious Isla, Johnathon." She turned to look at him, his eyes didn't falter away from hers. "Oh no, I guess he doesn't want to say anything to you," she sighed in a teasing, maniacal tone, grasping Johnathon's hand. My rainbow tears flowed like waterfalls down my face.

"Johnathon, I'll see you in Islathon. I love you," I cried out as they turned and walked out the door. I collapsed on the floor. I couldn't breathe, my heart was dead.

"Are you okay?" Lizzy asked helping me up to my feet.

"What happened?" Calvin asked. I was too stunned to speak. All I felt was a numbing pain. I felt like I was dying. In fact, I wished I had.

Chapter 19

Come Back to Me

WHEN WE GOT BACK TO THE HOTEL room, I went directly to the bedroom, to lie down. I could hear Lizzy and Calvin talking in the next room, like they were sitting right in front of me. Lyrics began rolling around in my head, so I grabbed my notebook and a pen. My pain flowed in ink.

Don't leave me now
Somebody wake me because I don't like it here
There's a feeling in the air that shakes me
It's hazy and in no way clear
I'm driving really fast, but I can't steer

Streams of white ribbons flying by
Air flowing through my hair
Going too fast feel like I could die
Deaths deep stare, I'm going nowhere

Don't go, don't leave me now
I will fight for us no matter how hard, or the pain I feel
Our love is strong I have hope that it will...be forever

I'm standing still on the highest hill with my will in my hands
It gives me a deep chill to see the liquid sands slipping through my fingers

You can't ask me to stay here when I can't see your eyes
I will fade away to another atmosphere
A shimmering light in the black sky
Without you I would rather die

So please don't leave me now
I don't know how to go on without you
You are a part of me can't you see
I am consumed by you, so please don't leave me

After I finished writing I fell back on the bed, in mental and emotional exhaustion. I kept picturing Jeziaka hexing my man and taking him away, over and over again. It was like someone was hitting rewind and replay. I couldn't get it out of my mind. Closing my eyes was that much harder. He was there. I could always be with him in my dreams. And just when he would reach out to me Jeziaka's hand would knock it down and he would disappear. I cried and cried till finally I fell asleep.

I began to dream, but the topic was different than what I had been thinking about when my head hit the pillow.

I was flying down to a long black SUV. Suddenly I was inside the vehicle. Lizzy and I were both in black, zipped up body bags. The automobile was parked behind a building somewhere. I watched as if I were floating above everything. Where we were looked familiar, but I couldn't quite grasp where it was. Calvin came to our rescue, unzipping the bags and getting us out. I was still numb from the ripping out of my heart and I almost didn't want to fight back or hide. Calvin ordered us to go hide as he pointed us in the direction of a building next door.

"Go! The others will be here soon," he growled. I didn't understand what he meant by the others. We did as he told us and Calvin stayed to fight. We shoved the door open enough to squeeze in. The dark maroon paint that was peeling at the bottom of the door flaked off onto my long

black pencil skirt. My eyes widened to see we were in a warehouse as Lizzy and I pulled the door closed and bolted it tight. Then we turned and ran to the middle of the warehouse and ducked down behind some stacked crates and boxes when we heard a banging noise. Suddenly, I was alone and calling Lizzy's name.

I unfolded my eyes, gazing around the room. Forgetting where I was briefly til my memory was jogged. As my memory returned it brought with it unbearable emptiness.

The warehouse image haunted me, leaving me freaked out and afraid. But I somehow felt like I had nothing to lose without Johnathon. I got up. It was really late, or early, depending on the perspective. I went into the room that Lizzy was staying in. Calvin was asleep next to her. They looked so close and in love. I went around to Lizzy's side.

"Lizzy," I whispered, touching her arm lightly. Her eyes opened.

"Lizzy, I know you think this is a dream, but it's not. If we are ever in a warehouse don't leave my side. Remember, stay with me no matter what happens," I demanded as I patted her hand. She closed her eyes again, so I went back to bed.

The next morning I awoke with a sharp realization that I had to go to work. I just couldn't do that. I decided to call in sick, picking my purse up and rummaging for my phone. I located it and dialed work. When Lissa answered, I told her I had the flu. She said she would reschedule my appointments. I thanked her and closed my phone, setting it on the nightstand. It wasn't hard to sound sick. My heart was sick with grief. If I was going to fight for him I had to learn my abilities. All I could think about was her kissing him; it was gnawing at me like a rat eating dead carcass. I knew it wouldn't go away unless I got out and did something. I called a client of mine that owned a private gym. She had told me I could use it exclusively any time I wanted. I would just have to go to her office to get the key. She worked at a building in downtown Asheville. I'd have to go alone so nobody could see what I could do. Heck, I didn't even know what I was capable of. But, I didn't want to go alone. If only Lizzy knew everything, she would go with me. If anyone could understand it would be her.

I got dressed and put my makeup on, all the time listening for movement in the other room. Before long Lizzy knocked on my door.

"Come in," I said, feathering my lashes with mascara.

"Good morning, don't you have to work today?"

"I did, but I called in sick," I replied as I put my makeup back in the bag. "Hey, is Calvin still here?" I asked

"Yes," she replied as Calvin came up behind her.

"I'm still here. What's up?" Calvin asked.

"I need to talk to you privately," I said, motioning for him to come in and close the door. Lizzy made a face and then walked off. He entered the room and sat at the foot of the bed.

"Do you think Lizzy could handle the truth about everything?" I asked.

"Yes, I was going to tell her last night when I kept stopping in the midst of our passion." I smiled, but frowned on the inside. I knew what it was like and how frustrating it could be for both parties, to want someone so bad it tore you up inside.

"Do you want to tell her, or should I?" I asked.

"I think I should be the one to break the news," he answered as he stood and strolled towards the door.

"Do you want your privacy, or should I be there?"

"You can observe if you want, but let me do most of the talking," he suggested, pivoting to face me. He spun back around and leisurely reached for the door knob.

"Hey---are you in love?" I asked just before he turned the knob. He then reversed and stepped to where I was standing, smiled and said, "I like her very much. Now come on." We went in the living room and Lizzy was sprawled out on the couch.

"Hey girl, we need to talk to you," I announced, perching beside her with Calvin on her other side. She scooted closer to him and gave him a kiss.

"Okay, about what?" she asked intrigued, but a little nervous. I picked up the remote to turn the volume down. My eyes fixated on the TV for a second or two. *I Love Lucy* was on and I used to love that show, well at least the reruns. Getting my mind back on the matter in hand I took a deep breath while Calvin began.

"Do you know why I stopped kissing you last night?" he asked, gazing in her eyes.

"No, I just thought that you wanted to wait, and that you were being a gentleman," Lizzy replied.

"Well I am, but I had to stop so that I didn't lose control," he explained as he caressed her hand. She turned towards him putting her knee up on the couch with one leg hung off.

"What do you mean by lose control?" Lizzy asked, with confusion in her voice. Her eyes were wide with anticipation.

"Remember you asked me why my skin was so cold?" he asked as her eyes fell on his hand in hers.

"Yes, you told me it was poor circulation," she replied with hesitation.

"Well it's not," he sighed as he stood up and in the blink of an eye was behind the couch standing directly behind her. She turned her head both directions baffled by what she had just seen. I sat next to her in silence and watched.

"What? How? How did you do that?" Lizzy stammered, staring at him wide eyed.

"Don't be scared. I would never hurt you," he breathed, sitting next to her again. She looked bewildered and frightened..

"What's going on?" she shouted jumping up and moving away from us.

"Lizzy calm down," I said standing and draping my arm over her shoulder.

"What are you?" she asked, glaring at Calvin.

"I'm---a vampire," he sighed, apprehensive about what her reaction would be. She hid behind me with her hands on my forearms, like she was using me to barricade herself.

"What? What do you mean? Like a suck your blood vampire, as in Dracula?" She was shaking and since she was holding onto me I was shaking, too. moving.

"Yes!" he replied sharply. His eyes dropped when he saw her revulsion.

"Lizzy, its okay. He won't hurt you," I explained, trying to comfort her.

She fell into the couch looking at the floor, then glared up at me. "Are you one too, Isla?" she asked as tears rolled down her face.

"No, not yet, but I will be as soon as Johnathon bites me, if I ever see him again," I sighed blankly.

"You mean Johnathon is one, too?" she asked, surprised as she held her hand over her mouth.

"Yes, but he lives by the code and won't bite me until we are married," I replied with sadness.

Calvin touched her and she jumped. Then he kissed her. First she began to struggle and then she melted. There was something about a vampire's kiss that could make you placid and tranquil despite your mood. I knew that a bite had to be the highest form of bliss.

"There's more. I am starting to feel things, because I bit him and drank his blood." Her eyes were big as saucers as I explained what I was going through. "I get waves of vivid vision, intense hearing, and I can read minds. I see rainbows around everything and even people's auras. I can even hear a dog bark from three miles away. But, it comes in waves. And each time it's different and stronger. I won't truly be a vampire til Johnathon bites me or I make my first kill."

"Your first kill?" Lizzy shouted and moved away from me.

"Lizzy! We won't hurt you," he sighed, pulling her to him. Calvin put his arms around her from behind. Her arms were stiff at her side.

"Johnathon and Calvin will protect us, from anything," I said reassuringly.

Her body language showed she hadn't accepted it, yet. Her guard was still up.

"Is Johnathon coming back?" she asked.

"I hope so," I sighed falling onto the couch. That question bounced around in my head and devastated my heart. I lost it, whimpering loudly with my head hung low. Those damn things had returned as usual. Sometimes I wished that emotion was something that could be shut down by the click of a button. It hurt too much to feel.

"I'm sorry, Isla! Please, don't cry," Lizzy apologized, not knowing that it would hit me so hard.

"He'll be back, Isla. I know he will," Calvin assured me, pulling my hair out of my tears.

My heart was breaking all over again. It was only last night, but it seemed like he had been gone longer. *What if he can't come out of her spell? How can I live without him?* I wondered as I got up from the couch. I started to go into the kitchen to make some tea and stopped.

"Isla, it will be okay," Lizzy said as I walked away.

I decided to go lay down and headed towards the bedroom. As I walked by the couch Lizzy and Calvin were cuddling. I guess it had registered and soaked in, or she didn't care. I shut the bedroom door and tossed myself down on the bed. I laid down and a wave pounded me. My eyes ached from the light coming in the window, so I got up and pulled the drapes.

I laid back down and continued crying. I couldn't stop the tears. I could also hear Calvin and Lizzy talking like they were right in front of me. I sensed the sound and vibrations of every little crick and crack in the hotel foundation it was driving me crazy. Hearing all of that along with every voice in the hotel and the cars on the road, was all too much for me. I buried my head in the pillow and pulled another on top of my head.

Lizzy was talking on the phone with work. I knew she was coming in to talk to me.

Knock knock "Come in Lizzy," I sighed, peeking out from under the pillow.

"How did you know it was me?" she asked after she opened the door. I pushed my head back down into the pillow.

"Isla, Sarah from my work wants to talk to you," she said, handing me her phone. I pulled my head out of the pillow and took the phone as I rolled onto my side.

"Hello Sarah. Yeah, I remember you. Really? Okay, I'll be there in a while. Bye." I closed the phone. "She told me she needed to talk to me in person about Johnathon," I said, feeling puzzled.

"Well, that works out well, because I need to pick up my check," Lizzy responded as she retrieved her phone from my hand.

Calvin appeared leaning inside the doorway. She smiled at him then ran and jumped on me.

"Lizzy!" I screamed as she dug her knee into my side. I had known she was getting ready to pounce on me, but I hadn't predicted where her knee would land.

"We have to go to Jaggers," I said to Calvin. He casually nodded like he knew.

What could she possibly tell me that I didn't already know? I had to find out. I couldn't help but sense an uneasiness in Sarah's voice when she spoke to me. She sounded scared. I caught a chill as I thought about it.

"What time do y'all want to go?" Calvin asked.

"I don't know. What time is it?" I asked.

Lizzy looked at her phone. "It's 4:30."

"Oh really? I thought it was early afternoon, like 2:00," I sighed. "Lizzy, can you get off my leg. Its falling asleep," I moaned. She got up off my leg, but continued lying on me. Calvin took her hand and swiftly pulled her up to him.

They started making out, and flashes of Johnathon and I kissing and the electricity of his glacial lips came to me. Once again my eyes got glossy.

"Alright, you two. Go out there and make out. I need to refresh my makeup and watching you two is making me miss him so badly. The tears are wrecking my makeup." I sighed.

"I'm sorry," she replied, looking down guiltily as she closed the door behind her. All I really wanted to do was lie back on the bed and never move again. At least not until he came home.

No such luck, I had to get up. I got up and dressed all in black. I picked up my purse just in time to realize my phone was vibrating. I pulled it out and saw a number that didn't ring a bell. I answered it anyway.

"Hello," I said reluctantly.

"Hi, is this Isla?" a pleasant woman's voice asked.

"Yes."

"I'm a friend of Johnathon's. You were supposed to come by and meet me tonight. My name is Serinya."

"Oh, yeah. How are you?" I asked with surprise.

"Great, well the reason I'm calling is I did a tarot reading on Johnathon the other day."

"What did it say? Did you tell him?" I asked, hesitant of all that I might hear.

"Yes! He was here. He shuffled the cards. The cards read that he would be ripped away from his love. From you, but he would find you again. Isla, he will find you again, soon."

"He will? When?" I delightfully asked.

"Talking to you now I'm getting the feeling of danger. You could be walking into some tonight, so be careful and use your new-found powers."

"O...kay," I stammered. I was stunned. My stomach began to tighten.

"One other thing, keep your friends by your side no matter what happens....Are you still there?" she asked.

"Yes. Thank you," I responded. She knew everything. I was astounded by all she had told me.

"Please, call me at this number if you need me in any way," she said, sincerely. I scratched my head and thought, *I wonder what kind of danger I'm walking into.*

"I will. Thank you again."

We said our goodbyes and I closed the phone and threw it in a different purse. I opened the door and went into the living room. Lizzy was on the couch.

"Where is Calvin?" I asked, glancing around the room.

"He had to feed so he could be with me. He'll be back soon," she sighed. She appeared to be in a foggy haze, staring at the blank TV screen.

"Are you having trouble accepting what they are?" I asked. She didn't answer, she stared off aimlessly. "Hey, I felt the same at first," I murmured as I softly touched her back. "I thought I was in a dream or a movie. I mean, I've seen plenty of vampire movies and they all had different aspects of weaknesses and powers. After I was attacked by Sigrid I started to think I might be in a movie."

"You were attacked?" she asked, eyes wide.

"Yes! Not once, but twice. Oh, actually it was three times. Twice by Sigrid, Johnathon's illegitimate brother. And once by Neco, who is the vampire that killed Johnathon's mother," I explained.

"How did you get away?" she asked, gaping at me.

"Johnathon saved me. Anyway, for the longest time I wanted to look around for the director or producer so they would tell me what to do, and point me in the right direction. I just knew I was in a movie, in a land of make believe. It was pretty shocking to find out that vampires are real, not to mention that I'm in love with one. In the beginning I thought I just needed to find the writer to figure out what part I played in all this. I only wish it was that easy," I expressed nervously.

"This isn't gonna be easy is it?" she asked, slumping back into the couch.

"No! Something this complex could never be easy. Hey, just be glad that Calvin doesn't have a jealous brother," I sighed, with my hand on my forehead.

"I just can't believe they're real," she voiced, resting her chin against her hand. She seemed to be in another world.

"It took awhile for me to realize that this was real, something I could touch or be touched by," I agreed as I leaned back and crossed my legs and arms. We were still staring at a blank TV, so I kept talking. "The moment Johnathon kissed me it changed me forever." I sighed and giggled a little as I elaborated, "I drive him insane trying to push him to bite me, all the time. Honestly, I love pushing him to the edge. When you love someone and you can see forever in their eyes. And forever is actually possible, if you become what they are. I'm willing to risk it," I murmured. "The fire we have between us burns so deeply. I know I can't grow old and die without him. And now that I have him, I would die to be like him, to be with him," I confessed. While I was spouting off at the mouth I pictured Jeziaka kissing his lips and how there was a humongous hole where my heart used to be. I shoved that image aside, threw my hands in the air, stood and said, "That's why I have to fight for my man." I grabbed my purse, slipped my arm through the strap and pulled it over my head and secured it tightly to my body. I was glad I had changed bags, because I wouldn't lose it and it wouldn't be in my way. Plus it was the bag with the weapons in it. "Now that I've gotten all of this off my chest I think I'll make a cup of tea, would you like one Lizzy?" I asked, walking into the kitchen.

"Sure, you make a great cup of tea." She smiled half heartedly and picked up the remote and turned the TV on.

All of sudden there was a knock at the door, she jumped and got up to peek in the peephole.

"Calvin's back," she announced as she opened the door. He came in and sat down, Lizzy practically sat in his lap.

"So, are you ladies ready to go?" he asked, eying both of us. After handing Lizzy her tea I stood next to the couch sipping mine.

"We'll go as soon as we finish our tea," I announced.

We drank our tea and headed out. On the way to Jaggers I doubled over from a sharp pain in my stomach. They didn't hear or see me writhing in pain. But a wave ran over me like a house being dropped on my head. This one was so powerful it knocked me for a loop. *They must be powered by adrenaline*, I thought to myself. Lizzy sat in front with Calvin so they couldn't see what was going on. All of a sudden I was bombarded with a vision of my wedding day. We were kissing in front of an altar in the garden of his castle, next to the Gazebo. It was exactly as I pictured it, my dress, the bridesmaids' dresses, what Johnathon was wearing, and the whole ambiance was fantasy perfect. *I know I'm seeing my future*, I told myself repeatedly. My daydreams or fantasies were mind-blowing and so authentic.

I was so caught up in my thoughts I hadn't noticed that the car had stopped until Calvin opened the door. He got in so fast it startled me.

"Here, I wanted to give this to you." He handed me a dagger that looked like a dragonfly, with blades on both sides. "You might need it," he said.

"You're probably right, it's better to have it and not need it then to need it and not have it." When I said that I remembered the gun and dagger I had not yet paid for from Michael. I couldn't remember where I'd left it. Holding the weapon and feeling the cold steel made the wave that much stronger, causing a sense of power I had never experienced before. It was as if my hands were glowing. Calvin smiled when he saw it how the dagger lit up in my hands.

"Just as I thought. I knew you had the magic touch. That dagger is very special," Calvin smiled gloriously at me and sighed.

I shook my head profusely in disbelief of what I was seeing and feeling. The dagger was glowing orange and looked like it was on fire. But it didn't burn my hand, actually the steal was quite cold.

I put it in my bag. It fit perfectly and was easily accessible.

"Thank you, Calvin," I said as I scooted up to get out. Lizzy was getting in as we were getting out.

"Hey girl, are you ready to go in?" I asked, standing outside the car. The parking lot was almost empty and the light of the full moon shone brightly in my eyes. There was a certain crispness to the night air. I took a deep breath and swallowed hard. It dawned on me that something was about to go down. I just had no idea what.

"Lizzy, no matter what stay next to me, don't leave my side," I commanded caringly.

"I had a dream you said that to me," she gasped with wide eyes.

"Really? So, please listen to your dream, and to me."

"I will," she said in an exasperated tone.

"Calvin, are you ready?" I asked.

He looked at me with black eyes, licked his teeth and smiled, "Yes!" We both knew there was going to be a showdown.

"Remember, you have tasted, you have the power. Don't forget what Jee Cee taught you," Calvin instructed. I felt like a champion boxer getting ready to face my opponent in the ring.

"I'm ready." I affirmed, taking Lizzy's arm.

Calvin held the door for us. As we entered the club it seemed as though the music stopped and every head cranked around to glare at us. It felt like a bar scene from a movie. It also may have been the wave messing with me. I saw Sarah in the distance, she strolled towards us.

"Hi Isla, I'm so glad you could come," she said. Something was different about her, but I couldn't put my finger on it. She seemed harmless with her shoulder length brown bob and her thin, frail body. Her facial expression changed noticeably as I had these thoughts about her. Oh, that's it! When I met her before she wasn't a vampire and now she was. *Lucky bitch! Oops, shouldn't have thought that.*

"What is it? Is Johnathon okay? Has he gotten away from Jeziaka?"

"HE'S NOT COMING BACK!" The sound of her voice echoed like I was at the Grand Canyon. My heart stopped and tears began to peek out of the corners of my eyes.

"What do you mean?" I asked, in major shock that she would say such a thing.

"I..." she paused and then retreated back towards the kitchen quickly.

I was hurt and baffled. "Lizzy, who do you trust here?" I asked, grasping for some hope. Her words had hit me hard. But I had to keep positive and know that was a lie.

"Him, that's Marcus." She pointed to the bar. I slapped her hand down.

"Don't point, let's just go over there," I sighed, trying not to draw too much attention to ourselves.

We went to the bar. "Hey Lizzy, you look like you're feeling better. So this must be the infamous Isla, Johnathon's desire," Marcus said with a deep Island accent.

"Hi, it's very nice to meet you, Marcus," I said, friendly and calm on the outside, while going crazy on the inside.

I reached out to shake his hand and the minute his frigid hand touched mine I summed him up in my mind: *Vampire*. He stared me down, I could literally feel his glare. He tilted his head back and to the side, his long black dreadlocks shaking from the movement. His pecks flexed under his bright blue and green Hawaiian shirt. After staring me down he turned to Lizzy and asked, "When are you coming back to work?"

"I don't know, I have some personal business to take care of first," Lizzy murmured, nervously looking around the around the room.

The door behind Marcus opened and Sigrid walked in from the back. My eyes widened with terror as I gritted my teeth and pushed a smile. He leered at me. He then handed Lizzy her check, never taking his eyes off me. I took a deep breath and looked to Calvin for comfort.

"Don't let him get you," he whispered in my ear. Observing Sigrid's eyes I noticed they were getting blacker by the minute. I grinned at him with an ulterior motive of reading his mind, but at that time the wave wasn't hitting me. *Perfect, when I need it, it goes away*, I sighed to myself.

He turned away, talking to Marcus. I grabbed Lizzy's arm.

"Is there a back door out of here?" I felt sweat on my forehead and the panic was rising in my throat.

"Yes, follow me," she whispered. She grabbed my wrist and pulled me. When she did I realized that Calvin wasn't with us anymore. We walked through the pool hall and everyone stopped shooting, drinking, or whatever they were doing to ogle us. We moved swiftly through that area and to the kitchen where the staff stopped and stared, too. I swear, one guy even sniffed the air as we approached. I don't think it was food he smelled. At that moment it occurred to me that it was a bit ironic that a vampire would own a restaurant, since they don't eat or drink. But then I figured it must be a great way to attract victims. I felt sure there were vampires in there that didn't live by the code.

"Lizzy, where did Calvin go?" I asked as she pushed a button beside a door that had an exit sign above it. She shrugged, saying nothing. We opened it, ran out, and closed it behind us. When we turned around there was an older gentleman dressed sharply in a double-breasted grey suit holding a big gun. We both gasped and clung to each other as he turned the gun on us. We stepped back and Lizzy walked directly into another man with a gun.

"Lizzy, you have really let me down," a tall man in a white suit carrying an even bigger gun grumbled. "How did you get away from me?" he asked as he jerked her arm nearly out of the socket. I still had her other arm and I had an iron grip on it. So when he jerked her, it jerked me.

"Christian, I can't be with you. I don't love you," she cried, scared out of her wits. Her eyes were squinting from the burn she felt from his relentless grip. Suddenly Calvin came out of nowhere and pulled her out of the Christophe's grasp and into his arms. His furious expression grew more evil when he saw her in another man's arms.

"Tie them up and put them in the SUV," the man in the grey suit bellowed, waving his arms towards the monstrous, night-colored automobile.

"Monty! Anthony! Torture them!" he demanded in raspy howl. A woman in a black and white striped suit walked up to us. Her short, spiky brown hair and piercing green eyes completed the look of a woman not to be messed with.

"What do we have here? This is the girl that put a damper on our plans? All because she walked in the wrong door at the wrong time," she stated in a soft and steady tone as she grabbed a handful of Lizzy's dark brown hair and pulled her down to the ground.

Lizzy screamed, "Stop, let me go!" I glanced over at Calvin who was ready to attack. I could see it in his eyes and his teeth grew as I watched.

Lizzy was screaming in agony. A hand came from behind me picking me up by my throat, choking me. I couldn't breathe as it clamped down harder and tighter. My eyes gushed as Christophe held me up higher and looked back at the older gentleman.

"Sal just shoot! Here, I'll hold her up for you!" he yelled in an Italian accent. My feet were dangling in the air, and when he turned away I kicked him violently in the head, not once, but twice. He let go of my throat and I landed on my feet. He went flying, and slammed up against the side of a dumpster. I guess I was lucky that a wave had come at that moment. I bent over, gasping for air. When I stood up Sal cocked the gun that he had pointed straight at me. I closed my eyes briefly, because I knew, I knew I was about to die. But, when I opened them Johnathon was right behind Sal. I gasped and admired him from afar. His rigidly carved features were breathtaking to me.

I pivoted to see if Lizzy was okay, I didn't see her or Calvin. Johnathon's eyes were jet black and his canines were glowing in the moonlight. *My heart is finally here,* I thought to myself and took a deep relaxing breath. Then Johnathon bent down biting Sal's neck and thrashing him around like a dog shakes a stuffed animal. If

I'd been standing any closer I would have been painted in blood. I stood there paralyzed, watching my man destroy another man.

And then all of a sudden a hand came from behind me and I saw a flash of white as it brutally covered my mouth and nose. I struggled and kicked then my eyes rolled back in my head and everything went black.

Chapter 20

Tears Kept Falling

EVERYTHING WAS BLACK WHEN I OPENED MY eyes. I tried to raise my arm and realized my arms were tied together. I attempted to chew through the rope but had no luck. The rope was way too thick. So I tried to tugging on it with my teeth. I was getting exasperated and frustrated. My eyes were full of water but suddenly I must have pulled on the right piece I felt it loosen. I was able to maneuver my hands out of the rope. I discovered I was in a bag when I felt the metal zipper teeth above my head. I ran my finger along it looking for the pull and couldn't find it. I figured it was on the outside. I remembered the dagger in my purse and felt for it. I was surprised to find that my purse was still wrapped around my body and the handle of the dagger was sticking out. I pulled it out and stabbed it into the thick fabric, ripping through the bag.

I crawled out, noticing there was another bag next to me. There was a muffled scream echoing from it. It was Lizzy. I recognized the crying. After unzipping it and getting her out. I untied her wrists. She threw her arms around my neck as I pulled her out.

"Isla, I was so scared. Where are we?" Her eyes were shadowed and smeared. I'm sure mine were just as bad. I wiped my eyes with my fingers. She did the same.

"We're in a big friggin' SUV. Let's get out of here!" I gasped looking through the dark windows, standing up examining my surroundings.

While I explored, I pictured Johnathon thrashing and tearing out Sal's jugular and the splatter of blood that painted the pavement. I wondered if he was looking for us. I had so much going through my head and it was changing rapidly. This was the SUV in my dream. It was very velvety and plush inside, just how I had imagined. I felt the material as we headed to the back. None of the other doors would open and the back door was our last hope. Flashes of my dream ran through my head and I hoped it would play out the same way. I pushed down on the handle, squeezing my eyes, hoping it would be unlocked and wouldn't make too much noise. It opened, and I sighed deeply. I stuck my head out the door looking to see if the coast was clear. I had a feeling that Calvin was going to show up any minute. I stuck my head back in to tell Lizzy to come on. We exited the vehicle slowly to make sure no one was coming.

"There you are," Calvin said, standing right outside the SUV.

"How long have we been missing?" I asked quietly. Lizzy stepped down out of the vehicle. Calvin and Lizzy hugged.

"Not long, about an hour or two," he answered. I peeked around the side of the automobile, nervously. "Don't worry, Johnathon and I took care of those mobsters, but one of the Giovanni brothers got away. I don't know which one, but there's only one left."

"Where's Johnathon?" I asked, putting the dagger back in my purse.

"Don't put that up, someone's coming. You'll need it," he muttered.

I felt it somehow, too. I pulled it back out, and heard a voice yell out.

"What the hell! Sal!" a distressed voice pierced the night. "Oh come on man, wake up! Where's Anthony?" the voice hollered, hoping to hear an answer, but Sal was dead. I could hear the anger building as he realized his family had been massacred.

Calvin looked at me with urgency. "Go! You and Lizzy hide wherever you can. Try the building next door," he muttered and motioned with his head then pointed. He kissed Lizzy and growled, "Go!"

"Okay!" I whispered.

"Will you come get us?" Lizzy asked Calvin with a trembling voice.

He held a finger up to his lips, "Shhh!" and then pointed with the other hand. We ran to the building next door. I slid the dagger back in my purse because I needed both hands to open the door and to hold on to Lizzy's hand. I was astounded when the door opened easily. I locked it behind us and as soon as we were in, a staggering feeling washed over me and I knew I had been there before. The boxes, lumber and furniture were all exactly the same as in my dream.

I gripped Lizzy's hand tightly. "Don't leave me, no matter what." She smiled and moved closer. We ran as far back into the warehouse as we could until we heard a crashing noise like the window on the door had been smashed in. I dove behind a stack of white crates that reached almost to the ceiling. Lizzy was next to me the whole time.

"I know you're in here," a voice shouted, not so far away from us. Evidently the place was huge because we hadn't made it that far from the entrance. My heart was thumping in my ears and Lizzy was digging her acrylic nails into skin.

"Ouch! Lizzy let up on your grasp, your hurting me," I whispered.

"Sorry, I'm just doing what you told me to do," she whispered back. I rolled my eyes and rubbed my wrist where she had dug her nails in.

"What do we do now?" she asked softly.

All of the sudden we heard shots fired. Our first thought was to hit the ground and lay down flat. Then he started shooting at the ceiling right above us and pieces of debris were falling to the concrete floor. Lizzy was holding her ears. I looked at her and said, "Don't let go," as I took her hand.

"Sorry, it was so loud," she mumbled, gripping my hand more tightly. I grimaced and stared at her. "Oh, I'm sorry." She loosened her grip a bit. I mouthed, thank you. She nodded.

I peeked over the corner of a crate and could see him coming closer. "Come on!" I whispered, heading off down the dark aisles, with Lizzy following very close.

"If I can't find you and kill you, I will smoke you out!" he screamed chillingly.

My heart stopped when I smelled smoke. Everything caught fire so fast it was following us, sneaking up on our every step. We ran as fast as we could to the back of the warehouse. We raced along the back wall looking for a door, just like in my dream. We were both freaking out, trying to find the door. The smoke and fire was coming upon us so rapidly. The smoke was smothering the air and suffocating us.

All of a sudden Lizzy yelled out, "Isla, I found it!" I heard her open the door as I ran down the wall to get to her. A super Wal-Mart would have fit in this warehouse. The place was enormous. As I got closer she yelled, "Hurry! I can't hold it any longer!" I sprinted towards the sound of her voice. "It's too heavy!" she cried. She went out and the door slammed shut precisely when I reached it.

I tried to open the door, but it wouldn't budge. I bent over gasping from the smoke inhalation. I came up as I inhaled and Jeziaka was standing right in front of me.

"Johnathon may have gotten away, but now I have his girl. I will take you and everyone will think you burned up in the fire," she muttered.

I started screaming and pounding on the door. "Lizzy! Help! Jeziaka's in here." I prayed that she heard me. I turned around and doubled over trying to breathe. Coughing and wheezing I stood to face my abductor. She didn't say a word as she reached out with one hand and touched me on my forehead. I closed my eyes and fell to the floor.

When I woke up I could see her face closely, she had me in a head lock and my feet were dangling. Looking down I could see the building was engulfed in flames, as we flew up into the sky.

"Where are you taking me?" I asked, scared that I would never see Johnathon or anyone ever again. She wouldn't even look at me, much less answer my question. Feeling the anguish of missing him, and him thinking I burned up in the fire was too much. My heart was cracking into millions of pieces.

Somehow I needed to let him know. *Calvin, if you can hear me, please let Johnathon know I'm alive and Jeziaka has me.* I repeated it over and over again in my head hoping he would somehow get the message.

We were in the air a long time. I was beginning to feel a little nauseous and light headed. The fact that I hadn't eaten anything for days wasn't helping the matter. I put my hand over my mouth just in case I was going to hurl, because getting it on her was not a good idea, she'd kill me for sure. Then I would never make it back to Johnathon.

"Please, I need food," I breathed to her, trying my hardest to keep from regurgitating. I envisioned Johnathon on his way to save. But I closed my eyes when I realized, he thinks I'm dead.

She let go of my arm and the hold she had on me, but still had my other arm. The morning sun was beginning to peak through the clouds.

We landed in the back yard of a beautiful white Victorian house. The scent of gardenias permeated the air. We walked up steep concrete porch steps to the back door of the house. A tall, truly remarkable looking woman, with dark brown hair and copper brown eyes, came to the door and opened it. She stepped aside as we walked in. Jeziaka clenched my arm unyieldingly.

"Did you bring lunch?" the woman asked, licking her teeth and staring at me.

"No, she's collateral," Jeziaka growled.

She shoved me down into a chair and tied me up. As she was tying me she noticed the dagger's handle sticking out of my purse. She pulled it out and swung it around at my face. I could feel the sting of the blade tearing at my skin. I dodged it the best I could. Then she began examining the knife.

"This looks familiar," she muttered, feeling the sharpness of the blade with her fingers.

She grabbed my hair pulling my head back and stuck the dagger to the side of my throat. I could feel the blade entering my skin, any deeper she would've killed me. Crying out in pain I squeezed my eyes shut hoping to go or wake-up somewhere else. She pulled it out of my skin and threw my head back. I fell over backwards, the chair was digging into my arms. Tears kept falling. Trying to hold them back was impossible.

"Lyza watch her! I'll be back in a minute," Jeziaka ordered, walking out of the room.

The woman Lyza picked me up and set the chair back on all fours. She got a glimpse of the blood dripping from my wounds. Her eyes went dark and she smiled, exposing her long sharp teeth. She extended her hand out and with her long thin finger swiped the blood, getting a good amount on the tip of her finger. She put it to her lips and tasted it squeezing her eyes tight in sweet rapture.

I thought to myself *this is it, she's gong to attack me.* That was not the way I wanted to die. I always thought it would be Johnathon who changed me, or killed me, because he lost control. Not this.

She got closer and closer to my neck, taking one hand and pulling my head back to expose my already sliced skin dripping of blood.

I closed my eyes and said in my head, "Johnathon, I love you and always will." The tears were cascading down my face. I could feel her ice cold breath on my skin.

"Stop! I told you she's collateral!" Jeziaka roared out as she marched in and impeded her from feeding on me just in the knick of time. Lyza stepped back, her head hung low in disgrace, and stomped out of the room like a spoiled child that didn't get her way.

"Are you related?" I murmured. She ginned and bit her lower lip.

"Yes, she's my sister," Jeziaka muttered, sitting back on the couch and eying me.

"Can I get some food?" I asked hesitantly. My stomach was hollering at me and I knew it couldn't hurt to ask.

"I'll call my niece and see if she'll pick you up a hamburger," she replied as she picked up the phone that was sitting on the pine coffee table in between us. She walked into the other room. I could hear her, but it was muffled. She came back in.

"Do you want fries?" she asked, which threw me for loop.

"That would be great! Thank you," I replied, trying not to ask too much of her.

"And fries," she said into the receiver and then hit a button, it beeped and she set it back down on the table.

I was sitting there, still and calm, then a wave hit me. It must have done something to my eyes, because Jeziaka looked at me intently, trying to read them.

"You have tasted blood or been bitten, one or the other. Which one?" she asked.

"Actually, I have tasted and been bitten," I sighed, peering around the room at the rainbows dancing off the lights. There was a lamp on the table next to the long brown leather couch. The lamp shade was hot pink and it put out an extremely bright florescent orange light. I squinted to stop the sting in my eyes.

"Did Johnathon bite you?" she asked as she picked up a magazine and began flipping through it.

"Yes, we were kissing."

"You mean he actually stopped?" she asked baffled.

"Yes, he doesn't want to turn me, he's keeping me from the pain."

"He's trying to keep you from the pain and he's causing it at the same time, how ironic."

"I guess so," I muttered, getting dizzy from the colors I was seeing. "Why do you want Johnathon so badly?" I asked her feeling a little powerful.

"He killed my brother, Neco," Jeziaka replied, then stood up. I could tell she was getting upset. She started pacing the floor. I noticed a painting of a beautiful dark haired woman on the wall, hanging above the couch. I wanted to ask about it, but thought it might not be appropriate for me to meddle.

The front door opened and in walked two girls. They hadn't seen me yet, but one made a comment about smelling human blood. Both the girls had long, wavy, brown hair. One had red and blonde highlights. Both were very pretty. The one with highlights came over to me.

"Hungry?" she asked as she held up a bag from Burger King.

"Yes," I replied, my mouth watering.

She put the bag behind her, licked her lips and said, "Me, too!" Her upper lip quivered and he eyes began to dilate. I swallowed and took a deep breath as I thought, *Not again.*

"Roshanna, don't tease her!" Jeziaka shouted, getting up to untie me.

She untied my hands then coiled the rope around my feet and the bottom of the chair. I didn't care, my hands were free and I was starving.

"Phedra! Go get her some water," Jeziaka ordered.

Roshanna plopped down on the couch and stared at me. She started making hissing noises by sucking the air through her teeth, then smiled at me mischievously as Lyza entered the room.

"Mom, I'm hungry," Roshanna announced in a whiny tone, looking for comfort.

"I saw some drifters over by Pisgah Forest," Lyza replied as she sat down next to her and played with Roshanna's hair.

"Phedra, do you want to go with me?" Roshanna asked as Phedra walked into the room and handed me a glass of water.

"Where? What are we doing?" Phedra asked. She looked like she was anxious and bored as she sank down and threw her legs over the arm of a big brown leather chair that matched the couch.

"We're going hunting!" Roshanna announced, getting up and walking to the door.

Phedra got up and followed. "Bye mom!" Roshanna yelled. Phedra waved as they walked out the white back door.

"Thank you for the burger," I said with my mouth full and covering my mouth with my hand. She wanted to say you're welcome I could feel it, but she didn't want to like me. I felt deep down inside she was starting to.

We talked a little more, but she kept her distance.

"You do know that Neco killed Johnathon's mom?" I asked.

"I know," she replied, but cut it short and left the room.

While she was gone I thought of Johnathon and what he was going to do if he thought I was dead. *Calvin I'm not dead! Johnathon I'm not dead!* I said repeatedly in my head hoping we were on the same frequency and that somehow I got through. *How am I going to get out of here? My parents, what is this going to do to them?* I thought to myself as the tears began to fill my eyes, again. I was so tired of crying. I pictured my mom crying and dad trying to scoop her up and put her back together again. My heart was breaking. I could never imagine what it would do to Johnathon, though. I know if it was me thinking he was dead, or no longer roaming the earth, I would kill myself. I had to get home fast.

Jeziaka came back and sat down on the couch. She looked like something was bothering her.

"Why are you crying?" she asked, staring me in the eyes.

"I'm dying inside," I replied, heartbroken and solemn.

"What do you mean?" she asked as she stood up and lit a cigarette.

"Can I have one of those?" I asked, motioning with my head.

"Sure." She handed me a cigarette and lit if for me.

"I don't really smoke except from time to time at work, and night clubs. It's a social thing for me," I murmured as I exhaled and watched smoke.

"Now, why are you dying inside?" Jeziaka asked as she sat down on the couch in front of me, like she was a friend sitting down to have a chat.

"Have you ever been in love?" I asked her as I watched the smoke circulate in the air. The patterns and swirls circling briefly distracted me from the pain of the cuts and my breaking heart.

"Yes, it was very long ago, his name was Edwin Secrete. It was before I became a vampire. I would have died for him, but instead he threw himself in front of a bullet to save me. After losing Edwin I turned away from God and Neco found me and invited me into his family.

"So you must know what this is doing to me? I'm worried about what Johnathon might do now that he thinks I'm dead. I love him more than anyone in the world could ever love anyone. He's my sun, my moon and stars. He's my Heaven. I miss my heart." She sat there still and quiet for a long time. I was very quiet, too. Then she got up and left the room.

I leaned down quickly untying the rope while watching for her, loosening it up just enough so I could get my legs out of it. She came back in. I quickly sat up. I felt like me heart was going to jump out and take off.

"He still killed my brother and he will pay," she replied as she sat back down.

Looking around the room I noticed my dagger sitting on a table by the door. All I had to do was wait until she left or went to sleep to get out of there.

Roshanna and Phedra returned from their hunt. Their white skin was blushed from their feeding. I was scared that I'd missed my chance to escape.

I could partially see through the window from the chair that I'd been tied to supposedly for hours. I could see it was getting dark again. I had held my bladder all day, but my eyeballs were beginning to float. I would have to make my escape soon. If I had to kill in order to escape, then that was just something I would have to do. I kept my eye on the dagger, without being obvious to anyone watching me. It was difficult. *If only I could make the dagger come to me,* I thought.

Jeziaka got up and told the girls something. I couldn't hear them, despite my best efforts. Then Jeziaka went out the front door. Roshanna and Phedra sat down on the couch talking about the drifter, how cute he was and how he resisted before they killed him. They looked like they were the same age as me, but I knew they weren't. Roshanna looked at me "I like your hair, it's a pretty color," she muttered, playing with her locks, twisting one around her finger.

"Thank you. I'm a hairstylist. I did it myself," I replied as I sniffled and ran my finger up under my eyes. My tears had halted for the time being. I wondered how long that would last.

"Where do you work?" I must have gone white at that question because they both looked at me peculiarly.

"The Hair Shop," I blurted out. It was not a good idea to tell them where I worked and I had to keep the name of my shop out of my head incase either one of them was reading my mind.

"Where is that?" Roshanna asked me, appearing to be interested.

"In Asheville, it's new," I replied.

A soothing feeling eased it's way through me seconds before the wave came. I heard an angel's voice. It was my dark angel and I knew it was him. No other voice captivated me like his did. The voice growled in my head, "Relax and get ready to make your move," the voice was breathy but strong. They both looked at me with confusion. I really had to see what it did to my eyes to make them look at me that way. Then the strangest thing happened. The front door opened just a crack, making the dagger shine like the sun. At the same time Roshanna and Phedra got up and went to another room.

I took my legs out of the rope, grabbed the dagger as quietly as I could, then opened the door just enough to squeeze out. I ran like I'd never run before. Running through a dark forest, I suddenly felt like someone was following me. So I jumped in a river to cover my scent.

It was so dark I could barely see anything. I was tripping over branches and rocks but I managed to not fall. When I got to the other side of the ravine, I heard footsteps above me I decided against climbing up. I thought it was a better idea to follow the river bank. Then I came across a bridge and saw a car pass on the overpass. So I climbed up the side of the bridge and waved down the first car that came my way.

A white Mercedes stopped and I ran up to the car, not even noticing what direction I was going or needed to go. I looked in the window as I came up to the car. It was a woman with salt and pepper hair probably, in her late forties to fifties. She smiled warmly, so I opened the door and got in.

"Hello dear, where do you need to go?" she asked as we drove off down the road. Peering back I checked to see if we were being followed, thankfully there was no one.

"Asheville," I replied, praying that we were going in that direction.

"You're in luck, that's where I'm headed," she answered and smiled at me.

"Thank God, I was so scared you would be going the opposite way."

I took the strap of my purse over my head and rummaged through it for my phone. The dagger slipped out and fell on the floor board. She slowed down when she saw it.

"Don't worry, that's just for protection," I assured her. I picked it up and put it in my purse. I held my phone in the other hand, then set my purse on the floor. She relaxed and kept driving.

"You don't look like you would hurt anyone anyway," she murmured, smiling.

"Of course not, I'm a lover not a fighter," I replied, smiling back.

"What were you doing out there anyway?" she asked as she turned down the oldies station that was playing on the radio.

"I'd been kidnapped and I just escaped," I answered bluntly.

"Oh dear, do you need to talk to the cops?" she asked.

"No! No, please I just need to get back to my fiancé, he thinks I'm dead."

"Where do you need to go?" she asked as she glanced at me and then back at the road.

"I'm staying at the Hyatt off 276."

"Is that where you're living?" she asked in a motherly tone.

"No, just staying there for a while. Sorry, I need to make a call," I said as I opened the phone.

"Go ahead, dear," she replied, focusing on the road. I dialed my mom's cell phone. It rang and then the recording said it wasn't a working number.

"Is everything okay?" she asked, observing the puzzled look on my face as I glared at my phone.

"No, my mom's cell phone isn't a working number. I don't understand."

I closed my phone and when I did, it shut off. The battery was dead. *Maybe, that's why it wouldn't connect*, I said to myself

"Do you have a cell phone?" I asked.

"No dear, I wouldn't know what to do with one," she sighed and giggled a bit, which caused me to laugh. But my laughter was short lived when I thought about Johnathon going off the deep end with the news of my death and what he would do.

I thought, I better tell him and Calvin telepathically that I was on my way home. I hoped they would here me. *Johnathon I love you, I'm on my way home. Calvin, I'm not dead, please don't let Johnathon go anywhere.* I said it over and over again in my head, and hoped it would work. I would just die if anything happened to Johnathon.

"Man, I'm tired," I mumbled. I hadn't slept in more than twenty four hours.

"Go ahead dear, lay back and get some rest. I'll let you know when we're almost there," she said warmly.

"Okay, thank you."

As I laid my head back on the headrest a wave hit me, and it occurred to me I had not experienced any dreams in a wave at least from what I could remember. The wave had to intensify them somehow. With that last thought, I was out.

In my dream I was walking down a street that I didn't know. There were street walkers everywhere standing provocatively in windows. The streets were lined in tall street lamps. The air was brisk and murky and the sky was black with very few stars, but was lit up by a crescent moon. I stumbled on some stairs that led up to a tall black door with red light and steam almost bursting out of every crease and corner like fire seeping through the edges. Something was drawing me to the door. I opened it and heard strange chanting in another language, it was eerie. The huge room was dark, but with candlelight scattered throughout. I looked down on this enormous room from a balcony. Everyone there that I could see was looking in the same direction, watching something. I couldn't quite see what it was they were observing so intensely. Curious as to what it was, I went to another balcony further up, but still my vision was blocked by people in the way. I had an undeniable desire to see what was going on, so I went to the next and last balcony.

When I saw what it was, my heart stopped. It was Johnathon hovering over a pool of water. There was a man standing off to the side eating cloves of garlic like candy.

"You must swim and feed, the order is your choice, just as it is your decision to die," a big voice echoed.

"Johnathon! No!" I screamed.

I sat up with my eyes opened wide in shock as my tears began to fall.

"Are you okay dear? I stared straight ahead with a blank look on my face. "Hello, are you okay?" the woman asked as she tapped me on the shoulder.

Everything was blurry and had rainbows around it when I opened my eyes. My heart was pounding so hard it sounded as if someone was beating on a hollow door with their fists.

"We need to go faster! I have to get there now!" I hollered. Those salty drops were pouring down my face. I was scared and furious all at the same time.

She stepped on the gas pedal. We were going about fifteen miles over the speed limit. I was praying that we didn't get pulled over because that would hold us up more. When we pulled up to the hotel, I saw the limo parked in the closest parking place available.

"Thank you so much for the ride," I said, picking my purse up off the floorboard.

"You're welcome, dear. By the way, my name is Jean Smith," she said and then smiled.

"My name is Isla Van Burren," I sighed. She gave me a hug. I was sniffling and wiping my eyes. My emotions were going haywire. No matter what I did I couldn't control them.

"Well go on! I hope everything works out for you," she said as I opened the door and ran up to the entrance.

There was a young couple on the elevator, when I got on. They gawked at me the whole way up to my floor. I must have looked awful, I hadn't even seen a mirror in days, much less showered or put any make-up on at all.

I searched my purse for the key to the room, as they watched. The elevator door opened to my floor and I smiled halfheartedly at them as I got off. I sprinted down the hall to our hotel room, put the key in and opened it. When I walked in I must have been too quiet because Calvin and Lizzy were on the couch and hadn't heard me come in. He had his arm around her and she was weeping loudly.

"Did somebody die?" I asked smiling. They both turned around in surprise.

Lizzy jumped over the couch and into my arms.

"Isla, I thought you were dead. I'm so sorry I let the door close."

Calvin joined in on the hug.

"Isla, I'm so glad you're alright, where have you been?" Calvin asked with concern in his eyes. His cold touch was comforting, but made me yearn for Johnathon's touch.

"Jeziaka captured me as the building went up in flames. Where is Johnathon?" I sighed, terrified and wiped out.

Calvin and Lizzy looked at each other with worry in their eyes as they lowered their heads. Then Calvin put his arm around me.

"He's gone. He thought you were dead. He was devastated and said he would be with you soon, then took off," Calvin explained with his hand on my sleeveless shoulder. I closed my eyes and the tears began sliding down.

"I know where he's going and what he's going to do," I revealed bleakly. "We have to go to Amsterdam! Now!" I gasped, pulling my phone out of my purse and dialing, before I remembered it was dead.

I ran into the bedroom and plugged it into the charger. While it charged I cleaned up, changed into some black pants and a fitted, black and white shirt with black boots. I put some make-up on and put my hair up in a high pony tail. Then I threw all my clothes in my bag, as fast as I could.

Lizzy came in and sat on the bed. "Do you need any help?" she asked.

"Yes! Lizzy, grab all our stuff that might be scattered throughout the suite and put it in the bag," I commanded as I walked into the kitchen to get a glass of water. I needed to wet my whistle. I was hungry, but didn't have time to eat. Every second was ticking away and I had to get to him before it was too late.

"I need a bag for the dirty clothes," she said as she opened the kitchen cabinets looking for one. "So, why do you think he's in Amsterdam?" she asked as she tossed some clothes in a plastic bag.

"I had a dream on my way here."

"What happened to you anyway?" she asked.

"Jeziaka kidnapped me and I thought for sure she was going to kill me. I was being held in a house somewhere, I never really knew where the house was because I escaped at night, and I couldn't really see much. The river led me to a bridge so I waved down the first car that came my way, and a nice lady brought me here. I'll tell you more later, we have to get going." I didn't have the time to get into too much detail.

"I'm so glad you're alive," Lizzy sighed, as she gave me another hug and was not letting go. "I love you, and I'm so glad you're back," she said with tears in her eyes. "I thought I had lost my best friend, forever," she murmured.

"I love you too, girl. But, we've got to get going," I repeated, patting her on the back, as we embraced. She let go so we continued gathering our things.

"Do you think they will let us go earlier? I mean, it's a different date on the ticket, right?" I asked.

"It shouldn't be a problem. I don't think there's a date on it anyway," she assured me as she leaned down to pick up a piece of clothing off the carpet by the couch. While I washed the few dishes in the sink.

"You do have your passport with you, right?" I asked, hoping we didn't have to go pick it up.

"Yes! As soon as I got the tickets I made getting a passport my first priority. I keep it in my purse."

"Me too! The day after you asked me I put in for it," I remarked. "Where is Calvin?" I asked, looking around the room. I wanted to make a cup of tea, but knew I didn't have time.

"He went to go do something. But he's on his way back. He might even be waiting out front."

"Okay, let's get out of here," I said as I checked to make sure we got everything.

We grabbed the bags and all of our stuff and headed down stairs. When we got to the car Calvin was standing with the door open. He took the bags and put them in the car. I started to get in, but he stopped me and hugged me.

"I'm so glad you are alright," he said.

"Thank you, me too," I replied as I started to get in the car. Although I wasn't alright, I was quite far from it.

Lizzy started to get in with me. "I know you want to ride up front with Calvin. Go ahead, I'll be fine," I murmured.

"Are you sure?" she asked, torn and unable to make up her mind. "Okay, we'll keep the privacy window down so we can talk." I could tell she was nervous about leaving me alone.

"I'll be okay," I sighed and gave her a dismal smile. "Let's go," I said as I got in. She jumped in and we were off.

Calvin rolled down the privacy window.

"I think Johnathon went to tell your parents. You might want to call them, and let them know that you're okay," he said urgently.

"I tried, but my battery was dead. I hope my phone was on the charger long enough," I muttered as I pulled it out of my purse. Then it occurred to me that my boss, June, needed to know that I wasn't coming to work for a while.

"Do you think my boss thinks I'm dead?" I asked as I dialed my mom's cell.

"I don't know news travels fast," Lizzy replied, turning around to look at me from the front seat. "It was on the news about the fire and I'm pretty sure they said your name," Lizzy stated.

"Really? So everyone must think I'm dead? I need a drink," I sighed as I made one. I filled a glass with ice poured in some vodka and then cranberry juice.

After I drank half of it, I dialed my mom and she answered.

"Mom, it's Isla. I'm okay."

"Oh my God! Johnathon told us you died in a fire. Where are you?" she shouted, relieved and franticly overcome with tears of joy.

"Mom, I'm okay, but Johnathon doesn't know I'm alive and he has gone to Amsterdam to kill himself. We're on our way to the airport. I have to stop him," I explained, beginning to panic more and more as I told her.

"He was destroyed and beaten down when he came to tell us. I had no idea he would go to that extreme," she sighed, happy yet a little confused.

"How long will you be gone? Did you call work?" she asked, wanting to know the whole story.

"I don't know. I'll call work as soon as I get off the phone with you," I assured her.

"Your father was so devastated, he cried and I've never seen him cry like that." Tears ran down my face as I picture him crying.

"Please let him know I love him and I'm safe," I uttered with compassion.

"I will, I love you. Please be careful," she implored. When I heard her say be careful I remembered the card reading Angel had done for me and how many 'be carefuls' were in it. And that they were all about my trip to Amsterdam.

"I will, don't worry. I'll call you when I get there," I promised. But, I wondered if that was even possible to do.

"Okay, I love you," she said sniffling through the phone.

"Love you too, bye."

I closed my phone and then remembered I had to call work. I opened it back up and dialed. Lissa answered.

"Hi Lissa, this is Isla."

"We heard you were dead. I heard it on the news," she said loudly, confused but happy.

"No, I'm okay, but my fiancé thinks I'm dead so he's going to kill himself. I'm on my way to Amsterdam to stop him. I don't know when I'll be back. Just tell June it's an emergency, and I have to go."

"Okay, please be careful," she said reluctantly. "Bye, Isla."

"Oh, please tell Angel I'm alive and well."

"Yeah, she was pretty upset. We all were," she added caringly.

"Talk to you soon," I said.

"Bye, see you soon. Be careful," she instructed and then hung up.

I closed my phone and sat back in instant relief. Then Johnathon's face flashed to me, snapping me back to my mission. *Dear Lord, let me get there in time*, I prayed in my head. I repeated it quite a few times.

"Is everything all taken care of?" Lizzy asked, up on her knees leaning over the seat.

"Yes, and no. After I get Johnathon back in my arms again, then everything will be alright," I replied, leaning back and staring off into space. "Are we almost there?" I asked Calvin.

"Yes, we're pulling up to the airport now," Calvin announced.

"Lizzy and I will go in and try to switch out the tickets. Would you please bring the bags in, Calvin?"

"Sure! No problem," he replied, getting out to open the door.

"I'll meet y'all inside," he said as he shut the car door behind me, got in and drove off.

Lizzy and I went in. "Which airline is it?" I asked Lizzy who was holding the tickets in her hand.

"International Airlines," Lizzy read out. I scanned all the check in counters signs and the long lines waiting.

"There it is. Hey look it's the shortest line," I said, motioning with my head. We walked over and got in line. In front of us was two business women in suits. In front of them was a man who seemed annoyed that he had to wait. He was fidgety and doing all kinds of things to make little annoying sounds. First he started hitting his keys against the tall silver pole that held the rope to keep us in formation. When he observed the scornful faces gawking at him he stopped. Then he started jingling the loose change in his pocket. Finally the woman in front of him was done and he moved up to the counter. Everyone was thrilled that he wasn't going to bother us, anymore.

"I'm thirsty, do you want anything?" Lizzy asked.

"No thank you, I'm good," I answered and she turned and ran over to a soda machine. By the time she got back we were next in line.

"Can you believe what a bottle of water costs here?" Lizzy asked and then showed me the receipt.

"Wow that's a lot. I thought that you went to the soda machine," I commented.

"I did, but it didn't have water so I had to get it from a sandwich shop," Lizzy said and then began guzzling it down.

"Next please. May I help you?" the lady asked as we approached the counter. She had short and wavy dark brown hair, a pleasant smile, and pretty blue eyes.

"We have tickets to Amsterdam. Is it possible to use them today?" I asked as Lizzy handed them to me and I passed them on to the lady.

"Sure, we can take care of that," she replied as she typed with one hand.

"I also want to purchase one more ticket," I said, handing her my debit card.

A few minutes later she said, "Okay, your plane boards in twenty minutes, you better get going." She handed me the tickets. "There you go. Your plane is boarding now at Gate B23 and it takes off at 8:35. You better run!" she murmured as she put my label address through the handle of our black bag.

I turned to Lizzy and Calvin had just appeared behind her. I handed them their tickets.

"Thanks Isla! I'll pay you back," Calvin said surprised that I had purchased a ticket for him. I smiled and patted him on the side of his arm.

"Let's go!" I shouted with urgency. We started walking quickly through the airport. There were people everywhere making it hard to get through the crowd fast enough.

"We better catch a shuttle," Calvin suggested, pulling Lizzy and I towards the door of the shuttle.

"Calvin, do you know where the S.P.I. meetings are, in Amsterdam?"

"Yes, do you think that's where he'll do it?" he asked.

"Yes, my dream was very specific. It was definitely in the Red Light district," I replied as I sat down on the dark grey upholstered bench and held onto the pole as we flew through the airport to our gate. Lizzy just peered around in silence, smiling.

"Yep! That's where they meet," Calvin agreed.

When we were in line for the security check, I got worried about the dagger he had given me and the rest of the weapons. I couldn't recall where they were. I had packed in such a haste I never paid attention.

I looked at Calvin with wide eyes and he communicated to me silently that the weapons were in the checked bag . We went through without any problems. My mind was racing thinking about all these things.

When we got to the gate they were loading. The last people in line had just walked down the ramp as we approached. We went straight on, didn't have to wait in line at all. That part was cool. All of our seats were together. We got situated in our seats and put our belts on. The plane was on the runway waiting for clearance to take off. I had a feverish nagging feeling that something strange was going to take place on that plane. But, I chalked it up to my anxiety and my desperation to get there to stop Johnathon. I sat there waiting for the plane to take off and my mind was racing thinking about so many things. It seemed weird to me to be able to take weapons on a plane even in checked luggage. I pondered on it for a while. If someone was going to highjack a plane they could easily check there weapons, take over the plane and go where they store the luggage and be totally armed very quickly.

After the plane took off, I was fidgety and bothered by premonition of impending danger. My weary eyes began to get heavy so I fell asleep. I began to dream. *I could see a really bright light. Johnathon was standing in it and he looked like an angel. His white, long-sleeve shirt was open and he was wearing a light colored tee-shirt* under it. *The gleaming light was shimmering around his silhouette. The wind was blowing the sides of his shirt out to each side and it looked like he had wings. He smiled and took my hand. We were walking through the garden on his estate. He pointed to a cluster of white lilies.*

"Is that what you want in the flower arrangements around the gazebo?" he asked with his chilled arm around me.

"Yes, they are beautiful!" I exclaimed as I looked out over the garden at all the splendid blooms. "I also would like those fiery red and orange roses. They're stunning. Or maybe I'll have those in my bouquet only. After all they were amidst the first roses you gave me, before our first date."

"I remember. It sounds perfect, my sweet. You can walk this pathway down to the gazebo after all the bridesmaids and the rest of the wedding party," he said, waving his hand in the direction of the walkway.

"I would like to get married at dusk," I replied pulling him close and wrapping my arms around his light. Then it all became clear, he was the light, the sun wasn't even shining, it was actually dark outside.

We walked over to the gazebo.

"I'll be standing here, waiting for you," he breathed, grinning from ear to ear.

I smiled, but tears kept falling.

Suddenly I woke up, grabbed my purse, pulled out a pen and paper and began to write...

Tears Kept Falling (Duet)

Isla: You were in front of me
You vanished before my eyes
Now you think I'm gone never to return
You saw me burn and you felt my cries

Johnathon: I can't go on without you
I couldn't save you
Therefore I want to die

I will never say goodbye

Harmony: (Unison) Chorus:
I'm coming to be with you
You are my dream never dead
Pictures of our love like a movie in my head
Can't you hear me calling I closed my eyes
and the tears kept falling

Isla: I'm not gone I'm right here
I'm on my way to stop you from doing
what I think you're going to do
For once I will be the one to save you
You are my light when the sun goes down,
guiding me leading me around

Johnathon: I can show you love like it should be
I'll put white lilies in your hair, you'll see
Show you the world with all the joy it could bare
Fighting the odds we know life can sometimes be unfair

Harmony (Unison) Chorus:
I'm coming to be with you
You are my dream never dead
Pictures of our love like a movie in my head
Repeat: Can't you hear me calling I closed my eyes,
and the tears kept falling

Epilogue

Descending

*T*HIS IS GOING TO BE A LONG *ride*, I thought to myself.

"This plane needs to fly faster," I mumbled. I couldn't help but wonder if I was too late. I had to keep that thought out of my head.

Calvin and Lizzy were talking and kissing. So I just kept to myself. I didn't want to be a third wheel. From my window seat I stared out at the clouds, seeing pictures of him and things that reminded me of him in the patterns. I pictured his eyes and the waves crashing. I couldn't wait to surf those waves again and feel his cold hands on my face, his frigid lips to mine. I had to save him from turning both our lives upside down. *Please Lord don't let it be too late.*

"Isla, do you want something to eat or drink?" Calvin asked.

"Actually, I am hungry," I answered feeling extremely fatigued from everything I had been through.

"They came by with the beverage cart, but you were asleep," Lizzy remarked, looking over Calvin at me.

"Do you think they'll come back?" I asked, peering over the tops of the chairs. I observed how many empty chairs there were on the plane. It seemed that only a quarter of the chairs were full. It was a pretty vacant flight.

"I'm sure they will," Calvin replied. No sooner than the words left his mouth a tall, blonde flight attendant approached us.

"Would you like a turkey or chicken sandwich?" she asked me, smiling warmly.

"I'll take turkey, please, and a water. Thank you," I replied, returning her smile. But I knew there had to be some coldness in my smile. I didn't mean to be gloomy, it was uncontrollable. I was going crazy. So much of my life depended upon whether or not I was late.

"Okay, here you go," she said as she handed me a sandwich in plastic wrap and a bottled water.

"Thank you," I repeated before she turned and walked away.

"The movie is getting ready to start. I got you some earphones," Lizzy said, as she handed them to me.

"What movie?" I asked. She had already put her earphones in her ears and couldn't hear me. I shrugged my shoulders and did the same.

She switched seats with Calvin. He didn't mind. He knew we would be chatting during the movie. The movie was called *The Diary of Passion*. It began in a little white house on a secluded beach somewhere. A beautiful blonde in her early thirties was sitting on the front porch imagining a man sitting next to her sipping lemonade. He was tall with dark brown hair and had an award-winning smile. She was sitting there alone staring at the empty chair as her head hung low. Then it flashed to her standing all in black, surrounded by family and friends next to a casket. That's all it took! The flood gates were instantly opened. I was crying so hard Lizzy handed me a small box of tissue. I cradled my head in my hands, picturing myself in the woman's position. I was terrified.

"How long did they say this flight was?" I cried out loudly as I wiped my tears away. I made an attempted to shake the emotion off, but it was holding on for dear life. It was like a large scorpion was clamping down on my heart with its pinchers and at the same time continuously stinging me.

"I don't know, it's a straight flight. It might be eleven hours, I think," Lizzy responded. Her eyes were watering too, but nowhere near as much as mine.

Calvin leaned over Lizzy, "Isla, are you okay? Don't worry, the S.P.I. meets on Friday nights, so we have time. We'll make it." He could tell I was falling apart at the seams. "Watch the movie and relax," Calvin suggested as he patted my arm. The movie was making it worse, but I didn't have anything else to do.

I leaned back, ate my sandwich and watched the movie. But, I focused more on the sandwich, how it tasted and looked. I barely paid attention to the screen. I chewed each bite slowly with my eyes closed, attempting to enjoy the taste. But it was bland and didn't satisfy me.

At the end of the movie I couldn't hold back my emotions. What little I had seen of the movie had triggered the motion picture playing in my head. Lizzy was crying, too. We looked at each other and laughed out loud.

"Are you okay?" Lizzy asked, seeing that I hadn't stopped crying. "Cheer up, we'll stop him. I just know it," she assured me, putting her arm over my shoulder, which made me sob even more. I knew one thing for sure; this was going to be the longest ride of my life. "Here's a magazine if you want to get your mind off of it," Lizzy offered, trying to distract me.

"Thank you. Maybe that will help," I sighed as I took it and began thumbing through.

It was *Vogue* which had become nothing but advertisements.

"OOoo, I like those shoes and that coat," I expressed, pointing. "These magazines must to have subliminal messages in them somehow. They can do it with audio and now visual," I said to Lizzy, trying to get my mind off everything.

Calvin got up to go to the restroom. Lizzy looked at me with a serious expression.

"Do you want to be a vampire?" she asked, quietly scrunching down in her chair. I looked around and thought to myself *The seat behind us is empty. Who is she trying to be quiet for?* But I decided to play her game and scoot down in my seat, too.

"Yes, not necessarily because I want to drink blood, but to be with him forever," I whispered.

"Have you tasted blood, besides Johnathon's? What does it taste like?" she whispered.

"Yes. It's salty, sweet and a little bitter, but in a good way," I explained as I licked the tip of my finger and tapped the top corner to turn the page. I continued flipping through the magazine, in order to hide my eyes. I didn't want to tell her I had tasted hers. Or maybe that was in a dream. I couldn't even remember anymore.

"Now that you have tasted it, do you crave more?" she asked in a low whisper.

"Yes. I'm beginning to crave it and I have been experiencing feelings of exuberance."

"What does exuberance mean?" she asked.

"It means unrestrained enthusiasm," I explained. Her eyes were wide and she was paying close attention to everything I said.

"Oh! So, do you still like food?" she asked, looking at my half-eaten sandwich in front of me.

"Sometimes, but I have to remind myself to eat because I forget to. Almost like---I don't need to anymore. My body used to let me know when I needed to eat. But, now it's backing off."

"What about killing, do you think you'll be able to do it, to feed?"

"I don't know, maybe I will work at a blood bank or something. What about you, do you want to be one?"

"I guess so. I do know I want to be with Calvin, but I'm scared."

"I am, too. I'm more scared of being without Johnathon and growing old," I began staring out the window and trailing off into my thoughts.

Calvin came back and sat down.

"What did I miss?" he asked.

"We were just talking about becoming a vampires," Lizzy whispered to him.

"How do you feel about it?" he asked Lizzy.

"I want to be with you, so of course I want to be one," she admitted as she swallowed hard.

"You're probably going to make her wait just like Johnathon is making me wait, aren't you?" I asked Calvin.

"What did you think of the movie?" he asked, changing the subject.

"It was good, it was sad and emotional," I said, handing my trash to the lady walking by with a bag.

"It must have been, because you both look like you've been crying," he murmured with a grin.

"Oh, we have," Lizzy confirmed as she checked her eyes in a compact.

"It made it really hard on me, though. I miss Johnathon so much," I sighed, beginning to tear up again.

"Don't start again," Lizzy pleaded, touching my arm softly.

"I won't," I assured her, but I leaned my head over on her shoulder and cast my pain all over her. I couldn't stop. Suddenly, I sat up and wiped my eyes. "Calvin, please try to read his mind and tell him don't do it and that I'm alive," I cried. I was desperate.

"I'll try. I tried earlier and there was something blocking it, like there was a wall up," Calvin revealed.

"What exactly did you see?" I asked him, begging for more information.

"He was standing in front of a tall black door, he would reach for the handle and hesitate and walk away and then try it again, but never actually turned the knob. There was such sadness in his eyes, but something was holding him back."

"Maybe he heard my plea and he can feel that I'm still alive. Perhaps he read your mind subconsciously and doesn't realize it. Please go try again. Tell him we're on our way and that I love him--please," I begged as my voice cracked.

"I'll try," he answered, getting up swiftly and zooming off across the plane. It caused such a sweep of air that it blew magazines and papers of out of other passengers' hands and belongings.

I couldn't get the image out of my head of him standing in front of the tall black door. "Please, Johnathon. Don't do it," I whispered to myself, grasping my head with both hands, my fingers sliding softly into my hair. I squeezed my eyes and tried to telepathically reach him.

"Do you have a headache?" Lizzy asked me.

"No." Just as I answered a wave hit me. I peered up at all the lights that were on irritated my eyes severely.

There were rainbows around every light and the auras around everyone on the plane illuminated a multi-colored mist in the air.

Out of the corner of my eye I saw a man who had no aura. He was two rows back, across the aisle. Glancing around the airplane I confirmed he was the only one that did not have one. I had an uneasy feeling about him. He had short black hair, dark skin, and a little mustache. He was wearing a button down shirt that was white with gray stripes, and gray pants. I could hear different voices all throughout the plane. There were two older women talking about each others kids and grandchildren. A few seats over was a middle aged man yelling at his laptop because it was locking up. An airline attendant with reddish-blonde hair was hoping the hunk in first class had noticed her. I could hear everything. But nothing came from that man with no aura who just sat there like he was waiting for something.

Calvin came back and sat down.

"I really think I got through this time, something changed in his eyes."

"Where is he?" I asked.

"It looked like he was at Sigrid's house."

"He lives in Amsterdam?" I asked confounded. "I just always assumed he lived at Castle Le Daine. I mean it's not like its not big enough for both of them. You could get lost in that house. Is Sigrid there?" I asked.

"No, I don't think so," Calvin said as he stood up to let Lizzy out to go to the restroom. He sat back down next to me. "We will get there in plenty of time to stop him. Stop worrying," he said smiling.

"I hate to say it, but our worries aren't over yet. You see the man two seats back on our left with dark hair?

"Yes." He was quiet. I could tell he was reading his mind. He turned quickly back to me. "This might be bad."

"I know. This plane is about to be hijacked," I said, catching my breath. I knew that the time had come to finally see what these powers could do. "The question is, should we take him down before or after?" I asked Calvin.

"We wait," he replied sternly, and prepared for the unexpected.

Lizzy had come back from the restroom and stood in the aisle waiting for Calvin to move so she could sit back down.

"What did I miss?" Lizzy asked, getting comfortable in her seat.

"Something is about to happen, here and now," Calvin whispered.

"What do you mean?" she asked befuddled.

"Just get ready and do what we tell you to do," Calvin ordered under his breath.

Suddenly, we heard a scream. We all stood up in the aisle to see what the commotion was. The man with no aura was holding a box cutter to a woman's throat, the same blonde flight attendant who had brought me my food.

"My name is Sonsta Rueben. Get the pilot or I kill her right now!" The sharp steel razor was entering her skin. As I jumped over Lizzy, a big man walked by quickly.

"I'm Freddy Andrews, I'm the sky marshal," he announced as he held out his badge. "What do you want? We don't want anyone to die here." The man didn't speak, he just pushed the sharp blade harder against the woman's neck. Freddy stepped back, pulled out his gun and pointed it at Sonsta's head. "We're not going to have a problem here!" the sky marshal ordered.

I glanced at Calvin, then he was gone and behind Sonsta.

"Come out from behind him, you don't need to help, sir," the sky marshal reprimanded Calvin.

Calvin reached down in a flash of movement and took the box cutter out of the man's hand. The woman took off quickly down the aisle. The sky marshal then took both of Sonsta's hands behind his back and wrestled him to the floor. As Sonsta fell, he dropped something. It landed next to my foot, so I picked it up. It was a black plastic box with one red round button about the size of a pill box. It looked like it was some kind of trigger. I handed it to the sky marshal.

"What's this for?" he asked Sonsta.

"It's for the bomb that will go off thirty minutes before we land, unless I disable it first. So what do you know, we're going to die after all," he announced with a sneer. Lizzy gasped and so did eye, in silence. Calvin came back over to comfort us. Every other person that could see and hear what was going on stared with their mouths gaping open.

The sky marshal grabbed him by the front of his shirt, twisting it tightly around his throat. "Tell me where it is! How can I disable it!" he yelled at him, expecting him to just come right out and tell him. Sonsta clammed up and wouldn't speak. Calvin was trying to read his mind. He was staring at him intently.

"This guy's mind is locked up like a bank vault. I can't read anything on him," Calvin muttered frustrated. "I'm going to do some searching. I'll be back." He disappeared in a flash.

Lizzy and I just stood there stunned.

"Okay," I said.

"That time was really fast," Lizzy said, shocked.

"Oh, heck yeah, I want to be a vampire," I announced quietly to Lizzy as we sat down.

"So--- This is it. If he can't find it we're going to die. I won't get to see Johnathon ever again," I sighed as my eyes filled with tears.

I looked down so the tears wouldn't run down my face. *Goodbye Johnathon, I love you. I'll see you in Islathon*, I said to myself.

"If Calvin would bite us we wouldn't die, right?" Lizzy asked.

"You're right, but it would take too long for us to turn. We would die before the change was complete," I sighed, staring at the back of the seat in front of me.

"I don't want to die," she cried painfully, shaking and bighting her nails.

"I don't want to not roam the earth. I can't say bye to Johnathon, my parents, and my friends." I began to go through home movies in my head. Johnathon was always behind the scenes watching me. He stood on the sidelines as I watched the happiest moments of my childhood. My vision changed to a dreamy night, the night Johnathon and I would be able to show our love fully and he would sink his teeth into me. I was lost in intense passion in my mind when all of sudden I heard a loud voice roar out, *Calvin can fly, too!* It sounded like Johnathon's voice. His voice echoed in my heart. His smooth velvet voice was music to my ears.

"It's not over yet," I smiled as I patted her hand.

"It's okay, we have to face that this is it," she moaned, leaning her head back and closing her eyes..

"No, Calvin can fly just like Johnathon, we have a chance," I insisted.

"Do you think he could hold us both?" she asked, excited and nervous at the same time. She leaned over with her hand clamped around my arm.

"I sure hope so," I said, looking around to see if the sky marshal was still sitting behind us. He wasn't, but Sonsta was still handcuffed to the seat.

He glared at me; it was an evil stare. I could see in his eyes that he didn't care that he was about to die or anyone else for that matter.

"If Calvin doesn't come back soon we're going to look for him," I announced to Lizzy.

"How will we get past him?" she motioned towards the sky marshal who had returned to the chair next to Sonsta.

There were a lot of empty seats on this flight so not too many people had heard the hijacking go down, or knew about the bomb. I looked at my cell phone for the time. I saw it was 11:35 a.m. and we would land in about five hours or so. Luckily my cell phone changed automatically to the correct time zone.

Calvin returned. "I found it, but there is no way to stop it, it's hooked up to the landing gear. As soon as it goes down . . . B O O M!!" He sat down and Lizzy sat in his lap and cuddled up into his chest.

"I'm scared!" she whispered to him.

"Lizzy and I had an idea," I said.

"What?" he asked, but I could tell he had read our minds already. Before I could respond he answered. "It would be hard, but we could try. We'll have to go down to cargo or luggage to take off."

"What about the other people on the plane? They're all going to die," I sighed, scared for their lives.

We heard another commotion going on behind us. We all got up slowly.

The sky marshal was torturing Sonsta with the box cutter. Tell me where it is," he demanded in a deep throaty voice. They were eyeball to eyeball. The marshal stuck the knife into his skin. Calvin was suddenly behind him and tapped him lightly on the shoulder.

"Where did you come from? Please go back to your seat, sir," the marshal ordered, perturbed by the fact that he had to ask him once again.

"I found the bomb," Calvin announced as he took his arm. The marshal retracted the box cutter with the other hand and put it in his pocket. They took off in a flash.

They were so fast that the people that had seen them were shaking their heads in disbelief.

Lizzy and I sat down again. I prayed quietly to myself. Then it dawned on me, as a wave began to hit me. I bet I can go as fast as Calvin.

"Okay, I'm going to try something," I sighed getting ballsy again. The wave was returning stronger than ever, feeding on the adrenaline in my body. She looked at me like a puppy with her head tilted and wondered what was going on in my mind.

"Your eyes look glazed over," she said as she got closer to my face. "It looks like there are waves in them." She leaned back away from me.

"I won't hurt you, don't worry." I touched her arm gently, letting her know everything was going to be okay.

I stood up pulling her up with me. We got out into the middle of the aisle. I took her arm and wrapped my arm around it tightly. "Hold on," I whispered as we zoomed off. The wind blew by my face and it felt as if it were going a hundred miles an hour. A burning sensation had developed on my cheeks. Then we stopped. I stepped cautiously getting my bearings after being grounded again. Lizzy looked confused and amazed.

"Whoa, that was so cool," she breathed. Her eyes were wide and bloodshot and she looked a little drunk as she balanced herself against me.

I heard voices not far from us, and one was Calvin's. We slowly walked around the corner. Calvin saw us and turned the sky marshal around so he couldn't see us.

Calvin mouthed, "Stay here," and poof, they were gone.

"What did he say?" Lizzy asked.

"Stay here," I replied.

"Oh, I thought he said steer," Lizzy responded and then busted out laughing. She was always in good spirits no matter what was going on. "I like that set of luggage," she announced as she pointed at some candy apple red luggage. To me they were neon. I had to look away because of the brightness.

"That surprises me, I thought for sure you would have chosen those over there," I said pointing. They were pink with black décor, very cool.

"Oh, I didn't see those, you're right. Are we going to be able to get our bag?" she asked, scanning for it.

"Probably not, it's going to be hard enough for him to fly holding us both," I replied. Although, I wondered just how strong a vampire really was.

"Yep, it'll be hard, but I know we'll be fine," Calvin said as he appeared into our view. His skin was flushed and he had a strange look on his face.

"The dagger's in your bag?" he asked reminding me.

"Don't you mean the weapons are in your bag? I better get them," I replied, heading over to a huge pile of luggage. Our bag was about third from the bottom.

"Is this it?" Calvin asked, pointing to it.

"Yes," Lizzy replied. Calvin pulled it out so quickly the other suitcases barely moved.

"Grab anything you need that can fit in your purse and doesn't weigh a ton," Calvin suggested.

I unzipped it and grabbed some clothes, the dagger and a few other things. But I didn't see the guns. There was a typed letter from the airport security that basically said that they had confiscated the guns. And until I could produce a license for the use of a weapon, I couldn't get them back. There was a phone number to call if I had any questions. But since I had no license I wouldn't be calling, which meant I pretty much had just lost the guns.

"They confiscated the guns! Oh, well." I zipped up the bag after stuffing all I could fit in it. I was happy I carried a big purse.

"I'm afraid I left my purse at my seat," Lizzy sighed as she gritted her teeth and stared at me. I could tell she was relieved that the guns had been taken.

"It'll be okay, we'll get another gun later," Calvin said to me as he patted me on the back. "I'll go get your purse, wait here," he said to Lizzy and then zipped away. Lizzy and I sat down on a grey perforated ledge.

"I'm glad we're down here, it's hard looking at the other people knowing that everyone is going to die," Lizzy said, beginning to tear up.

"Don't think about it," I told her as I repacked my purse and then pulled the strap over my head to wrap it around my body. It was light, but bulky.

Calvin came back around the corner.

"We have about two hours before the bomb goes off," he said, preparing us. He clenched my wrist and threw his arm around Lizzy.

"Shouldn't we take off sooner?" I asked.

"We can, but it would be best if we were lower to the ground so we could land on top of a building, just in case," Calvin suggested.

"You don't have much faith in your flying abilities," I said, snickering at him.

"I've never held up two people before," he said. I could tell he was getting a little frustrated with me, but he grinned, anyway.

"I think you're more powerful than you give yourself credit for," I muttered.

"Yeah, you're probably right," he agreed, putting his arm around both of our shoulders as he squeezed in between us to sit down.

"What are you all doing down here?" the sky marshal yelled as he walked up. "Get back to your seats," he ordered, taking my arm and pulling me up to my feet.

Calvin jumped to his feet and stood in front of us. He stared the other man in the eyes. "You need to go back to your prisoner," Calvin commanded in a low hypnotic tone. The marshal nodded, "I have... to go check on the hijacker," he sounded blasé and dazed. Then he just turned around and walked away.

"That was cool. I thought for sure we were going to have to go back to our seats," Lizzy said, jumping on Calvin's back and kissing his neck. I watched his eyes change instantly from light brown to black.

"His eyes changed," I said to Lizzy who slowly slid off his back to the floor and peeked around to see them.

"I want to see," she said playfully.

Calvin just smiled and kissed her.

"It's getting close," he announced, staring in the direction of the bomb.

"Maybe you should try one more time to disable it," I said, looking at Calvin giving him my puppy dog eyes. Although there was no need to try to persuade him. He cared for the lives of people, generally. I could see in his dilated eyes that he was tormented by an unsolvable strife. It didn't matter how strong his powers were this was something he couldn't deactivate.

"I'll try one more time, but if it doesn't work hit this button and jump." He pointed to a big red button that had in black letters the word DON'T across it. I looked at him like he was crazy and giggled a bit. "I'll catch up," he said, dryly.

"Uh, what did you just say?" I stammered. "You want us to jump without you?" I asked, not wanting to do that at all. I was terrified of heights. At the salon our stations were up on platforms. And I didn't have to stand next to the ledge to feel like I was falling. Calvin zoomed away without a word.

My eyes were the size of saucers. I felt the sweat form on my brow and I was beginning to hyperventilate. I was holding my chest like I was having a heart attack. Suddenly Calvin came rushing at us, the whole thing looked like it was in slow motion, despite his super-natural speed. He pushed that button causing a big window to open up in the floor to the side of where Lizzy and I were standing. I was frozen.

"Get ready," he yelled. The wind was roaring and made a loud humming sound.

"Okay," I shouted. But I wanted to yell *heck no*, as I stood there staring down at nothing but clouds. We were just coming out of the clouds. I breathed a sigh of relief when I saw a city below. Lizzy grabbed my hand and squeezed. We both looked at each other with wet worry in our eyes.

¡This is it!" Lizzy said. Then all of a sudden a big wind swept us out the window. The wind was smashing against our faces and blowing us wherever it wanted while we plummeted down. I screamed bloody murder, we both did. I had such a feeling of terror. And then suddenly, I calmed down some. I looked around and saw how peaceful it all was. Then I closed my eyes and pictured Johnathon's face. We were still falling and the ground was getting closer. I looked around and didn't see Calvin. Lizzy was still screaming. I thought to myself, *This isn't the way I want to die.*

BOOK TWO
ISLATHON

BOOK THREE
BLACKHEART

BOOK FOUR
WOUNDED DRAGONFLY

Here's a sneak peak at
Islathon
the tantalizing sequel to
Twisted Dream
Dead Moon.

Islathon

by Chelsea Raine

Preface

I could see the city lights getting closer and brighter as we plummeted out of the sky. With my eyes closed I saw every moment of my life like a movie rolling like wildfire through my mind. Johnathon was there through every step, even when I took my first baby step. I remembered my first tears over peer pressure or a crush. The first time I rode a bike and mom almost fell on her face because she didn't want to let go. Through everything I saw in the pictures in my brain, he was there. A shadowed figure standing in a corner or by a tree on the curb in front of my house. Johnathon was there. He was my dark angel waiting in the wings. Then everything changed and I went *into* his eyes. I saw myself being thrown around fiercely by his waves. After trying hard instinctively to keep my head above water, I gave up. As I slid under the blue waters looking up at the sky through the windowpane of the surface. I thought to myself, *At least I had my moments with my dark angel.*

Chapter 1

The Rescue

THE WIND BEGAN TO SLOW. WHEN I opened my eyes I was back in reality. My heart was in my throat and what I was feeling was off the charts. I glanced at Lizzy, she was looking the other way and then I saw Calvin holding her hand. I took the deepest breath I think I have ever taken in my life. The next thing I knew he had come behind her and gotten in between us taking both our hands tightly in his.

He yelled, "Do you see that building coming up? We're going to land on the roof."

I could barely see it. "Why is it so dark?" I yelled, looking at him instead of down.

"It's six hours ahead here," he announced.

My heart began thumping hard and sporadically in my chest. "What do you mean? What time is it?" I hollered, beginning to freak a little.

"Probably 10:30," he hollered.

"Do we have time? What time does the council meet?" Lizzy yelled.

"Midnight," he hollered, then looked straight ahead.

"Here we go! Get ready!" Calvin shouted. The building got closer and closer. As it neared I felt hot, almost like I was on fire. A wave hit me like a ton of bricks. I could see every detail of the building like I was lying down staring at the grains of sand in the pavement roof top. Then it happened again. I got ballsy and let go of Calvin's hand. I let go, but he didn't. He looked at me strangely.

He didn't actually say anything, but he asked me. *Are you sure you're ready?* And I heard it plain as day in my head.

Yes, I'm ready. I answered him back without moving my lips. He slowly let go, his fingers slid down my palm then to my fingertips and he let go. I was flying by myself. I was exhilarated that I was flying on my own. The building came upon me quickly. I wasn't really sure how to land. I'd never done anything to that magnitude before. It was all overwhelming to me.

.

He and Lizzy touched down on the roof, as if they were walking. I was just about to land, when I heard a loud explosion and saw a blast of fire in my peripheral view. Suddenly a gust of wind caught me, pulling me back up. The eruption of the after blast shot me, spinning me, rolling me, and smashing my head and body against the pavement.

I got up and dusted myself off. *I hope I can land better next time.* I ran my hand across my forehead and everywhere else that was exposed feeling for blood. My hand was clean when I glanced at it. *Man I'm amazed that I didn't get hurt.*

"Isla, are you okay?" Lizzy shouted out as she and Calvin ran up to me.

I looked up at the smoke and fire blazing in the sky and watched the sparks and debris fall to the ground. Tears began to build in my eyes. I looked up to God.

"God bless them all," I murmured and bowed my head in silence as my tears fell. Calvin and Lizzy joined me in mourning.

"If only we could have saved them all," I uttered loudly and it echoed off the other buildings. Calvin touched my arm lightly.

"We had to save ourselves. We have to get going," he sighed.

"Let's go," I replied as I was gasping for air. Even though I was on such a high from flying by myself, I was sad for the lives lost.

I marched to the end of the building.

"Where are you going?" Calvin asked.

"Come on, we did it before and it was only you flying us," I said, ready to go again.

"Let her if she thinks she can," she remarked softly as she brought her head up and gave me a halfhearted smile. Calvin took her hand, kissed her, then grasped her hand securely. I was getting anxious watching their signs of affection. I just couldn't wait to be back in Johnathon's arms and I was terrified that we wouldn't make it soon enough.

We took off into the sky. Although I was scared and gloomy, the lights of Amsterdam were irrefutably breathtaking.

This is amazing!" Lizzy sighed loudly.

"I just wish there was something we could've done to save all those people," I called out looking over at Lizzy and Calvin.

Both their heads lowered. "I did all I could do. I tried everything," Calvin hollered in a harsh tone glaring my way.

"I know! I'm not putting any blame on you. I just wish the situation hadn't arose at all," I shouted. He nodded his head agreeably. I was so upset and distraught by the occurrences that had taken place that I couldn't enjoy the fact that I'd actually made it to Europe. I was too sad to take all of it in joyfully. But, I knew I was missing out on the beauty that was before me, and there was nothing I could do to change it. I felt guilty to be alive because of the lives that had just been taken.

"Don't focus on that anymore! Just concentrate on why we came here to begin with!" Lizzy hollered, staring at me.

"You're right," I agreed reluctantly.

"We're coming up to the red light district, it's just up ahead," Calvin yelled, motioning a few blocks up.

The hawks were back, bigger than ever. I hadn't felt them in a long time. They were stronger than what I had remembered, maybe because they were accompanied by waves of elusive exuberance laced with sadness. My adrenaline was on a high.

"What time is it?" I asked as we lightly touched down in a back alley so no one would see and point.

"It's 11:30," Calvin announced.

"Are you sure?" I asked, walking really fast as soon as my feet touched the ground.

"Yes," Calvin replied, practically dragging Lizzy behind him trying to keep up with me.

"Where is it?" I asked Calvin.

"It's near a café. At least that was where they used to meet years ago," he said, pulling Lizzy and I close as we passed by a group of shady men on the street. They were saying some of the most outlandishly crass stuff to each other and anyone that walked by. I think they were drunk or high as kites. Some of them looked as though they hadn't bathed in a while.

"Hey babe, how much?" one tall, dark haired guy yelled out and that was the nicest remark that came out of their mouths. I'm not sure how many there were, but I speculated there to be more than ten and less than twenty. That was at a glance. I looked at Calvin's back or the ground, most of the time. I didn't want to accidently glare at one of them in the eyes. But, Calvin stared them down as he pulled us through the pack. They backed off and moved out of our way.

We went down the street a ways. "This is it," Calvin murmured as he stopped in front of a café. It was boarded up. The cafe looked to have been a happening place at one time, judging by the walls of fliers of well-known bands on the front windows.

"It's right through here," Calvin said, pointing and leading us into a dark back alley. I didn't hesitate. I had to get to Johnathon before he ruined both of our lives.

We walked up some creepy, wooden stairs to a tall black door. The door was exactly the way I had dreamt it. The black lacquered door had red lights shooting out the edges, and the door handle glowed fiery red. I cringed when Calvin reached for the handle. I could hear chanting as he opened it. I felt my heart in my head as we entered the room. It was dark except for candle lights flickering sporadically throughout. And it still wasn't producing enough light for me to see. I could barely see my hand in front of my face. I followed the light that was further up ahead. There were more stairs to climb. Calvin helped Lizzy and I by holding our arms and walking us up. I remembered the balconies from my dream as we approached a long hall with theatre balcony rooms off to one side. There was two, tall, black and chrome lamps lit brightly at the end of the hallway. I could see, so I broke away from Calvin's grip and as I started to turn around to run my ankle bent the wrong way and caused me to shriek loudly and fall. I laid there holding it and screaming.

"Isla you only have five minutes left. You're not gonna make it," Calvin murmured touching my ankle with his icy hands. His touch was startling at first then numbed the pain.

"Yes, I am!" I growled and jumped up on to the other foot. I hopped to the furthest balcony skipping the first two like I'd dreamt. I struggled to get to the last balcony, but I was driven by desperation. Once I was in, I had to take blood red carpeted stairs down to the window, and there were a lot of steps. I leaned on the corners of the stadium chairs as I made my way down.

I thought to myself, *This is going to be difficult.* I carefully, but as fast as I possibly could went down the stairs to the black framed window awning that was decorated with beet red velvet curtains. The top corners of the awning were decorated with black and white wooden carved designs.

I had to climb on top of a long table to get to the ledge. I looked out over a stadium lit with candles everywhere. There were so many people standing in black cloaks that if it hadn't been for their occasional movement it would have just look like empty space with stars. I was searching and scanning the room in a panic. Then some of the people moved aside and I could see what they were watching.

It was Johnathon. He was bending down to bite the man who had been eating cloves of garlic like candy. The dirty sweaty man was so bloated I could smell him from wear I was. It was enough poison to kill him instantly. There wouldn't be anything slow about it.

One single tear slowly dripped from his eye and froze on his skin. I couldn't necessarily see the tear, but I felt it and my heart dropped suddenly. He was on the verge of stabbing his canines into the man's throat. I yelled at the top of my lungs, "JOHNATHON! NO! I LOVE YOU!" I cried out with one arm up to sky and the other holding onto the awning so I wouldn't fall, as I leaned out.

He stopped just as he started to bite down and looked up into my eyes. He shoved the man out of the way and within seconds was by my side. He took me in his arms and kissed me. Every nerve in my body tingled as he embraced me. My peace had returned.

"I thought you were dead," he breathed, pulling me into him so tightly I felt us become one. He gently kissed me and I became limp in his arms. I couldn't stand on my good leg anymore. He held me up off my leg. He must have read in my mind that I was hurt. The chanting got louder, but he didn't stop. It didn't matter what was going on around us. We were alone in our own world. The energy was obvious in my head as I saw us as lightening people. Every vein in our bodies lit up and the light splintered through us. When our bodies ignited we were blinding to the naked eye. At least that's what I saw and felt.

"Move in with me, Isla. I don't ever want to be separated from you again. When I thought I lost you nothing mattered anymore. Beautiful flowers in my garden looked only to be shriveled, brittle twigs. My heart turned black. I knew that I'd become a ruthless killer, again, if I didn't take my own life. I contemplated drowning myself in the waters of Islathon. Without your touch and the love you showered down upon me, I wouldn't care for humanity, ever," he breathed, buckling his arms around me tenaciously. His body smothered mine in endless bliss. His Siberian touch created ice in my veins and I had a chill so overpowering my whole body quivered. But I didn't care. I was in heaven.

"I love you, Johnathon. Without you I would have nothing to ever look forward to. Every light would be bleak and dim. Music would be just dry noise. The feel of cold would be just that, complete and utter death," I whispered as tears slid down my face. We kissed and he began to lose control, but instead of pushing me away as he always did, he pulled me in closer til the hunger subsided. He rested his head on my shoulder and buried his face in my neck.

"I have missed you so, my sweet," he sighed and his arctic breath on my throat invoked a burning sensation in my skin. I had to put my hand over it to supply instant heat. He looked me in the eyes and asked, "What happened? How did you get out of the fire?" His icy fingers delicately stroked my face, causing chills up my spine.

"Jeziaka captured me as the building burned down. She held me hostage in a house somewhere. I escaped at night and couldn't see much. A nice lady picked me up and took me back to the hotel. Calvin told me where you were and I knew for once, I had to save you. I tried to reach you in your mind many times. Couldn't you feel that I was still alive?" I asked, puzzled that he had tuned me out that much. Devastation made him deaf to his extraordinary senses.

"I thought I heard you, but I thought it was my mind playing tricks on me. I had seen the building burn down. I was completely destroyed. The news of your death marooned me into an emptiness so vast there was no bottom," Johnathon whispered as he gazed deeply in my eyes. My heart pounded so hard and my tears continued to slide. Then I reflected on the request he had just bestowed upon me.

"Wait! Did you just ask me to move into Castle Le Daine? Did I hear right?" I asked, remembering that I hadn't acknowledged his request. "Yes, I'll move in with you," I whimpered and sniffled. Johnathon, I don't ever want to be away from you," I screeched, squeezing him tightly.

We kissed and it was as if I was a fireplace and he sprinkled lighter fluid on me, causing an explosion of sparks shooting all over the sky, lighting it up. We hadn't even noticed Calvin and Lizzy standing there waiting for us to stop loving on each other.

"Where are we staying?" Lizzy asked as she cuddled up to Calvin and smiled at me.

"We'll stay at the Old Church, Sigrid's house," Calvin blurted out.

I spun around on my good foot and glared at Calvin with shocking expression. Johnathon was behind me holding my waist, his hands gave away for my quick move, but he didn't let go. "Sigrid's house, are you insane?" I shouted and shot him a strange look. "I know not to go into the Lion's den. He wants to kill me or make me his. No! I'm not a glutton for punishment," I sighed and then took a deep breath as I realized. *I am a glutton for punishment. I'm a slave to love.* I thought to myself.

"Don't we still have reservations at the American Hotel Amsterdam?" Lizzy asked, looking like she was going to fall out any minute. I could see the jetlag in her eyes. I was experiencing a hint of it myself.

"I can tell you the history of that particular hotel. Do you want to hear?" Johnathon asked, holding me, leaning up against a post.

"Sure," I replied, interested, plus I was just so happy to hear his smooth beautiful suave voice again.

"My cousin Cornelius Steinigeweg built the original hotel in the early 1900's. I didn't know him all that well. After he died his immediate family fought over who would get it. The dispute ran so long that the place went under. It was later bought and refurbished by Willem Krobout and H.G. Jansen. However they have established a room in his honor. They call it Steinigeweg Hall. There are some pieces of his art and antiques in a museum nearby, the Rijles museum," Johnathon announced as he rested his chin on my shoulder from behind me staring out at Lizzy and Calvin.

"Was he a vampire?" I inquired softly in his ear.

"Yes! He was also the founder of S.P.I," Johnathon replied breathily.

"So did he die or is he a vampire?" I asked, a little confused. Johnathon grinned at me.

"In that time when someone was turned, they were dead to society. There was a funeral and everything. He started his own society," he sighed and chuckled a little.

"Guess who's moving in?" Johnathon asked Calvin.

"I figured she would be. I hope you don't mind if I ask Lizzy to do the same," Calvin asked Johnathon.

Johnathon nodded and grinned. "That's fine we have plenty of room." You could tell Lizzy was flabbergasted. She stood there speechless smiling ear to ear and gazing at Calvin.

"Yes, I would love to," she sighed as she kissed him passionately.

"That'll be awesome! We'll all live there. Plus Jee Cee and Lexi too, right? That would be incredible!" I said, getting lost in Johnathon's eyes.

"Let's go to the Old Church," Johnathon said in that soft, velvet voice I had missed so badly. He held me tight, kissing my neck and then my lips. I felt relaxed, but my heart was banging on the inside of my chest. I was calm and then there was a part of me that was totally terrified about going to Sigrid's house.

"Isn't that where Sigrid lives?" I asked again.

"He's not there," Johnathon promised protectively.

"Are you sure? I can't handle getting captured again and being taken from you." I enfolded him in my arms.

"Isla, don't worry. If he shows up I'll protect you and get you out of there," Johnathon whispered.

He gazed into my eyes and I was surfing those waves again, splashing in the cool waters of his heart. I was drowning. And I didn't want to be saved.

We turned and began to walk up the stairs. Johnathon noticed me limping and stopped.

"What happened, my sweet? Can you walk?" he asked sympathetically.

"I sprained it trying to get to you in time. I can hop."

"No need. I'll carry you," he replied as he swiftly picked me up and carried me up the stairs to where Calvin and Lizzy were standing and talking at the entrance of balcony. I put my arm around his neck and tucked my head in close to his cool, statuesque body.

He carried me down the long hallway and down the steep stairs. Calvin and Lizzy were already standing at the opened black door, waiting for us. I did wonder why he was going so slow. Just being cautious, I guessed. We walked down the last flight of stairs out onto the street. Every light down the still street illuminated iridescent vapors in the early morning air.

"I should be a pro at carrying you over the threshold by the time we get married," Johnathon sighed, snickering under his breath.

"That's true, you do carry me whole lot. How far is it? I can hobble if it's not too far," I murmured, resting my head on his shoulder.

"It's right around the corner. Are you sure? I was just playing. I'd carry you forever, if you wanted me to," Johnathon sighed. I nodded and bit my bottom lip as he delicately set me down to stand on one foot.

"You're so sweet. I think I can hop for a bit," I sighed and grimaced from a twinge of pain that shot up my leg. But, I kept my head down to hide my expression. I didn't want to burden him any longer.

"We're gonna start walking," Calvin announced leering at Lizzy, pulling her into his arms and nibbling playfully on her neck. I could tell they wanted to be alone. They weren't the only ones.

We literally walked around the edge of the building and there it was. It was an old gothic church, creepy and beautiful at the same time. It was actually called Oude Kerk which means *Old Church*. It was a 13th century church, but rebuilt in the 14th century, Johnathon informed me as we approached the yard packed full of gravestones.

Johnathon opened a very squeaky black wrought iron gate. I got chills when I heard the medal on medal squeal. We all walked up to the door. Well, I limped. Johnathon held my arm gently as he helped me up the wide rock steps to the front door. The door was like a saloon door, only it was also wrought iron, only it was bronze. It had a big padlock across it. He opened the lock by the wave of his hand. On the other side was another door. It was wide and heavy made of dark walnut. It flew open as we came to it. When we entered, it was like stepping back into medieval times. There were tall-backed black leather chairs lined up against the wall. Hanging on the wall were colorful hand-painted brass shields and swords. There were beautiful murals of gorgeous landscapes on several walls. I sat down on the couch right inside the door, it was made of dark wood with deep red velvety upholstery. Calvin and Lizzy walked off down the hall, we stayed behind.

Johnathon offered me his hand to stand up. He backed me up against the wall.

"I want you, Isla. When I thought you were gone I never wanted to breathe, feed or care about anything ever again. All that was left of me was better off completely dead," he breathed.

My breath caught when I heard him say he wanted me. "That's why I had to save you this time. If I had been too late, I would have let all of the vampires in that room devour me til death!"

"Isla, I can't wait to spend the rest of eternity with you," he whispered, then kissed me long and sweetly. I was captured in deep rapture. He was a dark angel swooping down to wrap his huge wings around me. He was my peace, my happiness.

"You're my heaven, Johnathon. I could never imagine my life without you. I can't wait until we get back to Asheville and we can go to Islathon."

"Do you want to get married there or the castle? We could even get
married here in Amsterdam, if you would like," he suggested, gazing in my eyes.

"No, I definitely see us getting married at Castle Le Daine," I said, remembering my dream about us planning the wedding together and standing out by the gazebo. Inside I was kicking myself for not taking him up on his proposal of getting married there in Amsterdam. Then I wouldn't have to wait to become what he is. But, I saw our wedding a certain way and that was exactly the way it would be.

"Do you want to wait til next year to get married?" he asked.

"We can wait til April 25th as long as we're living together." I hugged him tightly. "I'm so happy," I sighed, jumping up off my foot and wrapping my legs around his waist. I gave him dragonfly kisses all over and the fireworks began. Our kisses were getting intense and hard. The heat was rising as he was devouring my lips.

All of a sudden, Johnathon was across the room leaning next to the fireplace mantel, breathing heavily. I was discombobulated by his sudden retreat as I balanced myself on the wall.

He peered up at me and noticed my attention was on his eyes and turned his head. His teeth were sharp and long, his eyes black as a night sky.

"I want you more than anyone or any blood I've craved in my whole existence," he murmured in a deep and sultry voice, convulsing with each breath.

"You need to eat," I sighed, hopping up to him and caressing his back.

"I do need to feed," he growled while blocking his face.

"Then don't wait! Feed on me!" I cried out, standing in front of him making him look at me as salt water slowly dripped from my eyes. My heart was in my throat waiting for his reply.

"I can't! I can't be sure to stop in time. I could kill you," he growled. His hunger was showing. I could tell it was torture for him. It was hurting him to keep from consuming me. And in his decision of not bowing to his thirst, I backed off. I rotated on my toe, hopped out the front door and shut it behind me. I needed some air.

I stood there breathing in the brisk air with one hand on the old, cracked wood railings holding me up. I wiped the tears from my eyes with the other. Gaining my composure seemed unlikely. The door crept open with a high pitched shrill. I looked behind me and saw nothing. I turned back around then felt something around my waist. I froze, then looked down to see Johnathon's hands.

"Isla, come back in it's getting cold out here," he whispered in my ear. A chill ran through my entire body. The hawks were back and I was upset. I faced him and gazed into his eyes.

"I'm gonna have to go feed soon," he murmured, looking down.

"I know," I uttered solemnly. "Where will you go?" I asked, accepting the inevitable that he would leave me once again.

"Calvin and I will go find some killers and if we can't find anyone we'll hunt. You both can stay here if you like," Johnathon suggested as he took my hand and threw my arm over his shoulder and walked me back inside.

"No, I would rather go to the hotel," I replied, scared of being at that house without protection.

"Okay, I'll take you there," Johnathon sighed, peering down the long dark hallway looking for Calvin and Lizzy.

"How long do you think it'll take you to find a murderer? Where are you going to go?" I asked again because he hadn't answered me. I limped to the couch and was just about to sit down when Johnathon pulled me back to him and picked me up, cradling me in his arms.

"Come here baby. I want to love on you some more," he whispered with a grin. I felt so empowered, and so incredibly at peace in his arms.

"Please don't ever let me go," I whispered to him.

"I'll never let you go, Isla," he sighed, kissing me passionately then stopping abruptly. The waves in his hungry black eyes were furiously smashing.

"Isla, I have to eat soon," he growled, eying my neck.

I leaned my head back to make the vein bulge out even more. Saliva was dripping from the corners of his mouth and his spiky teeth. Even though he was looking at me as if he were to attack at any minute, which was what I hungered for, he was still beyond dreamy in my eyes.

He gave me a quick kiss and laid me on the couch. He moved away from me rapidly.

"I have to go," he growled, opening the door and walking out onto the porch. I stood quickly wondering where he was going and moaned when I accidently stepped down on my bad ankle. I limped to the door and went out looking for him. He was supposed to take me to the hotel, so I was confused as to where he had gone. I didn't see him.

He was far away from me and my heart was already missing him. I turned around swiftly because I'd realized I had set my purse down. I nearly walked right into Calvin who was standing right in my face, ready to attack. Lizzy was standing by the door on the inside. Calvin stepped back two steps, he purposely counted and retreated. He twisted his head and looked at Lizzy. He smiled then walked out to join Johnathon who was then waiting at the tall iron gate.

"Toss me my bag, would ya?" I called out to Lizzy.

She turned her head and took a step back grabbing my purse off the couch. She handed it to me and I thought I saw a shadow move behind her. I froze with wide eyes and then jerked Lizzy, pulling her through the doorway and out onto the porch. She took my arm and helped me down the steps, through the gate and out to the road.

"I guess we'll catch a cab," I murmured and then whistled loudly at the cars passing by. After a few fruitless tries, I decided to give it one last attempt. It wasn't long before a cab pulled up. I opened the door and Lizzy got in. I looked back to see if I could see him. I jumped when Johnathon surprised me with a kiss and handed me a letter in an envelope. I started to open it.

"Please, open it a little later," he sighed caressing my cheek with the side of his chilly hand.

"What is this? You're not leaving me again, are you?" I asked with concern in my eyes and my heart suddenly in my throat.

"No Isla, it's nothing like that. I had written it when I thought you were dead, although I did slip something else in," he explained with a grin then kissed me. "It's a love letter," he replied as he and Calvin turned to walk away.

"Johnathon, I want you! I need you!" I shouted and my eyes filled with water. He rushed back to me and held me tightly in his arms

"I love you! We'll meet you at Dolphin's Coffee Shop just as soon as we take care of our problem," he sighed, his voice was breathy and deep.

"I love you!" I breathed and then he kissed me sweetly. His fingertips left mine as he turned and walked away, again. "Baby! Let's just meet at the hotel?" I hollered, before I got in the cab.

"Okay, we'll see you in a bite," Johnathon snickered a bit after he realized what he had said. Lizzy and I both laughed as we got in. I watched him til they vanished.

"Where are you ladies headed?" the cab driver asked.

"We need to go to the American Hotel Amsterdam," I replied, staring at the envelope in my hand.

The dark-skinned, dark-haired cab driver smiled and said, "Yes ma'am," Then he hit the meter. We sat back as he took off. I was holding the envelope he had given me. It was too heavy to be just a letter. To the left of the meter read a sign "cash only" in big red letters.

"OH CRAP!" I gasped under my breath.

"What's wrong?" Lizzy asked curiously.

"I don't have any cash," I whispered, hoping that Javier hadn't heard me. His name was next to the sign.

"What are we going to do?" Lizzy whispered loudly.

"Do what?" he asked us. We just looked down like we hadn't heard him.

"Are you going to open that or what?" Lizzy asked me impatiently.

"Okay." I pulled back the seal and looked in. There was cash and lots of it. I breathed a sigh of relief as more tears began to fall. I didn't count it. I was more interested in the letter, but knew it had to be a couple grand. Opening the letter I noticed it was stamped shut like an old fashioned seal, except it was in blood not wax.

The letter read:

My dearest Isla,

> *Now that you have gone, I can't go on. My heart beats, but it will beat no more. Although, I can always land on my feet, the ground will only swallow me whole. I know you are free, free of me in so many ways, free of the pain I could cause, free of the pain I won't give you. If only I had listened to you and just done it. I wanted so much to give you immortality on our wedding night. Now, I see no way out. I will close my eyes for an eternity in honor of your name and all the love we've shared in such a short time. I can't cry anymore, my tears won't fall. When I cry out your name there is no call.*
>
> *I am a black hole, empty and alone without you. The way your lips tasted and the fluids within will haunt me till the end. I only know from you, not where I begin. Please wait for me on the other side. I know from our past it will be a crazy ride. With only your love by my side. My love for you will grow and continue by and by.*
>
> *With all my love forever and an eternity*
> *Johnathon Daine*

P.S. I meant every word with everything that I am. It's so amazing to hold you again. We have a wedding to plan, and a honeymoon, too. Just let me know your fondest wishes and they'll all come true.

With tears streaming down my face I held the letter to my chest. I knew he would return soon. I felt as if I was holding him to me.

"Everything okay?" Lizzy asked. She could tell I was having mixed emotions.

"I just feel safe and peaceful holding it to my chest. Just give me a few moments," I sighed.

"So I guess that means yes?" Lizzy asked curtly, in a sassy tone.

"I'm sorry, everything is hunky dory," I sighed. She then smiled and picked up the envelope that had fallen down between us. She nonchalantly opened the envelope and counted the money.

"Wow, there is like five-thousand dollars in here," she whispered, handing it back to me.

"Really?" I sighed then reached in the envelope and counted out half and handed it to her.

"This is for me, really?" she asked, surprised and touched.

"Yes, see the post-it," I replied holding up the money. On the back of the last bill was a yellow post-it that read 'Give half to Lizzy,' Calvin wanted her to have money, too.

She read it and got teary eyed. She took the money and put it in her wallet.

"Wow! They're both angels," she breathed, grinning at me.

"Yep! They're our dark angels," I sighed, and Lizzy nodded with a smile.

"Here you go ladies." Javier pulled the cab over to the curb in front of the most awesome hotel I had ever seen. It looked like an amusement park from the outside. I was excited to see how it was inside.

"That will be thirty-five Euros," he announced. We both looked at each other. "That is fifty American dollars," he explained with a thick accent and then smiled, revealing his rotten teeth. I gave him a hundred. "I don't have change for a hundred," he murmured.

"It's okay, keep it," I replied. He grinned even bigger and the sight of his teeth turned my stomach a bit.

"Here's my personal cell phone number. If you need a cab later on or anytime you're here," he said, handing me a card. I slipped it in my purse.

"Thank you. We might call you tomorrow," I replied as I got out. Lizzy followed close behind me.

We grabbed our purses and started up a long walkway lined with red and purple tulips. A little white boat was docked by the moat that went all the way around the hotel. We strolled slowly, because of my limp. Lizzy held the tall, glass door open for me. My eyes were as big as saucers seeing how beautiful and magical the place was. It was like we'd stepped into the wonderful world of Oz. The lobby was open and expansive with high vaulted ceilings and glass elevators on each side of the check-in counter. The sofas in the middle of the lobby were big and plush, black velvet with large gold and silver pillows. The couches were surrounded by large leather chairs. There was a huge flower arrangement of red, orange, and white flowers on a round table behind one of the couches. The floor was shiny black marble with white flecks and I could see my reflection in it as I hobbled to the counter.

"This is cool," Lizzy announced, looking all around.

"Yeah! I really like this place," I replied, setting my bag down by my feet as we made it to the desk.

"How may I help you?" the woman behind the desk asked us with a nice smile. She had reddish-brown hair with blonde highlighted bangs.

"We're great! We have reservations for a room. Actually could we get an upgrade to a suite?" I asked nicely and smiled as I handed her our drivers licenses.

"Sure, we can bump you up to a suite. Two bedroom okay?" she asked.

"That sounds great," I replied. I handed her my debit card. She swiped it and handed it back.

"If you girls need anything my name is Sharamey. Here is my card. That's my cell," she said, handing it to me and pointing it out on the card. She was our kind of people, I liked her right away.

"Sharamey, our boyfriends will be soon. Would you send them to our room?" I asked, smiling while peering around the hotel.

Sure, what do they look like?" she asked, typing and looking around the room at the same time.

"They're both tall with dark hair and eyes, and pale skin."

"I'll keep an eye out for them," she said, skimming the room. "Here are your keys, is four enough?"

"Yes, that's perfect. Thank you!" I replied as I leaned down to pick up my bag. Lizzy was standing with her back to me checking out everything. I handed Lizzy hers and Calvin's keys.

"If you all need anything, a guide or buddy to hangout with, just give me a call. By the way, I think your men just came in," she motioned to the huge glass front doors. She looked down to hand me some pamphlets about the sights and information on the boat that travels around the hotel. And when she looked up the guys were right behind us.

"Hey baby, I missed you," Johnathon whispered, then kissed me. When I turned around I noticed Sharamey had an expression of shock on her face.

"What's wrong?" I asked her.

"How did they get here so quickly?" Sharamey asked, pointing her finger at them, baffled.

"What do you mean?" I asked, smiling.

"I don't know." She shook her head and continued, "Alright you're all checked in. Go up the elevator to the fourth floor. Your room is four twenty-five."

"Great! Thank you!" I turned around to Johnathon and he picked me up in the air.

"Do you know what that number means?" Johnathon asked me as he brought me back down kissing me sweetly.

"I don't know. What?" I asked, baffled.

"That will be our anniversary. Remember, that's when I proposed to you?"

"Oh! That's cool," I replied with a big smile as he set me down gently on my good foot.

We turned to walk to the elevator. Johnathon wrapped his arm around mine to help me, so I wouldn't put too much weight on my ankle. Calvin and Lizzy were lagging behind, kissing and playing around. Luckily, I had given Lizzy and Calvin their keys.

"Let's not wait on them," Johnathon suggested, hitting the four on the number panel. We were the only ones on the elevator.

I stared out the window as we went up. Johnathon put his arms around my waist and playfully nibbled on my neck. I couldn't take it anymore. I turned around and nearly knocked him over jumping up on him. We kissed madly. Then the elevator door opened to our floor. I slowly crawled down him, fixed myself up a little and we were in our room and on the bed so fast it made my head spin. He got up and shut the bedroom door. If Calvin and Lizzy came in they would know to not disturb us.

We kissed and played around a long time. We ventured a little further than we had before. We were both going crazy, crazy for each other. We laid back and talked about everything from wedding plans to how I felt about the pain that I would experience when he finally turned me.

"I want to just take you now, but I can't do that to you," he said, lightly caressing my arm with his frigid fingers. I was hot and bothered and it felt like ice running along my skin, without the wet feeling.

"Are you cold?" he asked me, pulling the blanket over my legs.

"A little, you know what your hands do to me. Burn me and freeze me at the same time," I sighed breathily.

"Fire and ice baby," he whispered, softly running his finger down my neck. It made me sizzle.

We were kissing when we heard the other door open in the next room. Calvin and Lizzy were talking as they came in.

"Hey guys, we know you're in there," Lizzy shouted.

"Yes! We'll be out in a little bit!" I shouted back.

"Well y'all hurry, we want to go check out some coffee shops," Lizzy hollered.

"I'm tired. I kind of want to wait til tomorrow to check out the coffee shops," I sighed, pulling the cover over my head.

"Isla, we can stay in if you want to," Johnathon said, crawling under the blanket with me.

"Y'all go out without us," I yelled.

"What?" Lizzy asked as she opened the bedroom door. "What did you say?"

We were still under the covers. He started tickling my tummy and I was giggling and thrashing around under the covers. His chuckles were almost musical.

"We're not going tonight," I shouted and continued fighting Johnathon's hands off me. I was extremely ticklish and his icy fingers on my bare skin was shocking. I was screaming and laughing loudly.

Lizzy pulled the covers back.

"What are ya'll doing under there?" Lizzy asked with a strange expression on her face. We were laughing because he kept tickling me.

"Nothing!" I replied pulling the covers back over our heads.

"Well, you two have fun. We're going to go check out some coffee shops," she announced with exasperation, trying to make us feel guilty. It didn't work.

"Have fun!" I yelled. They closed the door to the bedroom then the door to the room.

"They're gone," I said, throwing the covers off and jumping up to my foot. "Lets get naked!" I shouted, trying to balance.

"Isla, you know I definitely wouldn't be able to handle that," he sighed with a huge grin. "Isla, you're too much." He chuckled gazing up at me.

"I know, but it would be fun to fantasize or talk about," I breathed, feeling extremely frisky.

"Yes. But, no taking clothes off. Please," he begged firmly, then reached up inviting me to lie back down.

"You're such a party pooper. Okay," I sighed sadly, sitting back down on the bed against the sand-colored, wooden headboard. I jumped down off the bed and grabbed the one night gown I brought with me.

"Isla, that time will come," he promised as I held up the long, black silky night gown. He grinned mischievously.

"You can watch," I teased as I pulled my black and white shirt over my head. He quickly turned away. I slipped the gown over my head and it lightly slid down my body. The satiny material clung to my curvy figure. He turned to look at me with a boyish grin then jumped on the bed and laid down.

"By the time it comes, you're probably going to go so crazy and you'll accidentally kill me instead," I joked, as I got back on the bed and laid beside him.

"No, if I think that I might kill you, I would never bite you," he sighed as he sat up some.

"What do you mean?" I asked with a sour expression.

"I mean, I'll be well fed before our wedding night," Johnathon explained firmly, looking up at me as I rolled over on top of him.

"If that's what it takes," I whispered, gently kissing his chest.

"I'm so glad you saved me," he said with a boyish grin as he brushed the hair out of my eyes and kissed me.

"I was glad to return the favor, besides I could never see another day without you."

As I lay there in his arms another wave came over me, but this was a bit different. Gazing in his eyes I saw myself splashing around in his waves. Little rainbow-like filters surrounded his eyes.

"Isla, are you feeling it again?" Johnathon asked as he examined my eyes.

"You know I am," I said. "Why, do you think Jeziaka is coming for us again?" I asked reading deep into his mind.

"What? Oh, yeah. She has figured out where we are," he sighed, staring in my eyes. He looked like he was captivated by my eyes. "Your waves are beautiful," he whispered, his peaceful smile mesmerized me.

"Don't change the subject. She's coming because her dad told her where we are, right?" I questioned upset that he hadn't warned me.

I wanted to know everything. And his voice was calming and eased my panic of confusion from all the voices I was hearing. I was picking up voices from all over and couldn't decipher who or where they were coming from. It got to me at times. I wanted to pull my hair out. There were other times I just wanted to fly away.

"Let's do it then," he blurted out.

"What? Do what?" I asked, dizzy and confounded by everything I was seeing, hearing and feeling.

"Lets fly. We haven't done that in a while," he suggested in a deep breathy voice. I grinned and took his hand.

"Okay, a quick one. I need to get some sleep, if Jeziaka is coming to either take you away again, or kill me. I'm going to need my rest to fight her off."

"Isla, don't worry. Her spell won't work on me this time."

"Why? How do you know? What makes this time so different?" I asked as I got up and put my shoes on.

"Don't you know?" he asked, testing me.

I read his mind. "Yes. You're under my spell," I answered.

He nodded then went to the balcony, opened the door and took my hand.

"Ready?" he asked. I smiled and didn't have to say a thing.

We were weightless, floating in the steamy moonlight. It was a little chilly. He pulled me close pointing out the lights of Paris off in the distance.

"How are you now under my spell, but you weren't then?" I asked.

"I've seen your waves," he said, glancing over at me.

"So now that I have you under my spell, can I make you my love slave?" I teased giggling seductively.

"Yes, you can!" he replied, kissing my lips softly.

"Okay! You are my love slave. I want you to bite me, now!" I ordered. His eyes glazed over and he looked away. He turned back to face me.

"If that's what you wish?" his voice was monotone and robot-like.

"Yes! Yes! That's what I want," I exclaimed passionately, grabbing his shirt and pulling him to me.

He got in front of me, held me tight, and kissed me long and hard.

"Are you ready?" he asked, breathing heavily. His eyes went black and his teeth grew.

"Yes! Please!" I sighed, holding my breath.

He moved the hair from my neck, tilted my head back. My heart pounded so hard it felt like it was in my throat. He licked from the bottom of my earlobe down to my pulsating vein. I felt his teeth; I closed my eyes and inhaled a big sharp breath. I sighed to myself.

"Finally....!"

Acknowlededements

I would like to thank God for his amazing blessings and the gift of life. I will love You and praise You always.

Thank you to my Grandparents who have been and will always be my role models as long as I live. I love you both and cherish every second I spend with you. You have helped me in so many ways.

Thank you Dad for loving me and being the best Dad you knew how to be. I love you and pray that you will find love again.

To our Lexi, I love you and cherish you. I will do whatever it takes to make sure you have an amazing life.

Thank you to my sis Kristi, I love you and I know things would have been different if we had grown up together. All my love to Paris, Garrett, and Bart.

I love being a hairstylist. To me it is the most fun and instantly rewarding job out there.

Here it goes, if I leave a name out let me know and I will make sure to mention you in Islathon book two. These are not in any specific order.

Thank you and all my love to: (my editors)Bonnie Mays, Kim Hedge, Vicki Hall (friends/clients/family) Janie Cook, Jolie Blake, Vallerie Riggan, Annie Brecht, Judy Crowson, Donnie Radcliffe, Donald Radcliffe(Pops) and Ginny,

Angie Dunn, Cindy Thomas, Christina Atkinson, Erin Bay, Shannon Wells, Evalise, Sharamey Sandridge, Gordon Orem, Jackie and Stacey Knobel, Jo Robertson, Jenelle Little and Family, Denny Rockwell, Kristie Tallman Kent, Lara Marx, Laura Kencel and family, Wanda Kirk, Connie Williams, Cathy Carwile, Michelle Lamoureaux, Ashley Miles Radcliffe, Patti Peterson, Julia Pearson, Rachel Allen, Rick Warren, Ron Yearout, Russ Blakely, Tammy Kinnerson, Tatum Willis, Mary Lou Willis, Brandy Fields, Vallerie Swietzer Hill, Venessa Patterson and Beej Jordon, Caitlin Traylor, Shelly Degrasia, Lucy and John Howie, Sean Harral and family, GYPSY, Trisha Kvasnicka, Tammy Alley, Martha Binder, Tina Trivett, Rosie Adams, Brenda Mitchell, Terry Flannigan, Tammy Alley, Meagan Thomas, Dave and Brenda Thomas and Dana and Laura, Brittney Martin, Helen Lasky, Marybeth Gradziel, Cindy Bridges, Jeri Hopper, Kathy and Larry Hall, Stacy Long, Gayle Peterson, Elias and Bethany Dancey, Robin Yarborough, Diane Ange and family, Arlene Hairfield, Dorothy Tate, Walter Gerheart, Forrest Mitchell, Chris Masconi, Susan Faison, Steve and Teresa Quigley, Brenda Perkins, Jerry Hewitt, Christine Harris, Margaret Forest, Julia Williams, Ginny Cope, Diantha Girard, Cindy Wayne, Lori Lepore, Erin Grimes, Chris and Jennifer Wicks, Jessica Statzer, Susan Snyder, Linda Spainer, Laura Golden, Lori Culpepper, Haleigh Culpepper, Julia Leys, Brandy Pierce, Paula Robertson, Sharon Benter, Terry, McKayla, and Justin Dunford, Barbara Carpenter, Jordon Rogers, Lucy Willkinson, Amber Mitchem, Chris Turner, Ashley Thompson, Becky Williams, Rhonda Skinner, Cherie Greenwood, Peewee Offutt, Susan Gokey, Debbie and the girls

A SPECIAL THANKS TO: Jason Wakefield, Andrea in Heaven, Maggie and Toozy Wakefield, Cindy Thomas, Wanda

Kirk, Sheila Rundlet, Connie Williams, Laura Kencel, Jo Robertson, Kim Hedge, Laura Golden, Greg Radcliffe, Terry Dunford, Ollie Crum(the Ollie's) Linda Ross, Vickie Hall, Janie Cook, Vallerie Riggan, Annie Singletary, Bob White. Without your help, publishing would not have been possible.

Manufactured By: RR Donnelley
Breinigsville, PA USA
July, 2010